MORE PRAISE FOR KAY HOOPER AND *AFTER CAROLINE*

"Kay Hooper's dialogue rings true; her characters are more three-dimensional than those usually found in this genre."
—*The Atlanta Journal*

"Kay Hooper gives you a darn good ride, and there are far too few of those these days."
—*Dayton Daily News*

"Peopled with interesting characters and intricately plotted, the novel is both a compelling mystery and a satisfying romance."
—*Milwaukee Journal/Sentinel*

"Kay Hooper has crafted another solid story to keep readers enthralled until the last page is turned."
—*Booklist*

"Joanna Flynn is appealingly plucky and true to her mission as she probes the mystery that was Caroline."
—*Variety*

AFTER CAROLINE

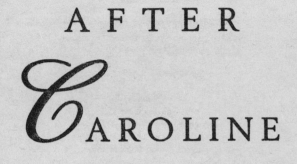

Kay Hooper

BANTAM BOOKS
NEW YORK TORONTO
LONDON SYDNEY AUCKLAND

After Caroline

A Bantam Book

PUBLISHING HISTORY
Bantam hardcover edition published December 1996
Bantam paperback edition / October 1997

ISBN 0-553-58857-5

Published simultaneously in the United States and Canada

Bantam Books are published by Bantam Books, a division of Random
House, Inc. Its trademark, consisting of the words "Bantam Books" and
the portrayal of a rooster, is Registered in U.S. Patent and Trademark
Office and in other countries. Marca Registrada. Bantam Books, New
York, New York.

PRINTED IN THE UNITED STATES OF AMERICA

OPM 10 9 8 7 6 5 4 3 2 1

To my friends,
Catherine, Linda, Iris,
and Fayrene—
because connections
matter.

AFTER CAROLINE

$\mathcal{P}$ R O L O G U E

✦　✦　✦

July 1

IT WASN'T MUCH to cause such a drastic effect. Not much at all. A small spot on the road, maybe a smear of oil that had dripped down when some other car had inexplicably paused here where there were no side streets or driveways or even wide shoulders to beckon. She never saw it. One moment, her old Ford was moving smoothly, completely under her control; the next moment, it was spinning with stunning violence.

She was jerked about like a rag doll, and clung to the steering wheel out of some dim conviction that she could somehow regain control over the vehicle. But the sheer force of the spin made her helpless. It seemed to go on forever, the summer green of the scenery revolving around her wildly, the anguished scream of tires on hot pavement shrill in her ears. Other cars cried out in response, their tires shrieking and horns blaring, adding to the cacophony blasting her.

And then there were actual blows as the whirling car began to strike stationary objects, the overgrown shrubbery that lined the street at first, and then small trees. Harsh shudders shook her and the car again and again. The spinning slowed, she thought, but then the undercarriage snagged something that refused to give or let go, there was an ungodly wail of tortured metal, and the car flipped—not once, but over and over, as violently as it had spun on its wheels.

She didn't realize she had closed her eyes until the car jolted a final time upright, rocked threateningly, and then went still with a groan.

In that first instant, she understood the phrase "deafening silence"; all she could hear was her own heart thudding. Then, as though someone had turned up the volume, the sounds of people shouting and car horns filtered into her awareness. She opened her eyes cautiously, blinking back tears of fright.

The sight that met her gaze was appalling. The windshield's shatterproof glass had simply vanished, and she could see with terrible clarity the long hood of her car now crumpled back toward her like some monstrous accordion, with unbroken headlights pointed bizarrely toward the sky. The passenger door had also been forced inward, so that she could have easily rested her elbow on it without even leaning to the right. And though the driver's door seemed amazingly whole and unharmed, she knew without even looking back that the rear of the car had also folded in, so that she was encased in a tight box of collapsed metal.

She forced her hands to let go of the steering wheel and held them up to eye level, warily examining her fingers one at a time until she could convince herself that all ten were present and working properly. Then, as the voices came nearer to what was left of her car, she shifted a bit, carefully, waiting for a pain or some other indication of injury.

She even managed to feel down her legs, bared by her summer skirt, and searched for damage.

Nothing. Not a scratch.

She wasn't a religious woman, but staring around her at something that didn't even look like a car anymore, she had to wonder if perhaps something or someone hadn't been watching over her.

"Lady, are you all right?"

She looked through the glassless window into a stranger's concerned face and heard an uncertain laugh emerge from her mouth.

"Yeah. Can you believe it?"

"No," he replied frankly, a grin tugging at his lips. "You ought to be in about a million pieces, lady. This has gotta be the luckiest day of your life."

"Tell me about it." She shifted slightly, adding, "But I can hardly move, and I can't reach the door handle. Can you get it open?"

The stranger, a middle-aged man with the burly shoulders that come of a lifetime's hard work, yanked experimentally on her door. "Nope. There isn't a mark on this door, but it's been compressed in the front and back, and it's stuck tight. We're gonna need the Jaws of Life, sure enough. Don't worry, though—the rescue squad and paramedics are on their way."

Distant sirens were getting louder, but even so she felt a chill of worry. "I had a full tank of gas. You don't think—"

"I don't smell anything," he reassured her. "And I've worked in garages most of my life. Don't worry. By the way, my name is Jim. Jim Smith, believe it or not."

"It's a day to believe anything. I'm Joanna. Nice to meet you, Jim."

He nodded. "Same here, Joanna. You're sure you're okay? No pain anywhere?"

"Not even a twinge." She looked past his shoulder to watch other motorists slipping and sliding down the bank toward her, and swallowed hard when she saw just how far her car had rolled. "My God. I should be dead, shouldn't I?"

Jim looked back and briefly studied the wide path of flattened brush and churned-up earth, then returned his gaze to her and smiled. "Like I said, this seems to be your lucky day."

Joanna looked once more at the car crumpled so snugly around her, and shivered. As close as she ever wanted to come . . .

Within five minutes, the rescue squad and paramedics arrived, all of them astonished but pleased to find her unhurt. Jim backed away to allow the rescue people room to work, joining the throng of onlookers scattered down the bank, and Joanna realized only then that she was the center of quite a bit of attention.

"I always wanted to be a star," she murmured.

The nearest paramedic, a brisk woman of about Joanna's age wearing a name badge that said E. Mallory, chuckled in response. "Word's gotten around that you haven't a scratch. Don't be surprised if the fourth estate shows up any minute."

Joanna was about to reply to that with another light comment, but before she could open her mouth, the calm of the moment was suddenly, terribly, shattered. There was a sound like a gunshot, a dozen voices screamed, *"Get back!"* and Joanna turned her gaze toward the windshield to see what looked like a thick black snake with a fiery head falling toward her out of the sky.

Then something slammed into her with the unbelievable force of a runaway train, and everything went black.

There was no sense of time passing, and Joanna didn't feel she had gone somewhere else. She felt . . . suspended, in a kind of limbo. Weightless, content, she drifted in a peaceful silence. She was waiting for something, she knew that. Waiting to find out something. The silence was absolute, but gradually the darkness began to abate, and she felt a gentle tug. She turned, or thought she did, and moved in the direction of the soft pull.

But almost immediately, she was released, drifting once more as the darkness deepened again. And she had a sudden sense that she was not alone, that someone shared the darkness with her. She felt a featherlight touch, so fleeting she wasn't at all sure of it, as though someone or something had brushed past her.

Don't let her be alone.

Joanna heard nothing, yet the plea was distinct in her mind, and the emotions behind it were nearly overwhelming. She tried to reach out toward that other, suffering presence, but before she could, something yanked at her sharply.

"Joanna? Joanna! Come on, Joanna, open your eyes!"

That summons was an audible one, growing louder as she felt herself pulled downward. She resisted for an instant, reluctant, but then fell in a rush until she felt the heaviness of her own body once more.

Instantly, every nerve and muscle she possessed seemed on fire with pain, and she groaned as she forced open her eyes.

A clear plastic cup over her face, and beyond it a circle of unfamiliar faces breaking into grins. And beyond *them* a clear blue summer sky decorated with fleecy white clouds. She was on the ground. What was she doing on the ground?

"She's back with us," one of the faces said back over his shoulder to someone else. "Let's get her on the stretcher." Then, to her, "You're going to be all right, Joanna. You're going to be just fine."

Joanna felt her aching body lifted. She watched dreamily as she floated past more faces. Then a vaguely familiar one appeared, and she saw it say something to her, something that sunk in only some time later as she rode in a wailing ambulance.

Definitely your lucky day. You almost died twice.

Her mind clearing by that time, Joanna could only agree with Jim's observation. How many people, after all, go through one near-death experience? Not many. Yet here she was, whole and virtually unharmed—if you discounted the fact that the only part of her body that didn't ache was the tip of her nose.

Still, she was very much alive, and incredibly grateful.

At the hospital, she was examined, soothed, and medicated. She would emerge from the day's incredible experiences virtually unscathed, the doctors told her. She had one burn mark on her right ankle where the electricity from the power line had arced between exposed metal and her flesh, and she'd be sore for a while both from the shock that had stopped her heart and from the later efforts to start it again.

She was a very lucky young lady and should suffer no lasting effects from what had happened to her; that was what they said.

But they were wrong. Because that was the night the dreams began.

NE

"*CAROLINE?*"

It wasn't the hand on her shoulder that made Joanna Flynn turn; it was the utter astonishment in the voice that had called her by another woman's name. Astonishment and something else, something she sensed more than heard. Whatever the emotion was, it prompted Joanna to respond.

"No," she said. Then, driven by something she saw in the man's face, she added, "I'm sorry."

He, a fairly nondescript man with reddish blond hair and blue eyes that were only now losing the expression of shock, took his hand from her shoulder and nodded a bit jerkily. "No," he agreed, "you couldn't be. . . . *I'm* sorry. Sorry. But you look so much like—" He stopped, shook his head. He offered her a polite, forgive-me-for-bothering-you smile and brushed past her to keep walking.

Joanna watched him striding away and felt vaguely troubled without even knowing why. People were mistaken for other people all the time, she knew that, and just because it had never happened to her before was no reason to let it bother her now. But she couldn't seem to get his shocked expression out of her mind.

She stood there on the virtually deserted Atlanta sidewalk in the hot September sunlight for much longer than she should have, gazing after the stranger she could no longer see, before she finally managed to shake off her uneasiness enough to continue on toward the private library where she worked as a researcher.

It was just another odd thing, that was all. Just another item to note in the column of her life reserved for strange occurrences—the column that had been filling up with items since her accident two months before.

Some of the items were minor ones. Her restlessness, very unusual for her. The vague but increasingly strong sense of urgency she felt. Her anxiety, churning within her for no reason she could pinpoint.

But the biggest item was the dream. It had begun the very night of her accident, and though it had been sporadic those first few weeks, it was a nightly occurrence now. Always the same, it presented a sequence of images and sounds, always in the same order. It was not a nightmare; there was nothing innately terrifying about the images or how they were presented. Yet Joanna woke each morning with her heart pounding and a sense of fear clogging her throat.

Something, somewhere, was wrong. She knew it. She *felt* it. Something was wrong, and she had to do something about it. Because if she didn't . . . something terrible would happen.

She didn't know what, but she knew it would be something terrible.

It was so damned vague, it was maddening. So vague that it should have been easy to dismiss as nothing more than the distorted but unimportant ramblings of the unconscious mind. Joanna had never paid much attention to her dreams, and she wanted to be able to ignore this one as easily. But she couldn't.

Her doctor said that odd dreams were to be expected. After all, she had suffered a blast of electricity strong enough to stop her heart. The brain was filled with electrical impulses, and it made sense that those impulses could have been scrambled by thousands of volts from a power line. He was sure there was nothing for her to worry about.

Joanna just wished she was as sure.

❖　　　❖　　　❖

The roar of the ocean was deafening at first, smothering all other sounds. The house, perched high above the sea, was beautiful and lonely and awoke in her a confusing jumble of feelings. Admiration, pride, and satisfaction clashed with uneasiness and fear. She wanted to concentrate on the emotions, to understand them, but felt herself abruptly pulled back away from the house. It receded into the distance and grew hazy. Then a brightly colored carousel horse passed in front of her, bobbing and turning on its gleaming brass pole, as if to music she couldn't hear. She smelled roses and from the corner of her eye caught a glimpse of the flowers in a vase. Then the roar of the sea abruptly died down until the loud ticking of a clock could be heard. She walked past a colorful painting on an easel, her steps quickening because she had to . . . get somewhere. She had to . . . find . . . something. She heard sobs, and tried to run forward—

Joanna sat bolt upright in bed, her arms reaching out, her heart pounding against her ribs. She was shaking, and her breath rasped from her tight throat. And inside her was pain and a terrible grief, and over everything else lay a cold, black pall of fear.

Her arms slowly fell while she tried to calm down. The fear and pain and grief faded slowly, leaving only the familiar uneasiness behind, and Joanna tried to reassure herself. It was a dream. Just a dream.

But the dream had changed, and its impact on Joanna had changed as well. The sense of fear had been a part of the dream all along, but this time there had been more. The grief was new, and the pain, and what she had felt while the dream had played out before her, the overwhelming feelings of anxiety and urgency, that was different, too, so powerful now that she couldn't even try to ignore what she felt.

More than ever, she was certain there was something she had to do. She didn't know what it was, but the urgency was so strong that she actually threw back the covers and swung her legs over the side of the bed. She hesitated for a moment when she realized what she was doing, then went ahead and got up. It was morning anyway—albeit very early morning. Five-thirty.

In the kitchen of her small apartment, she put coffee on, then wandered into the living room and turned on a couple of lamps. It was a pleasant room, with comfortable over-stuffed furniture and an eclectic collection of knickknacks from all over the world. Aunt Sarah had loved to travel, and every summer she had packed up her niece and jetted off to some remote corner of the globe.

Joanna's friends had always envied her her Aunt Sarah, who had certainly not been a conventional parent. And Joanna had enjoyed her unorthodox upbringing. But in a small, secret corner of her heart, she had envied her friends, because all of them had a mother and father.

She wandered over to the cold fireplace and, with her index finger, traced the edge of a silver-framed photo of her Aunt Sarah that was on the mantel. The shrewd eyes gazed out at her, and the warm smile stirred memories, and Joanna felt disloyal somehow for the childish idea that her aunt had not been enough, that her childhood had been missing something vitally important.

Still touching her aunt's photo, Joanna turned her gaze to the other silver-framed picture on the mantel. Her parents. Her mother had been younger than she was now when the photo had been taken. Fair and delicate, she stood in the protective shelter of her husband's arm, her smile glowing. Lucy Flynn had married her childhood sweetheart, and had been head over heels in love with him until the day she died. One of Joanna's most enduring memories was of the sound of her mother's voice speaking softly to her husband and calling him "darling."

As for Alan Flynn, what Joanna remembered most about him was his laugh, deep and contented. He had adored his wife and child, a fact neither had questioned. He had always been there, for both of them, never too busy or too preoccupied by his job as an attorney to spend time with his family.

Joanna reached over to touch the silver frame holding her parents' picture and wondered, as she had so many times before, what would have happened if a judge's illness had not given her father time off on that sunny June morning. Time to happily gather up his wife and take her sailing in their small craft. She wondered why fate had placed her far away that day, gone with Aunt Sarah on an impulsive trip to Disney World. She wondered why the weather service had not warned of a storm coming or, if it had warned, why her father had not taken heed. She wondered why he, an expert and experienced sailor, had been unable to bring the little boat safely back to shore.

With a little shock, Joanna realized that it had been twenty years.

She was roused from her thoughts by the coffeemaker hissing as it completed its cycle, and she turned away from the mantel and her memories. The dream had left her in an odd mood, she decided. That was all, just an odd mood.

But she was more uneasy than ever as she went to fix herself the first cup of coffee of the day, because the feelings she remembered from that tragedy of her childhood had not felt so strong since then as they did on this quiet morning. She felt pain, grief, wordless anger. She felt bereft, abandoned. It was as if something had ripped open an old, old wound inside her, and Joanna felt as raw and adrift as she had felt on that June evening when Aunt Sarah had held her and cried.

As if it had happened again.

✧   ✧   ✧

The first week in September passed, then the second. Joanna managed to keep up a good facade, she thought, but inside, her nerves were jangling. The dream came nightly, and with it the anxiety she couldn't shake, the sense that something was very, very wrong. More than once, she caught herself looking up from her work and listening intently, almost straining to hear something, and yet with no idea what it was she tried so hard to hear.

And then there were the other things. Odd things she couldn't explain. Like why a child sobbing in a grocery store because its mother wouldn't allow candy suddenly had the power to yank at her emotions. And why a whiff of cigarette smoke awoke in her an urge to inhale deeply. And why she began wearing skirts more often than slacks, when she had always disliked skirts. And why she felt a jolt of surprise whenever she looked in a mirror, as if what she saw wasn't quite right.

She felt like a pressure cooker, the force inside her building and building until she could hardly bear it, until it was dangerous, until she knew she had to do something about it. But she didn't know *what* to do, and the frustration of that ate at her. It wasn't until the middle of September that the dream haunting her offered a clue.

✧   ✧   ✧

The roar of the ocean was deafening at first, smothering all other sounds. The house, perched high above the sea, was beautiful and lonely and awoke in her a confusing jumble of feelings. Admiration, pride, and satisfaction clashed with uneasiness and fear. She wanted to concentrate on the emotions, to understand them, but felt herself abruptly pulled back away from the house. It receded into the distance and grew hazy. Then a brightly colored carousel horse passed in front of her, bobbing and turning on its gleaming brass pole, as if to music she couldn't hear. She smelled roses and from the corner of her eye caught a glimpse of the flowers in a vase. Then the roar of the sea abruptly died down until the loud ticking of a clock could be heard. A paper airplane soared and dipped, riding a breeze she couldn't feel. She walked past a colorful painting on an easel, her steps quickening because she had to . . . get somewhere. She had to . . . find . . . something. She heard sobs, a child's sobs, and tried to run forward, but she couldn't move—and then she saw the signpost, and she knew where she had to go—

Joanna woke to find herself sitting bolt upright in bed, her arms outstretched and her heart pounding painfully. Slowly, her arms dropped, and in the silence of the dark bedroom, she heard herself whisper a single word.

"Cliffside."

   ✦   ✦   ✦

Like a weird movie signpost, crooked letters on an old splintered board. *Cliffside.* It wasn't very much to go on. There were probably hundreds, if not thousands, of towns bearing that name in the United States alone.

But a research librarian had the tools and knowledge to sift through all the possibilities, and Joanna wasted no time beginning what she expected to be a lengthy search. Luckily, her workload was light at the moment, and so she was able to spend hours at the computer and microfiche machine.

It was a customary part of her job, spending hours combing through information, and Joanna was glad. Not only because it made her task easier, but because she could search for a dream signpost without arousing any undue suspicion. No one around her could possibly guess what was going on in her head, the anxiety and uneasiness. No one could possibly imagine that she woke each night from an eerie dream with a cry locked in her throat and panic tearing at her breathing.

By every outward sign, Joanna's life was normal. She went to work each day and home each evening. The face she saw in the mirror was unchanged, her smile nearly as quick and easy as it had always been. Her coworkers noticed nothing unusual about her intense focus or the preoccupation that often kept her working through her regular lunch hour. And since she had no family and had kept herself too busy recently to see much of her friends, no one spent enough time with her to realize that in actuality her life was anything but normal.

But Joanna knew. She felt oddly out of control, as if she were adrift in a current, helpless to choose her own direction. She was being carried along, whether she wanted to be or not. Toward a place named Cliffside. She had never really believed in fate, but as the days passed, it began to seem to her as though fate demanded that she concentrate all her energies on one thing alone. Finding Cliffside.

But why? Haunted by a dream, her life virtually taken over by it, Joanna couldn't begin to understand what was happening to her. She had to believe it had something to do with her accident, since the dream had started afterward, but that didn't explain *why*. In her more frustrated moments, she couldn't help but wonder if all that electricity had simply scrambled her brain, yet even then something deeper inside her refused to believe that. Her accident had somehow been a catalyst, but the dream was no mere accidental pattern of electrical impulses in her brain.

It meant something. And until she understood what that was, Joanna knew that her life would not be her own again.

She threw herself into the search for Cliffside, trying to match the rocky, surf-pounded shoreline in her dream to an actual place. By eliminating all the landlocked Cliffsides from her initial list, she was able to cut the list in half, and eliminating all states with a low-lying coastal plain cut it again, but there were still dozens of towns named Cliffside left, each of which had to be checked out individually for characteristics matching those in her dream.

It was a slow, painstaking process. And by the middle of the third week in September, with Cliffside still elusive, Joanna had begun to seriously question her sanity. She didn't feel like herself anymore. Favorite foods no longer appealed to her. She found herself drawn to colors she had never cared for. And for the first time in her life, she'd begun to bite her nails, a nervous habit so unlike her that it frightened her. She was filled with anxiety and tormented with a sense of urgency that was knife-sharp each morning when she woke from the dream and diminished only a little throughout the day.

Cliffside. It was like a lodestar, hovering before her to entice and compel. Everything else in her life had shrunk to insignificance.

By the following Sunday afternoon, she had to take a break from the pile of books and clippings cluttering the living room of her apartment, and drove to a shopping center a few miles away. She didn't need to buy anything in particular, but she was tired and discouraged and not looking forward to the coming night, and splurging on a new bottle of perfume or bath oil sounded like a good idea.

It felt like a good idea too. Then, as she came out of the department store with her purchases in one of those little paper bags with twine handles and the store's elegant logo printed in foil, a chilly hand grasped her arm.

"Caroline?"

This time, a woman's shocked face met Joanna's startled gaze. She was a beautiful and exotic looking blonde with catlike eyes the slightly unreal green of tinted contact lenses, wearing a two-hundred-dollar silk blouse over faded blue jeans.

"No," Joanna said. "Sorry."

The woman's hand fell and her shock faded as she smiled politely. "Excuse me, I thought you were—someone else." She laughed a little, obviously still shaken, then murmured another apology and went into the store Joanna had just left.

Joanna found herself looking at her own dim reflection in the glass of the door as she gazed after the stranger. Caroline again. That, she thought, stretched coincidence a bit thin, to be mistaken for this Caroline twice in such a short span of time. But even that didn't bother her as much as the shock of the man and woman who had mistaken her for Caroline. Why had they looked that way? Why would they feel such stunned incredulity at believing she was this woman?

Who was Caroline? And why did Joanna have the feeling that that was the most important question of all?

✧   ✧   ✧

"Oh my God." Joanna was hardly aware of speaking aloud, but since she was alone in the microfilm room, it hardly made a difference. There was no one to hear her. No one to see the shock she knew her face held. Checking references to Cliffside in Oregon in *The Portland Citizen-Times*, she had reached the previous July without a reference. Then she had found something.

> Caroline McKenna, 29, *was killed July 1 when her car went out of control on a rain-slick highway not ten miles from her home. A prominent resident of the coastal town of Cliffside, Oregon, and very active in community affairs, Mrs. McKenna is survived by a husband and daughter. Memorial services will be held July 4 in Cliffside.*

Caroline. *Killed the day of my accident.*

A woman named Caroline, who had lived in Cliffside, Oregon. A woman who had been killed in a car accident on July 1. A woman who might very well have looked enough like Joanna that two people had been shocked to have seen her—alive and walking the sidewalks of Atlanta.

And a haunting, compelling dream containing a signpost that said Cliffside.

Joanna stared at Caroline McKenna's obituary, reading it again and again. It wasn't much information to sum up a life—or a death. A car accident. A young and vital woman killed before her time who had left behind a husband and daughter. An end to promise.

Why did it tug at her so? In many ways, their lives seemed opposite. Caroline married with a child, Joanna single and childless. Joanna with a career, Caroline apparently occupied by community concerns. They lived on opposite sides of the country, one in a small town and the other a major city. Yet on the same July day, both had been involved in car accidents. One had survived. The other had not.

A woman she had never known had died three thousand miles away, their lives seemingly unconnected despite their being the same age and possibly being physically similar—and yet Joanna felt the strongest compulsion she had ever known to learn more, to find out about Caroline and Cliffside. It made no sense to her, no sense at all.

She made a copy of the obituary and automatically labeled a new file folder to add to the others containing material she had collected. This folder was labeled simply *Caroline,* and it struck Joanna powerfully that the first item of information to be placed into it was Caroline McKenna's obituary.

She closed the folder and set it aside, then went back to scanning the newspaper for any references to Cliffside and Caroline. Nothing. As far as *The Portland Citizen-Times* was concerned, the only thing of consequence to happen in Cliffside during the entire year through July was Caroline's death.

In August, however, there was a brief article about the planned expansion of Cliffside's small medical clinic; a new wing would be added, thanks to a bequest from Caroline McKenna. In her will, she had left to the clinic a piece of land adjoining the existing structure and more than enough money to build, equip, and staff the new wing. It would contain a lab and the latest diagnostic tools, as well as a cardiac care unit and trauma center.

The article, which Joanna copied and added to Caroline's file, offered at least some information about Caroline, however indirectly. She'd had money, that much was certain; the projected cost of the clinic's wing was somewhere in the neighborhood of three million dollars.

Three million dollars.

"There's one difference between us," Joanna heard herself murmur wryly.

The article also seemed to indicate that Caroline either had been interested in funding medicine in general or had felt pretty strongly that her community had needed its medical services expanded. But whether she had funded other causes wasn't clear; there was no mention of any other charitable bequest. And no mention of whether Caroline had left any part of her estate to her husband and child.

It wasn't until the following day, when she was working through her lunch hour, that Joanna gained computer access to Cliffside's newspaper and town records and began to find the information she had been looking for. Information about the town and its people, from climate and economy to how many marriages, baptisms, and burials were recorded at City Hall.

And a photograph of Caroline McKenna, taken the previous year when she and her husband had posed with a group supporting Cliffside's community theater.

She could have been Joanna's sister.

Dark rather than fair, the dead woman nonetheless shared Joanna's features, the shape of her face, even her slender build. On the computer screen, Caroline's delicate features were distinct. Her face was slightly heart-shaped, her dark hair worn in a smooth shoulder-length style some inches shorter than Joanna's much lighter blond hair. She had large eyes and a tender, almost childlike mouth, and there was an air of fragility about her.

Her husband, Scott McKenna, stood on her right. He was a darkly handsome man in his mid-thirties, well built and taller than Caroline by some inches despite her high heels. The dark suit he wore made him look not so much somber as . . . aloof. He was smiling faintly, but there was an odd aura of remoteness surrounding him, and though he and his wife stood side by side, they were not touching.

As she looked at the two people and the group around them, Joanna slowly became aware that the restless urgency she had felt for so many weeks had become a conviction so powerful she didn't even try to fight it. For the first time since waking from the accident, she knew exactly what she had to do, and the relief of that was stunning.

In order to get her own life back, she would have to go to Cliffside and explore the life of another woman, a woman who had died the day they had both been involved in car accidents. Joanna didn't know why, but she was certain that she and Caroline were somehow connected, and that until she understood that connection and the reason for it, she would never be at peace again.

$\mathcal{T}$WO

✧ ✧ ✧

$\mathcal{H}$OLLY DRUMMOND CAME OUT of her office and cast a critical eye over the front desk, more out of habit than the need to supervise. Bliss Weldon, the day clerk, was, despite her absurd name, both efficient and utterly reliable. And in fact, the desk was quiet, with Bliss working intently at the computer. No phones ringing, no guests offering plaintive grievances. Everything was peaceful, just the way a hotel manager preferred her establishment to be.

Holly consulted a page on her clipboard and nodded to herself. Only one guest was due to check in this afternoon, and she was booked into a small suite for the next two weeks, with the possibility of a longer stay. Which was fine, just fine. This time of year, guests tended to be sporadic, and anytime Holly could declare a 50 percent occupancy rate during the off-season, it was satisfying to both her and the owner.

She walked through the lobby toward the veranda doors, pleased by the elegant and comfortable atmosphere

surrounding her. Called simply The Inn, the hotel was
more than fifty years old, but no expense had been spared
in renovating it less than five years ago, and it was a beautiful place. From the marble floors to the wallpaper, only the
best of materials had been chosen, and a well-trained staff
kept the place running with smooth, quiet efficiency. The
Inn had a four-star rating and a firm reputation for provid-
ing the ultimate in comfort for its guests.

It was, in fact, one of the major tourist draws for the
area. Beautiful scenery, peace and quiet, and The Inn
brought visitors to Cliffside, and the visitors brought
money to boost the local economy. Generally speaking, it
was a fine relationship all around.

Holly went through the open doors and out onto the
seaside veranda. Chaise longues and groupings of tables
and chairs were placed invitingly under the protective roof
as well as farther out where the October sunshine was
bright and warm. A dozen or so guests relaxed out there,
some reading newspapers while others drank coffee and
talked.

Holly nodded to the waitress keeping the guests supplied with whatever they wished and went on. Her destination was a chaise at the edge of the veranda, where a lean,
copper-haired man relaxed in the sunlight. He wasn't
alone; a girl of about eighteen sat on the foot of his chaise
and flirted for all she was worth, encouraged by his lazy
smile of amusement.

Holly felt herself frowning, and smoothed out the expression as she joined them, saying pleasantly, "Hi, Amber.
I thought you had a drive scheduled for today."

The slender blonde jumped to her feet, her expression
both guilty and defiant. "I told my parents to go without
me. Who wants to look at miles and miles of scenery? I was
just telling Mr.— I was just telling Cain that I was thinking
about walking down to the stores and doing some shopping."

"It's a nice day for it," Holly said, her tone ever so

slightly dry. At the moment, she felt every one of the twelve years between her and this girl.

Amber shoved her hands into the front pockets of the very brief shorts she should have packed away a month before and smiled brightly. "I thought so. Cain, would you—would you like to go?"

Cain Barlow chuckled, and his lazy voice matched his smile when he said, "Haven't you heard the latest psychobabble? Men are hunters and women gatherers; that's why you love shopping for its own sake, and we hate it."

Amber looked down at him, her bafflement painfully evident. "Oh. Well . . . maybe we could walk along the cliffs later?"

"Afraid you'll have to count me out, Amber. I have to drive into Portland this afternoon."

"Oh." Amber summoned a smile and clearly hoped it was devastating. "Some other time, then."

"Sure."

The blonde offered Holly another of those half-defiant looks, then left them and walked across the veranda toward the building.

"Do you suppose she learned to walk that way by watching old Mae West movies?" Cain mused.

"I think she just lets her hormones rule," Holly said. "That and wearing heels three inches too high. You shouldn't encourage her, Cain. Hearts break very easily at eighteen."

"Encourage her? I was sitting here minding my own business and waiting for you to come back when she came over and practically dropped into my lap. What was I supposed to do? Offend one of your paying guests by being rude to his daughter?" He reached up a hand to touch Holly, but she shifted away with a faint shrug of impatience, and Cain's eyes narrowed. "Obviously, you think I should have chased her away."

Instead of claiming Amber's former seat at the foot of

Cain's chaise, Holly sat down on another one near his. "I think you charm without a second thought," she said.

"Holly, she's a kid, just a kid. And twenty years younger than me."

"All the more reason for you to be careful." Holly looked down at her clipboard, frowning.

Cain laced long fingers together over his flat middle and looked at her for a moment. He wore an expression of acute detachment, with only his brilliant green eyes alive in the stillness of his face. "Okay. Noted, for future reference. Now, hadn't *we* planned a walk along the cliffs before that phone call interrupted us?"

"I can't."

"Let me guess. The call was from the master?"

Holly looked at him, still frowning. "It was Scott. Why do you have to be so mocking whenever you mention him?"

"Because I don't like him," Cain told her pleasantly. "And I don't like the way you drop everything and run to him whenever he whistles."

"That isn't fair. He's my employer. And he's having a tough time right now," Holly said. "Since Caroline was killed—"

"Since Caroline was killed, the entire town's been heaping sympathy and understanding on poor Scott's grieving head," Cain said, definitely mocking now. "And the son of a bitch is milking it for all he's worth."

"That's a terrible thing to say."

"Isn't it? And a genuine pity it's true."

Holly surged to her feet, hugging the clipboard as though it were a shield. "Look, I just came back out here to tell you I have to meet Scott at City Hall and go over some things about the new wing for the clinic. It shouldn't take more than an hour or so. If you're still here then—"

"I won't be. Like I told baby Amber, I have to drive into Portland." Cain didn't move as he looked up at her. He sat relaxed, watchful—and Holly had no idea what he was thinking.

She never did. It was enough to drive a woman crazy. She nodded. "All right, then. Lunch was . . . fun."

"Yeah. Of course, it would have been more fun if we'd ended up in my bed for dessert. But you don't seem to have the time—or the taste—for sweets these days, do you, Holly?"

"You're busy too," she said defensively. "How many times have you had to go to L.A. or New York in the last weeks? Stop making it sound like it's all my fault we hardly see each other." She heard herself sounding like a neglected woman and made a fierce effort to keep that note out of her voice. "Look, we both have careers, and—"

"We were both busy a few months ago and still managed to find the time," he said, his voice hardening. "Before poor Scott began to depend on you for everything."

"You're not being fair," she said, knowing she was repeating herself.

"No, probably not. But then, I'm a selfish bastard myself. You've told me so often enough." He shrugged, dismissing the conflict as though he really didn't care whether it was resolved. "You run along and help Scott with his current problem. I should probably conserve my strength anyway. It's a long drive to Portland."

Holly turned away and took two steps before stopping. *Damn, damn, damn.* Hating herself, she turned back. "Are you staying long in Portland? I mean—will I see you tomorrow?"

"I'll probably be back late tonight," he said.

She waited for an instant, until it became obvious that was all he was going to say. Then, reaching for dignity, she nodded. "Have a good trip. Drive carefully."

Those brilliant green eyes softened just a little, and he nodded. "We'll none of us ever be quite so nonchalant about driving as we were three months ago, I suppose. Don't worry, I'll be careful."

It was harder, this time, to turn away from him, but she did it and left the veranda briskly. She felt his eyes on her until she was inside, but she didn't look back or even pause. She had a job to do, after all, she reminded herself. She worked for Scott McKenna, who owned The Inn as well as various other properties and businesses in Cliffside, and if he needed her help in planning the new wing for the town's clinic, well, then she'd help him.

She could feel the rift between her and Cain widening.

Holly was halfway across the quiet lobby when the front doors opened. She heard one of the bellmen outside saying something about bags and parking a car, and then a blond woman came in. Holly stopped dead in her tracks, vaguely aware that her mouth had dropped open, that she was staring incredulously, but she was so surprised she couldn't seem to do anything about it.

The blonde came several steps into the lobby, saw Holly, and stopped a bit uncertainly. She was about Holly's own height, an average five-six, with lovely honey-gold hair pulled back off her face in a simple style, and her casual slacks and sweater showed off a slender, almost delicate figure. Her face was more heart shaped than oval, her unusual tawny eyes large and dark-fringed, and she had a sensitive, vulnerable mouth.

Before Holly could gather her wits, the woman gave an uneasy little laugh and asked a question in a soft voice with a strong Southern accent.

"Was it something I said?"

Holly blinked. How strange to hear such an alien voice come out of a mouth that was all too familiar, she thought. "Oh   no. God, I'm sorry. It's just that you look an awful lot like someone I used to know."

"Used to?"

"She died a few months ago."

"Now *I'm* sorry."

"It's all right. We weren't . . . close." Holly smiled and stepped forward, holding out her hand. "I'm Holly Drummond, manager of The Inn. Please call me Holly."

The blonde shook hands, her grip firm. "Nice to meet you, Holly. I'm Joanna. Joanna Flynn."

"Well, Joanna, welcome. If there's any way I can help

make your stay with us more enjoyable, I hope you'll let me know." The words were conventional and professional, but Holly always meant them, and that sincerity came through.

"I will, thanks." Joanna Flynn smiled. "What I mostly want now is to settle in, unpack, and get the kinks out of my legs from the drive. Maybe I'll see you around later?"

"I'm usually around," Holly told her with a laugh. She watched Joanna head for the front desk, and after an instant continued on her own way. It was a fairly short walk, just a couple of blocks to City Hall, and Holly needed both the exercise and the air—to clear her head. And to figure out how to warn Scott. Hell, how to warn the town.

Hey, guess what? There's a new guest at The Inn, and if you colored her hair dark and put in blue contact lenses, she'd be Caroline! How about that . . .

"Dammit," Holly barely heard herself whisper, "what'll he think when he sees you, Joanna Flynn? What'll he feel . . . ?"

◇ ◇ ◇

The fourth-floor suite was lovely; it was composed of a sitting room, a bedroom, and a bath, and it was spacious and comfortable. Despite its quaint name, The Inn was a full-service hotel complete with twenty-four-hour room service and cable television, according to the friendly bellman, and if there was anything she required to make her more comfortable, anything at all, she had only to ask.

As soon as he left, Joanna began settling in. She unpacked and put away all her things, turning on the television to CNN for background noise while she briskly worked. When that was done, she went to the French doors in her bedroom that opened out onto a little balcony, and stepped out to contemplate her ocean view.

Down on the right was the tile roof that partially shaded the veranda; down and straight ahead were a couple of acres of green lawn, then the rocky cliff tops and, beyond them, the ocean. There was a beach at the base of the cliffs except at high tide, the bellman had told her, but it was narrow, the path down to it somewhat difficult, and few guests ventured down there more than once.

Joanna turned her head to the left, her gaze following the cliff tops south. She froze, hardly breathing, and for a long moment just stood there staring. Then she eased back into her room as if careful movement was required to keep something dreadful from happening. She went into the sitting room and sat down at the little desk where she had placed the notebook.

She had never kept a journal before, but it had occurred to her that it might be a good idea here. To organize her thoughts. To keep things clear. Drawing a breath, she opened the notebook carefully and smoothed the page. She used the pen thoughtfully provided by The Inn and dated the top of the page. She didn't really think about what she wanted to say, she just began writing.

> *Today I arrived in Cliffside. Here at The Inn my bedroom has a little balcony overlooking the ocean. And from that balcony, just exactly as it was in my dreams, I can see the house.*

✦　　✦　　✦

Even from a distance, it was an impressive house.

Joanna sat on a smooth-topped boulder atop the cliffs about halfway between The Inn and the house from her dreams, and stared at it. It was still nearly a mile away by her judgment, and from this angle the trees between it and Cliffside's main road hid part of the beautiful landscaping she had seen from her bedroom balcony, but it was still beautiful.

Vaguely Victorian in style just as The Inn was, it had a roof with many peaks, countless windows sparkling in the sunlight, and a wide, ocean-side porch with, no doubt, a spectacular view. From where Joanna sat, the house should have looked bleak; it seemed almost to perch on a rocky promontory, standing in lonely isolation, with frothy ocean waves crashing against the base of the cliffs far below. Yet it didn't look bleak so much as . . . dignified.

Still, Joanna's feelings about the house were distorted, shaped by the dream that had tormented her for so many weeks. It seemed to her dark and menacing. It made her wary, almost afraid.

Joanna drew her knees up and wrapped her arms loosely around them, listening to the thunder of high tide battering the cliffs and feeling the cool ocean breeze. The sun was setting over the ocean, making the windows of the distant house glow reddish, and Joanna felt a faint chill that had nothing to do with the falling temperature.

Caroline's house. She didn't know how she knew she was looking at the house where Caroline had lived, but she was positive of that fact. And there, presumably, lived Caroline's husband and daughter.

In the three months since her death, they had no doubt begun to cope with her loss, but Joanna knew her own appearance was bound to cause some . . . distress. Even the bellman and desk clerk at The Inn had been startled by her, and as for Holly Drummond, the attractive brunette had looked as though her knees had nearly buckled in shock.

Joanna hadn't thought very much about her impulsive decision to come here during all the busy days of preparation, but as she sat there on the rock gazing at Caroline's house, she felt more than a little panic. What did she hope to gain by coming here? Would her being here exorcise the ghost of Caroline McKenna from her dreams—if it was the dead woman's ghost?

She had the uneasy idea that by coming to Cliffside so impetuously, she had started something that had immediately grown beyond her control, and for an instant she was sorely tempted to go back to The Inn, get her things, and catch the first plane heading to Atlanta, where she belonged. But before she could give in to the spurt of panic, a voice recalled her attention.

"Excuse me, but you shouldn't—"

Joanna turned her head quickly, hardly surprised by this time when the man who had approached without giving his presence away broke off abruptly, a look of shock on his face. He was a tall man, broad shouldered and athletic in build. He had very dark hair and very dark eyes, and though his lean face was too rugged for conventional handsomeness, there was something unusually compelling about him.

Beyond him, at the edge of the woods, Joanna saw a Blazer parked on a narrow dirt trail she hadn't even noticed until then, and though the lettering on the vehicle's side wasn't entirely clear at this distance, the large logo was.

"You're a policeman?" she asked, surprised by the lack of a uniform. He was, in fact, very casual in jeans and a light nylon windbreaker open over a dark T-shirt.

He nodded slowly and took a couple more steps toward her so that they were no more than a few feet apart. The shock had faded from his expression, but he was frowning slightly. "Sheriff. Griffin Cavanaugh." His voice was deep and just a bit harsh, though whether that was usual or he was emotionally disturbed by her appearance was something Joanna had no way of knowing.

"I see. Am I doing something wrong, Sheriff?"

He didn't answer immediately, those dark eyes fixed on her face so intensely she could almost feel the touch of them. But then he said almost mechanically, "You shouldn't sit so close to the edge. It isn't really safe. We had somebody fall right about here no more than four or five months ago."

Since heights never bothered her, Joanna hadn't hesitated to sit so close to the edge of the cliff that if she swung her right leg, it would have dangled out into thin air. But his words caused her to glance down at the jagged, surf-pounded rocks far below, and she shivered a little. Without wasting another moment, she scrambled off the rock and stood before him.

"The person who fell," she said, "did he or she . . . die?"

Sheriff Griffin Cavanaugh nodded. "We lose one every

five years or so," he said, his voice still a bit remote. "Tourists without the sense to stay back."

Joanna felt defensive on behalf of all tourists. "There's no sign. If it's so dangerous, why isn't this area posted, Sheriff?"

His dark eyes narrowed slightly, and this time there was nothing detached in his tone when he said, "Because every time I post it, either the wind or a vandal does away with the sign. You're from The Inn, aren't you?"

"Yes, I'm staying there."

"Then you should have read the warnings posted on the inside of your door. The cliffs behind the hotel have guardrails, and all guests are advised not to wander from that property. You're on private land now."

Joanna glanced toward the distant house involuntarily.

"Yes, his land," the sheriff said, following her glance with one of his own. "It isn't posted, but trespassing is strongly discouraged. This area can be treacherous, Miss—?"

"Flynn. Joanna Flynn."

He nodded. "Miss Flynn. We would all prefer it if you confined your walks around the cliffs to hotel grounds. For your own safety."

"I understand." She had no intention of saying more, but when the sheriff started to turn away, she heard herself say, "Sheriff? I've encountered quite a few surprised reactions today, including yours."

"You resemble someone who used to live around here," he said readily enough.

"So I've been told. Holly Drummond said that the woman I look like . . . died."

"Yes. Three months ago." Whatever he may have felt about that fact, Griffin Cavanaugh kept it to himself; his expression was calm, his voice without emotion.

"Forgive me, but what was her name? And how did she die?" Joanna didn't know why she was pretending ignorance about Caroline, except that she was reluctant to let anyone in Cliffside know that she had traveled thousands of miles to explore a tenuous connection with a dead woman.

"Why do you want to know?" he demanded bluntly.

"It seems I look enough like her to be her sister." Joanna managed a shrug. "I'm curious."

"Her name was Caroline McKenna. She was killed in a car accident. The highway was slippery; she was driving too fast and lost control of her car. Anything else you want to know?"

Joanna didn't let his rather harsh tone dissuade her. "Do I really look so much like her?"

He looked her up and down quite deliberately and thoroughly, then said, "Dye your hair black and change the color of your eyes and her own mother wouldn't have been able to tell the difference."

She didn't know if it was pain or anger she heard in his voice, but whichever it was warned her that she had gone far enough. "I see. Thank you, Sheriff—for the warning and for the information."

"Don't mention it." He looked beyond her, where the sun was sinking rapidly. "It'll be dark soon. It happens suddenly this time of year. You should head back to the hotel."

Joanna knew a dismissal when she heard one, and she decided to obey. She was here for at least two weeks, after all; there was plenty of time to explore. But before she could do more than begin to turn toward the hotel, he stopped her with a question of his own.

"Why are you here, Miss Flynn?"

"Vacation."

"In October?"

"I like fall vacations."

He frowned at her. "You're Southern."

"Don't you like Southerners?" she managed lightly.

The sheriff ignored that. "Georgia, I'd say."

Without meaning to, Joanna answered the implied question. "Yes, Georgia. Atlanta, as a matter of fact. But we haven't tried to secede from the Union recently, so I don't see that you should have a problem with my being here."

His hard mouth curved in a faint smile at that, but the amusement was short-lived. "You've come a long way just to spend your vacation in a place with nothing to recommend it but the scenery."

"That is surely my own business, Sheriff. But if you must know, I plan to vacation in every state eventually. It's the best way I can think of to see the country. Oregon just happened to be my first choice in visiting the West Coast."

"And Cliffside?"

Joanna couldn't tell if he believed her or not. She shrugged. "The Chamber of Commerce made it sound like a nice place, and all I wanted was a pretty coastal spot where I could relax. Good enough?"

"For now," he said. "Good day, Miss Flynn."

"Sheriff." She turned and headed toward the hotel, making a determined effort to move casually. At first, she was tempted to chalk the sheriff's interest up to small-town caution, but that reasoning didn't hold water when tourism was so vital to the local economy. A more likely possibility was that he found the sudden appearance of a woman who looked eerily like Caroline McKenna to be far more than coincidental.

It occurred to Joanna only then that there would no doubt be many people in Cliffside who would feel the same suspicion.

She reached the neatly trimmed lawn of The Inn and paused to look back. The sheriff was still standing there where she had left him, but he wasn't looking after her. He was instead gazing off toward that lonely house in the distance.

❖   ❖   ❖

For the first time in weeks, Joanna slept all night without waking, but when she did wake around eight the following morning, it was with a niggling sense of unease as well as the memory of having dreamed again. Not everything this time, at least not that she remembered, but definitely the carousel horse and paper airplane, and there had been rose petals drifting downward like rain.

She lay there for a long time in her comfortable bed, listening to the low roar of the ocean and staring at the ceiling, thinking about the previous day and trying to weigh her impressions of Cliffside and the people she'd met. Judging by all the reactions she'd earned, it seemed obvious that Joanna was going to find many people who had known Caroline. Which meant there would be many sources of information.

If Joanna could only figure out what questions to ask.

She got up, showered, and ordered breakfast from room service. And she drank her final morning cup of coffee while standing in the open door of her balcony and looking off toward Caroline's house. She continued to feel uneasy when she looked at it. But that didn't stop her from considering the best way to approach the place.

Trespassing was "strongly discouraged," Sheriff Cavanaugh had said. Okay, but he'd also said the land wasn't posted. So *legally* she wouldn't be breaking any laws if she just wandered along the cliffs in that direction. Of course, the good sheriff could argue that she'd known better—if she got caught.

Briefly and somewhat ruefully amused at herself and this unfamiliar recklessness, Joanna left her room and took the elevator down to the lobby.

Holly Drummond was standing near the front desk and greeted her cheerfully. "Good morning, Joanna."

Joanna was very aware that the other woman was looking at her in a measuring way that was probably completely unconscious and doubtless due to the resemblance to Caroline. It made her a bit uncomfortable, but she reminded herself silently that she had better get used to it.

"Hi, Holly. Listen, I was wondering. If there's any information I need about Cliffside and the surrounding area—"

"You can ask me or whoever's running the front desk," Holly said. "Most of the staff know the area pretty well, in fact. We don't have a concierge, but there are lots of brohures over there by the house phones, and any of us vould be happy to help you. What do you want to know?"

That's a good question. "Oh . . . nothing in particu-ar, at least right now." Reading curiosity in Holly's ex-pression, Joanna managed a laugh. "I'm a research ibrarian back home, so I guess it's an occupational hazard hat I tend to research the places where I spend my free ime. No matter how hard I try to relax, I always end up in ι library reading about the town founders. Absurd, I ‹now."

Holly smiled. "I don't know, it sounds more enjoyable :o me than playing golf or buying a lot of junk you don't ιeed, which is what most people seem to do."

"Yeah, but my friends tell me I really should stop work-ng when I'm not getting paid for it."

"I know the feeling." Holly glanced somewhat ruefully Jown at her ever-present clipboard. "I never seem to be off Juty. But, hey, who promised us life would be fair?"

"My Aunt Sarah," Joanna answered seriously.

"Really?"

"Oh, yeah. She raised me, and to her dying day, she was absolutely certain that you get out of life what you put into it. Be fair to others and they'll be fair to you. You know, I once saw her face down a mugger by asking him in her best aunt voice why he was wasting his life robbing people. He followed her for a block trying to explain his reasoning."

Holly laughed. "She sounds like quite a lady."

"She was." Joanna smiled, then said, "Well, I think I'll go out and look at the ocean for a while."

"Now would probably be better than later," Holly said, "unless you like walking in chilly rain; the forecast prom-ises we'll get wet this afternoon."

"Thanks for the warning." Joanna waved and started toward the veranda.

"Joanna?"

"Yeah?"

Holly smiled. "Our library is three blocks down, just

past the courthouse. A casual walk or a very short drive. Just in case."

Joanna acknowledged the information with another wave and a smile, then went onto the veranda. Had she offered a good enough explanation for her curiosity? She wasn't sure, but it had been the best she'd been able to come up with, and would at least provide a reason for her to spend time in Cliffside's library *and* to ask questions. She hoped.

Low brooding clouds promised that the weather forecasters had gotten it right for once, and the gusty breeze carried on it the taste of salt from a rather stormy looking ocean. Joanna didn't linger long behind the inn, standing at the railing and gazing out for no more than five minutes before turning and beginning to follow the cliffs south.

Reaching the end of the lawn, she looked around warily, feeling absurdly guilty to be leaving hotel grounds and more than a little nervous. But that didn't stop her from moving on briskly once she was fairly sure that no one had noticed her. She kept back from the edge of the cliffs this time but remained always in sight of the ocean, her destination the woods.

The plan, such as it was, was to make her way through the woods until she was closer to Caroline's house. After that, Joanna didn't know what she would do. She had no intention of knocking on the door, of course, or even of being seen if she could avoid it. And she didn't know what she hoped to gain by trying to get closer to the house. But the more ground she covered, the more certain she was that there was something out here she needed to see, to find.

She had no way of knowing what that was, but she recognized it instantly when she emerged suddenly into a clearing that was separated by the lawn of Caroline's house only by another fifty or sixty feet of forest. Built within the half-moon clearing near the cliff's edge was a lovely gazebo, slightly oriental in design like a little pagoda.

And inside the gazebo, in colors so bright and fresh it

looked brand-new, was the carousel horse from her dreams.

Joanna moved forward without conscious volition. She went up the two steps, across a few feet of solidly built flooring, and lifted a hand slowly to rest upon a painted forelock. As far as she could tell, it was a genuine, full-sized horse from a carousel, the pole on which it was mounted fastened securely to the floor and ceiling beam of the gazebo.

"Now all I need is a paper airplane to sail by," she heard herself murmur.

"This was our place."

It wasn't difficult to tell who was more startled when Joanna turned her head. The little girl actually took a step back, her already huge blue eyes widening and her little face going paper white.

"It's all right," Joanna said involuntarily, not moving because she didn't want to frighten the child further. "I won't hurt you."

"You look like my mama."

She hadn't prepared herself even for the possibility of this meeting, and Joanna felt completely inadequate. She was gazing at a girl of no more than eight or nine, a girl who had lost her mother a scant three months before, and the poor kid was clearly on the verge of shock at finding her mother's virtual twin standing in the place they had apparently loved.

"My name is Joanna." She kept her voice as quiet as possible and allowed her instincts to tell her what to say. "I'm just a visitor in Cliffside. But they told me when I got here yesterday that I look like someone who . . . used to live here. Someone named Caroline. Was she your mama?"

The little girl nodded slowly, unblinking eyes still fixed on Joanna's face.

"I'm sorry you lost her. I lost my mama when I was about your age. My father too."

"In a—in a car accident?" Caroline's daughter asked hesitantly.

"No, it was another kind of accident. My father liked to sail, and one day when they went out together on a little boat, there was a storm."

"The boat sank?"

Joanna nodded.

The little girl frowned slightly and looked past Joanna for a brief moment. "Aren't you scared of the ocean now?"

"If I'd been with them, I suppose I would be. But I wasn't. And it was a long time ago."

"I'm afraid of cars. I don't ever want to get in one again."

"I can see how you'd feel that way," Joanna said, her heart going out to the grave little girl.

"My name's Regan. With a long *e*." The last was added somewhat defensively, and that was explained when she added, "Only one *e* and only one *a*, but everybody wants to spell it with two *a*'s and say it with a short *e*."

"I like it much better with only one *a* and a long *e*," Joanna said judiciously. "It's nice to meet you, Regan."

"You don't sound like my mama." Regan tilted her dark head a bit. "You don't sound like anybody around here."

"That's because I live on the other side of the country," Joanna explained. "In Atlanta, Georgia."

"Where the Braves are?"

Joanna smiled. "Yeah, where the Braves are. You like baseball?"

"Uh-huh. So does—so did my mama." Regan dug her hands down into the front pockets of her jeans and hunched her shoulders. "Daddy doesn't. He doesn't like anything except his work."

Hearing more in those last two sentences than the mere words, Joanna said slowly, "Sometimes when grown-ups lose somebody they love, they spend all their time working so it won't hurt so much."

Regan looked at her with an oddly adult discernment. "He worked all the time before the car accident."

Lesson: Don't talk down to the poor kid. Joanna nodded. "I see. Some people are like that."

Regan seemed pleased by the simple statement; she didn't quite smile, but nearly. "That's what my teacher says."

"Your teacher? Say, why aren't you in school today?"

"I'm being home-schooled," Regan explained. "Because of the car and the bus. School's on the other side of town, too far to walk, and . . . I heard the doctor tell Daddy not to make me get in a car or the bus until I was ready. So I have a teacher at home now. Her name's Mrs. Porter."

"You like her?"

Regan hunched her shoulders again. "She's okay. She likes one of those talk shows on TV, so I always take my morning break the same time so she can watch it."

"Do you always walk out here during your break?" Joanna asked.

"No, just sometimes." Regan hesitated, then went on a bit gruffly, "Mama's favorite place was this gazebo. When I was little, Mama took me to a fair, and I rode on the carousel. I liked it so much that she hunted and hunted until she found a carousel horse she could buy, and then she had it put here. So her favorite place could be mine too."

"She sounds like a pretty terrific mama."

Regan's face began to crumple, but she controlled it with a fierce effort. "Uh-huh."

Joanna pretended not to notice. "Regan, do you mind if I come out here sometimes? I won't unless you say it's okay."

"It's okay. You can even sit on the horse if you want. Mama did."

"Thanks, maybe I will." Before Joanna could say anything else, they heard the distant sound of a bell ringing.

"That's Mrs. Porter ringing the garden bell," Regan explained. "It means her show's over and I have to go home now."

"I see." Joanna smiled at her. "It was very nice meeting you, Regan. I'm sure we'll see each other again."

"You'll be in Cliffside for a while?"

"At least a couple of weeks."

"Good. That's good." Regan half turned, then paused and looked at Joanna with an odd hesitation. She seemed to be trying to make up her mind about something, and when she spoke, it was diffidently. "Joanna? How do you know when a grown-up is afraid?"

"I guess that depends on the grown-up," she replied slowly. "When I'm afraid, I sit very still and hope whatever scares me will go away."

"I have bad dreams when I'm scared," Regan said. "Mama did, too, I think. She had a lot of bad dreams last summer. Before the car accident."

"Regan—"

The bell rang again, and Regan said quickly, "I've gotta go. Bye, Joanna."

"Bye. . . ." Joanna stood there in Caroline's gazebo, her hand on the carousel horse, and watched Regan run off toward home.

THREE

✦ ✦ ✦

GRIFFIN CAVANAUGH SAT at his desk and looked out the window. Across the street and at a slight angle to the Sheriff's Department was the town library, the front door clearly visible from where he sat. He glanced at his watch and frowned.

Three hours she'd been in there. Not that it was such an unusual way to spend a rainy Wednesday afternoon, but tourists seldom considered a small-town library's resources as a possible source of entertainment when planning their vacation activities. And he very much doubted that Joanna Flynn was so bored after less than twenty-four hours in Cliffside that the prospect of spending three hours looking through back issues of *National Geographic* would hold much appeal.

So what was she doing in there?

He had noted down her license plate as a matter of course, but the car was a rental and he doubted there'd be any useful information to be had from the agency in Portland. If he were looking for information, of course. And if he had a halfway decent official reason for inquiring. Which he didn't.

Of course, that hadn't stopped him from calling Atlanta first thing this morning, counting on the brotherhood of his fellow police officers to answer a few unofficial questions about Joanna Flynn. The answers had been prompt and at least somewhat reassuring. She had no criminal record, and not so much as an unpaid parking ticket against her. One traffic accident last summer, totaling the car, but no one else had been involved and no charges had been filed against Joanna. She worked at a private library in Atlanta, rented an apartment where she had lived for some years, and always paid her bills and her taxes on time.

Born in Charleston, parents killed in a boating accident twenty years before, raised by an aunt. Had a current passport, and had traveled out of the country every summer during her teens.

And that, as far as the Atlanta P.D. was concerned, was all the relevant information about Joanna Flynn.

"Hey, Griff?"

"Yeah?" He didn't even try to pretend that he'd been engrossed in the paperwork on his cluttered desk as he turned and watched one of his deputies come into the office. Small-town life had certain advantages, and one of them, he'd discovered, was a laid-back attitude toward paperwork. And there was nothing urgent, anyway. "What do you need, Mark?"

"Ralph Thompson just called about those new parking spaces he wants beside his store; what did the town council decide to do about that?"

"Nixed the whole idea. Said it'd cut thirty feet out of the park."

"Well, you told him that from the beginning." Mark Beller sighed and rolled his eyes. "You know, I really don't want to be the one to give him the official word, if you don't mind. Ever since I wrote him up last month for blocking that back entrance, he's been treating me like I poisoned his dog or something."

Griffin glanced out the window again; her rental car was still parked in front of the library. "I'll go tell him myself," he said. "In person, to demonstrate my concern; he'll appreciate that. I need to stretch my legs anyway."

"It's raining buckets out there, you know."

"I won't melt." He pushed his chair back and got up, reaching for his windbreaker. On duty today, he was wearing dark slacks and a pale blue shirt, no tie. Though his deputies wore uniforms, Griffin stuck to street clothes that tended to be on the casual side; one of the perks, he maintained, of being in charge of all the town headaches. And though the mayor sighed heavily whenever they encountered each other, so far no one had objected to the way Griffin dressed on duty.

"I guess you've heard about Joanna Flynn," Mark said.

Griffin didn't let himself react. "What about her?"

"Well, that she's here. That if you dyed her hair black, she'd be the image of Mrs. McKenna."

Griffin, who hadn't mentioned his encounter with Joanna Flynn to anyone, wasn't particularly surprised; Cliffside's grapevine was second to none. "Yeah, I knew about her."

"People are wondering," Mark said innocently.

"Wondering what?"

"All kinds of things. Reincarnation is being discussed over at City Hall, seriously from what I hear. Twins separated at birth seems to be the favorite of the guys at the fire station—some of them have put money on it. And Janie says all her ladies at the salon are absolutely positive that Mrs. McKenna faked her death for some mysterious reason and has now returned to Cliffside to haunt somebody, but Ted at the bank thinks that last sounds a bit too unlikely."

"More unlikely than reincarnation?"

In an injured tone, Mark said, "I'm just sharing the sentiments of the town with you."

"What did they do, fax you all their ideas?" Griffin demanded.

Mark grinned. "Near enough. You wouldn't believe how many calls've come in since this morning. What should I tell 'em, boss?"

Griffin zipped up his windbreaker and settled his shoulders. "You tell them we don't butt into the business of innocent tourists, no matter *who* they happen to look like. Spread the word, Mark. I don't want anybody in this office adding fuel to the gossip."

"It won't need fuel," Mark said.

That was true enough, Griffin thought as he went out through the quiet lobby of the building. Gossip in Cliffside wasn't generally malicious, but it did get brisk whenever interest was aroused.

Joanna Flynn had definitely aroused interest.

Griffin didn't try to deny his own interest—to himself, anyway. And he didn't try to deny his apprehension. He sensed a matching uneasiness lurking just below the surface of Cliffside's calm, a tension that hadn't been there this time last year, and he was worried that an eerie replica of Caroline McKenna showing up here—especially now, so soon after her death—could only make things worse.

There was nothing he could put his finger on to explain what he sensed, and all his cop's instincts could offer was the awareness of silence where there should have been words, and sidelong glances closed and guarded. Everything *seemed* the same, at least on the surface. People smiled and greeted one another, and life went on as usual. But Caroline McKenna's death had somehow changed the town, and Griffin wondered if it could ever be as it had been.

The rain had slacked off a bit by the time he stepped outside, so Griffin was able to walk across the street without getting soaked. He went into the library, which was a fairly small building but held three floors, and saw no one except the middle-aged librarian, who was working at the desk.

"Hello, Sheriff," she said when she looked up and saw him. She was a pleasant looking woman, and her voice was unexpectedly loud and cheerful for someone who worked in the traditional quiet of a library. But then she reverted to type by adding severely, "You're overdue."

It took Griffin a beat to remember he'd checked out a few books a couple of weeks before. "Sorry, Mrs. Chandler. I'll get them back in tomorrow, I promise."

"Have you read them?"

"No," he admitted sheepishly.

She closed her eyes a moment in anguish. "Well, don't bring them back in unread, for heaven's sake. If anyone needs them, I'll call you—but read them before you turn them in!"

"Yes, ma'am."

"Meek doesn't become you," Mrs. Chandler observed.

"I'll try to work on that." He smiled at her. "In the meantime, is Joanna Flynn here?"

"Yes," she replied, making no pretense of not knowing who he was talking about. "She's upstairs with the microfilm reader. Seems to know her way around a library."

"What's she reading up on?"

"Town history, so she said. Asked about the town founders, and which families could trace their roots back. Said the property around here was lovely, and wondered who owned what. She copied a few maps and plats. She seemed pleased that we keep the birth, death, and marriage records here instead of City Hall. And the newspaper morgue." Mrs. Chandler paused, then added deliberately, "Strange how much she looks like Caroline, isn't it? If it weren't for the coloring and the voice . . ."

"Yeah." Since Griffin had no good official reason for wanting to talk to Joanna, he didn't offer one. He merely nodded to the grave librarian and made his way upstairs to the second floor, where most of the town's archives—such as they were—were kept.

The old stairs and floorboards creaked beneath his weight, but the woman at the microfilm machine was so intent on what she was doing that she obviously didn't hear his approach. Griffin paused a few feet away and studied her, trying to be objective. It was unexpectedly difficult. Even under harsh fluorescent lighting, her hair gleamed gold, and despite frowning in concentration, she was lovely. Yet even in profile, the resemblance to Caroline was amazing. A long-lost twin? Looking at her, it didn't seem so unlikely.

He might have risked money on that possibility himself if he hadn't known with fair certainty that Caroline had never had a sister.

Griffin drew a breath and walked toward her at about the same moment as she realized she was no longer alone. She started when she looked around and saw him, and perhaps that was why her hand moved suddenly—or perhaps she had quite deliberately made sure he wouldn't see what it was she had been reading with such intentness.

He wasn't happy to realize he suspected the latter.

"Sheriff. Fancy meeting you here."

"Miss Flynn." He sat down in a chair near hers and in that moment caught the light scent of her perfume. He liked it, but it also unsettled him for some reason he couldn't immediately put his finger on. Then he realized. He had expected her to smell of cigarette smoke.

"Oh, please, Sheriff, call me Joanna." There was dryness rather than friendliness in her tone. "I mean, since we're apparently fated to turn up in the same places day after day."

Griffin's silent debate was a brief one; he decided not to let her sarcasm get under his skin. Not today, at any rate. "I'm not following you around, if that's what you think," he told her. "My office is across the street, and I saw you come in here. Do you realize you've been here for at least three hours?"

"So?" she demanded somewhat belligerently.

"So I thought you might be ready for a break. Why don't I buy you a cup of coffee?"

She eyed him uncertainly. "Is this a trick question?"

He laughed despite himself. "No. Look, I was ready to take a break and I thought you might be too. There's a cafe just down the street where they happen to make great coffee. What do you say?"

After a moment, she shrugged. "Sure, why not. Just give me a minute to put things back where I found them."

"Through for the day?" he asked mildly.

"I think so. Spending *more* than three hours in a library on my vacation, even on a rainy day, sounds a bit too obsessive, wouldn't you say?"

"That probably depends," he said, "on what you're looking for."

Joanna paused in rewinding a spool of microfilm and looked at him steadily. Then, in a reflective tone, she said, "Tell me something, Sheriff. Suppose you went to a quiet little town on vacation, and when you got there you discovered that you looked an awful lot like someone who had recently died. What would you do?"

"I think I'd do what you're doing," he replied, matching her thoughtful expression. "Find out all I could about that person, just out of curiosity."

She nodded. "Then why do I get the feeling you disapprove?"

"It isn't disapproval. If anything, it's concern. Caroline McKenna's death is still a raw wound to a lot of people."

"I imagine it is. Any death in a close-knit community is bound to affect a lot of people. Why do you think I'm in here reading back editions of newspapers instead of out asking questions? Because I don't want to upset anyone more than I already do just by looking like her." She drew a breath. "I had an unexpected encounter this morning. With Caroline's daughter. I don't want any more surprises, Sheriff. Not like that one."

He watched her nimble fingers coping with the microfilm. She had beautiful hands, he thought, but what he slowly said was, "It must have been difficult for you."

"More difficult for that poor little girl than for me, but I might have handled it better if I hadn't been caught by surprise."

"I see your point."

"And understand?" She folded up a stack of papers— undoubtedly copies she'd made of some of the information stored on microfilm, as well as the maps and plats Mrs. Chandler had mentioned—and put them into her large shoulder bag.

"I understand your reasons for trying to find out what you can about Caroline." He wasn't conscious of having used only the first name until Joanna looked at him thoughtfully.

"You knew her well?"

How the hell do I answer that? "Well enough. It's a small town, and I've lived here for more than nine years."

Without comment, Joanna got up to return the microfilm to storage, taking her shoulder bag with her. Griffin smiled grimly and got to his feet, waiting for her to come back. Yes, her reasons were perfectly understandable, but her attitude wasn't. Why should she be so cautious if her interest was so innocent and easily explained?

When Joanna came back, they walked downstairs, neither one of them saying anything. Griffin knew she was a little tense; he couldn't see it, but he could feel it. It bothered him that he could feel it. Was it only because she looked so much like Caroline that he felt this sense of knowing her? Was he feeling Joanna's tension only because he knew Caroline would have been tense in such a situation as this?

"Find everything you were looking for, Joanna?" Mrs. Chandler asked.

"Pretty much." Joanna nodded at the older woman. "I may be back, though, especially if it keeps raining. It looks like you have a fine stock of popular fiction."

"Not bad, if I do say so myself. You come back anytime. We'll be here," the librarian told her.

When they left the library, the rain had stopped, though the clouds continued to glower with the promise of more later, and the smell of rain was definitely in the air. Joanna paused for an instant and looked at her car, then said, "Hey, I'm in a one-hour parking zone."

"I noticed," Griffin said.

"I didn't. Are you going to give me a ticket?"

"No." When she sent him a wary look, he shrugged. "We usually don't bother to enforce the zone except during tourist season, when parking is at a premium. If you'll look around, you'll notice that nobody'd have to wait or circle the block looking for a place to park today."

She did glance around at the almost totally deserted street, and said, "I see what you mean. So you won't get all official if I leave my car where it is while we have our coffee?"

"This is my afternoon break," he said. "I won't get official at all unless somebody robs the bank over there."

Joanna turned obediently when he indicated the way, and walked beside him down the sidewalk toward the cafe a couple of short blocks away. "Is it usually a quiet job, being the sheriff of a small town?" she asked.

"Usually." He thought she was honestly interested, and so he added, "We're more apt to have arguments than crimes, and we need a judge so rarely he only works a couple of days a week. Off-season, that is. During the summer, it gets a bit more lively, but for the most part all I do is see to it that civic ordinances and regulations are obeyed, and that the kids from the high school don't get carried away on prom night."

She looked up at him rather curiously. "You said you'd been here around nine years, and somehow I don't see you as a small-town product. Were you born in Oregon?"

He shook his head, wondering if she was intuitive or if it just showed. "Nevada. Raised all over the place; my father's career army."

Joanna nodded, but before she could comment, an older lady walked past them going in the opposite direction, murmuring a polite hello to Griffin but looking only at Joanna.

"Not at all surprised to see me—but very definitely interested," Joanna noted somewhat ruefully, keeping her voice low. "Bet she knows my name. I didn't have to introduce myself to the guy who put gas in my car at the service station *or* to the librarian. Tell me something, Sheriff. Does *everybody* in this town know my name?"

"If anyone doesn't," he said, opening the door to the cafe, "they undoubtedly will by nightfall. And my name's Griffin—Joanna." He held the door for her, and when she responded to his last remark with a quick smile, Griffin had to fight a sudden urge to reach out and touch her. He managed to resist it, but he felt even more unsettled as he followed her into the cafe.

The cafe's young waitress also needed no introduction to Joanna, and her curiosity was absolutely naked as she led them to a corner booth and then reluctantly left them to get the coffee.

"Is it just me, or because you're with me?" Joanna asked him.

"It's just her," he answered lightly. "Liz is incurably nosy."

"I see." Joanna glanced around at the dozen or so customers in the place and added, "A nosy town you've got here, Sheriff. I mean—Griffin."

"Afraid so." He didn't have to look to know that everyone in the place was watching them, and most openly. "You'll be the hot topic of interest for at least a few days, I'd say."

She studied him with an intentness he found more than a little unsettling, and he wondered if she had any idea how strange it was to look at her. Unusual light brown eyes instead of blue, golden hair instead of black, but the features were almost identical. Christ, even the way she tilted her head thoughtfully was Caroline's mannerism. Yet the differences were just different enough to confuse the eye—and the ear.

"I suppose they *will* get used to me?" she offered hopefully.

"Bound to," he answered almost at random. Then, because he couldn't help himself, he added, "I don't suppose it's possible that you and Caroline were sisters?"

She lifted a brow wryly. "I admit I wondered about that myself. So I checked at the library and saw her birth certificate. She was born right here in Cliffside, to parents who practically founded the town. I, on the other hand, was born in Charleston, South Carolina, also to parents well rooted in their community—and three days after she was born. So unless there was incredible chicanery committed in two places thousands of miles apart and for no apparent reason, I don't see how we could be related in any way."

"I guess not," he said. "But for two women to look so much alike without being related . . . what are the odds?"

Joanna looked reflective. "I don't know. But if you consider the theory that we all have a double—or doppelganger—living somewhere on earth—"

"Please, let's not venture into science fiction."

Liz arrived with their coffee then, and Joanna didn't respond to his comment until the waitress had left. Then she said, "Yesterday's science fiction is tomorrow's science fact. Or don't you believe that?"

Deliberately, he said, "I believe answers are usually ordinary and almost always simple, Joanna. Being a cop in a much bigger place than Cliffside for a few years taught me that much."

"So you're a hardheaded realist?"

"If you want to call it that." He shrugged. "People are fairly predictable, on the whole, and their motives are seldom complicated. What you see is usually what you get. It makes my job easier."

"And what do you see when you look at me?" she asked him seriously.

"I see . . . Joanna Flynn."

After a moment, she smiled. "You're a bad liar, Griffin."

"I'm not lying." He tried to keep his voice even. "Caroline McKenna is dead. Unlike most of the people in this town, I saw her body, so I couldn't begin to convince myself that you're her. Even if I wanted to."

Joanna's smile had vanished. She looked down at her coffee, frowning. "I'm sorry. I didn't mean to remind you—"

"Of something painful? I was a cop in Chicago for nearly five years, Joanna; I've seen a lot of bodies. I can talk about her—and what that wreck left of her—without going to pieces."

She looked at him, grave now. "Given your job, I'm sure you can. But when I said you were a bad liar, I didn't mean I thought you literally saw Caroline when you looked at me."

"Then what did you mean?" He knew he was so tense it showed, and he knew his voice held a harsh edge despite all his efforts to sound detached. Most of all, he knew that his quick denial of any pain about Caroline's death had sounded jarringly untrue.

"What I meant was that you hadn't gotten past the—the features I shared with Caroline. When you look at me, when anybody in this town looks at me, they see Caroline's face. They see somebody who looks like Caroline looked. Nobody knows *me*. Nobody here has any idea who Joanna Flynn is, so they don't see me at all."

After a moment, Griffin nodded. "Okay, fair enough. It's . . . disconcerting, I admit." And no doubt explained his own turbulent feelings, he thought. His brain was just trying to reconcile images of two women who happened to resemble each other even though he knew they had to be different in other ways. That was all.

"How do you think I feel? People look at me as if they know me. They assume things. Do you know, when I went to the drugstore just before the library, the clerk automatically got a pack of cigarettes and pushed it across the counter to me?"

"Caroline smoked," Griffin heard himself say.

"Yeah, so I was told when the clerk realized what she'd done. Mrs. McKenna smoked, she said, and she'd just assumed . . ." Joanna sighed. "The poor kid didn't know where to look, and neither did I. It feels peculiar, let me tell you."

Griffin hesitated, then said, "Does that mean you're going to cut your vacation short?"

She sipped her coffee, those big golden eyes fixed unwaveringly on his face, and didn't answer until she had set her cup back on the table. Then she merely said, "No."

"If we make you so uncomfortable . . ."

Joanna shrugged. "If it gets too bad, I can always leave. In the meantime, according to the Chamber of Commerce, Cliffside offers just what I need—wonderful scenery, peace, and quiet."

"And if the people around here go on making you feel peculiar?"

"Then I'll spend all my time staring at the scenery or reading peacefully on the veranda at The Inn."

He wondered if he'd ever get used to her voice and that lazy accent. It was oddly pleasing, but startled him every time she spoke. "Is your life back in Atlanta so hectic?"

Her eyes lit with amusement, and her lips curved in that brief, just slightly crooked smile that was nothing like Caroline. "As a matter of fact, my life is pretty tame. I work in a private library."

He nodded, trying to look as if he hadn't already known that. "So why the need for peace and quiet?"

"Oh . . . maybe it's not so much that as just a change of scene. And it's so noisy in a big city." She shrugged again.

Griffin wished he believed her, but his cop's instincts were telling him that Joanna's reasons for being here were hardly as simple as the need for a change of scene. There was nothing he could pinpoint, no obvious indication that she was hiding something, but he was certain she was. Despite the little he had been told about her blameless life, he was certain that it was no coincidence Joanna had come to Cliffside. She had a reason for being here, and he had the unhappy idea that he wouldn't like it when he found out what it was.

"You're staring at me," she murmured.

He shifted his gaze to his coffee, realizing only then that he hadn't even tasted it yet. "Sorry."

"So, tell me about Caroline."

It caught him completely off guard, and when he looked quickly at Joanna, he knew she had intended to do just that. "Didn't you find out all about her at the library?" he asked stiffly.

"Oh, I found out a few things. That she was on a lot of committees. That she was highly respected in this town. That she was intent on improving the quality of medical care here. That she was a concerned parent, involved in her daughter's school."

"And all that isn't enough for you?"

Joanna shook her head very slightly. "None of it tells me who Caroline was, not really. I still have a lot of questions about her. What did she do with her life besides serve on committees and paint scenery for the school play? Did that fulfill her? Did she have hobbies, interests? Did she like animals? What about music, art—did she like those things? Did she love her husband? Was she happy?"

Griffin drew a breath. "Why ask me?"

"Because you won't go to pieces talking about her," Joanna said quietly. "That's what you said, isn't it?"

Goddammit. "I can't answer your questions," he told her.

"Can't—or won't?" Then she shook her head a little before he could decide how to answer, and said, "Sorry, I shouldn't push. It looks like you've got another nosy person in your town, doesn't it?"

Griffin frowned at her. "Joanna, I meant what I told you at the library. Don't go around town asking questions about Caroline. There are too many people you could hurt."

"Is that an order from the sheriff?"

He couldn't read very much in her expression, but he

had the distinct feeling that he had made her mad. "No, it's a request from me."

She inclined her head slightly. "Noted. And now, I think I'd better head back to the hotel. Thank you for the coffee."

"Don't mention it," he said.

Joanna didn't offer to shake hands with him outside the cafe when they parted company; she merely said, "See you around," and strolled off down the street toward the library and her car.

Griffin stood there for a moment looking after her, until it occurred to him that every patron in the cafe, as well as Liz, was watching him watch Joanna. He was tempted to turn around and glare at everybody, but finally just walked away in the opposite direction so that he could tell Ralph Thompson he couldn't have those extra parking spaces he wanted.

Fifteen minutes later, having listened patiently, until Thompson finally ran out of breath, to a diatribe on the consummate arrogance and utter ignorance of the town council, Griffin walked back to the Sheriff's Department. Joanna's car was no longer parked in front of the library, so he could only assume she had returned to The Inn.

He retreated to his office without speaking to anyone and closed the door behind him, fighting the impulse to lock it. He took off his jacket and hung it on its peg, then sat down at his desk and unlocked the top drawer. Inside were a few confidential files, but he didn't reach for any of them. Instead, he pulled out a piece of pale blue notepaper. It was folded once, the crease worn because he'd opened and closed it so many times. He opened it now, and read the rounded, almost childish handwriting with the ease of someone who had long ago memorized the message.

Griffin,
I must see you. Meet me at the old barn at noon.
Caroline

He closed the note and returned it to his desk drawer, then leaned back in his chair and stared out the window.

It was raining again.

✧   ✧   ✧

"Damn this rain," Scott McKenna said.

"You live in Oregon," Holly reminded him. "It rains a lot here."

"Too much. I should go back to San Francisco."

"Where it doesn't rain at all, of course. And where there are earthquakes to boot. Besides, you've lived here for twelve years. Your roots are here."

"Are they?"

Holly looked up from the keyboard and watched him for a moment. He was standing at the window of his study, gazing out at the drenched garden beside his house. He was a strikingly handsome man, with dark hair and hooded gray eyes, and there was something remote in the very way he stood. He always looked alone, she thought, even in a crowd. It was something she had noticed about him from the first day they'd met.

"Well, the majority of your money's here anyway," she told him. "You have to run things."

He turned his head and looked at her, that direct, measuring stare that no longer unnerved her. "You could handle most of it alone," he said.

"What, you mean the stores, the greenhouse, the lumber mill, *and* the new wing for the clinic, to say nothing of The Inn? News for you, boss—I don't want to handle it all."

Scott smiled slightly. "I know. But you could."

"Yeah, right." She finished entering figures from her clipboard into the computer on his desk, and said, "Okay, that's everything, I think. All the estimates and bids, the materials lists, including the list from the medical supplier. Cost of grading, even landscaping."

"Thank you, Holly."

"No problem. I don't mind, Scott, really." She might have said more, but the door opened just then and Scott's daughter looked in. As always these days, Regan was solemn, her dark blue eyes large and unreadable.

"What is it, Regan?" Scott asked a bit abruptly.

"Mrs. Ames says I can stay up tonight and watch all of that movie if you say it's all right." Her voice was flat, without expression.

Scott didn't ask what movie, he merely nodded. "It's fine."

Without another word, Regan departed as suddenly as she had arrived.

Holly sat back in his desk chair and looked at her employer. He was gazing out the window once again, his aloof expression daring her to comment. Never one to refuse a dare, Holly said, "Does the housekeeper always supervise Regan after Mrs. Porter goes home?"

"She doesn't need much supervision," Scott replied coolly. "She's an independent child, you know that."

"Independent, sure. She also lost her mother three months ago. Have you talked to her?"

"What would you have me say to her?"

Holly gave a helpless shrug even though he wasn't looking at her. "I don't know. All I *do* know is that she adored Caroline—and I've never seen her grieve for her mother. Not the day it happened, not at Caroline's funeral, not anytime since. Has she cried at all?"

Scott didn't answer immediately, but finally said, "I don't know."

"Scott—"

"Holly, I can't change my nature just because I've suddenly become a single parent. Regan was close to Caroline, but never to me. I'll do everything I can for the child, but I can't take Caroline's place."

She had known him for eight years, but looking at him now, Holly had no idea what—if anything—he was feeling. He had always been somewhat remote with his daughter, but hardly more so than he was with most other people; perhaps it *was* his nature.

"I know it's none of my business, Scott, but I can't help

being concerned. If you don't reach out to Regan now and help her get past Caroline's death, I think you'll regret it for the rest of your life." She got up from the desk, adding briskly, "And that's my meddling for the day. I'm going home."

"Drive carefully."

"Yes. I will." She went as far as the door, then paused and looked back at him. "Good night, Scott."

Still gazing out the window, Scott asked, "Does that arrogant artist of yours know how lucky he is?"

"I don't know."

He nodded slightly, as if her answer didn't surprise him. "Good night, Holly."

She went out, quietly closing the door behind her, leaving Scott alone.

❖   ❖   ❖

Joanna slipped the last sheet of paper into Caroline's file and leaned back against the pillows banked behind her, frowning. There was still precious little information in the file, not nearly enough to do more than sketch in a life. No color, no . . . texture. That was it, she decided; so far, she couldn't really feel the texture in Caroline's life.

In three hours, Joanna had managed to scan years' worth of Cliffside's weekly newspaper, so she had more information than she'd arrived here with—but as she'd said to the sheriff, none of it told her who Caroline had really been.

A wealthy woman, yes—in her own right as well as married to a wealthy man. A woman who had supported a long list of charities, most of them in the areas of medical research and treatment, probably because a younger brother had died of an incurable disease when Caroline was a teenager. A woman who had seemingly been at ease speaking in public. A woman who was known for her sense of style and who wore dresses more often than pants, at least publicly.

Facts . . . behind which lay only speculation.

Actually, Joanna had discovered far more about Caroline's character in casual conversation than by reading a recitation of facts in the newspaper. The clerk in the drugstore, for instance, had told her not only that Caroline smoked pretty heavily, but also that it was a nervous habit and that "she bit her nails, too, poor thing."

The clerk had boasted long, beautifully manicured nails, so her pity was easily understood. Joanna lifted her own hands and studied them, taking note of the neat, medium-length nails, only one ragged thumbnail evidence of her recent nibbling. Aunt Sarah had been quite definite in her ideas of how a young lady should present herself, and those had included well-kept hands and no nervous mannerisms.

Another difference between Joanna and Caroline? Caroline had apparently been nervous, at least in some ways, and Joanna had never been that. Except that for the first time in her life, she had caught herself chewing on her nails in Atlanta during the search for Cliffside and Caroline. An odd coincidence? Or something more eerie?

She shivered unconsciously and let her hands fall. Was it possible, she asked herself, to absorb another person's mannerisms? A person one had never met? No, surely not. Just as it wasn't possible to establish some kind of psychic connection with another person just because both of you "died" the same day. It defied logic and common sense.

Yet here she was.

She shook her head, forcing herself to stop thinking about elusive things and to concentrate on the facts she had gathered.

The guy at the gas station, once he'd stopped staring at her, had offered the information that Mrs. McKenna had been a real safe driver, everybody knew that, and it had been a real shock when she'd been killed driving so fast. Some said the car must have had something wrong with it, but he knew for a fact it had been okay, because his boss *and* the sheriff had practically used a magnifying glass to go over what was left of the wreck, and they hadn't found a thing wrong, not a thing. So she must have just lost control, that was what his boss and the sheriff thought. And wasn't it a shame, the whole town thought so. . . .

And the girl working in The Inn's gift shop had, in the middle of a long, involved description of her last visit to the town's clinic, mentioned that Mrs. McKenna had had terrible allergies and had to see the doctor often, especially during the spring and early summer. Of course, she always went straight in to the doctor while others signed in and waited, but nobody minded, truly, because she was so nice, and besides, it was she who had persuaded her husband to open the pharmacy next door, where they kept prices down, so everybody benefited. . . .

Lesson: Instead of asking questions, just talk to people.

It was something Aunt Sarah had taught Joanna, this inward acknowledgment of the lessons learned in everyday life. She had firmly believed that more could be learned from just observing life than any school had ever taught, and she had convinced Joanna it was true.

So . . . Caroline had had at least two nervous habits— smoking and biting her nails. A safe driver apparently driving a safe car in good working order, she had wrecked that car driving too fast on a slippery road. And she had suffered from allergies, the condition serious enough that over-the-counter remedies had apparently been ineffective.

A bit of texture. Not much, but some.

And to that, Joanna could add a few insights she had picked up since arriving in Cliffside. Caroline had been a good mother, devoted enough to have a playful carousel horse installed in one of her own favorite places. And if Regan's comments were anything to go by, it seemed obvious that Caroline had been the more loving of the two parents.

Regan . . . Joanna felt very uneasy about her. She missed her mother so desperately, and even though she had seemed to accept that Joanna was completely different in almost every way, the similarity of feature might well be enough to cause her to form an attachment. And even if a bond of that sort helped Regan now, it was bound to cause her pain when Joanna left.

Part of Joanna wanted to avoid the child for that very reason. But another part of her wanted to reach out to Regan, because she felt sure Regan hadn't even begun to deal with her mother's death. And because there was something in that sad little girl, some worry or knowledge, that tugged desperately at Joanna. She wanted to hold the child, to soothe and protect her.

Protect her . . .

How do you know when a grown-up is afraid?

"Caroline died in a car wreck," Joanna heard herself say aloud in a very firm, matter-of-fact voice. "There was nothing wrong with the car. It was just a tragic accident."

I have bad dreams when I'm scared. Mama did, too, I think. She had a lot of bad dreams last summer. Before the car accident.

"And Regan is just an unhappy, grieving little girl trying to understand why she lost her mother. Trying to find a reason it happened. Trying to make sense out of something so utterly senseless."

. . . the sheriff had practically used a magnifying glass to go over what was left of the wreck. . . .

"He was just being thorough, that's all. Just trying to find out what had caused her to lose control of the car, because he knew she wasn't a reckless driver. Not because he suspected anything other than an accident—and if I keep talking to myself like this, especially out loud, somebody's going to lock me up."

The sheriff, probably. He'd be happy to, she thought. More than happy to. She hadn't decided whether he simply didn't trust her or had another reason, but he definitely did not want her roaming around town asking questions about Caroline.

Why? Because he was protecting the sensibilities of the people in his town—or because there was something he didn't want her to find out? What if there was something to find out, something damning? He was the sheriff, after all; he'd know all the details of the "accident" more completely than anyone else. So maybe there *had* been something suspicious about Caroline's death, some evidence that it had not been an accident after all. Maybe even evidence of deliberate murder. And maybe the sheriff had kept that to himself because . . . because of what? Why would the respected sheriff of a small coastal town hide evidence of murder? Because he'd been involved in it himself? Because he was protecting someone else who had?

Joanna slid down on the bed and groaned softly. God, this was ridiculous! She had come three thousand miles to find out about a dead woman, and now she was driving herself nuts imagining that there might have been something deliberate about Caroline's accident when there wasn't so much as a hint that that was so. It was worse than ridiculous, it was . . . crazy.

Joanna had never been quick to judge, yet here she was eyeing this town and everyone in it with distinct suspicion. And why? Because she had a recurring nightmare filled with fear? Because she was convinced beyond all reason that Caroline had somehow reached out to her and needed her help? Because Regan, in her terrible, contained grief, reminded Joanna of the little girl she had been one hot June when her world had changed forever. . . .

She closed her eyes, feeling tired. It was barely ten o'clock and far too early for bed, but the day behind her seemed unusually long and filled with unfamiliar, uneasy emotions. And unsettling encounters. Regan. Griffin. A little girl almost paralyzed with grief, and a hard man with the darkest eyes she'd ever seen. What color were they? She hadn't been able to tell.

He saw Caroline when he looked at her, just as everyone else had, Joanna knew that. But he also saw . . . something else. Maybe, she thought, maybe he saw a little bit of Joanna there as well. . . .

She was walking along the cliffs toward the gazebo, staying out of the woods because the woods weren't safe. Behind her she kept hearing a gull cry, and finally she

*looked back over her shoulder, and she saw a girl with
long blond hair leap off the cliffs as if trying to fly. She
wanted to cry out a warning, but it was too late, the girl
was soaring out and down . . . and down. . . . And
standing on the cliffs where the girl had been was a man,
his back to her, and he started to turn, and she was so
terribly afraid. . . .*

Joanna jerked awake with a gasp, her heart pounding.
The clock on her nightstand told her it was barely midnight, and she could hear the low wail of the wind outside.
It wasn't raining, she thought, but the forecast had called
for storms all night, and it sounded as if they were on their
way.

She sat up, running her fingers through her hair. The
dream remained vivid in her mind, and with it a sense of
urgency even stronger than the one that had sent her across
the country in search of a dead woman.

"My God, Caroline," she murmured, "is that what happened? Did you see that poor girl pushed off the cliffs? Is
that why you were afraid?"

There was no answer, except the wind.

$\mathcal{F}$OUR

❖ ❖ ❖

$\mathcal{A}$T FIRST, Holly thought it was a dream. She was floating peacefully, listening to the wind and half-consciously waiting for the storm to arrive. She liked storms and always slept better during a stormy night. Then she felt movement, the bed beneath her shifting heavily, and she rolled onto her back with a little moan of annoyance.

Something touched her mouth, warm and hard and tasting faintly of coffee. She uttered another little sound, this one filled with pleasure, and decided she liked this dream. Someone was kissing her, only their lips touching, and he was awfully good at it. He aroused and enthralled her, seduced her, until her body felt hot and throbbed with a slow pulse that seemed to originate deep inside her. His mouth brushed hers, teased hers, his teeth nipping gently at her bottom lip, and his tongue enticed skillfully until she pulled her arms from beneath the covers to reach for him.

Her wrists were caught and held together, gently pinned against the pillow above her head, and Holly would have protested if she could have found the breath for it. His mouth was still moving on hers, possessing hers, and she thought she was going to burn up or explode or just melt into a puddle if he didn't do something to satisfy the frantic need coiling inside her.

Then, finally, his hand touched her breast, moving in a slow, lazy circle so that her nightgown offered a silky friction, and she whimpered at the waves of pleasure. As if they had all the time in the world, he kissed her mouth and caressed her breasts. Her back arched as she tried to push herself harder against his tormenting hand, and when he teasingly drew back, Holly moaned his name in frustration.

"Cain . . ."

"I'm glad you know who I am," he murmured, cupping her breast through her nightgown, his thumb rubbing slowly back and forth across the straining nipple. "I was beginning to think you were going to sleep through this. Open your eyes, Holly."

She did, staring up into the dark glitter of his eyes. She made one somewhat weak attempt to free her wrists from his gentle grasp, then forgot about doing anything about that and tried to think straight. "You're in my room," she realized.

"You didn't lock your terrace door. That's a bad habit to have, babe, even in a small town."

He kissed her again before she could reply to that, and Holly kissed him back hungrily. It seemed like forever since he had touched her this way, and her body demanded his with an all-consuming need she had no power to fight.

Even so, she heard herself mutter, "You can't just waltz into my room whenever you feel like it, dammit."

"Want me to leave?" he asked politely, finger and thumb pinching her nipple gently.

Since Holly was convinced his will was equal to anything—even self-denial—she wasn't about to call his bluff. Fiercely, she said, "If you walk out on me now, I'll never forgive you!"

He kissed her, not teasing now, and released her wrists.

Before she could grab him, he drew back, pushing the covers off her and looking down at her in the dimness of her bedroom. The only light came from a lamp in the hall that she always left on, and the glow provided just enough illumination for them to see each other.

Cain had undressed before getting into bed with her, and she wished there was more light so she could really look at him. But memory closed the gap between what she could see and what she touched when she reached out to him. He was hard, flesh smooth and taut over well-defined muscles, and her fingers savored the journey along his arm and shoulder and to his chest.

Holly knew his body almost as well as she knew her own, but she always felt a sense of discovery when she touched him, as if he was new to her every time they were together.

"I'm glad you're here," she murmured.

"Are you?" He pushed the narrow strap of her nightgown off one shoulder and pressed his lips there. "I wanted to make you come to me, but . . ."

"But?" She pulled her arms free as he pushed the other strap down, and felt the warm slide of silk as he eased the gown to her waist. And she almost forgot the question when he reached out and slowly trailed his long fingers from her collarbone down between her breasts to her navel.

A low, rough laugh escaped him. "But I knew you wouldn't come to me, not now, and I couldn't wait. You're making me crazy, you know that?" Suddenly impatient, he pulled the gown completely off her, dragging the material from under her before she had time to raise her hips, and threw it aside.

Holly wanted to deny the accusation, or at least ask him what she was doing to make him crazy, but his mouth was on her, on her throat and her breasts, and the only sound she seemed capable of making was a whimper of raw triumph. He knew just where to touch, how to touch, knew just what her body craved from him, and he gave her what she needed.

The pleasure washed over her in waves, each one more intense than the last, and when he finally came into her, it seemed to Holly that she had wanted him forever. Her body welcomed him, moved with him in a rapt, rhythmic dance he had taught her. Until Cain, she had never felt the delights her body was capable of, and she wondered if he knew that. Or even if it would matter to him.

She looked up at him dazedly, her nails digging into his shoulders, wondering, as she always did, why he always watched her with such total absorption, wondering what it was he was so intent on seeing in her face in the naked moment when her pleasure peaked and she cried out in helpless rapture.

And then it happened, and she forgot everything except the blind, deaf, and dumb delight of her body. With a control that always maddened her, Cain waited for her, delaying his own release until she came back to herself. Only then did he let himself go, climaxing with a hoarse groan of elation.

It was some time before either of them moved, and then Cain simply rolled so that she sprawled out on top of him. It was a position he enjoyed on the rare occasions when they actually slept together, and since she enjoyed it as well, Holly hadn't complained.

Now, summoning the strength to move, she folded her hands on his chest and rested her chin on them. "Spending the night?" she asked.

"I thought I would. In case you can't hear it, it's storming outside."

Now that he mentioned it, she did hear thunder rumbling and rain pelting against the bedroom window. It was a restful sound to her, yet though she was completely relaxed, she wasn't sleepy. "I wouldn't make you leave even if it wasn't storming," she told him.

"No?"

"No." She smiled slowly. "But from now on, I'm locking the terrace door."

He chuckled. "So I should wait to be invited, huh?"

"I have my reputation to consider," Holly said, solemn. "Living here in the hotel does have its drawbacks, and being under everyone's eye is one of them."

Cain was threading his fingers through her hair, spreading the silky strands over her shoulders and back. "Do you really think there's anyone in all of Cliffside over the age of twelve who doesn't suspect we're lovers?"

"Probably not. But I refuse to confirm their suspicions."

"So I sneak out in the morning?" he asked wryly.

"Well . . . you can slip out the terrace door and meet me on the veranda for breakfast. Nobody has to know you didn't walk over from your place. *Did* you walk over, by the way?"

"Yeah."

She hesitated, then said, "I wasn't sure . . . I mean, after yesterday, I had the feeling you weren't liking me very much."

A flash of lightning brightened the room for a brief second and lit his eyes like a cat's in the dark. "I wasn't," he told her with a touch of dryness. "Like I said, you're making me crazy."

"Because I have to work for a living?"

"No. Because you can't see through Scott McKenna."

Holly drew a breath. "See through to what? Cain, Scott's been nothing but good to me. Never so much as a harsh word. What is it I'm supposed to see?"

"He's a taker, Holly. He always has been and he always will be."

"A taker? I don't understand what you mean." Suddenly uncomfortable, Holly got herself off Cain and pulled the covers up around them.

Cain didn't try to stop her, turning on his side and propping his head on a raised hand in order to see her better. "Don't you? Haven't you ever noticed that Scott's life is carefully arranged so that Scott is rarely troubled by anything? You take care of The Inn, Dylan York and Lyssa Maitland take care of most of the other businesses—and you can't wait to help out poor Scott when they have to be out of town."

"Those are our *jobs*, Cain—"

"You're all at his beck and call twenty-four hours a day. He has a housekeeper, maids, and gardeners to run his house. And if you think Caroline wasn't the only parent in that house, think again. Now that she's gone, what happens? When Regan is too terrified to get into a car or school bus, does he try to help his kid? Does he even give her a hug, or hold her hand while they're burying her mother? No. He just hires somebody else, a teacher this time, and expects her or the housekeeper to put *their* arms around that poor little girl."

Holly was too honest to deny the justice of some of what he said, but it didn't make her very happy to admit that. "All right—say he's everything you claim he is. But, Cain, I still work for the man. And it's . . . upsetting that you're always so hostile toward him."

After a moment of silence, Cain reached over and cupped her cheek. "I'll make a deal with you, babe. You do just the job he hired you to do, and I'll keep my mouth shut about him."

"Just the job—"

"You're the manager of The Inn—and that's a full-time job. You weren't hired to wrangle contractors and suppliers for the clinic's new wing, or run over and water the plants in the nursery, or handle problems at the lumber mill when that manager's out sick. You were hired to run this hotel. So run it. And the next time poor Scott calls asking you to enter data in his computer because he never learned how to type, suggest he hire a temp to do it. Or a full-time secretary; he seems to need one."

Holly chewed on her bottom lip. "Lyssa and Dylan should be back within a few days, so things *will* get better—"

"That isn't the deal, Holly."

"Don't back me into a corner, dammit!"

Cain shook his head. "Jesus, you're a stubborn woman. Look, all I'm asking for is a compromise. Things keep going the way they have been, and we see each other maybe once a week; at least if you cut back to only *one* job, we might be able to spend a little time together."

"I want that. But—"

"But what? I'm willing to make some time for us. My next show isn't until the spring, and I do most of my painting during the day while you're running this place. That leaves us evenings and weekends—*if* you're willing to set aside that time." He looked at her steadily. "Are we worth that much?"

Holly had known all along that she would cave in; this was the first time in the eight months since they had become lovers that Cain had shown any desire to have more of a relationship than being occasional bedmates and lunch dates, and she couldn't even pretend that didn't matter to her.

"Holly?"

She nodded quickly. "All right. From now on, I promise to try my best to do only the job Scott hired me to do, and not be at his beck and call. Good enough?"

For an answer, he leaned over and kissed her, then settled back on his pillow and pulled her into his arms. "Notice I'm not crowing in triumph," he observed.

"Wise of you," she remarked, cuddling up to his side. "There's nothing worse than a man who crows when he gets his way."

Cain chuckled.

She closed her eyes and listened to his heart beating beneath her ear. But when he spoke again in an almost idle tone, it chased away the first tendrils of sleep that had crept over her.

"You haven't mentioned Joanna Flynn. Does she really look as much like Caroline as people have been telling me all day?"

Holly made her own voice matter-of-fact. "Amazingly

like her. Blond hair and yellowish eyes, and a Southern accent you could cut with a knife, but fix the coloring and she'd be Caroline's twin."

"Mmm. Well, I'm sure I'll run into her sometime."

"I imagine so." Holly was silent for a long moment, then said, "Cain? Why have you never painted me?"

As if he'd been waiting for that question, Cain answered it immediately, his tone light. "I don't know enough about you yet, babe."

"Oh." Holly said nothing more, but long after Cain's even breathing told her he was asleep, she lay awake and listened to the storm that continued to rumble outside. And the thoughts chased themselves through her mind until she wanted to scream aloud to relieve some of the pressure inside her.

She wanted to believe that Cain's hostility toward Scott was, as he said, anger because the other man took advantage of her. She really wanted to believe that. But she was very much afraid that it simply wasn't true. She was very much afraid that the woman the two men had in common was not her—but Caroline.

Cain didn't know it, but hardly more than a week after Caroline's death, Holly had gone to his house to see him. He hadn't been at home, but she had looked into his studio through the window, and had seen, for the first and only time, a portrait of Caroline.

He had, it seemed, known enough about her.

❖   ❖   ❖

The storms had spent all their fury by Thursday morning, and Joanna ventured out after having breakfast in her room to find the sun shining. She stood at the edge of the veranda, breathing in the clean scent of the breeze and staring out past the cliffs at the ocean. It was a beautiful sight, a beautiful day, but she couldn't summon much enthusiasm for either.

She had slept only fitfully during the night, and though she had dreamed again after finally going back to sleep, it had not been of a woman pushed from the cliffs. No, she had dreamed the same dream that had driven her here in the first place, of the house and the cliffs and carousel horse, and roses and a painting, and a paper airplane. A clock had ticked loudly through it all, and a child had sobbed miserably. Only the signpost had been missing, but Joanna supposed that made sense. She was here, after all, and no longer needed a signpost as guide.

As always, the dream left her restless and anxious, so to her, the day felt overcast rather than sunny, and the pounding of the surf against the rocks seemed to throb in her ears uncomfortably. She wanted to back away from that sensation and to put some distance between herself and those dangerous cliffs. She wanted to do *something*.

She was tempted to return to the library and finish going through back editions of the local newspaper. She had been reading an interesting bit about how Scott McKenna had started a greenhouse business locally, supposedly because his wife loved flowers so much, when the good sheriff had interrupted her, and so she hadn't copied that part. And she definitely wanted to look back—when had Griffin said? Four or five months ago?—and find out all she could about the poor woman who had fallen (been pushed?) from the cliffs.

But she didn't want to go back to the library so soon, not when Griffin could, apparently, look out his office window and see her. Spending a rainy afternoon in the library was one thing—a bright sunny day was another thing entirely.

After a moment's thought, Joanna nodded to herself. Shopping, of course. Tourists always shopped. So she'd just stroll into town and see what all the stores had to offer. And talk to people.

Griffin's warning aside—and damn the man for assuming she had the sensitivity of a stone!—Joanna had no intention of asking direct questions about Caroline, not unless whoever she was talking to brought up the subject first. Which most anyone was likely to do, given the resemblance, of course. Still, she was unlikely to cause anyone pain by talking about a subject they brought up themselves.

"Well, it's about time you—"

Joanna turned around, surprised, to encounter Holly's surprise.

"Oh, sorry. You know, I hate to tell you this, Joanna, but not only do you look like Caroline from the front, you look like Amber from behind."

"Amber? You mean that girl who runs around here in shorts?"

"That's her. I was going to tell her it was about time she packed away her shorts—only it was you."

"She has to be ten years younger than me," Joanna objected. "And you can't possibly believe I move like her. Please say you don't believe that."

Holly chuckled. "No, no. It's just that your hair is the same shade and length, and you have the same build. She's probably at least a couple of inches shorter, but with the heels, who can be sure?"

Joanna sighed. "That's all I need, to look like somebody else. Is there a hairstyling salon around here? Maybe I could dye my hair flaming red."

Holly laughed again. "Don't do anything rash."

"Oh, I won't. I'm a very prudent woman, not given to doing rash things." *Except flying three thousand miles to get to know a dead woman . . .*

"Another lesson from Aunt Sarah?" Holly asked curiously.

It was Joanna's turn to chuckle. "One of many. Always think things through—and sit up straight, and get your elbows off the table."

Holly pursed her lips in a considering manner. "I'd say that Aunt Sarah taught valuable lessons."

"I've learned to value them," Joanna said. "She also taught me to be a shrewd and energetic shopper. How're the stores in town?"

"Eager for your business," Holly replied cheerfully. "Honest, though, the clothes at On the Corner are first-rate; the manager gets them from L.A. and San Francisco—even New York, Atlanta, and New Orleans. And if you're looking for things rather than clothes, try One More Thing; it's a little antique shop, and sometimes they have some really great stuff. Both places are on Main Street, like most of the shopping in the area."

"Sounds good, thanks."

With a slightly guilty expression, Holly said, "I should probably tell you that the owner of The Inn also owns On the Corner. But I don't get kickbacks for sending customers in, I promise."

"Too honest for your own good, I see."

Holly sighed. "Just a highly developed sense of guilt."

"Well, never mind. I need a new sweater, especially if the temperature stays this chilly, and On the Corner sounds like just the place to get one."

"They have some beautiful sweaters." Holly smiled at her. "And they'll deliver here if you don't want to carry shopping bags."

"Terrific. Then I'll walk into town instead of driving. Thanks a lot, Holly."

"My pleasure. Have fun, Joanna."

Waving to the brunette, Joanna went back into the hotel so that she could get her purse and go out the front of the building to take the most direct route into town. Within five minutes, she was back outside and on her way to town, walking briskly. It did occur to her almost idly that the man and woman who had mistaken her for Caroline in Atlanta were possibly managers or buyers from a couple of the stores here or had some other type of job that had taken them three thousand miles away.

Or else there had been some bizarre coincidences at work.

Joanna felt distinctly wary of encountering those two people here in Cliffside. Because once she did, it would undoubtedly take no time at all for the news to get round town that she had been mistaken for Caroline in Atlanta—which made her decision to "vacation" here suspect, to say the least. Still, there was nothing she could do about the situation except hope they were still away and would remain away for the next couple of weeks.

Joanna reached town after ten minutes or so, having encountered no one. The place was neat, with clean streets and sidewalks and attractive storefronts. It took her only a moment to find the sign for On the Corner at the end of the next block.

But she lost all interest in clothes at the first store she came to, and stopped on the sidewalk as though she'd run into a wall. The store itself was not particularly interesting to her; it appeared to specialize in wicker things, from baskets to furniture. But in the front window, propped on a brass easel, was the painting from Joanna's dream.

✧   ✧   ✧

"Of course, we had to have it," Kellie Hayes told Joanna as they both stood admiring the painting. "The little girl in a field of flowers, that basket in her lap. We thought it'd be perfect for the store. Mr. Barlow didn't want to sell it, but he finally agreed to let us display it in the window. Of course, he doesn't need to sell everything he paints—so much money these artists make at big shows in San Francisco and New York!—and he said this was a favorite, so not for sale at any price."

"I don't recognize his name, but I know nothing about modern artists," Joanna said. "Is he very famous?" This had to be important, she thought. The painting done by a local artist had to mean something, or else why had it been a part of the dream? What was the connection to Caroline?

"Oh, yes, dear, very famous. And he never does seascapes, isn't that odd with him living on the coast? It's his portraits he's famous for, people all over the country have commissioned him to paint them. He does things like this one, of course, to please himself, and I've heard he accepts a student now and then, though I've never seen strangers about his place. But anyway, he's been in lots of magazines about artists and art. They do say he's even one of the artists under consideration to paint the president's portrait. Can you imagine? Not that he'd be impressed, of course."

"Wouldn't he?"

"Oh, I don't think so. He's a very charming man, Mr. Barlow, and handsome, but he does have a way of looking at you sometimes that makes you feel he might be laughing at you inside. Not really unkind, just as if he thinks most of life is a pretty good joke."

"You sound as if you know him very well. So, he's lived here a long time?" Joanna kept her voice casual.

"Let me see, when did he buy his little house?" Kellie frowned in thought as she gazed at the painting. "It must have been four or five years ago, at least. He only spent summers here the first few years. Then, about a year ago, well . . ."

Joanna nodded encouragingly. "Something changed?" She had always been able to "read" most people quickly with a kind of intuitive understanding, and Joanna was leaning on that ability heavily right now. Within a minute of saying hello, she had known that Kellie would happily talk about anything or anyone suggested to her; she was a born gossip and likely to be completely aware of everybody's dirt.

Kellie laughed. "Well, I guess it's no secret. It was obvious that Mr. Barlow noticed Holly Drummond sometime that summer—have you met her yet, Joanna? She manages The Inn—and when fall came, well, he just stayed on. They make a very nice couple, though people do say he'll never marry her and she's wasting her time thinking otherwise. Personally, though, *I* think there's something that keeps him here, and she's such a bright, pretty girl."

"You're probably right," Joanna told her. "Um . . . is there another place in town that displays Mr. Barlow's work?"

"Oh, no, dear, he says he's not about to become Cliffside's local artist and have the tourists taking pictures of him. But if you're interested, I think Sam might have something you can look at. He runs the bookstore two doors down, you see, and I believe he has a book with pictures of some of Mr. Barlow's work in it." Kellie smiled.

Joanna bought a basket.

❖ ❖ ❖

"I must say, you look an awful lot like Mrs. McKenna," Sam Atherton said, shaking his head. He seemed a bit wary, but the resemblance clearly intrigued him, and he couldn't take his eyes off Joanna. "She was a nice lady—and a regular customer. Was always in here buying books, mostly for Regan. That little girl does love to read—and what a vivid imagination. Do you know, she once told me there were fairies living beneath the cliffs?"

"With me, it was always trolls," Joanna said, following him toward a rear corner of his crowded bookstore. "There was a bridge near the house where I lived, and I was convinced trolls lived under it."

His smile was perfunctory. "Sounds like you and little Regan would get along fine. Me, the most I ever imagined was that I played shortstop for the Giants. Here you go, Joanna—this book has quite a lot about Cain Barlow in it."

"Good, just what I wanted," she said, taking the fairly heavy book from him. "And do you have some kind of history of the area?"

"Sure," he said after what seemed to her a slight hesitation. "Over here, against the wall . . ." He led the way to the other side of the store, still talking casually—and still glancing at Joanna. "I guess you're probably tired of hearing that you look like Mrs. McKenna, but it really is the most amazing thing. People can't stop talking about it."

"I can't help being interested in her," Joanna said.

"I guess you would be. Can't say that I knew her all that well, even though she'd been a customer for years. She was always nice, like I said, but she didn't talk about herself."

He was trying, Joanna thought, but she wasn't really buying his disinterest. Whether he knew more about Caroline than he was willing to say or had merely disliked her and didn't want to reveal that, it seemed clear to Joanna that he wasn't being nearly as open and casual as he seemed to be. She had the distinct impression that he was weighing every "casual" word before he spoke it, and that he wouldn't give away anything he didn't want her to know.

But why? What was it he didn't want her to know?

"What about Mr. McKenna?" she asked, casual herself.

Sam's rugged face never changed expression, but his eyes went shuttered and his voice turned decidedly cool. "Well, about him I couldn't say much at all. Not much of a reader. He comes in now and again, but not often. Always perfectly pleasant, but . . . kind of cold, I guess you'd say."

Definitely doesn't like Scott McKenna, and doesn't care if I see it. "He owns a lot in town, doesn't he?"

"Oh, yeah. The lumber mill about ten miles from here. Quite a bit of land. On the Corner and a couple of other stores. The Inn and several cottages he rents out summers. And then there's the greenhouse." Sam frowned, those guarded eyes briefly narrowed. "You know, that's kind of funny now that I think about it. All the things he owns in this town, and the greenhouse is the only thing Scott Mc-Kenna put his name on." He looked at the shelf in front of him and pulled out a book. "Here you go, Joanna—the best history of the area that I carry."

"Thanks, Sam." Joanna went to the counter with him to pay for the books, still chatting casually, this time about nothing in particular. Sam wasn't the only one who could present a calm and untroubled front, she decided. She could too. But inside, she felt more than a little uneasy. Maybe she was just being fanciful, imagining an ominous meaning behind what was likely no more than the natural wariness toward a stranger, but she couldn't help thinking that there was no reason for Sam to be guarded with her . . . or was there?

A few minutes later, she stood outside the store on the sidewalk, the two books—bagged—in her basket, and eyed the next store. She'd found one gossip who would no doubt talk to a post, and one bookseller who had talked without saying very much at all; what could she expect to find in the old-fashioned drugstore besides a soda fountain?

✧   ✧   ✧

"Your Aunt Sarah sounds a lot like my Aunt Alice," Mavis said, industriously wiping the immaculate counter in front of Joanna's cherry Coke. "With a saying or proverb for everything. It does tend to make life simpler, though, doesn't it? I mean, having an answer for most every question."

"It does give you rules to live by," Joanna agreed.

"That's what I keep telling my boyfriend, Danny. He says the commandments are enough to worry about, but what I say is, the people who came before us had a few things figured out, and why shouldn't we listen to them? My Aunt Alice lived through the depression and wars and—well, I think she'd earned the right to be listened to."

"Oh, I agree. Aunt Sarah never gave me bad advice, never."

"Neither did Aunt Alice." Mavis smiled at Joanna with an obvious feeling of sisterhood. "Wouldn't they both be pleased to hear us quoting them?"

Joanna nodded. "Definitely. Aunt Sarah always said that fame was the number of people who remembered you after you were gone."

"Isn't that the truth." Mavis shook her head, then blurted out, "Oh, gosh, Joanna, you sure look like her!"

"Caroline? So I hear."

"You don't sound like her, not a bit, and you're so relaxed and friendly where she was sort of shy, I guess—"

"Shy? I read somewhere that she spoke in public quite a lot."

"Oh, she did—at least, pretty often. Committees and the PTA, that sort of thing. But when it was one-on-one like this, just casual-like, she always seemed shy, at least to me. Quiet, hardly talked at all. Didn't smile much. She was beautiful—I mean, hey, look in the mirror!—but kind of . . . subdued. She just didn't sparkle, know what I mean?"

"I think so," Joanna said slowly.

"Except when Regan was with her, of course. She did love that little girl, and it really showed."

"I keep hearing that." *Is that why Caroline wanted me here? Because of some danger to Regan? But what could it be?* "I met Regan, and she seemed . . . sort of frozen. Very alone. I had to remind myself that she still had her father."

Mavis's cheerful smile faded and she looked away from Joanna, not quite guarded but definitely uncomfortable. "Oh, yeah, she has him. But from what I've seen and heard, the poor kid might as well be a complete orphan. I've never seen a man with less interest in his own kid."

Another one who didn't like Scott. "You mean, just now? Or—"

"No, he's been that way most of Regan's life. I guess some men should never be fathers. Everybody figures Caroline wanted kids and he just went along with the idea, the way he went along with all her ideas."

"Was Caroline so . . . persuasive?" Joanna asked slowly.

"With men she was." Mavis's gaze returned to Joanna, and she made a little sound that might have denoted unwilling admiration. "She had that way about her, you know? Sort of helpless on the outside, and always needing a man to do one thing or another for her. Why, even the sheriff was more or less at her beck and call."

"They were close?" It took an effort, but Joanna kept her voice only mildly interested.

Mavis looked thoughtful. "Well, I heard once that they were *very* close, if you know what I mean. But I never saw anything to prove that, and honestly, it might have been just gossip. All I know for sure is that he always seemed to have time to help her if she needed him. But I have to say, that's true of most everybody in Cliffside. He's an awfully good sheriff, Joanna. And he finds out things, you know? I mean, we don't have a lot of crime here, but Sheriff Cava-naugh gets to the bottom of what we do have pretty quick. My Danny, he says the sheriff is like a terrier after a rat when he's trying to solve a problem."

Great. Just great. And he's suspicious of me.

"Sounds like he's suited to his job," was her only comment.

"I'll say. We're lucky to have him."

Joanna nodded in casual agreement, but her thoughts were anything but casual. A terrier after a rat equaled a man dedicated to the truth, but if that man had been involved with a victim of a so-called accident, even supposing he had not been involved in causing that accident, just how deeply would he dig for the truth?

"Another Coke, Joanna? Or something to eat? It'll be lunchtime soon, you know."

"I'm not really hungry," Joanna said, conjuring a faint smile. "I think I'll go on with my shopping now that I've rested."

"For a little town," Mavis offered proudly, "we have some pretty good stuff, don't you think?"

"Yeah," Joanna said. "Oh, yeah."

✧   ✧   ✧

It was after two o'clock when Joanna came out of On the Corner to find Griffin leaning back against the store's old-fashioned railing and quite obviously waiting for her. She was empty-handed, all her purchases having been left in the store behind her to be delivered to the hotel, and the bits and pieces of information she'd acquired today were a jumble in her head.

Even more, she was trying to decide if the wariness she had sensed at times today had been real or her imagination. If she had imagined it, it was no wonder, given her state of mind. But if she had not imagined it, then what lay behind it? Because she was a stranger who looked like Caroline? Because she was asking questions? Because something other than an accidental death had happened in this nice little town?

All she knew for sure, as she stood on the sidewalk, was that she felt wary herself. Especially now, confronting this man. She didn't consider herself much of an actress, but she was determined to maintain her pose as simply a tourist enjoying the visit to his town.

So she didn't hesitate to say, "We've gotta stop meeting like this, Sheriff. People will begin to talk."

"As opposed to what they've been doing?" Not waiting for a reply, he asked, "Enjoying your shopping, Joanna?"

"Immensely," she said. "I bought a lot of stuff, really good stuff."

"I'm curious," he said. "What're you going to do with the basket? And with the clock in the shape of Cliffside's courthouse?"

"Have you been following me?" she demanded.

"Not at all, I was merely on my daily rounds. Making sure the good citizens of Cliffside were all safe and happy."

Joanna glanced around at the downtown area, fairly busy on this sunny Thursday afternoon, and wasn't surprised to catch a number of covert looks directed toward her and the town sheriff. The problem was, what should have struck her as simple and genuine interest in someone who looked oddly like Caroline was beginning to seem sinister to her. To *feel* sinister. As if everyone but her knew something, some dark secret they didn't want her to find out.

I'm just imagining things. Jumping at shadows.

"They look fine to me," she said, lying.

"I'm good at my job."

For the life of her, Joanna couldn't tell how strong Griffin's sense of humor was. So far, he hadn't so much as cracked a smile, and the very dark eyes were completely unreadable. It left her uncertain as to just how serious his supposed curiosity was. Was he suspicious of her actions, or was he, in fact, merely being a small-town sheriff?

Finally, she shrugged and said, "I can always use another basket. *Everyone* can always use another basket. And the clock is simply my souvenir of Cliffside."

"I assumed," he said, "your souvenir of Cliffside would be the paperweight you bought at Merton's."

"That should teach you not to assume. The paperweight, with its replica of The Inn inside, is obviously a souvenir of where I'm staying. Specifically where I'm staying, I mean."

He nodded gravely. "And the needlepoint pillow? I understand it represents the architectural marvels of our little community theater."

"The needlework," Joanna said, "is exquisite."

"Umm. May I ask what is this fixation you have with buildings?"

Still not so much as the glimmer of a smile. He had a great poker face, this sheriff. Joanna cleared her throat. "Look, all those things just happened to appeal to me, that's all. Surely there isn't a crime against buying things you like."

"No. I just find it rather surprising. I would have sworn you weren't the kind of woman who would buy tacky tourist souvenirs."

"Well, obviously you were wrong."

"That is possible. I'll even admit I was wrong—if you can explain to me what possessed you to buy the little box covered with seashells."

"A . . . souvenir for a friend back home?" she ventured.

"Male or female?" he asked with detachment.

"Female. Why?"

"She likes poker?"

Joanna blinked. "She wouldn't know a straight flush from three of a kind. Why?"

"You didn't even bother to look inside it, did you?"

"Well . . ."

"Joanna, if you'll open that little box, you'll find a deck of very . . . adult playing cards inside."

"No wonder Tony asked me if I was sure that was what I wanted," Joanna murmured, remembering the clerk's uncertainty.

"And would your friend enjoy the gift?" Griffin asked politely.

Joanna sighed. "Let's just say I should have been paying closer attention."

"You know, you didn't have to buy something in every store just because you went in."

"What makes you think—"

"I believe it was the box of nails you bought in the hardware store that finally convinced me. I think they have nails in Atlanta, don't they? Probably not much different from the ones we have here."

Joanna was trying hard to keep a straight face, but he began smiling then and she lost it. She had a niggling suspicion that her laughter had an edge of hysteria to it, but he didn't seem to notice and at least it eased the tension inside her. When she finally leaned against one of the railing's posts and tried to catch her breath, he held out his handkerchief with a grin.

"Didn't mean to make you cry."

She wiped her watering eyes and sniffed, trying to swallow a final giggle. Definitely hysteria. "Oh God, don't start me off again. You don't play fair, you know that?"

"Hey, you could have explained the nails," he said. "A loose floorboard in your room at The Inn, for instance. It's not my fault you couldn't think on your feet."

"Don't give me that. You were determined to break me up, weren't you? Completely deadpan, and me trying to explain absurdities." *Keep it light. Keep it casual.*

Griffin accepted his handkerchief when she returned it, and said a bit ruefully, "I was half hoping you *could* explain them. Joanna, did you take a course in how to get information, or does it just come naturally?"

She sighed. "I didn't upset anyone with questions, Griffin, I promise. Is it my fault if they just started talking about Caroline? With me looking so much like her, it'd be a miracle if nobody said anything. What was I supposed to do, interrupt whenever anyone said her name?"

"Don't try to tell me all this was accidental," he said.

"You've been working this town with all the deliberation of a census taker."

"Let's not get nasty, Sheriff."

"Am I smiling?" he demanded.

She looked hard. "Well, a little bit—behind the eyes."

He closed the eyes briefly and sighed. "We've got to talk about this. Look, why don't I buy you lunch? I know you haven't eaten yet, and I've . . ."

"You've been following along behind me and missed lunch too," she said when he broke off.

"Something like that," he said, unrepentant. "I feel like Italian. How about you?"

"I haven't seen a sign of an Italian restaurant in town," she said, looking around. "Where is it?"

"About fifteen miles up the coast highway toward Portland. What do you say? Want to save the other side of the street for tomorrow?"

"What'll everybody think if we just drive off?" she asked.

"They'll think we're hungry," he said dryly. "I'll have to let my office know where I'll be—and you don't seriously believe that information will stay inside the Sheriff's Department, do you?"

After all the conversations behind her, Joanna knew exactly what he meant. "No. Oh, no. There don't seem to be very many secrets in this town." *Except the one that counts?*

"Not many." He took her arm and began leading her down the sidewalk in the direction of the Sheriff's Department. "By the way, I do wish I'd been privileged to meet your Aunt Sarah. Sounds like quite a lady."

✧   ✧   ✧

They were about ten miles from Cliffside when Griffin pulled the Blazer off to the right side of the road where the shoulder was wide and cut the engine. Joanna looked around, seeing only the twisting road beginning to climb ahead of them, a sheer drop to the ocean on their left, and a forest on their right.

"Why are we stopping?" she asked.

"Something I thought you should see. It'll just take a minute." He got out of the Blazer and walked across the street to the narrow shoulder on that side, where a low guardrail was the only barrier.

Joanna followed him slowly, reluctant. She knew what he was about to show her, and she wasn't at all sure she wanted to see it. She looked at him rather than anything else when she joined him, watching the ocean breeze ruffle his dark hair, noting the distant look in his dark eyes.

What did she mean to you, Griffin? Were you lovers?

"This is where her car went over," he said. "She was heading toward town and apparently lost control on that last turn over there. The car was going so fast that the guardrail was no barrier at all, it just sheered off."

Is that pain in your voice or anger?

Joanna looked at the long section of guardrail that was newer than the rest, then swallowed and looked past it and over the cliff.

This section of the cliffs was even higher than those behind The Inn, and far below, the rocks were incredibly jagged, vicious points thrusting upward. They would have torn a car to pieces.

Joanna stared down for a moment, feeling dizzy, feeling her heart thudding rapidly. *Is this why I'm here, Caroline? To prove you died here by someone else's hand?* Because she was sure, suddenly. Sure that Caroline McKenna had been murdered.

She closed her eyes for an instant, and half turned as she opened them so that she was looking at him. His face was hard. "Why did you think I should see this?" she asked, her voice sounding more normal than she had any right to expect.

"You're so curious about Caroline." His voice was a little harsh, matching the stone of his face and the bleakness of his eyes. "This is where she died. There wasn't much left of the car, and even less of her, but we managed to piece together enough of both. Enough of her to identify her, and enough of the car to figure out what had happened."

"You're sure it was an accident?" she asked, unable to keep from asking the question.

Griffin frowned at her. "She didn't try to kill herself, if that's what you're suggesting. They aren't very visible now, but there were clear skid marks from the middle of that last curve all the way to this point. She was trying to stop the car—she just didn't get it done."

"Do you think—" Joanna bit her lip for a moment, then went on. "Is it possible that someone could have forced her off the road? That someone could have caused the accident?"

"You mean another driver, drunk or playing insane games?"

Joanna hesitated, then nodded. "Is it possible?"

"Anything is possible, Joanna. But it isn't very likely. There were no signs of anything like that."

"You looked?"

"Of course I looked—what kind of cop do you think I am? I had to explain what must have happened to a number of people, including her husband. They pay me to know how to figure that stuff out."

"I only meant—"

"Look, nobody had tampered with the car. We found no damage not consistent with the car hitting the rail and going over onto the rocks; no flecks of paint from another car, no sign of a blowout prior to the crash, nothing. It had been raining. The road was wet, she was driving too fast and lost control. End of report, Miss Flynn. End of story."

"I'm sorry," she said, reaching out instinctively to touch his arm. "I didn't mean to imply anything, to question your competence. It's just that everybody said she was a safe driver, and—"

"She made a mistake. It happens."

"I guess you're right." Joanna didn't say anything more while she followed him back to the Blazer and got in on her side. Then she said, "You were definitely right to warn me about the cliffs being dangerous. First that other woman, and then Caroline."

"What other woman?" Griffin paused after putting the vehicle in gear to frown at her.

"You said somebody had fallen four or five months ago," she said.

"Yeah," Griffin said, pulling the Blazer back onto the road and continuing on their way. "But it wasn't a woman. The victim was a man."

$\mathcal{F}$ IVE
✦　✦　✦

IT WAS DIFFICULT for Joanna to enjoy lunch after that, but she tried. She told herself that the dream had most likely been caused by her own unsettled state of mind. Caroline had died going over the cliffs, Joanna knew that at least one other person had also died on those jagged rocks, and so her own anxious emotions had conjured a nightmare vision of a woman—a blond woman—also plummeting to her death.

Simple. Probably, she decided, the dream had been wholly hers and none of Caroline's—and just a dream. A nightmare welling up out of tensions and fears, as most nightmares did. After all, she had dreamed virtually meaningless dreams for most of her life, and just because one particular dream had sent her here didn't mean that all her other dreams had to be anywhere near as unusual.

It didn't convince her, but Joanna's ability to focus helped her to concentrate on the here and now. And since Griffin's mood seemed to change once they reached the restaurant, she forced herself to at least appear relaxed and untroubled.

"My Aunt Sarah would say that when a cop buys you lunch, he's probably just trying to get your fingerprints," she said when the waitress had left them in a corner booth at Donatelli's with menus. With the lunchtime rush over and the dinner crowd still a couple of hours away, they had the place virtually to themselves.

"Did she offer that along with lessons on keeping your elbows off the table?" Griffin asked dryly.

"Absolutely. She also taught me how to cook, sew, drive, dance, sail a boat, and ride a horse."

Griffin's brows went up. "You know, I had the impression your Aunt Sarah was the elderly-maiden-aunt type—hair in a little bun, specs on the nose, support stockings—but I think I was off base."

"Wildly." Joanna could hardly help but smile. "First of all, she was no maiden; she buried four husbands. And she was barely sixty when she died four years ago. She had bright red hair and favored short skirts and high heels—and since her second husband was a cop, I imagine she knew what she was talking about when it came to you guys."

"You mean she specifically warned you against cops?"

"*Against* cops, no. But I do recall her saying that a cop's natural instinct was to be suspicious. So if you brought me all the way out here just to get my fingerprints . . ."

"I could have got them before now if I'd wanted to," Griffin responded with a faint smile. "Why should I? Something tells me you don't have a criminal past."

"Cop's intuition?"

"Whatever. Am I wrong?"

"No. I've never even cheated on a parking meter." Joanna sighed. "God, that sounds dull."

"Law-abiding, not dull. Speaking on behalf of policemen everywhere, I thank you."

Joanna chuckled and then looked down at the menu. "What's good here?"

"Just about everything, especially the shells and cheese . . ."

The waitress came to take their order a few minutes later, and when she'd gone, Joanna decided it was time to try to clear the air with Cliffside's sheriff. She was still unwilling to confess that she had come all the way to Oregon specifically to find out about a dead woman, but Griffin's lurking distrust was something she didn't like. She didn't like it because he was the sheriff and could, therefore, make her life difficult; and she didn't like it because . . . well, because she didn't *like* it. Something about those dark eyes gazing at her in suspicion bothered her more than she wanted to admit, even to herself.

The problem was, she wasn't sure how much she could tell him without making him even more suspicious.

"Tell me something," she said. "Why does it bother you that people are talking to me about Caroline?"

"It doesn't bother me," he said immediately. "And I gave you my reasons for . . . disliking it. People could be hurt—"

"Griffin, credit me with an ounce of sensitivity, would you please? I'm only talking to people who talk to me, and I never bring up the subject of Caroline myself."

"With the resemblance, it'd be a miracle if nobody brought it up. You said so yourself."

"Well, but what's wrong with talking about her? What's the harm in Sam Atherton telling me Caroline bought books for Regan, or Mavis telling me Caroline was shy one-on-one, or Julie telling me that Caroline favored blue and green and loved silk? Who is that going to hurt?"

"No one," he said, admitting that with obvious reluctance. "But . . ."

"But what?" Joanna waited a moment, then said, "Is it me you're suspicious of? My motives? Griffin, what nefarious purpose could I have in asking questions about Caroline?"

He leaned back with a sigh, and a slight smile tugged at

his mouth. But his very dark eyes were abruptly shuttered. "I can't think of a single damned one."

"Then what are you worried about?"

After a moment of silence, he said, "I don't know, Joanna. But something tells me there's more to this than you're willing to say."

It startled her a bit, but Joanna tried not to let that show. "My only interest in Caroline is that she looked enough like me to have been my sister, and I'm curious about her. I'll probably keep on talking to people, but I promise you I'm harmless. Okay?"

Griffin nodded slowly. "Okay."

"Good." She saw their waitress approaching with salads, and added, "So we can talk about something else."

"Yes," he said. With an almost visible shrugging off of his suspicion, he said lightly, "I have to hear more about Aunt Sarah."

"Well," Joanna said, "when she was a teenager, she actually ran away to join the circus. I was the only kid in Charleston with an aunt who could juggle oranges *and* stand up on a galloping horse's back. I was really popular in show-and-tell."

He chuckled. "I'll bet you were. She raised you?"

"Since I was nine. My parents were killed in a boating accident." Joanna nodded her thanks to the waitress and picked up her fork. "Luckily for me, Aunt Sarah had always been a part of my life, and she was entirely willing to be my legal guardian."

Griffin nodded, but said, "Still, nine is awfully young to lose both parents. It can't have been easy for you."

Joanna didn't respond immediately, thinking about how fresh those old wounds felt now, and had felt since her accident. Twenty years, and yet the ache of missing her parents hurt as much now as it had when she had first realized they were gone forever. As a child, she hadn't understood the finality of it, not really, not for a long, long time. Even with Aunt Sarah there, a loving presence, she had often thought of something she wanted to tell her mother, something she wanted her father to see, and the shock of remembering they were gone had remained sharp as a knife's stabbing cut for years afterward.

Three months since Caroline's death; had Regan faced the finality of it yet? Had her father—or anyone—held her while she sobbed in grief and loss? Did she cry herself to sleep every night and wake up aching after dreams of happier times?

"Joanna?"

She looked across the table at Griffin, and scrambled to recall what he'd said. "Oh—no, it wasn't easy. Losing someone you love never is."

For an instant, his dark eyes were naked with feeling, and Joanna felt caught up in what she saw there, tangled in his pain. It wasn't so unusual for her to feel an empathic sense of someone else, to sense and understand what they were feeling, but never before had she looked into someone else's eyes and felt his pain so acutely that she nearly cried out.

As it was, she must have looked shocked or somehow unsettled, because Griffin leaned back suddenly and turned his gaze downward to fix on his plate. When he looked at her again, his eyes were veiled once more. "No," he said, almost casual, "you're right about that. I see a lot of loss in my job, and it's never easy."

Joanna couldn't have matched his feigned nonchalance to save her life. She began eating automatically, tasting nothing. Was it Caroline? Had he loved her so much that her death had caused this awful anguish inside him? Or were his feelings about her and her death more complex than simple grief? Joanna wanted to ask him, but somehow couldn't put the question into words.

The silence didn't go on long—surely it didn't—before she managed to say calmly, "Having Aunt Sarah helped a lot. She wasn't really a motherly sort of woman, but she thought of life as an adventure, and if I learned anything from her, I hope it was that."

Lightly, he said, "You came three thousand miles alone just for a vacation; that sounds pretty adventurous."

Since she didn't want him to think that particularly unusual, she said, "Oh, that's nothing. My high school graduation present from Aunt Sarah was a trip to Egypt. I went alone, with nothing but her list of places to see and people to introduce myself to. She had a lot of friends over there, so I didn't lack for escorts, but I went most places by myself."

Griffin was smiling. "Definitely adventurous."

For the first time, Joanna wondered what her aunt would think of this situation, and the answer came swiftly. She would commend her niece for having the gumption to journey across the country in search of the meaning behind disturbing dreams, but she would urge caution because Joanna was, after all, surrounded by strangers. Strangers who had all known Caroline.

Particularly this stranger.

Joanna conjured a smile in response to his. And kept the conversation firmly on the subject she knew best and could casually discuss throughout the length of a meal and a drive back to town in the company of a disturbing stranger who hid his secrets all too well.

"Maybe, but Aunt Sarah was the true adventurer. Do you know, she once rode across India on an elephant? And she was the only person I ever knew who had actually been to the North Pole. The South Pole too. And Madagascar. Have you ever known *anyone* who went to Madagascar? If there really had been dragons at the edge of the earth, she would have found them. . . ."

✧   ✧   ✧

On Friday morning, after a quick stop by the library, Joanna began "working" the other side of Main Street. The sense of urgency that had brought her to Cliffside had not abated at all; as she awoke every morning it seemed even stronger. She had to do *something* to try to ease that tension, and the only thing she could think of was to keep trying to find out about Caroline—particularly her death.

Her murder. Somewhere in all this was an answer, Joanna knew. Somewhere was the reason she had been driven to come here.

She just had to find it.

There were a number of stores on this side, including two jewelry stores, what was once upon a time a five-and-dime, a store that made signs, two tourist-type stores selling souvenirs and other like items, and a couple more clothing boutiques.

At first, Joanna thought she'd have the same fair success as the day before in gathering bits of information about Caroline, but that optimism was soon proved wrong. The first store she went into was one of the clothing boutiques, and while the young clerk (whose nametag read Sue) was professional and polite in asking her if she needed help, she also retreated immediately when Joanna said she was "just looking." And for the next fifteen minutes or so, Joanna was uncomfortably aware of being watched.

Not stared at. *Watched.*

She actually drew a breath of relief when she was once more outside on the sidewalk, and couldn't wait to move along, away from the windows, so that she no longer felt those unblinking eyes on her.

It's because I look like Caroline. That's all.

Squaring her shoulders and conjuring a friendly smile, Joanna went into the next store, which was one of the souvenir-filled ones. This time, the lone clerk remained behind his cash register, reading a newspaper and listening to the oldies station on his quiet radio.

Joanna was so conscious of his disinterest that she picked up a souvenir at random, not realizing until she got up front that her prize was a cast-iron doorstop in the shape of a beaver. Thinking that maybe such an absurd choice would break the ice, she approached the cash register and said hi to the middle-aged man.

"Will this be all, ma'am?" he asked, polite but unresponsive.

"Yes, thanks." She watched him begin to ring up her

purchase, adding casually, "You have some very nice things here."

"Thank you, ma'am. That'll be thirty-eight fifty, ma'am."

She handed over two twenties and tried again. "My name's Joanna."

His mild blue eyes were unreadable as he handed her the change and a sturdy bag containing her doorstop. "Yes, ma'am. Thanks for coming in."

There was, Joanna thought, something very, very deliberate about his unresponsiveness, almost as though it had been rehearsed. He seemed a little too studied as he turned away indifferently and picked up his newspaper again, dismissing her so completely that she felt almost invisible.

Back out on the sidewalk, Joanna cradled her awkward purchase against one hip and stood eyeing the next store with a little frown. One of the two jewelry stores. What would she find in there?

She found Mr. Landers, who was pleasant and who told her a sweet story about Regan and a necklace the little girl had got for her mother. But when Joanna tried to probe his feelings about Caroline, his affable smile faded a bit, and his eyes turned guarded. She was a nice lady, that was all he said. And when Joanna mentioned Scott, Mr. Landers abruptly recalled some business he had to take care of in the back, and was there anything else he could do for her?

Joanna left without buying anything. This was very . . . odd. She could hardly believe that Main Street divided Cliffside into helpful and unhelpful sides, so she could only assume that something had changed since yesterday to make these people wary of her. Had Griffin returned from their lunch and quietly spread the word that her questions about Caroline weren't to be answered?

If he had, why? Why were her questions so dangerous?

And if he had not, then why was she meeting with so much unresponsiveness today? Because small towns were naturally resistant to questions, and her interest in Caroline and her family was considered excessive? Was she merely being politely warned off? Or was there something more sinister in the closing ranks of Cliffside's citizens?

More than a little unnerved, Joanna entered the next store, another clothing boutique. This time, she was met with a smiling face. The youngish clerk introduced herself in a friendly manner as Linn, and she didn't hesitate to admit that she knew who Joanna was.

"I expect everybody knows by now," she said frankly. "With you looking so much like Mrs. McKenna, that's hardly surprising, is it? Is there anything special you're looking for, Joanna?"

Answers! "No, not really. Maybe a new sweater. It's cooler here than I expected."

She was led to sweaters and several were suggested. Linn's manner was brisk and friendly, but quite business-like. She didn't seem disposed to chat, and when Joanna tentatively broached the subject of Caroline, Linn replied vaguely and politely excused herself to attend to another customer.

By the time Joanna selected a sweater almost at random and took it to be paid for, she was unsurprised to see Linn's smiling face and guarded eyes. But the confirmation of her expectations was nevertheless disturbing—so much so that Joanna turned back toward The Inn rather than continue shopping.

As she walked, she tried to concentrate on what she knew or had heard—mostly yesterday, although the stop at the library had provided at least one bit of information.

The tourist who had fallen to his death had been named Robert Butler, a businessman from San Francisco. He had, apparently, been walking too close to the edge and slipped. Nobody seemed to think there had been anything more to his death. An accident. A sister came up to claim the body. End of story.

Other than that, she had found out that it was very likely that the man and woman who had mistaken her for Caroline in Atlanta were Dylan York and Lyssa Maitland, two of Scott McKenna's employees. Both, she had heard,

were currently out of town on business for him, and there
had been some vague mention of the East Coast.

They were due back soon. Too soon.

And Joanna had also discovered that Caroline had
bought a little antique box at One More Thing about a
week before she was killed. Was that important? She didn't
know. It was just another piece of the jigsaw puzzle, one
more fact to add to the rest.

Joanna wondered if she'd ever be able to put the pieces
together and find out what the picture *was*.

✧   ✧   ✧

It was Friday afternoon when she met Cain Barlow.

After having a solitary lunch in her room at the hotel,
Joanna was more than ready to find a quiet place and just
let the sea breezes clear her jumbled thoughts. She ended
up buying a newspaper and trying to read that on the cool
veranda, but found her thoughts wandering again and
again from the news of the day. The news didn't seem too
important here, she thought, at least not today.

It was almost four o'clock when restlessness drove her
from the veranda. With daylight saving time still in effect,
there were still a couple of hours of light left, so she wasn't
worried about getting caught in the dark. She moved
toward the cliffs but turned north instead of south, fighting
her urges because she was determined not to wander in the
direction of the McKenna house. Not now. Her head was
stuffed with details about Caroline as it was, and she
needed to sort through them.

She stayed back a few feet from the edge of the cliffs and
just strolled north. Since Cliffside's Main Street was set a
slight distance inland, there was room between the town
and the jagged cliffs for a number of widely spaced cottages, each an individual design so that the overall effect
wasn't one of mass production but originality. Most were
privately owned by townsfolk, and she'd been told that
nobody would mind if she walked up that way.

There was, actually, a narrow footpath that wound
along the irregular coastline a safe distance back from the

rocks, so Joanna followed that. She had passed a couple of the cottages, seeing no one, and was about to turn back toward The Inn when, through the trees that had begun crowding the coastline here, she saw another cottage. And saw him.

He had his back to her, his attention fully on the painting on his easel even though he didn't seem to actually be working on it, and Joanna found herself walking toward him without really thinking about what she was doing. And she didn't think about what she was saying when she blurted, "I thought you never painted seascapes."

He turned quickly, brilliant green eyes widening and then narrowing as they fixed on her face. He was a good-looking man, tall and well built, his coppery hair cut much too neatly for an artist.

"Damn," he said in a deep, pleasant voice, drawing the curse out.

"I'm sorry, I didn't mean to sneak up on you," she said. "I'm—"

"Joanna Flynn," he supplied.

She sighed. "Why do I even bother to *try* saying it? I've hardly had to tell anybody who I was since my first day here." She eyed him and couldn't resist saying, "And you're Cain Barlow, local artist."

He had a sense of humor; there was a laugh in his eyes when he responded in a polite tone, "Just so, Miss Flynn."

"Oh, call me Joanna. Everybody does."

"All right, Joanna. I'm Cain." He hadn't taken his eyes off her face, and shook his head now in a gesture that was not quite disbelief. "Forgive me for staring, but from an artistic viewpoint it really is . . . fascinating."

"From my viewpoint too," she told him a bit ruefully. "It's odd enough to look so much like somebody else, but when you find yourself surrounded by people who knew that other person . . . well, let's just say it's been an experience."

"I imagine so."

She glanced past him at the painting. "If I'm disturbing you, I'll go away."

Cain shook his head. "I was finished for the day. Just brooding."

"I was told you didn't paint seascapes," Joanna said, repeating her first remark as she studied what was definitely a seascape. Like all his work she had seen so far—the painting at the basket shop and photographs in the art book she'd bought—this one was filled with color and life. Unlike other seascapes she had seen, his depiction of a promontory north of his cottage, ocean waves battering its rocky base, was not done in dark shades of gray and blue but in unexpected swirls and splashes of warm, brilliant colors.

"I don't paint many," Cain said. "The sea doesn't really inspire me."

"If this is what you can do when you aren't inspired," she said, "I would love to see what you consider a result of true inspiration."

"Know anything about art?" he asked in a neutral tone.

Joanna smiled at him. "Don't worry, I won't madden you by saying that I don't know art but I know what I like."

"It's a true enough statement from most people."

"From me too, I suppose—but I won't say it." She returned her gaze to the painting and went on slowly. "This . . . makes me feel. I noticed the same thing with your painting in the wicker shop. All the color and life just seem to leap right off the canvas."

"I'm glad you like it, Joanna." He was absently cleaning a couple of brushes with a paint-spattered rag as they talked.

She heard a slight note of constraint in his voice and thought it probably made him uncomfortable to hear his work talked about. According to what little she had read about him, Cain Barlow was one of those rare, amazingly gifted artists who painted to satisfy a creative demon inside him; he didn't care about commercial success beyond being able to earn enough to live on, and it was said that art critics respected him for not giving a damn about their opinions.

Or anyone else's, probably.

Joanna took her gaze off the painting and looked at him, reminding herself that one of his paintings had appeared in the dream that had brought her here. So, what did he have to do with Caroline?

"Now you're staring," he said, a little amused.

"Sorry. Something just occurred to me. The painting at the wicker store . . . is the little girl Regan?"

"You've met her?"

"Briefly, the other day. Shook up both of us. Is it her in the painting?"

"She didn't pose for it," Cain replied. "But she gave me the idea when I saw her in a field one day. She was picking flowers for her mother."

"I guess you knew Caroline."

"Everyone did. Surely you've realized that by now." He began putting away his brushes in a case, his movements methodical and unhurried. "It's not only a small town, but Caroline could trace her roots to its beginning. That still counts for something in a place like this."

Joanna nodded slowly. "I got that feeling. But, you know, it's funny, a lot of the people I've talked to said that they didn't really know her. Was she as shy as all that?"

"Shy? No. I'd call it repressed. She married right out of high school, and beyond being allowed to mother Regan however it suited her, I doubt she was given many choices in her life."

Joanna was more than a little startled, both by his words and by a note of definite anger in his voice. Did it come from a purely benevolent interest in a woman who had touched something in him? Or had Cain Barlow known Caroline McKenna much better than the gossips in Cliffside had realized?

Before she could even begin to frame some kind of question, an interruption presented itself in the form of Amber

Wade, who came down the path from The Inn wearing her usual very short shorts and very high heels and swaying on the latter probably more than even she intended due to the uneven trail.

"Oh," she said when she reached them, an uneasy and unfriendly glance at Joanna followed immediately by a glowing smile at Cain. "I thought you'd be alone, Cain."

"Joanna stopped by for a visit," he said casually. "Have you two met?"

"Not officially," Joanna said. "But we're both staying at The Inn. Hi, Amber."

"Hello. I've seen you around." Amber looked at Cain's painting. "Oh, how pretty," she said.

"Thanks," said Cain with a faint smile.

"I wish you'd paint me. Oh, Cain, why won't you?"

It occurred to Joanna that Amber said "oh" so often because the syllable pursed her lips as though she were ready to be kissed. It also occurred to her that Cain was being hotly pursued by a young lady with all the subtlety of a flamethrower.

Lightly, he told Amber, "I never paint anyone between the ages of thirteen and twenty."

She looked confused. "Why not?"

"The growing years. Never the same from one day to the next—and it's a hopeless task to try and get that on canvas."

Amber was too young to be able to hide anything, including disappointment and a lack of comprehension. "Oh. But—"

"Why don't I walk you ladies back to the hotel?" he suggested. "It's getting late, and I'm supposed to meet Holly there anyway."

Joanna thought about saying she wanted to walk farther up the coast before going back, but a quick glance from his vivid green eyes told her that Cain was asking for her help. Glad that she herself had survived being eighteen, she murmured that she'd be glad of the company and watched Amber fume silently.

"Give me five minutes to put this stuff away," he told them.

"Need a hand?" Joanna asked.

"No, thanks, I've got it." And he did, vanishing into his cottage with the painting in one hand and his easel and equipment in the other.

"He and Holly make a nice couple, don't you think?" Joanna asked the younger girl, mildly curious as to whether Amber knew of the relationship.

"She doesn't appreciate him," Amber replied instantly.

"No?"

"No. She's always busy and—and she frowns at him a lot."

Joanna didn't bother to remark that if Amber had seen those frowns, it was doubtless because she herself had been hanging around Cain—and probably too close for Holly's comfort. Instead, she merely said, "Well, outsiders never really understand relationships between a man and woman, do they?"

"I'm very perceptive," Amber told Joanna. "Psychic, even."

Joanna kept her expression grave. "I see. And you think Cain needs a . . . change of girlfriend?"

Amber actually went red, and Joanna couldn't tell whether it was because Amber had honestly believed her crush had gone unnoticed by others or because she didn't expect Joanna to be so blunt. "I," she said, chin lifting high, "would support and appreciate his artism!"

It was getting more difficult to keep a serious face, but Joanna tried, resisting the temptation to tell Amber that unless she believed Cain to be autistic and she meant to support and appreciate that, the word she probably wanted was "artistry." Or just "art," maybe.

Cain came back out of the cottage about then, sparing Joanna the need to come up with some kind of response, and the three of them started back up the path toward the hotel. The path was really too narrow for all of them to walk abreast, but Amber stuck close to Cain's right side, and since he directed most of his conversation to Joanna, she had to walk fairly close on his left.

At no time was he even slightly rude or condescending toward Amber, yet he managed to subtly demonstrate to the girl that she was out of her depth with both him and Joanna by launching a rather lively discussion on the current state of American politics. He and Joanna disagreed on a few points, which led to some spirited debate, and by the time they reached the hotel lobby, Amber wore an expression somewhere between stricken and frustrated.

"See you later, Amber," Cain said, polite but unmistakably indifferent. "Joanna, how you can say that new bill is even remotely necessary—"

"Bye, Amber. Well, of course it's necessary, Cain. The states can't agree how to handle it, there must be a million different laws and all of them confusing. Without some kind of accord on the issue, we're just going to have more of these ridiculous court cases dragging on for years. . . ." Joanna looked past him and added dryly, "She's gone."

He sighed. "I hated to do that. Holly says hearts break easily at eighteen."

"They do," Joanna agreed. "But rarely into a million pieces, and they tend to heal as easily as they break. God, she's so *young.*"

"Even for eighteen, I know. Thanks, Joanna. That's the second time the kid's turned up at my place. The first time I was inside and just didn't answer the door when she knocked."

Joanna couldn't help but smile. "I was glad to help. How much longer are she and her parents staying here, do you know?"

"Another week or so, I think. If this was summer, there'd be at least a few more kids her age staying here. But it's October, she's bored stiff, and she's got it in her head—"

"Yes, I know, artists are such romantic figures," Joanna finished with a soulful expression.

"The bane of our existence," he confessed with a sad look.

"Yeah, right, I'm sure the burden is unbearably heavy," she told him with spurious sympathy. "I'll leave you to bear it alone, shall I? It was nice meeting you, Cain."

"The pleasure," he said, "was all mine, Joanna."

She lifted a hand in farewell and headed across the lobby toward the elevators, thinking it was no wonder both Holly and Amber found the artist fascinating; he had charm to spare. But what she still didn't know was why one of his paintings appeared in her dream, and what his relationship with Caroline had been. Friend? Or lover?

❖ ❖ ❖

It was Saturday afternoon when Griffin found Joanna sitting on a bench in Cliffside's town park with a cocker spaniel puppy asleep in her lap. There was a canvas tote bag on the ground beside the bench, a bat, a dirty softball, and three ragged baseball gloves piled on the ground nearby, and she had one raised foot propped on a huge pumpkin.

"Don't tell me you bought *him*," Griffin said, sitting down beside her.

"No, I'm only puppy-sitting," Joanna replied gravely. "It seems that the regularly scheduled activities of the Cliffside softball-playing, kite-flying, and pumpkin-carving club were interrupted by commerce. Mr. Webster stopped by with an offer of five dollars to the group if they wanted to rake his yard, and everyone decided to go. Since Travis here was deemed too young to attend, I offered to sit with him."

Griffin, recognizing an apt description of the small group of children usually to be found in the park on Saturday afternoons, shook his head slightly. "The pumpkin isn't carved," he observed.

"Apparently, they were going to carve it—in practice for Halloween—until it was discovered nobody had access to a knife. Mothers being what they are. And nobody had a kite, hence the need for five dollars."

"Ah. And how did you get involved?"

"I just stopped by to feed the birds and got drafted to be umpire. Has anybody paid attention to Jason Riordan's pitching, by the way? That kid's got quite an arm."

"If I know Jason's father, and I do," he said casually, "Jason's pitching will definitely be encouraged."

She smiled faintly and looked down at Travis in her lap, idly toying with the sleeping puppy's long, silky ears. "I like this town," she said, not at all sure she did at the moment, but saying the expected thing.

"Not bored yet?"

"Not at all. I told you I generally lead a pretty quiet life even if I do live in a big city; this suits me very well."

"Especially while the shopping is good? I hear you gathered a few more souvenirs yesterday."

"And every one a gem," she said lightly, wondering what his reaction would be if she described in detail her unnerving morning. Then again, he no doubt already knew.

"Including the doorstop?" He made his voice mildly curious. "I suppose every home needs a good doorstop, but I would have thought a foot-high cast-iron beaver would be hell to get on a plane."

"I thought I'd ship it," she murmured. *Yeah, he definitely knows.*

Griffin nodded with hardly a trace of a smile. "I suppose it goes with your decor back in Atlanta?"

"Absolutely."

He would have kept up his assault on her dignity, but Cliffside's kite-flying and pumpkin-carving club returned just then to reclaim their property, and it was some time before it could be decided who would carry the heavy pumpkin home. Griffin finally settled the matter himself by promising to see to it the future jack-o'-lantern was transported safely to their school on Monday morning, there to be carved under the supervision of a teacher.

"Very diplomatic," Joanna commended him when the children had collected their belongings—including a still-sleeping puppy—and rushed off. "Will you deliver the pumpkin yourself?"

"Probably," he said.

Joanna chuckled, getting to her feet and picking up the canvas tote bag she seemed to be carrying in lieu of a purse. "And you'll leave it here until then?"

"Might as well," Griffin said, walking beside her as they headed toward Main Street. "Where are you off to, more shopping?"

"Not exactly. I'm heading to the hardware store to return that box of nails."

"Wrong size?" he asked politely.

"Oh, I thought a box of washers would do just as well."

"Do for what?"

She gave him an innocent look. "For the same reason I got the nails."

Griffin found himself torn between a sigh and a laugh. "Joanna—"

"Are you on duty today?" she asked.

"On call, not on duty. Why? Need help picking out the washers?"

"No, I was just curious to know if the sheriff worked weekends."

"Only when he has to." Griffin looked at her, wondering why it was that jeans and a big sweater looked so good on her when the same outfit had made Caroline look childlike. It was the strangest thing. And strange how her eyes were so expressive when Caroline's had been dark and quiet. In fact, he was beginning to believe the resemblance he and others had seen was not nearly as powerful as they had first imagined.

"My God, it *is* you!"

They had reached Main Street's sidewalk, and both turned in surprise to see a man somewhere in his thirties, of medium height, with pleasant features and reddish blond hair walking toward them quickly. His eyes were fixed on Joanna, and it was clear he was startled.

Griffin looked at Joanna just as she sent him a quick

glance, and something tightened inside him. There was recognition in her golden eyes, and guilt.

"I thought it had to be you," Dylan York said as he reached them. "When I got back home this morning, and everybody was talking about you, said you were Southern—"

"Have you two met?" Griffin asked with stony control.

"Not exactly," Joanna murmured.

Dylan stuck out his hand and introduced himself, adding to Griffin, "I saw her in Atlanta, Griff. Lyssa and I both saw her within a week. And both of us called out Caroline's name without thinking—it was such a shock, you know? Of course, we got hold of ourselves pretty quick, but it was really unnerving. Nice to meet you, Joanna, believe me; I had half convinced myself you were a figment of my imagination."

"I'm . . . glad to be real," she told him with one of her brief smiles.

"It can't be an accident you're in Cliffside, Joanna," he said, finally releasing her hand. "Do you mind if I call you Joanna?"

"Of course not." She had not looked at him, Griffin realized, since that first guilty glance.

"Good, I'm Dylan. Lyssa's not going to believe this. We both work for Scott McKenna, you know."

"So I heard," Joanna said. "As for why I'm here . . . let's just say I was curious."

He frowned. "I'll buy that, but how did you know where to go? I mean, neither Lyssa nor I told you Caroline's last name or mentioned this town at all. And you didn't know who we were, since we didn't bother to introduce ourselves. Neither of us said much to you beyond Caroline's name before we bolted. So how did you know to come to Cliffside?"

That's the best question I've heard lately. Griffin waited for her to answer it, and he wasn't surprised when she managed to avoid doing so.

"Don't you believe in fate, Dylan? I'm beginning to." She smiled.

Obviously charmed by the smile, Dylan said, "I've never really thought about it, but—"

"Sometimes the place you end up in by accident is the very place you were meant to visit," she said lightly. "I have a friend who claims there are patterns in life, and that sometimes we get caught up in them. I guess that's what I'm doing here."

"Okay," Dylan said, clearly baffled. "But how did you—"

He hadn't intended to say anything to get her off the hook, but Griffin heard himself ask, "Dylan, is that your car parked across two spaces? What's wrong with you?"

"Hell, Griff, I saw Joanna and—"

"Joanna isn't leaving Cliffside today, you know; you can talk to her later. But if one of my people drives by and sees you parked illegally—"

"Okay, okay. I *do* want to talk to you later, Joanna."

"Anytime," she said.

Griffin watched the other man lift a hand and head back toward his car. Then, not particularly giving a damn what anyone thought, he put his hands on Joanna's shoulders, turned her to face him fully, and said, "Let's have it, Joanna." He knew his voice was harsh, and he probably looked mad as hell, but he didn't give a damn about that, either. Right now, all he cared about was getting a few answers.

She shook her head slightly with a rueful look. "You know, I knew it made sense that the two people who called me Caroline in Atlanta *had* to be from Cliffside. Had to live here. Must have known her. And just happened to be in Atlanta for some reason. It made sense. In fact, it was the only thing that made sense. And that meant, of course, that eventually they'd have to come home. I was just sort of hoping it wouldn't be quite this soon."

Griffin shook her, and he didn't try to be gentle about it.

"Goddammit, Joanna, I want to know what you're doing here!"

"I told you what I'm doing here. I'm on vacation and I'm finding out about Caroline." Her voice was steady, and her gaze met his calmly. "Want to call the library where I work and ask them if I'm on vacation? I'll give you my boss's name."

He didn't let her distract him. "You came here deliberately, didn't you? You came here knowing you looked like a dead woman."

She hesitated, but finally nodded. "Yes, I knew I looked like Caroline after Dylan and Lyssa mistook me for her. And—I found out she'd been killed. That's one of the reasons I came."

He stared down at her, trying to understand this. "How did you know who Caroline was, where she was from? How did you find out she'd been killed?"

Joanna glanced around as if she felt the weight of watching eyes, then looked back at him. She didn't seem so calm now. She seemed uneasy, guarded. "I . . . found out."

"How?"

"Newspapers, public records."

"Joanna, if all you knew was the name Caroline, how in hell could you find out anything more?"

"You wouldn't believe me if I told you," she said.

"Try me."

Joanna lifted her chin. "All right, dammit. I started having the same dream, over and over. And in that dream, I saw a signpost, and the sign said Cliffside. And when I finally managed to track down Cliffside, I saw her picture in a newspaper and Caroline's obituary. That's when I decided to come here."

"Why didn't you tell me?" he asked slowly, not at all sure he was believing any of this.

"Tell you what? That I came three thousand miles to find out all I could about a dead woman because we looked alike and because—"

"Because?"

She drew a breath. "Because, as near as I can figure, Caroline and I died on the same day. But I was luckier than she was. They brought me back. And that night, I had the first dream about Cliffside."

Six

SHE SAT BACK in the visitor's chair in his office and said, "What's everybody going to think? That you're arresting me?" Not that she really cared, and she doubted he did.

"It was the closest private place I could think of," he said, repeating what he'd told her when he had marched her in here nearly fifteen minutes ago. The door was closed, and so far they hadn't been disturbed by deputies or anyone else.

"You've just started a new round of gossip," she told him. *I'll bet* nobody *talks to me after this.* "You looked very fierce out there."

"I think I had a damned good reason to look mad as hell." His voice was still harsh.

"And I've said I'm sorry. I'm sorry I didn't tell you all the truth before now, but I just didn't want to sound like a lunatic." She eyed him thoughtfully, frowning. "And since I think you're still reserving judgment on that question, I was probably right to keep quiet."

"I don't know what I think." Griffin shook his head without smiling. "It's the wildest thing I've ever heard, Joanna. Just the incredible coincidence of you and Caroline looking so much alike and being involved in car accidents three thousand miles apart at roughly the same time—"

"Exactly the same time," Joanna insisted firmly. "You say the doctor couldn't determine the exact time Caroline died, that it was somewhere between noon and one o'clock that day. I was wearing a watch when that power line hit the car, and my watch—like my heart—stopped at three thirty-five. That's twelve thirty-five Pacific time." She would have said more, but stopped because of the look of surprise on his face. "What?"

Griffin cleared his throat. "Caroline was wearing a watch. There were no signs of damage from the accident, so we couldn't use it for time of death, but . . . it had stopped at twelve thirty-five."

Joanna laced her fingers together in her lap and looked down at them for a moment, then returned her gaze to Griffin's face. It wasn't so unexpected, yet she still felt shock at having it verified. She and Caroline really *had* died at the same moment. "I couldn't have known that," she pointed out carefully. "It wasn't in any of the newspaper articles."

"No, it wasn't."

She nodded. "So. Caroline and I looked alike, we were born three days apart, and twenty-nine years later we both had a car accident the same day. I survived my accident without a scratch—but a power line damaged in the crash fell on the car, and I was electrocuted at three thirty-five. Very possibly the exact moment of Caroline's death. The paramedics brought me back. Caroline wasn't so lucky."

"And you started having the dream that night?"

Joanna had already described the dream to him, and so nodded again. "That night. By the time it had been going on for weeks, I had to do something about it." She hadn't mentioned her strange compulsion about coming to this place, the overwhelming urgency, and didn't now. Griffin already thought she was off her rocker; there was no need to confirm that. "It was when I was trying to find Cliffside that for the second time in Atlanta, someone—Lyssa Maitland, I assume—called out Caroline's name when she saw me. After that, I found Caroline's obituary, and . . ."

"And decided to come out here. Because of a dream."

"Because of everything."

"Do you honestly believe Caroline is communicating with you from beyond death?"

Despite her own uncertainties on that score, Joanna felt her teeth grind together at the open skepticism in his voice. "I don't know what's beyond death. Maybe there's nothing. Before July first, that's what I thought, that death was just the end. I didn't believe there was anything, any kind of existence after death. I don't know what I believe now, not about that. Maybe it isn't even about that. Maybe . . . maybe there was just some kind of weird resonance between her and me, a connection because of all the similarities. Maybe each of us does have a double in the world, and maybe we're joined to those doubles in some way we'll never understand. *I don't know.* All I know is that on July first, I made it back from something we call death, and she didn't. And I know that if we weren't connected before that day, we somehow touched each other that day. In that moment. And I can't explain any of this any better than that, *Sheriff*."

If the cold dislike in her voice bothered him, he didn't show it. "But you think she wanted something of you?"

"I think she was afraid. I think she was in a lot of pain a long time before that car went over the cliffs. I think there's something wrong here in your pretty little town." Joanna drew a breath. "And I can't show you a shred of evidence proving any of that, either."

Griffin shook his head, but said, still with open skepticism, "Say you're right. Say Caroline was afraid of something, that she was unhappy. She's gone, Joanna. Nothing that you or I could do is going to bring her back. So what do you hope to accomplish by trying to find out about her now?"

"Something's wrong here," she repeated deliberately. "I don't know what it is. I don't know who it involves. I don't know why I can't just pack my bags and walk away from it. All I do know is that I have to be here, and I have to try to understand who Caroline was, what her life was. I don't have a choice about that."

"We all have choices," Griffin told her roughly.

"About some things. Not about this. I haven't felt so strongly about anything in my entire life. I'm sorry you don't understand."

"How can I understand? You're talking about subjective things here. Feelings, senses, beliefs. There's not one thing in all this that I can hold in my hand and say, 'Yeah, this is real.'"

Joanna leaned forward, planted her elbows on his desk, and said, "I'm here. I'm real. Explain that."

As much as he would have liked to, Griffin could offer no other explanation for her presence here except an incredible string of coincidences—and if he offered that one, he'd be calling her a liar. Something he hardly wanted to do. The fact remained that if she had indeed come here deliberately, *something* had helped narrow her search for Caroline. Otherwise he didn't believe she could ever have found this small town. He would check out her story, of course, as far as he could, but unless Joanna had excited some undue attention in getting here—like laying a heavy bribe on Dylan and Lyssa's hotel manager, for instance— he doubted he'd find anything to either confirm or disprove what she claimed.

"All right," he said finally, hearing the reluctance in his own voice. "I'll accept that you came here because of a signpost in a dream. I don't like it, but I'll accept it. I'll even accept that you believe there's something wrong here, or was. You've been talking to people about Caroline for days now; have you found even a hint of anything wrong?"

Joanna hesitated, wanting to ask him if he'd warned the

townspeople not to talk to her. But she wasn't quite ready to ask that question. Maybe because she didn't want to hear the answer.

"No, not really. Vague things, but nothing you could hold in your hand. Regan thinks her mother was afraid, but you don't have to tell me that poor kid's swimming in grief. There've been a few things said about Caroline that bugged me, but nothing drastic. Maybe she didn't have a great marriage, and maybe she wasn't close to many people around here, but she seems to have loved her daughter and she seems to have had a busy life."

"Well, then?"

"Don't ask me to be logical," she told him, trying not to sound as tense and defensive as she felt. "I can't be. But I'm sure there's an answer here—I just haven't found it yet. Probably because I'm not looking in the right place." She paused, then leaned back in her chair and said slowly, reluctantly, "And then there's you."

He was startled. "Me? What about me?"

Joanna didn't take her eyes off him. "Were you in love with Caroline?"

He didn't get indignant or angry, and he didn't seem surprised. He merely looked at her for a moment, as if he had expected the question, then said evenly, "No, I wasn't."

Joanna wished she believed him. "Then there must be some other reason for it."

"For what?"

"The way you look when you talk about her. The tone of your voice. I don't know you very well, Griffin, but I do know pain when I see it. And I see it in you. Something about Caroline—or her death—has affected you profoundly." She didn't ask the question, just watched him and waited. For a moment she didn't think he was going to respond, but finally he did.

"Caroline sent me a note that morning, asking me to meet her at an old barn just off the coast highway. At noon."

Joanna felt more tension creep into her, even though she couldn't tell much from his level voice and those dark eyes. What did he feel about this? She drew a breath, and asked cautiously, "Was that usual?"

"Dammit, no. We weren't involved with each other."

She still didn't believe him. His words told her one thing, but his voice and those veiled eyes told her something else. "Then why did she want to meet you at such an odd place?"

"I don't know."

"Didn't she say—"

"I didn't meet her." Griffin visibly forced himself to pause a moment to regain his calm, then went on. "I had a minor emergency come up here, and the next thing I knew it was well after twelve. I figured she wouldn't have waited so long, so I didn't bother to go."

"Correct me if I'm wrong," Joanna said, still feeling her way cautiously, "but I get the feeling you didn't attach too much importance to her request."

Griffin's mouth twisted bitterly. "No, you aren't wrong."

"But if you didn't know what it was about—"

"The meeting place was odd, but there didn't seem to be any particular urgency. If I thought about it at all, I just assumed she was going to be on her way to Portland or somewhere else and the barn was handy. As to what it was about, she was on a half dozen different committees and it wouldn't have been the first time she'd wanted to talk to me about a zoning ordinance or what permits she'd need for a PTA-sponsored carnival."

"Wouldn't she have come here to your office for anything like that?"

"I don't know. Yes, probably. Christ, how do I know what she wanted to talk to me about?"

Joanna heard guilt and self-blame in his voice now and thought she could guess where it was coming from. "You believe if you had met her, she wouldn't have been killed, don't you?"

"I believe . . . I should have been there. If I had met her at the old barn at noon, it's unlikely she would have been coming down the coast road like a bat out of hell at half past."

"You can't know that."

"No, but it's a good bet I'm right."

"There's something else, something else that bothers you," Joanna said, after a moment's thought, trying to read him. "What is it?"

Griffin sighed. "At the time, there was nothing. But, looking back now, it seems to me that Caroline was . . . jittery that last week or two before she was killed. Much more so than usual."

Joanna sat up straighter. "You mean all this time I've been saying there's something wrong here and you *agreed* with me?"

"No, that's not what I mean. There was nothing going on here, Joanna, no grand conspiracy involving Caroline. She was jittery, that's all. She must have had something on her mind, something she wanted to talk to me about. It could have been anything—"

"Anything that made her more nervous than usual?"

"Joanna, there was no sign of something serious being wrong, not that I noticed. Hell, not that anyone noticed. Nothing had happened out of the ordinary—"

"A man had fallen from the cliffs not long before that," she reminded him.

"I told you, that happens every few years. Why do you want to connect it to Caroline?"

"Because it happened around the same time as her death, and I'm looking for . . . drama. A catalyst." Joanna recalled her dream about the girl falling from the cliff, and couldn't help wondering if it meant something she hadn't considered. Not the fact that a woman went over the cliffs, but the fact that someone was *pushed*. "I suppose there was no sign that that man's death wasn't an accident? I mean, murder was never considered?"

Griffin stared at her for a moment, less incredulously than he might have done a couple of hours earlier. "No."

"Did you check him out?"

"For what? For dying in Cliffside?"

"Griffin—"

"He was a tourist. He'd been staying at The Inn less than a week when he wandered too close to the edge of the cliffs and went over. That was all there was to it."

Joanna put her hands up briefly to massage her temples with a gentle touch; she was getting a headache. Not at all surprising, really. She tried to concentrate. "Tourist. He was here alone?"

"Yeah. Is that sinister? You're here alone, you know."

She felt her teeth grinding again, but refused to let his sarcasm throw her off track. "Had he been doing the usual tourist stuff?"

"He didn't buy a cast-iron doorstop."

"Griffin."

"What usual tourist stuff?"

"Whatever unaccompanied male tourists do around here. Was he here for the hiking? The scenery? I hear the fishing's good; did he have fishing equipment?"

"I don't know. Look, as far as I remember, there was nothing odd about the man. Nobody had spoken to him beyond pleasantries, but he had plenty of ID, and when I called his sister in San Francisco, she came up and claimed the body. No mystery, Joanna."

"Caroline didn't know him?"

"Nobody around here—" Griffin broke off abruptly and frowned.

"What?"

His frown deepened, and the fingers of one hand drummed restlessly on his desk. Then he shook his head. "Christ, now you've got me questioning the most ordinary things. Just because Scott spoke to the man briefly in town a week or so before he was killed doesn't mean there has to be anything diabolical about it."

"Scott McKenna?"

Griffin nodded, still scowling. "They passed each other outside one of the stores in town. Spoke just a few words, I think; I was too far away to be able to tell even if I'd paid close attention."

"But—that's a connection with Caroline," Joanna pointed out.

"Yeah? What if the guy just asked Scott the time? Would that be a connection?"

"You don't know what they said."

"No, but it's a damn sight more likely to have been something innocent than something ominous."

Joanna was about to press him on that point, but he frowned suddenly, and she said, "You've thought of something. What?"

"Butler was from San Francisco," he muttered. "A businessman from San Francisco. Scott's originally from San Francisco, and still does business there from time to time."

Joanna felt the first real surge of hope since she'd arrived here. "That's enough of a connection to check out, isn't it?"

Before Griffin could respond, his phone buzzed, and she listened to a brief one-sided conversation that seemed to indicate the mayor was in search of his sheriff.

"Ask him to wait a minute, please," Griffin said finally. He punched a button and put the phone down, then got up and came around the desk to her. "Joanna—"

She stood up. "It's all right, I need to go anyway. Nails to return, you know. Paranoia to cultivate."

"I don't think you're paranoid," he told her.

"No, that would mean I thought I was being persecuted, wouldn't it? I'm just being haunted, in a sense. And you think I'm imagining things, at the very least, and that I'm crazy at worst. Is that supposed to be the lesser of two evils?"

He put his hands on her shoulders. "Stop it. I'm not taking any of this lightly, I promise you. But without more to go on than your dreams and my guilty conscience, there isn't much I can do, Joanna."

"I know, I know." She managed a smile. "Hey, maybe I'll get lucky and ask the right person the right question. In the meantime, the mayor's waiting to talk to you."

"Yeah." He hesitated, lifted a hand briefly to touch her cheek, then let her go and went to open the door for her. "I'll see you later," he said.

"I'll be around."

Griffin closed the door behind her and slowly went back to his desk. He sat down and picked up the receiver, but instead of immediately punching the flashing button that was the mayor, he buzzed one of the administrative assistants. "Shelley? Could you hunt up that file on the dead tourist last summer? The one who went over the cliffs behind The Inn, yeah. See what info we've got on his business in San Francisco, and see if we can get more details. And one more thing." He hesitated, then swore inwardly. "Pull everything we've got on Scott McKenna, all the public records. And see what you can find out about who he does business with in San Francisco. No, no hurry. Thanks."

He almost forgot about the mayor, despite his flashing button.

His Honor wasn't happy with the sheriff.

❖   ❖   ❖

If she'd been asked why she'd picked that afternoon, with hardly more than an hour or so of sunlight left, to return to Caroline's gazebo, Joanna wouldn't have been able to offer a really good answer. Answers aplenty, but no really good ones. Because she needed a brisk walk with the salt breeze blowing away cobwebs. Because she didn't know where to go next or what to ask when she got there. Because Regan with her helpless, suppressed grief was haunting her as much as the dream did, and she wanted to see and talk to the child again.

Because Sheriff Griffin Cavanaugh had touched her cheek.

She walked briskly through the woods at a safe distance from the cliff's edge, trying not to think for a while. Her head still ached faintly despite the aspirin she'd taken at the hotel, and she knew it was the tension of the last days. Even so, stopping the thoughts and questions racing through her mind seemed about as easy as halting a runaway train with an uplifted hand.

She reached the gazebo and went inside, finding herself absently stroking the painted forelock of the carousel horse as if it were real. It was sort of like a worry stone, she realized, her fingers tracing the swirls of colorful mane. A way to keep the fingers busy while the mind drifted. She wondered if Caroline had thought the same, and was somehow unsurprised to hear the answer aloud.

"Mama used to do that."

"Hello, Regan."

The little girl came slowly up into the gazebo, but only far enough to lean against one of the posts as she looked at Joanna. "You remembered my name," she said.

"Of course I did. Do you remember mine?"

"Joanna. I thought I'd see you before now, Joanna."

Hearing the faint note of accusation in that young voice, Joanna answered quietly. "I thought it might be easier for you if I stayed away."

"Why?"

"Because I only *look* like your mama."

Regan considered that for a moment, her big, dark blue eyes grave. Then she nodded. "You don't have to worry, Joanna. I know Mama isn't coming back." She dug her hands into the pockets of her jeans and hunched her shoulders in what seemed to be her usual posture.

"It's all right to miss her, Regan."

"Daddy doesn't miss her," the little girl replied.

"Some people," Joanna said, "have trouble showing what they feel. But that doesn't mean they don't feel. Maybe your daddy is like that."

Regan shrugged. "Maybe. But I heard Mama tell him he didn't have a heart. That's like the Tin Man, right? You can't feel without a heart."

"Everybody has a heart." Joanna had no idea if she was saying any of the right things, only that she had to try to reassure Regan. "Some people just can't open theirs and let other people in."

"I don't think my daddy likes me." Regan's voice quivered suddenly.

"Of course he does, honey."

"How do you know?" she demanded fiercely.

"Because daddies always love their little girls. Just like mamas do."

"Even when they're bad?"

Joanna wanted to go over and put her arms around this little girl, but held herself still. "Little girls are never as bad as they think they are," she told Regan gently, suspecting that the child somehow blamed herself for her mother's death and her father's apparent remoteness.

"I was bad, Joanna. I was awful bad."

"Honey, you could never do anything bad enough to make your mama and daddy stop loving you. I promise you that." *Whether it's true or not, dammit, she has to believe it!*

Regan drew a breath and let it out, relief easing her features, and Joanna was glad she had said it. She was also glad she hadn't asked what the child had done that she considered so bad. Probably, it was nothing serious—few things really were when you were eight—and the sooner she put it behind her, the better.

As for other questions, no matter how tempted she might be, the one person in all of Cliffside Joanna had no intention of questioning about Caroline was this little girl, so she merely changed the subject and said, "It's a little late for you to be out here, isn't it?"

"I come out to watch the sunset sometimes. It's pretty, isn't it?"

Joanna turned her head to look at the reddening western horizon and nodded. "Very. And the water looks like glass."

"I know. Mama said—"

"Regan."

They both started, and Joanna turned her head back

swiftly to see a tall, darkly handsome man approaching the gazebo. He was virtually expressionless, only a slight frown drawing his brows together. He gave Joanna one very long, direct look, and if her resemblance to Caroline disturbed him in any way, it wasn't apparent. His gaze went to Regan, and he spoke in a measured tone.

"Mrs. Ames has your supper ready now, Regan. It's time to go home."

There was no fear in Regan when she looked at the man who could only be her father, which rather relieved Joanna. In fact, there was a feminine version of his own measuring consideration in her darker eyes, and her more delicate brows had something of the level command of his.

She looks more like him than Caroline, even if it's more expression than features.

Regan turned her gaze to Joanna and smiled unexpectedly. "I have to go now, Joanna."

"I'll see you later then, Regan."

"Okay. Bye." Solemn once more, Regan left the gazebo and walked past her father without looking at him. She disappeared into the woods between the little clearing and the McKenna house.

"The resemblance," Scott McKenna said, "is remarkable."

Fairly or unfairly, Joanna had formed an opinion of this man, and it wasn't a positive one. So when she met his intent gaze now, it was with the first feeling of real hostility she had known since arriving in Cliffside. "I'm more different from Caroline than like her," she said flatly.

Scott's eyes narrowed. "Yes, I see that."

"Do you?"

He nodded. "Caroline was almost always reserved and seldom showed her emotions. Somehow, I doubt the same could be said of you. What you feel shows plainly in your eyes."

Deciding not to question him on that point, Joanna leaned an elbow on the carousel horse with the air of someone making herself comfortable. "I met Regan here the other day. I hope you don't mind my trespassing."

"And if I do mind?"

"I'll remember that. The next time I walk over here."

"I could call the sheriff," he said.

"Yes, you could. He warned me himself, as a matter of fact, that trespassing was discouraged."

"Well," Scott said, "just as long as you know that."

"I do. I don't care, mind you, but I know."

As with Regan, his smile was unexpected. "You don't like me very much, do you, Joanna? I wonder why—since you've known me a grand total of about four minutes."

"I have such a character flaw, I'm afraid. I make snap judgments."

"And I've been found wanting?" Still smiling very slightly, he said, "Things always appear distorted when outsiders try to look in—especially into a marriage."

Since she had said something very similar to someone recently, Joanna could hardly disagree with that. But she could question. "Is that what I'm looking into?"

"Oh, I think so. You hear from people around here that Caroline was unhappy and I was . . . distant. You see Regan look at me with no feeling. And you assume I'm at fault. That I'm the ogre, the villain of the piece."

"And are you?" she asked.

Scott McKenna's smile deepened for a moment. "Why, yes, Joanna. I am. Just because everybody says I'm a cold bastard doesn't mean it isn't true."

For one of the very few times in her life, Joanna couldn't think of a thing to say.

Scott glanced toward the setting sun, and said, "It'll be dark soon. The cliffs are more than usually dangerous after dark. You'd better go back to The Inn, Joanna. It was a pleasure meeting you." He turned around and walked away.

Joanna stared after him.

❖   ❖   ❖

Sunday was a rainy, intermittently stormy day, which did nothing to allay Joanna's uneasy restlessness. She couldn't go outside for more than ten minutes at a time, and her room had begun to feel very small and unbearably close to her. It was as if the walls were closing in on her, adding their pressure to the tension already stretching her nerves taut. And there was something else.

Tick. Tick. Tick. Just as in the dream, there was a clock ticking in her head now, a constant reminder of time passing. And she had the unnerving idea that it was ticking faster today than it had yesterday and the day before that. Urging her on, compelling her to do . . . *something*.

And not knowing what the something *was* was driving her crazy.

When she did finally escape her room, it was to find a few townspeople along with hotel guests in the game room playing poker, apparently a frequent event. It gave her an opportunity to talk to some new faces, to try to get more information about Caroline; more than anything else, it gave her *something* to do.

Not that she was very successful—at gathering more facts, that is. She won huge imaginary stakes in several games, but the perfectly pleasant people she talked to had nothing to say about Caroline. And they had nothing to say in a rather pointed fashion, deflecting the subject neatly when Joanna managed to raise it. They offered her friendly smiles and guarded eyes and asked if she wanted another card.

Joanna realized she was biting her nails again.

✦   ✦   ✦

Amber had never been so bored in her entire life. There was nothing to do in this godforsaken place, absolutely nothing. She shifted in her chair for the third time and sighed heavily.

Her mother looked up from the book she was reading and, patiently, said, "Honey, why don't you go and find something to do?"

"Like what? Drown? In case you hadn't noticed, only the ducks are happy out there."

"I didn't say go outside, Amber. It's after eight o'clock anyway, too late to go outside. But the game room is still open, and the gym. They're having those card games still. Or you could go swimming. You're always wanting to go swimming at home."

"Because of the lifeguards," her father said without taking his gaze from the television. "None here to watch her model that almost bathing suit of hers."

Amber felt her face flame, hating him because he was right. The indoor pool here had no lifeguard, just a middle-aged security guard keeping an eye on things from behind the glass of his office. It was disgusting. And not at all like home, where the local pool had college boys for lifeguards.

A bit plaintively, her mother said, "Well, then, why not the game room? They have lots of stuff in there, Amber. Jigsaw puzzles. Video games. Table tennis. You could—"

Amber lurched to her feet, the picture of a teenager willing to go anywhere if she could only escape from that pathetic note in her mother's voice. "Oh, all *right*. I'll go."

She thought it was an excellent performance.

"Be back by eleven," her mother reminded her.

Amber left the living room of the two-bedroom suite and went into her room, shutting the connecting door behind her. She picked up her keycard from the dresser and slipped it into her pocket, wondering if either parent would bother to look into her bedroom before they went to bed as usual at eleven.

Yes, of course her mother would.

Amber smiled as she left her bedroom. Okay, then, she'd *be* in her bedroom, as ordered, by eleven. Innocent as the driven snow. She'd be freshly showered and sweetly perfumed, smelling good in all the right places. And when her parents went to bed, she'd put on that lovely dress she'd bought yesterday in town, the filmy one with the short skirt, and then she'd slip out the terrace door, so nobody in this nosy hotel would see her. And she'd leave.

And with any luck at all, she'd never come back. Never.

She went down the carpeted hallway toward the lobby and the game room, feeling so restless and edgy that she didn't know if it was laughter or tears simmering beneath the surface. But definitely excitement. The whole world looked different to her tonight, and she said hello brightly to a few fellow guests as she made her way to the game room, amused when they were surprised by her friendliness.

They don't know. Nobody knows.

How wonderful to have such a delicious secret! She looked with pity and triumph at the ordinary people in the game room, vaguely sorry that they had not—surely had not—felt what she felt now. They couldn't possibly know, couldn't understand.

It was thundering. She loved the sound. But the storm would be over long before midnight, of course. It had to be. This was her night, and her night would be perfect.

Cheerful, she accepted a challenge from a middle-aged woman to play Ping-Pong, and even let the older woman win. Feeling generous, she even played a second game, and lost that one as well. Then she spent a few minutes working on a jigsaw puzzle someone had left uncompleted on the puzzle table. She played a video game for half an hour or so but was unable to sit still for long.

Restless, she wandered around, watching the poker players for a while and going often to the terrace doors to look out at the darkness where the storm wailed and grumbled. She got a Coke for herself and continued to wander around as she sipped it.

It was after ten when she finally headed toward the lobby and the hallway that would take her back to her room. Because her mother would have to find her innocently in her room at eleven, of course.

She giggled to herself, pausing in the lobby to glance back once more at the ordinary people, pathetically content with their ordinary lives. But what she saw was something else. She probably wouldn't have noticed anything odd about it if she hadn't been so edgy and excited, but she was and so she noticed.

"Wonder what he's doing with that," she mused under her breath. Then she shrugged, her interest fleeting, and continued on toward her room. She was already trying to decide which of her three favorite perfumes she should wear tonight.

❖   ❖   ❖

By late that evening, with rain blowing against the windows and thunder rolling almost continuously, and her thumbnail gnawed down to the quick, Joanna was more than ready for bed.

That night, the dream was a bit different. All the symbols were there, looming and contorting like objects in a funhouse mirror. Ocean waves crashed, the big house overlooked the sea, rose petals drifted downward. The colorful painting, now clearly the little-girl-with-flowers done by Cain, sat on its easel. The clock ticked loudly, a child sobbed miserably. The colorful carousel horse bobbed and spun on its striped pole, and a paper airplane soared and swooped as if on manic air currents.

But this time, a gull was screeching loudly, angrily, the sound violent and repeating over and over, like an echo. . . .

Joanna woke with a start to see the gray light of an overcast morning outside her window, and even though it was only a little after seven, she didn't try to go back to sleep. She was wide awake and already so tense that she caught herself chewing on the other thumbnail. Swearing, she threw back the covers and got up. Anything was better than lying in bed feeling overwhelmed.

Even being on her feet feeling overwhelmed.

Deciding to go downstairs for her morning coffee rather than call room service, she took a hot shower that failed to relax her, and dried her hair, leaving it loose this morning mostly because she was too jittery to do anything with it. Once or twice while she was using her loud dryer, she thought she heard that gull screaming again, and it occurred to her that maybe what she was hearing was an emergency siren.

Accustomed to the sounds of sirens in Atlanta, she found the thought of them here oddly disconcerting. Even upsetting. Fire trucks? Ambulance? Griffin's Blazer?

When she came out of the bathroom, she didn't hear anything that sounded even vaguely like a siren, but got dressed quickly nonetheless. She put on jeans and a ribbed turtleneck sweater with a flannel shirt worn open, and laced up her walking shoes because she intended to get out of the hotel even if she had to walk in the rain.

It was only then that she went to her bedroom balcony and opened the doors to look outside.

It wasn't raining, though the sky was gray and a brisk breeze was blowing in off the ocean, laden with moisture and salt. And though the surf pounded out there with its usual fury, it seemed oddly quiet. Joanna couldn't see anyone on the veranda below, but to the north of The Inn, just off hotel grounds, there was quite a crowd.

A rescue vehicle. A fire truck and ambulance. Griffin's Blazer.

She didn't meet anyone at all in the hall or elevator, and the lobby was deserted when she hurried through it toward the veranda. At one side of the veranda, those hotel guests and staff members up early enough to be aware of what was happening were gathered together under the shelter of the roof, drinking coffee.

Joanna saw Holly and her assistant, Dana, standing with the group, both looking very subdued. Everybody looked very subdued. In fact, one woman seemed to be crying. Joanna started to head toward them, but then she caught sight of Griffin out at the edge of the hotel's lawn.

The guests might have been warned to keep back, but Joanna didn't care. She hurried across the veranda, down the steps, and onto the wet grass, her gaze fixed on him. He was wearing a long black rain slicker this morning but was bareheaded, unlike the deputies out near the edge of the cliff who wore broad-brimmed, plastic-covered hats with their slickers. The stiff breeze ruffled his hair, and as she approached him, Joanna thought he looked tired and grim.

"Griffin?"

He half turned quickly, and though his expression didn't change, something seemed to flare in the darkness of his eyes when he saw her. He didn't move to meet her, but when she reached him, he rather surprisingly took one of her hands in his, the grip strong.

"What's happened?" she asked.

"You shouldn't be out here, Joanna," he said quietly. "We've asked everyone to keep back." But he didn't release her hand.

"But what—"

"Griff?" A tall, rather thin man with wet dark hair approached them from the cliffs, his slicker flapping against his legs. Joanna had dimly been aware that he had just been pulled by rope up over the edge of the cliffs by rescue workers, and she thought he had been lowered the same way.

"Let's have it, Doc," Griffin said to him.

The doctor sent Joanna a look of faint surprise out of tired blue eyes, but then shook his head and said, "You saw what I did. What do you need me to tell you?"

"Was there any evidence she'd been drinking?"

She? Joanna began to feel very cold.

"Griff, you know she had been soaked from the surf, so there wouldn't have been a smell if she'd drunk gallons. I can't tell about alcohol or drugs without lab tests."

"How was she killed?"

The doctor glanced again at Joanna, then said flatly, "The fall killed her, unless I find something I'm not expecting in the post. Jesus, Griff, she fell about a hundred and thirty feet."

"Was she pushed?" Griffin's voice was unemotional.

Startled, the doctor said, "I don't know. With all the damage from the fall, it'll be difficult to find any evidence if she was. But I'll look."

"Thanks, Doc."

The tall man lifted a hand in acknowledgment and turned back toward the cliffs, just as the men on the edge there began working the ropes again.

"Griffin? Who is it?" Joanna asked.

"I thought it was you at first," he told her in that same unemotional voice, his grip on her hand tightening a bit. "But it's a girl staying here. Amber Wade."

Joanna turned her shocked gaze back to the cliffs in time to see a rescue basket hauled up over the rocks. The body strapped into it was wrapped completely in a fluorescent orange blanket, but from one end trailed long blond hair.

$\mathscr{S}$EVEN

$\diamond \quad \diamond \quad \diamond$

"$\mathscr{Y}$OU'VE GOT TO BE KIDDING," Cain said.

Griffin sighed. "I'm doing my job, Cain. Answer the question."

Cain glanced at Holly, who was sitting beside him at a table on The Inn's veranda, then looked back at the sheriff, who was sitting across from them. "You're asking me if I pushed that kid over the cliff?"

"I'm asking where you were from about eleven last night until seven this morning," Griffin repeated. "Look, everybody knew she was after you. Her father said she could have slipped out last night after they thought she was asleep. Her room is separate from theirs, it has a private door opening onto the veranda, and she's apparently slipped out before."

"She didn't come to see me," Cain said. "Last night or any other night. For God's sake, Griff, do you honestly believe I encouraged that poor kid? That I asked her to meet me somewhere—while it was raining cats and dogs, let me remind you—and then killed her?"

"Where were you, Cain?"

"I was at home. At the cottage, all night."

"Alone?"

"Yes, alone, damn you."

Holly leaned forward. "Griff, surely it was an accident?"

He looked at her for a moment, then shook his head. "I don't think so. If she had slipped, she would have fallen straight down. We found her so far out that she must have gone over with some force."

"Then maybe she jumped."

"It's a possibility. Teenagers commit suicide every day, unfortunately." He returned his steady gaze to Cain. "But I have to cover all the possibilities. Consider all the imaginable equations. And one of those is that somebody pushed her."

Spacing every word for emphasis, Cain said, "It was not me."

Holly was shaking her head. "You can't think Cain would have hurt Amber. She had a crush, that's all. A teenage crush, the kind we all had growing up. Even if anyone had considered that a problem—and no one *did*—she was leaving here with her parents in another week."

"I'm not saying someone planned to kill her, Holly," Griffin said. "It could have happened in a moment of rage."

Cain stiffened, his vivid eyes fixed on the sheriff, and his voice was very quiet when he said, "Oh, now I get it. I lost my temper—once—and decked some guy acting like an asshole at one of my showings, and now I'm labeled as somebody who can't control his rage."

"You put him in the hospital, Cain," Griffin observed just as quietly.

"He hit his head on the corner of a table when he fell."

Griffin nodded. "I know that. And I doubt you're any more likely to act out of rage than I am myself. But look at this from my perspective. Everyone in this hotel—and half the people in Cliffside—knew how Amber felt about you, because she made it obvious. She did everything but hang around your neck whenever she was near you, and if you were here, she was somewhere nearby. Whether or not you encouraged her, she *could* have become a problem. I have to take that into account."

"Fine," Cain said. "But take this into account as well. I didn't consider Amber a problem. She was a kid with a crush—period. It was easy enough for me to avoid any difficulty by not being alone with her, and that wasn't hard at all. Ask Joanna, if you don't believe me; she helped me out—it must have been Friday—when Amber paid me a visit at the cottage."

"What was Joanna doing at the cottage?" Griffin asked before he could stop himself.

There was a sudden glint of amusement in Cain's green eyes. "Want me to paint the heart on your sleeve so everybody can see it?"

"Answer the question, Cain."

"She was just walking along the cliffs and stopped when she saw me working outside," Cain told the sheriff dryly. "And she was nice enough to walk back here with us when Amber made an appearance."

"I thought you said Amber didn't slip out to meet you," Griffin said.

Still a little amused, Cain wasn't disturbed by that accusing statement. "That's what I said, and what I meant. I never arranged to meet Amber anywhere at all, far less at the cottage. Friday was the second time she showed up there unannounced; the first time, I didn't answer when she knocked on the door."

Griffin nodded and got to his feet. He realized with annoyance that he was ending the interview not because he had no more questions and was satisfied with Cain's answers, but because he was uncomfortable beneath the other man's perceptive scrutiny. *Heart on my sleeve. The son of a bitch.*

"Griff?" Holly hesitated, then went on carefully. "I came up behind Joanna the other day, and until she turned around, I thought she was Amber."

It didn't surprise Griffin. When he had first glimpsed that broken body on the jagged rocks, blond hair streaming out . . .

"Something else to add to your equation?" Cain mused soberly.

"Yeah," Griffin said. "Something else." *And it's not adding up, Goddammit, it's just not adding up.* "If either of you remembers anything that might be important, let me know."

"We will," Holly said. She watched him turn away and walk out toward the end of the veranda, obviously heading toward the cliffs directly behind The Inn, where Joanna stood alone at the railing and looked out to sea.

"Do you really think somebody might have thought they were pushing Joanna to her death?" Cain asked her.

She looked at him and sighed. "It hardly makes sense either way, does it? I can't imagine why anyone would have wanted to murder Amber—or Joanna."

"But you think Joanna would be more likely?"

"I don't know." Holly frowned. "Maybe. It's just . . . well, Amber was only a tourist, a kid who hadn't really lived long enough to make enemies, if you know what I mean. She might have jumped, but who would have pushed her? Joanna, on the other hand . . ."

When her voice trailed off, Cain continued in a reflective tone. "Joanna turns up here, apparently just another tourist. But she looks eerily like a woman who was killed here a few months ago. And she's been asking a lot of questions about that woman. And maybe . . . somebody didn't like her questions?"

Holly felt a little chill at hearing her own reluctant thoughts voiced aloud. "Which would indicate—what? That Caroline's death wasn't an accident?"

Cain was frowning now, his gaze turned inward in a way Holly recognized; he always wore that look, she had learned, when he was listening to whatever inner voice drove him to paint.

"Maybe so," he said at last, slowly. "If Joanna was the intended victim rather than Amber, then it almost has to be connected to Caroline in some way. Because Joanna hasn't been making enemies around here, not that I know of. Certainly nobody's expressed the desire to get rid of her. So . . . what's wrong with this picture?" He brooded a moment. "What stands out in all this, what can't really be explained away, is Joanna's resemblance to Caroline, and the way she's been asking questions about her. As if she came here specifically to find out about Caroline."

"Did you hear about Dylan and Lyssa?" Holly asked him.

Cain nodded. "About them seeing Joanna in Atlanta, yeah. Very odd that she turned up here not long after that. Difficult to explain away as coincidence."

"How could it be anything else? Dylan said she couldn't have found out where he and Lyssa were from."

"Sure she could have," Cain objected. "If she was curious enough, she probably could have followed one or the other of them back to their hotel without being seen. And desk clerks have been known to provide information for enough bucks."

"I never thought of that, but you're right, of course. Do you think Griffin's thought of it?"

"Of course he has. Our small-town sheriff is nobody's fool—and he's a born cop, even setting aside his well-known trait of hating unanswered questions. I don't know what Joanna's told him, but you can bet he doesn't believe in the seeming coincidence of her showing up here when she looks so much like Caroline. And I can't say I'd blame him for wondering. It's beginning to bother me a lot."

Holly considered the question for a moment. "Why *would* she have come all this way if it was deliberate? Just out of curiosity? Because two strangers called her by another woman's name?"

"No, there has to be more to it." Cain frowned.

"Maybe I should ask her to pose for me. People talk about the damnedest things while they're being painted."

What did Caroline talk about? Holly wanted to ask the question, but didn't. Instead, she said, "Griff won't be happy with either one of us if we stick our noses into his investigation."

"No doubt about that," Cain agreed. "And especially if we focus our attention on Joanna. He's a bit touchy about her."

Holly smiled. "I thought he was going to hit you when you made that crack about the heart on his sleeve."

"I thought he was going to hit me too." Cain chuckled briefly, but added, "I shouldn't be amused. Men like Griff, when they fall, fall hard. It's probably driving him nuts if he believes she hasn't told him the truth. And even without those questions, it can't be easy for him, with Joanna looking so much like Caroline."

"What do you mean?"

Obviously surprised, Cain said, "I would have thought you knew, living here year-round. I mean, I knew years ago, even though I only spent summers here."

"Knew what?"

"That Caroline was in love with Griff at one time. She even considered leaving Scott."

Holly stared at him. Could she have been so wrapped up in her work that she'd been blind to what was happening all around her? Surely not. Even if she hadn't been close to Caroline, surely she would have noticed *something* if her employer's marriage had been on the verge of ending. Wouldn't she? "I never saw a sign of anything like that," she objected. "It must have been just gossip, Cain."

"No."

"How can you be so sure? I mean—"

"Holly, I know it was the truth because Caroline told me herself. Said she felt things for Griff she'd never felt for Scott." He shook his head. "Don't know why she confided in me, except that people tend to. They see me out painting somewhere and stop by to watch—which doesn't bother me, you know that—and they talk. You'd probably be surprised at some of the things I know about this town."

"It would seem so," Holly said.

Cain smiled at her. "Look, I wouldn't tell anyone but you what Caroline confided, especially since I don't think it was ever common knowledge. Caroline wasn't one to show her feelings in public, and she was too conscious of her good name to do anything to risk her reputation. Besides, they didn't end up together, so it was nobody's business but theirs."

"Did Scott know?" Holly asked.

"Caroline never told him, she said, and she believed he never guessed, that's all I know. It happened years ago, before Regan was born."

"I wonder what else I don't know about this place," Holly murmured, more than a little shaken.

"You've been busy," Cain said.

She looked at him, getting the point even though his voice had been offhand. "I guess I have. But I have been trying, you know. Since we made our little deal."

"I know you have." He smiled at her. "And it's much appreciated, believe me. But, Holly, the next time I ask you to spend the night at the cottage, do us both a favor and say yes even if you *do* have an important meeting the next day. Cops may well distrust an alibi provided by a lover, but it's better than no alibi at all."

"I could have lied to Griff and said I was with you," she observed.

"You could have. And that would have told me that you thought I could have had something to do with Amber's death."

Holly was surprised, but only for a moment. He was right. If she'd been worried about his whereabouts last night, she might well have leaped to his defense and claimed to have been with him. But since she knew he could never have harmed that poor girl, it had never entered her head that he might need help in proving his innocence.

"It's the nicest thing you've never said to me," Cain said, smiling.

Holly couldn't help but smile in return, and when he reached out to take her hand, she allowed her fingers to twine with his even though she knew they were being watched by several guests and staff members.

It was the first time she hadn't felt self-conscious touching him in public; progress of a sort, she supposed. Or maybe not. Because she wasn't really thinking about watching eyes. She wasn't even thinking about poor Amber's death and what it might mean.

Holly was thinking about Caroline. She was wondering if Caroline had gotten over her feelings for Griff in the years since their affair, or if she had merely transferred those feelings to someone else. Someone other than her remote husband. Someone who, perhaps, had listened sympathetically, who had offered a shoulder now and then. Someone who had admired Caroline's seemingly fragile femininity and had certainly appreciated her beauty and elegance.

Maybe someone like Cain.

Holly wasn't quite ready to ask that question, and she wasn't entirely sure why. Because it would be difficult to fight a dead rival, perhaps, or maybe just because she didn't want to hear that Cain had loved Caroline. All she knew for sure was what she *hadn't* known. She hadn't known Caroline nearly as well as she had believed.

She couldn't help wondering if any of them had ever really known Caroline McKenna.

✧   ✧   ✧

When Griffin reached Joanna, she was standing with both hands gripping the rail in front of her, her unfocused gaze directed somewhere toward the horizon. The strong, chill breeze whipped her long pale hair out behind her and drove color into her cheeks. When she spoke, her voice was a bit distant.

"You don't really think Cain killed that girl?"

"I'd be very surprised if he did," Griffin admitted. "But

I've been surprised before. I can't take anything for granted, Joanna. He said you were with him when Amber showed up—unexpectedly—at the cottage on Friday."

Joanna nodded. "He didn't encourage her, if that's what you want to know. He was careful not to hurt her feelings, but he did what he could to show her she was way too young for him."

"What did he do?" Griffin asked.

Joanna turned her head and looked at him, smiling faintly. "He got into a political discussion with me, for one thing. The poor kid was leagues out of her depth and knew it."

"And you're sure that's what he was trying to do—show Amber she was too young for him?"

"Of course. What else?"

Griffin decided not to give himself away twice in one day. Especially when he wasn't certain what it was he was feeling about this woman. All he was certain of was that she hadn't told him the whole story, and those unanswered questions nagged at him. How could he think about anything else where she was concerned?

Dragging his attention back to the matter at hand, he said, "Cain doesn't have an alibi for last night."

"Neither do I," Joanna pointed out. "And I'll bet the same could be said of most of the people in this town. You said between eleven last night and seven this morning, right? It was a stormy night and most everyone was probably in bed or curled up with a good book. Without an alibi."

"I know, I know." Griffin leaned a hip against the railing and looked at her. The scenery of Cliffside, breathtaking though it was, was familiar to him, but she was still unfamiliar—and fascinating. And she had an unnerving habit of stealing his breath more suddenly and completely than even the most splendid scenery could ever do, as well as drawing his attention away from the things he was supposed to be concentrating on.

Don't think about her. Don't. Not now. Not yet.

"Maybe nobody pushed her," Joanna said. "Maybe she jumped."

"It's possible." He forced himself to concentrate. "But . . . a girl like her, dramatic and self-important, isn't really the type. I could see her doing something destructive to Holly out of jealousy, or even striking out at Cain if he rejected her, but—"

"I don't think he did reject her," Joanna interrupted. "In fact, he went out of his way not to. He was more subtle than that, Griffin. He was sort of . . . indifferently friendly. He behaved as if he simply didn't notice she had a crush on him."

"She might have interpreted that as a rejection," Griffin said.

"The last time I saw her," Joanna said, "she was frustrated and feeling out of her depth, but she didn't seem angry or jealous—*or* despondent."

"Friday was the last time you saw her?"

Joanna nodded.

"Something might have changed over the weekend," Griffin mused. "Must have, in fact. I don't think she fell, so either she jumped or she was pushed. Suicide is probably more likely."

"But you don't believe that. Only because of the kind of girl she was?"

He hesitated, then sighed. "It's difficult to be sure because of all the rain we've had, and I could never prove it in court, but I found several faint marks at the edge of the cliff where she went over."

"What kind of marks?"

"Flattened grass, churned up bits of grass and mud. The kind of marks that might be made by two people, one of them much heavier than the other—and the lighter one struggling."

Joanna got a vivid mental image of two figures grappling with each other at the edge of the cliff, the wind and rain lashing them, lightning flashing, and she shivered. "It doesn't make sense. She was just a kid, a *baby*. Who could have wanted to kill Amber?"

"I don't know."

"No one saw *anything*?"

"So far, no one's admitted seeing anything. A couple of my deputies are going door-to-door questioning hotel guests, but I doubt anything will come of that. Like you said, it was a stormy night."

"Who found her?" Joanna asked.

"One of the hotel groundskeepers. He was about to go down and check the beach for storm damage, something he always does after a storm."

"So no help there."

Griffin shook his head.

Joanna looked at him, debating silently for a moment, then sighed. "I don't imagine this will help either, but . . . do you remember when I asked about the person who'd been killed here earlier this year? I thought it had been a woman, and you told me it was a man?"

"I remember. So?"

"So, the reason I thought it was a woman was because of another dream I'd had." She described the dream briefly, unable to tell from his expressionless face whether or not he believed her, but reasonably sure he'd put no more faith in dreams now than he had before. "I connected the dream with the other one I'd been having about this place and just assumed it had something to do with Caroline. That maybe she had seen a woman pushed off the cliffs; I even wondered if the dark man had wanted her dead because of what she'd seen. Then you told me a man had been killed instead of a woman, and I didn't know what to think. But when they brought up Amber's body and I saw her hair hanging out of the stretcher, I wondered if maybe it was her death I'd seen. Before it happened."

"A prophetic dream?" His voice was detached.

"I know, I know—you don't believe in them. But it *is* well-documented that people who survive serious trauma, especially something like a head injury, sometimes find themselves coping with extrasensory perception in one form or another when they recover. Maybe that's what happened to me. Maybe all that electricity blasted open a door to a room I never knew I had inside me."

He might easily have pointed out that what the electricity might actually have done was scramble or short-circuit the normal function of her brain, leaving her with weird dreams and illogical impulses. But Griffin didn't say that. He merely said, "I've seen too many strange things in my life to say it isn't possible, but it doesn't seem to help us any. You say you didn't see the man's face in your dream."

Joanna knew he didn't believe her, but at least he wasn't openly scoffing. "No, I didn't. I woke up just as he began to turn toward me."

"You noticed nothing special about him?"

She conjured a smile. "He didn't have red hair. That seems to let Cain out."

"If it was raining," Griffin said, "and you weren't close, how could you tell what color his hair was?"

Joanna's smile faded and she shook her head. "It . . . wasn't raining. I mean, the sky seemed overcast and everything was sort of gray and dreary, but there was no rain falling and definitely no storm."

Griffin frowned. "Amber was probably dead at least a few hours when we found her; that means she was killed before dawn. It was black as pitch outside last night, Joanna."

She drew a breath, conscious of another chill. "Well. I guess I didn't see Amber killed after all. You don't suppose . . ."

"What?"

Joanna made her voice light. "You don't suppose I saw myself take a flying leap off the cliffs, do you?"

Griffin reached out to grasp her shoulders. "No. Even if what you dreamed meant anything at all, Joanna, according to everything I've read and heard, dreams are almost always symbolic. Whatever you saw, it wasn't your own death."

"You sound so sure. How could you be so sure when you don't even believe the dream means anything?" She knew that she sounded shaken.

He shook his head slightly. "I didn't say I didn't believe it's possible that your dreams mean something. Maybe they do—how can I know? I have my doubts, natural doubts. But whatever I think about dreams, I'm absolutely certain that none of us can see our own death."

She wondered why he was so sure of that, but didn't feel much like having a philosophical discussion at the moment. It was easier and more comforting to just accept his certainty. "Okay. Then what could that dream symbolize?"

"Did you actually see the man push her?" Griffin asked.

"No. In fact, when I first turned in the dream, I didn't even see him. Just her, soaring off the cliff as if she were trying to fly. But then I saw him standing where she must have been, and when he began to turn toward me, I felt . . . absolutely terrified."

"And you thought—in the dream—that he had pushed her?"

Joanna nodded. "I was certain he had." Then she smiled wryly. "But then, I also felt that I had seen through Caroline's eyes. I mean, I felt sure I'd seen something that had already happened, something she had seen."

Griffin's hands tightened briefly on her shoulders, and then he released her. "I don't know which I'd rather try to believe—that you saw some past scene through Caroline's eyes or that you somehow witnessed Amber's death before it happened."

Try to believe. Not that Joanna could blame him, really. She had some pretty uneasy doubts herself. But she couldn't help feeling that the distance between them was more than just a couple of feet. "Probably," she said, "the best explanation for the dream is that I felt sure there was something wrong about Caroline's death, something inherently deadly about the cliffs, and all my worries kept my mind active all night. The blonde probably *was* me—just like the watcher was me. And the dark man on the cliff was probably the . . . the subconscious manifestation of my uneasiness. That's probably what I'd learn in Psychology 101."

He looked at her steadily. "Trying to convince me—or yourself?"

"Both, maybe?" She shrugged, but still felt compelled to try once more to make him believe her. "All I know is what I told you before. There's something wrong here in this town, something bad, and it has something to do with Caroline and her death. I know that. I *feel* it. Griffin, even you have to admit that three people going over the cliffs in only a few months—"

"Three people with no apparent connection to each other," he interrupted. "And there's absolutely no evidence that the first two deaths were anything but accidents."

Joanna frowned at him, tense with frustration. "No *apparent* connection. But what if there's one we just haven't found yet?"

"*We?* Joanna—"

Without giving him a chance to continue, she quickly laid out some of the thoughts she'd gone over and over in her head. "What could those three people have in common? Other than being here in Cliffside, I mean. We have a male tourist in his thirties, a female citizen of the town, twenty-nine, and an eighteen-year-old female tourist. Two of the three were staying here at The Inn, which is owned by the second's husband—but it's the only hotel in the town, so we probably can't call that significant. The first was killed early in June, the second on July first, and the third in early October. The first and third went over the cliffs within a couple hundred yards of each other, but the second was killed miles away."

Griffin didn't continue his objection. Instead, methodically, he said, "Two were on foot when they were killed, and one was in a car. One died about half past noon, one in the late afternoon, and one during the night." He paused. "So far, I don't see a connection."

"Well, if it was obvious, you would have seen it before now."

"Thanks a lot."

"You know what I mean."

He sighed. "Yeah. Look, I've gone all through the file on the first death—which, I gather, you've researched."

It wasn't quite a question, but Joanna nodded.

"Right. I didn't find anything odd."

"Neither did I," Joanna admitted. "But all I had to go on was newspaper reports. Were his belongings here inventoried?"

"As a matter of fact, they were, generally speaking. It wasn't a suspicious death, but his room here had to be cleared out. Why?"

"Was there any evidence he was here for the usual tourist activities? Did he have any fishing gear?"

"No. But before you call that suspicious, remember that some people actually want to rest on their vacation—and I recall his sister saying he'd been involved in an exhausting business deal just before he came up here."

Joanna sighed, feeling frustrated. "So his death was a simple accident. Caroline was driving too fast on a slippery road. And Amber . . . what about Amber? You don't think she fell or jumped, so—"

"So maybe—*maybe*—somebody pushed her. Maybe Doctor Becket will find some evidence of murder in the postmortem. Maybe we'll eventually find a witness. Or maybe not."

He sounded as frustrated as she felt, so Joanna didn't criticize his attitude; he was a hardheaded realist, after all, and with no witnesses and no real evidence pointing to anything but an accident, there wasn't a great deal he could do.

Griffin rubbed the back of his neck in a brief, weary gesture. "I could use a cup of coffee. How about you?"

"Definitely." She turned away from the railing and walked with him back up the lawn toward the hotel's veranda. They were both silent for some minutes, until they had their coffee and were seated at a small table under the shelter of the roof. It was still a chilly day, but away from the cliffs and the steady breeze out there it was much more comfortable.

"So what's next?" Joanna asked, sipping hot coffee gratefully.

Griffin took a swallow of his own before replying. "More of the same. Asking more questions, studying the medical evidence—trying to figure out what the hell happened to that girl."

Joanna didn't have to ask to know that he would concentrate his investigation on the victim. In the mind of most cops—and in reality—most deaths, even murders, were simple ones. Few were planned, with the vast majority occurring in the heat of emotion, on impulse. Somebody got mad, and somebody else got dead. Griffin had to assume that Amber had made somebody mad, and that's what he'd be looking for. He wouldn't look for a connection to Caroline, or to the man who had died here weeks before she had, because he didn't consider the deaths related.

It hadn't come together in her mind before now, but Joanna had a feeling—a strong but unaccountable and perhaps unreasonable feeling—that the deaths *were* connected. She didn't know why or how, but she was certain Amber had died because Caroline had died, and Caroline had died because a man named Robert Butler had died. Somehow, in some way she didn't yet understand, there was a pattern here, a series of connections tying the whole thing together.

Finding out why any one of them had died, she was sure, would provide the key to understanding why all of them had died.

She also had a feeling it would be better to keep her feelings to herself, for the time being at least. Griffin hadn't openly scoffed this time, but he didn't believe her, and he'd never be convinced by dreams and feelings, not when it came to murder. To satisfy him, she would need something more tangible. Something he could hold in his hand and say, "Yeah, this is real."

"Joanna?"

She blinked at him. "Hmm?"

"Where were you?"

"Oh, just thinking." She couldn't help but recall Amber's habit of saying "oh," and it made her suddenly self-conscious. She caught herself looking at Griffin's mouth and hastily lowered her gaze to her coffee cup. What was wrong with her, anyway? Even if she were in the market for a lover—which she wasn't—the last man in the world she had any business getting involved with was this one. Aside from his distrust, she had a job and a life three thousand miles away, and she'd return there in a week or two. Alone.

And then there was Caroline. The ghost of Caroline. She had known this man for years, and on the last day of her life she had arranged to meet him. Why? Had she trusted him enough to tell him what was wrong? Or had she wanted to meet him for more personal—and intimate— reasons?

Joanna felt a little chill as she reminded herself that she had only Griffin's word for most of this. *He* said Caroline had asked to meet him; *he* said he had been tied up and had missed the rendezvous; *he* said they had not been involved with each other; *he* said he had not been in love with another man's wife.

And it was his report that had labeled her death an accident.

Griffin leaned toward her and spoke just then, his deep voice holding a cop's hard-edged command. "Listen to me. You are not part of this investigation."

"Did I say—" She looked up at him to find his face as hard as his voice, and felt another touch of coldness that owed nothing to the weather. She didn't want to think this way, she *didn't,* but she couldn't help wondering if Griffin was warning her off because he didn't want her to find out the truth.

"You didn't have to say a word, it was written on your face." His voice remained stony. "Joanna, we have to *assume* Amber was killed—murdered. That means there could be a very dangerous person in this town, and I don't want you looking for him."

Joanna hesitated, but then nodded quickly when his eyes narrowed. "I know." And when he continued to stare at her, she added, "Look, I'm not a fool, and I don't have a death wish. Believe me, I don't want to meet up with a murderer."

Finally satisfied, Griffin relaxed and nodded. "Good."

"But I hope you mean to let me know what's going on while you investigate," she told him casually.

His smile was a bit crooked. "It's a small town, remember? *Everybody* will know what's going on while I investigate."

"They won't know what's going on in your head." She kept her voice mild. "And I have a hunch that's where all the important stuff will be." *Did you meet her that day, Griffin? Was it you she was trying to get away from when her car went over the cliffs?*

He lifted his coffee cup in a slight gesture that was an acknowledgment of her observation, but all he said was, "There won't be any important stuff unless I get cracking." He finished his coffee and pushed back his chair. "I'll see you later, Joanna."

"Sure." She watched him until he disappeared inside the hotel, then turned her blind gaze out to sea. No, she didn't have a death wish; she had already been as close to death as she wanted to get for a while. A long while. And she wasn't a fool. But she also couldn't sit idly by and wait for someone else to solve this puzzle, not when she felt so certain that it was the reason she was here. And not when she had her doubts even about the sheriff of Cliffside.

But she had no intention of angering Griffin by horning in on his investigation of Amber's death. No, she'd stay away from that one, at least for now. And try her best to stay out of Griffin's way. But she wouldn't sit idly by. Instead, she would concentrate her efforts on the two "accidents" Griffin considered closed cases. The death of a tourist named Robert Butler and the death of Caroline McKenna.

Investigating Butler's death would be more difficult, she thought, because he had been a stranger here and that meant almost all relevant information about him—and any connection between him and Scott, for instance—would be found in San Francisco, where he had lived.

Joanna wasn't quite prepared to go to San Francisco at the moment, or even to begin trying to get information by phone.

Which left Caroline.

She couldn't help but wonder about that. No matter what happened here, it always seemed that her focus was returned to Caroline eventually. *Either I've got a one-track mind, or . . .* Or what? Or fate was taking a hand?

Fate . . . or Caroline.

⋄　　　⋄　　　⋄

By the time Joanna finished her breakfast, the weather had improved considerably; the sun was shining, and the temperature climbed slowly toward sixty. She only wished she could say the same about her mood, that it had improved. But it hadn't. Amber's death had added more tension when she already felt as though she would snap at any minute.

Tick. Tick. Tick.

The sound in her head drove her out of the hotel, urging her to hurry. She only just managed to stop herself from running to her rental car, but it required an effort she was all too conscious of. And only the vivid awareness of what could happen to a speeding car on the winding coast road enabled her to drive slowly as she left The Inn.

I have to find out what's going on here. I have to. Before it drives me mad.

She intended to check out a couple of places outside town. The first place was one Griffin had mentioned, the old barn just off the coast road, where Caroline had

wanted to meet him just minutes before her car went over
the cliffs. It was her uneasiness about Griffin and his relationship with Caroline that made Joanna want to see it, as
well as her puzzlement about the place he claimed Caroline
had chosen to meet him. An old barn? It seemed unlike
Caroline to consider a deserted barn on the side of the road
to be useful for anything at all. And to ask a man to meet
her there?

It struck an off-key note, and all Joanna had to go on
was her intuition about things in Caroline's life—especially
those last few weeks—that seemed odd or out of character.

She didn't bother to ask directions of anyone; she just
began driving up the coast road toward Portland and kept
her eyes open. She expected to find it easily and did; no
more than a mile or so from the place where Caroline had
died, and hardly more than a hundred feet off the road,
was a ramshackle and apparently unused barn.

Joanna pulled her car off the road and parked near the
structure. For a few minutes she wandered around outside,
studying the area without looking for anything in particular. The place had a deserted feel to it, and it was very quiet
except for the rumble of the surf. A very unlikely place to
meet someone, she thought at first. But when she walked
around it, it appeared to her that there was an ideal parking place on the far side of the barn where a car—or even
two—wouldn't have been seen from the road, and it
looked as if it might have been used for that purpose. A
favorite parking place for teen lovers, perhaps?

Perhaps. She had known a few every bit as unlikely during her own teen years.

The warped door opened easily, and inside, Joanna
found that the building was being used to store hay. Bales
were stacked high, leaving only a relatively small space
roughly in the center of the building clear. The air was
thick with the slightly musty but sweet-smelling scent of
hay, and the interior was perfectly dry.

She didn't hesitate to explore, recalling from childhood
visits to hay barns how small "rooms" and chambers could

be made by arranging bales of hay. And sure enough, she found one. The entrance wasn't obvious, and it didn't appear to her to be an accidental arrangement of the bales, especially when a short "corridor" led her to one of the back corners of the barn where an eight-by-eight-foot-square room had quite obviously hosted more than one secret—or at least secreted—meeting.

It was a dim, shadowy place with barely enough light to see, the slight illumination provided by what little sunlight could find its way in between the warped boards of one outside wall. The loose hay on the floor was thick enough to provide a fairly comfortable bed, and Joanna found a rather luxurious plaid blanket folded neatly on a high shelf of hay bales. On the same shelf, she also found a shoe box containing an economy-size pack of moist towelettes and a varied selection of condoms.

"All the modern conveniences," she heard herself murmur aloud. Practical if not terribly romantic.

Common sense told her this was indeed a trysting place for teenagers, but the expensive quality of the blanket prompted faint uncertainty. It seemed to her more something an adult would have brought out here. She supposed a boy or girl could have brought it from home, but it didn't seem the sort of thing that wouldn't be missed from an average house, and why take the chance? A cheap blanket or throw bought new would have done just as well.

Possibly, her inner voice mused, *but that's just a guess. There's no evidence at all that sixteen-year-old Suzie didn't filch the thing from her mother's linen closet because all this hay was just too damned scratchy against her tender bottom.*

No evidence.

But somebody like Caroline, a fragile and dignified older woman, would certainly have thought of a blanket if this was her place to meet a lover. And she would have wanted to be prepared, to use protection and to have the means at hand to wipe away the damning evidence left by a lover. So a husband would suspect nothing.

And she might well ask that lover to meet her here on a warm July afternoon. A meeting that somehow went terribly wrong . . .

The possibilities were worse than disturbing; they made something inside Joanna tighten in pain. She couldn't be sure who Caroline might have met out here, but Griffin claimed she asked to meet him the day she died, and it seemed to Joanna that a woman wouldn't invite a man into her secret place unless it was a place he knew. A place he had visited before.

She left the box and blanket where she'd found them, turning away with even more uneasiness clawing at her. She didn't immediately leave the little room. Instead, she stood looking down at the thick hay underfoot for a moment. She couldn't have said what prompted her to begin scuffing her shoe through the stuff, and it was only after several minutes that she realized she was looking intently for . . . something.

No sooner had the awareness of her own actions penetrated than she caught the glint of light on something metallic, and she realized that her foot had uncovered a delicate piece of jewelry. It was a necklace, a fine gold chain with a small heart-shaped pendant.

Joanna knelt there in the hay and held it, squinting a bit in the dimness as she tried to make out the engraving on the front of the heart. Then she turned it slightly, and the words *I love you* seemed to jump out at her. After a moment, she turned the heart completely over, and saw more engraving on the back. This was more difficult to read, but finally she made it out. Two words only, engraved in script.

Love, Regan.

$\mathcal{E}$IGHT

❖ ❖ ❖

"$\mathcal{T}$ALK TO ME, DOC."

Doctor Peter Becket pushed his chair back as far as he was able in the tiny cubicle he used for an office whenever he was forced by circumstance to work in the basement morgue of the clinic. He rubbed his thin face with both hands, the gesture one of sheer weariness, and then peered up at Griffin standing in the doorway.

"We just brought her in a couple of hours ago. I haven't even opened her up yet, Griff."

"I know that. But you've done the preliminary exam, haven't you?"

"Yeah."

Griffin shifted impatiently. "Well?"

"Why're you pushing on this?" Becket asked, his voice mildly curious. "I mean, hell, I know she was just a kid, and I feel as bad about it as anybody else—but why does this matter so much to you?"

"It's my job. On my office door, on a shiny brass sign, it

says Sheriff. Says the same thing on my employment contract. The fine citizens of the town of Cliffside pay me to care when a tourist winds up smashed on the rocks."

Becket waited him out, then repeated, "Why does this matter so much to you, Griff?"

Leaning a shoulder against the doorjamb, Griffin muttered a curse under his breath and then sighed. "It matters because I've got a sick feeling that kid had help going over the cliff. Tell me I'm wrong. Please."

"I thought it was just an automatic question when you asked this morning," Becket said slowly. "What did you see out there that I missed?"

"The ground was a bit churned up, that's all."

"It had to be more than that. You wouldn't assume murder on the strength of something that vague."

Both his job and his nature made Griffin unwilling to lay all his cards on the table, even for a colleague and friend, so he merely shrugged and returned an evasive answer. "I'm not assuming murder now. It could have been an accident, an argument that ended in the girl being pushed over the edge. I just want to know if I should be asking a different set of questions, that's all."

After a moment, Becket let out a little snort. "Yeah, right. Which is why you haven't even given me time to do the post." He gestured slightly, waving away anything Griffin might have said in response. "Never mind. I've got enough worries on my plate without adding yours, thank you. Look, the preliminary exam didn't show anything conclusive. I found bruises on her wrist that *might* indicate somebody handled her roughly just before she died, and a few more on her shoulder I can't really explain. But nothing to say with any certainty that she wasn't alone out there last night. I expect the post to confirm she died from injuries sustained in the fall."

"Can you tell me if she had intercourse before she died?"

"We found her fully clothed," Becket reminded him.

"I know. But can you tell me if she had sex sometime in the hours before she died?"

Becket shrugged. "Possibly. Definitely if she did and her partner didn't wear a condom. You don't suspect rape?"

"Not really, since we found her clothed. But if you find any evidence of rape—"

"You'll be the second one to know."

"Thanks, Doc."

"Just go away for a while, will you? Except for the tox screen, I'll have a complete report for you late this afternoon."

"The tox screen—"

"In a few days, Griff. Go away, huh?"

Griffin went away. He chose not to leave by the rear entrance of the morgue, or "loading dock," where bodies were delivered for autopsies if death had occurred outside the clinic and were taken away to mortuaries afterward; even in a small town, death from accident or disease was a fairly regular occurrence, and there was something inherently depressing about those big, featureless double doors. Instead, he went upstairs and out the front of the clinic, waving to the nurse on duty at the desk but not pausing.

He didn't get into the Blazer immediately, but stood breathing in the crisp morning air and gazing around with the automatic attention of a cop. The small clinic was situated one street back from Main Street, one block over and behind the library, and had the entire block to itself. Beside and slightly behind it was the piece of land Caroline had bequeathed for expansion; Scott hadn't wasted time in carrying out his wife's wishes, having already cleared the land in preparation for the new wing even before her will was probated.

Griffin didn't think much about that. He absently noted that the bulldozers had apparently finished their part of the job, then got into the Blazer and headed back toward his office.

It had been a hellish morning, and the sick feeling in his gut wasn't getting any better. He'd felt as if a fist had punched him there when he had first glimpsed blond hair streaming over the rocks, when in that first terrible instant he had thought the dead girl was Joanna. The relief of discovering it wasn't her had been curiously numbing, and it had taken seeing her, touching her, and talking to her, to convince him she was all right and to make him feel less paralyzed.

But that sick feeling hadn't gone away. From behind, Amber might easily have been mistaken for Joanna, especially on a dark night. She might even have sounded like her if she'd cried out during the final seconds of her life. A scream such as the one she might have screamed would have no drawling accent, no expressive music, no unique personality—it would just have terror.

The only thing worse than being cursed with a vivid imagination, Griffin decided grimly, was to be cursed with an educated and experienced imagination. Amber had died violently; she might well have been mistaken for Joanna; and Griffin could see how it might have happened all too clearly in his mind.

That was one of the drawbacks of being a cop, this inability to sugarcoat anything. He had often wondered what quality of the mind or emotion was required to deliberately choose to be suspicious on a daily basis and to subject oneself to sights most people would have the good fortune never to see. Like torn and battered bodies. What made cops?

He knew the answer for himself, could easily pinpoint the place and time in his life when the urge to become a cop had taken root inside him. A summer he'd never forget as long as he lived had shaped him, he knew that. It had shaped him to hate evil, to mistrust more often than he trusted, to be suspicious of things that didn't add up, and to loathe unanswered questions. That summer had turned him into a cop, even though he had been a kid of fifteen.

He pushed the haunting memories out of his mind and forced himself to concentrate on what he had to do in the here and now. The first step, of course, was to gather information, as much information as he could. Then he would have to weed through everything, examine every minute detail of Amber Wade's life and death.

Asking Becket to check for any sexual activity prior to death was no more than a shot in the dark; Griffin didn't believe Cain had been sexually involved with her, and she'd seemed too fixated on him to have been having sex with another man. Rape seemed very unlikely, not in the least because rapists didn't normally dress their victims afterward. Though it was, of course, possible that she had been attacked, raped, and killed, then dressed and pushed over the cliff in an effort to make her death appear accidental. Still, given the weather last night, that seemed unlikely.

But even if she *had* had sex sometime last night, where would the information get him? Her partner *might* have been a secretor, which would give them a blood type from semen left in the body—but so what? Without an admitted or suspected lover in custody, what good would that knowledge be?

Brooding, Griffin parked the Blazer in its accustomed spot at the Sheriff's Department and went inside. He was met outside his office door by Gwen Taylor, one of his deputies, and she followed him inside with her usual doleful expression.

"I've got most of the statements here if you want to go through them, boss."

"Any surprises?" he asked, hanging up his jacket.

She smiled. "That'd be too easy, wouldn't it? Mark and Megan are beginning to fan out from The Inn just for the hell of it, knocking on doors and asking if anyone knew the girl, if anyone saw her yesterday or last night, but considering the weather—"

"Yeah, I know." Griffin took the statements from her and sat down behind his desk. "Did Neal find anything down on the beach?"

Gwen shook her head. "Nada. If there was anything to find, high tide washed it away."

"Okay. Thanks, Gwen."

She went as far as the door, then paused and looked back at him. "Um, boss? Shelley's still there at the hotel, and she says Mr. Wade has started asking when they can take their daughter's body home."

Something inside Griffin's chest tightened, and for a moment he couldn't answer. A natural reaction of relatives, and one he'd seen before too many times. The urge to escape the scene of death and horror, to go home and, please God, find it had all been just a terrible nightmare. Griffin tried to imagine what it must be like for a parent to have a child die by violence, then shied away from the attempt so violently that it was almost a physical movement. Not something anyone could imagine—or want to feel, he thought grimly. And then to know her body would be further violated by an autopsy . . .

"Tell Shelley to be as vague as possible; there's no need to say we're waiting for the results of the postmortem. She can tell them we're investigating the circumstances of their daughter's death, that we'll be as quick and thorough as we possibly can."

"What if they aren't satisfied with that?"

"Then I'll talk to them." He didn't want to. God, he didn't want to. Because there was nothing he could say to them that would help ease their pain. Absolutely nothing.

Gwen nodded and left without saying anything else.

Griffin looked after her for a moment, reluctant to begin reading statements he already knew would prove less than useless; he had good, well-trained deputies, and if they hadn't noted anything of importance, he wasn't likely to disagree with their assessment. He had to go over everything, of course, even if it was a waste of time.

But he couldn't help wondering if he was making a mistake in investigating Amber's death as he would any other. Was Joanna right? Was the death of this teenage tourist connected in some way to the death of another tourist months ago—and to Caroline's death?

All his training and instincts said no. And so far, the evidence confirmed that. They'd only begun getting some information from San Francisco, both about Robert Butler and about Scott McKenna's business dealings there, but so far there was no connection. And how Amber could be even remotely connected to either man was something Griffin couldn't imagine.

Other than the fact that all had died going over the cliffs, there was absolutely nothing to link those three people, or their deaths. But Joanna's certainty, even based as it was on the intangible stuff of dreams, nagged at him.

The simplest answer was usually the right one. But what if, this time, the answer was complex and obscure? What if there *were* connections between the three deaths, the three people, and those connections were so enigmatic or well concealed they could be glimpsed only in the soaring imagination of a dream?

What if Joanna held the key to three deaths?

And what if the wrong person knew that?

❖   ❖   ❖

It was midafternoon when Joanna came out of Landers' Jewelry Store downtown. She was about to walk toward the library, where she had left her car, when she looked across the street and saw Griffin and Scott McKenna. Instinctively, without a thought as to why she was doing it, Joanna glanced both ways quickly and then crossed the street toward the two men.

Although roughly the same height and build, they made an interesting contrast, she thought as she neared them. Scott was almost feline in his elegant, rather cold good looks, aloof and detached in the way cats often were. He was dressed in a dark suit unrelieved by any hint of color, and his face was expressionless.

Griffin, casual as always in dark slacks and a light-colored shirt beneath his customary windbreaker, looked rugged, more powerful physically and, despite his own closed expression, curiously more animated than Scott, as if his life force couldn't be contained or controlled as the other man's seemed to be.

They didn't like each other. *No, it's more than that.*

Scott hates Griffin. Joanna felt it as she stepped up onto the sidewalk through a break in the railing near them, the iciness coming off Scott like wind off a glacier. But his voice was perfectly calm, even pleasant, when he spoke, obviously answering a question asked of him.

"You'll have to forgive me if I can't recall a day more than four months ago, Sheriff. The interim has been . . . difficult."

"Butler died a few days after I saw you speak to him here in town," Griffin said, ignoring the reference to Caroline's death. But his voice held a note of tension. "I would have thought that would fix him in your mind."

"Afraid not. Sorry." Scott smiled thinly. "I assume one of us must have asked the time."

Griffin looked rather pointedly at Scott's left wrist. "You wear a Rolex, don't you?"

"Yes."

It was Griffin's turn to smile thinly. "Butler wore one too. It was on his wrist when he died, and judging by the pale skin underneath the watch, he wore it all the time."

Joanna was standing less than three feet away from the little confrontation, watching and listening intently without making any attempt to hide her interest. She thought both men were aware of her, but their attention remained fixed on each other.

Scott shrugged, just a bare lift and fall of his shoulders. "Maybe his kept time badly. Or maybe he asked me where he could get a decent cup of coffee. There were so many tourists around town then, I really don't remember what one may or may not have said to me. But I do wonder why you're asking about it now. I was under the impression that that investigation was closed."

"Maybe I closed it too soon," Griffin said.

Again, Scott shrugged. "That is, of course, your call to make. Reopen your investigation if you still have questions. But I can't answer them for you. I never met the man."

After a moment, Griffin nodded. "All right. But we've

had another death now. Another *accident*. Mind telling me where you were last night?"

One of Scott's eyebrows lifted slightly, but he remained otherwise expressionless. "At the house, naturally."

"Alone?"

It seemed at first Scott wouldn't answer. But finally he did, his voice a touch less pleasant than it had been. "Dylan and Lyssa were there until nine or so. After that, there's no one to give me an alibi, if that's what you're asking. The housekeeper had retired for the night."

He didn't mention his daughter, but Joanna assumed Regan had gone to bed by that time and that Scott didn't feel that had to be explained. Then her attention sharpened as Scott went on.

"I heard about the girl, of course. It's a pity—but I didn't know her. To my knowledge, I never even saw her. Satisfied, Sheriff?"

"For now," Griffin said.

"Then I'll be going." Scott walked past Griffin toward Joanna. Those chilly gray eyes touched on her briefly, and he nodded slightly and said, "Joanna," in remote greeting, but didn't pause. He walked to the end of the block and turned the corner, presumably heading for his parked car, and vanished from their sight.

"You've met?" Griffin's voice was a bit harsh, and when she looked at him, it was to see him flexing his shoulders unconsciously, the way a man would who had held himself too stiffly for too long.

Joanna halved the space between them and stood leaning back against the railing as she faced him. "Briefly. The other day, when I was talking to Regan at Caroline's gazebo. It was a considerably less frozen encounter than this little meeting, I think."

He grimaced faintly. "That obvious, huh?"

"Oh, no, not at all. A twenty-foot billboard with We Hate Each Other printed in giant letters would have made the point with more subtlety."

"I hope you're exaggerating."

"Well . . . maybe a bit. But it was painfully obvious. Why do you think I crossed the street so fast? I had the odd feeling you two were about to start swinging. Tell me, who hates the other more, you or him?"

"What kind of question is that?"

"A nosy one. Want me to answer it? I think if Scott McKenna felt like running somebody over, you'd be first on his list. And I think you hate *because* you're hated more than for any other reason."

"It's a little hard to feel positive about somebody who hates your guts," Griffin admitted.

"And he hates your guts because . . . ?"

"I don't know why."

"No?"

"No," Griffin said with just enough firmness to make her disbelieve him. "But, to be honest, even if he wanted to be pals, I wouldn't be interested."

"Why not?"

Griffin looked as if he wished he hadn't made that last comment. And sounded like it as well. "Never mind. Just a clash of personalities, I expect. As I assume you heard, Scott claims no connection with or knowledge of Butler, and claims to have been home all night alone. Something I doubt I could disprove even were I inclined to."

"Which you're not?"

Griffin shook his head. "Aside from the fact that I just can't see Scott out behind The Inn in the middle of a stormy October night for any reason—and far less to push an eighteen-year-old girl to her death—there isn't so much as a whisper of a connection between him and Amber."

Joanna wasn't really surprised. If a connection existed, she had a hunch it was indirect and not easily visible. "You're probably right," she told the sheriff. Then, thoughtfully, she added, "You seem to be a lot more certain than you were this morning that Amber's death wasn't accidental. Are you?"

"No. The postmortem found injuries consistent with death as the result of a fall. We'll get a lab report in a few days that'll tell us if she had any drugs in her system, but the doc tells me not to hold my breath."

Joanna frowned. "So there's no evidence to indicate it wasn't either accident or suicide. Then why did you question Scott McKenna so specifically about last night?"

"All part of a standard investigation."

She looked at him a moment. "Oh? Do you normally ask someone completely unconnected to the victim if they have an alibi?"

"When there's even a remote possibility that this victim or her death might be tied in some way to an earlier victim to whom he *did* have a connection—yes."

"A remote possibility. I guess dreams and hunches fall under that heading."

Griffin was reluctant to admit that he was, in fact, searching for factual evidence to connect Butler to someone in Cliffside—in particular Scott McKenna. Unless he found that evidence, of course. So he merely said, "Well, they are outside the range of normal police work, you know."

"Yeah." Joanna brooded for a moment, not quite sure she wanted to bring up the next subject but having already talked herself into it.

"What's on your mind, Joanna?"

She looked around them at the nice, peaceful little town of Cliffside, at the few people moving about on this cool October afternoon, and sighed. Just how much *did* go on under the surface here, undetected by the sharp-eyed gossips of Cliffside? With every day that passed, she was more and more certain the answer was a lot. This place had secrets. Secrets people were no doubt anxious to preserve. And what would happen if any of those well-protected secrets was exposed?

Especially to the wrong person.

You're the logical person to ask questions of, Griffin. But what if some of this town's secrets are yours? What if I can't trust you?

What choice did she have, really?

Joanna fished in the pocket of the flannel shirt she was

wearing in lieu of a jacket and held up the necklace she'd found in the old barn. "Recognize this?"

He looked at the heart charm for a moment, then took the necklace from Joanna's fingers and examined it more closely, checking the inscription before he answered. "Caroline's. She wore it a lot." His tone was impersonal.

Joanna struggled to match his tone and kept her gaze fixed on his expressionless face. "Uh-huh. According to Mr. Landers in the jewelry store, Caroline had one inscribed from her for Regan's birthday a couple of years ago. Then, for Caroline's next birthday, Regan marched into the jewelry store, dropped a handful of quarters on the counter, and asked that an identical heart be inscribed from her. Mr. Landers complied, accepted about three bucks' worth of quarters with a grave face—and held the bill for the difference, knowing that either Scott or Caroline would come in later and pay him. Caroline did."

"Yeah, that story made the rounds. So?"

Joanna took the necklace back from him and absently wound the chain around her fingers. "So when was the last time you remember Caroline wearing this?"

"How would I remember—"

"Come on, you're a cop. You notice details. When was the last time you saw Caroline wearing this?"

"Why does it matter?"

"Just answer the question—please, Griffin."

He shoved his hands into the pockets of his jacket and frowned at her with the inward-turned gaze of someone concentrating. "It was . . . okay. Okay, I've got it. This past Easter Sunday. I saw her here in town, with Regan, both of them dressed for church—and they were both wearing the heart necklaces."

"You don't remember seeing Caroline wearing the necklace after that?"

"No. Why, Joanna? And where did you get it?"

"I found it." She stared at the little heart charm. *Easter Sunday*. So, Caroline had had the necklace in early April and could have lost it anytime between then and her death on July 1. Sometime during those three months she must have been in that little room in the old barn where lovers met.

"Found it where?"

Joanna dropped the necklace back into her pocket. "I'll give this to Regan the next time I see her. I think she'd want to have it."

"Joanna, where did you find the necklace?"

She met his frowning gaze and wished she could believe that he had not been Caroline's lover. It would, she thought, help make all this so much easier if she could believe that. If she could trust him. But the doubts wouldn't leave her alone. Caroline had, after all, asked him to meet her at the barn the day she was killed, at least according to him.

Steadily, trying her best to read his reaction, Joanna said, "I found it in the old barn. There's a little room in one of the back corners, a room formed and hidden by bales of hay. Did you know?"

"I haven't been near the place since some kids cornered a loose horse in there summer before last," he said, with nothing in his face to suggest a lie. "A room?"

Even assuming he was being truthful, Joanna wondered why he hadn't checked the barn out just as a matter of course when Caroline was killed. The only answer she could come up with—and it assumed his innocence in Caroline's death—was the guilt he seemed to feel about what had happened. Maybe, she thought, his guilty conscience had made him consider the barn as only a place where he *should* have been, not where Caroline had been minutes before her death.

If he had nothing to do with that death, of course.

"A room," she confirmed. "A room where at least one pair of lovers has been meeting."

"How do you know that?"

"Evidence, Sheriff." Joanna managed a wry smile. "A nice thick blanket—and a box of condoms."

He let out a short laugh. "Well, at least they're being careful."

As far as Joanna could tell, his amusement was genuine and completely unself-conscious, but it didn't do much to ease her tension. She kept her attention fixed on his face when she said mildly, "Considering that I found the necklace in the hay back in that little room, does it occur to you that Caroline might have been one of those lovers?"

He looked surprised, but not shocked or disbelieving, and even his surprise was brief. "I suppose she could have been," he said slowly. "Most of the people in this town would probably tell you she wasn't happy in her marriage."

"Is that true or just gossip?"

"If you're asking me if Caroline confided in me about her marriage," Griffin said, "she didn't. I know she was unhappy years ago, but after Regan came along, she seemed to . . . I don't know . . . focus all her attention on the kid. She and Scott seemed fairly distant with each other, at least in public, but maybe that was the kind of marriage she wanted."

"Or maybe just the kind of marriage she had." Joanna didn't wait for a response, but added, "So she might have been meeting someone at the old barn?"

Griffin shrugged. "Maybe. It doesn't seem like the sort of place she'd pick, but there aren't many places around here where she would have had a decent chance of keeping the meetings secret. Anyway, if she did have a lover, so what?"

"So maybe that's someone you should have talked to about her death."

"With no evidence it was anything but an accident? And ask what, Joanna?"

"I don't know. If he saw her that day. If she'd seemed upset—*you* said she might have been more nervous than usual in the days before she was killed. So, why? What was on her mind? Don't you think that's important to know, Griffin? And don't you think a lover might have known?"

"I think a lover might have known," he agreed. "*If* something was bothering her. But even supposing I knew who the lover was—and if he exists, he's sure as hell kept the relationship to himself—what justification do I have to ask him anything at all? Even if we assume that Caroline lost control of her car because she was upset, there's absolutely no evidence it was anything but an accident—and the law doesn't prosecute people for saying the wrong thing or not offering a shoulder when one's needed."

"What if her having a lover means something else?" Joanna kept her voice matter-of-fact and speculative. "Maybe just having a lover is what got her killed. What if Scott found out? Where was he when Caroline's car went over the cliffs?"

"He was at the house, as usual on a weekday."

"Was he there alone?"

Griffin nodded. "Pretty much. It was the housekeeper's day off. Regan was home, but she'd had a cold, and she spent the afternoon in her bedroom. Lyssa was here in town at the store, and Dylan was in Portland. There was a gardener working at the house, but he couldn't say if Scott had left anytime that day. I did check all this out, you know. And so what? Like I said, her death was an accident, Joanna. She was driving that car. Nobody tampered with it, and there's no evidence anyone drove her over the cliffs. Which means *no crime was committed*."

Something he'd said sounded a false note in Joanna's mind. "Regan was home sick? And Caroline wasn't there for her?"

Griffin frowned a moment, then shook his head. "The kid wasn't that sick. I mean, Caroline probably wouldn't have hesitated to leave her there in the house with Scott for a few hours. Regan was getting over a cold, that's all."

Maybe that was all, Joanna thought, but it still seemed to her that Caroline wouldn't have left her child without a very good reason, not if she'd been ill. Which was a bit of evidence—in her mind anyway—that Caroline *had* been upset about something that day.

But it was obvious Griffin didn't agree with that. And it was equally obvious to Joanna that he wasn't going to pursue new information about Caroline's life unless and until he could be convinced her death had not been an accident.

He hadn't been Caroline's lover, he said. Maybe that was true. Or maybe it wasn't. He probably hadn't been involved in her death. Probably. Which wasn't to say, of course, that he hadn't covered up one or more facts about that death, for whatever reasons. So Joanna still couldn't trust him. Still couldn't completely believe what he told her.

And yet she wanted *him* to believe *her*. Wanted him to put aside his cop's training and instincts and believe something he couldn't hold in his hand. He didn't have to believe in her dreams, but . . . but he could believe in her. Couldn't he? She wanted him on her side in this, however illogical that was.

"All right," she said with a shrug, deliberately nonchalant. "But I think even the possibility she had a lover should tell us something important."

"Like what?"

"Like there are definitely secrets in Cliffside. If a woman like Caroline could have an affair that nobody caught on to, then we have to assume there's a lot going on beneath the surface of this town."

"Maybe."

Since she didn't want him getting the idea she intended to go on probing into Caroline's life and death, Joanna deliberately directed his attention to the most recent death. "So what does that say about Amber's death? I mean, the reason it happened. Awful as it is, could you have a closet rapist around here?"

"If so," Griffin said unemotionally, "and she was attacked by him, she either managed to fight him off or else she went over the cliffs during the struggle. Amber was a virgin."

Joanna got a sudden, vivid image of Amber saying "oh," in what she probably had imagined to be a sexy manner, her lips pursed and eyes liquid, and felt unexpectedly shaken. All the dumb clichés echoed in her mind, poignant because they were so damned true. *Died before she lived . . . innocence preserved forever . . . more child than woman . . .*

"Joanna?" Griffin reached out to grip her shoulder with one hand. "Are you all right?"

"No, I'm not." She managed a shaky smile. "How long do you have to do this kind of thing before you can look at investigating somebody's death as just an interesting puzzle?"

"I've been in police work more than fifteen years." He paused, then added, "It's not getting any easier."

"Then how do you back away from it? How can you be objective if the—the living presence of the victim won't leave your mind?" She was asking the question of him personally, and he seemed to realize that.

"A basic rule of police work is that you can't be effective as a cop if the case or the victim is too close to you. If it's too personal, you can't be objective at all, and there's a danger of seeing things the way you want them to be instead of the way they are."

"You mean like 'Caroline's death was an accident'?" The words were out before Joanna could stop them, and she regretted saying them the instant he let go of her shoulder and shoved his hand back into his pocket.

"Is that what you think? That I missed something because I was too close? I told you, Joanna, I wasn't involved with Caroline."

Joanna didn't know if she should feel relieved that he sounded merely impatient rather than angry. She held her voice steady. "What I meant was, you felt—and maybe still feel—a lot of guilt about her death. You said as much, said you had a guilty conscience. And maybe it's easier for you that it was an accident. After all, if something happened at that old barn while she was waiting for you to show up, something that directly or indirectly caused her to drive recklessly, then it might have been something you could have prevented. If you'd been there. So it's a good thing it was an accident, isn't it? Nothing you might have done differently would have changed the outcome. Because it was just an accident."

Griffin turned and walked away.

She didn't look after him. Instead, Joanna continued to lean against the railing and gaze at the spot where he had been for several minutes, until a sudden chill breeze reminded her it was getting late. And colder. Much colder.

"Damn," she said softly.

        ✦   ✦   ✦

"You could spend the night," Lyssa Maitland said.

He shook his head slightly, the gesture controlled as all his gestures were, and stretched languidly as he sat on the edge of the bed. "No, I can't."

Watching well-defined muscles move under his sleek skin, Lyssa thought as she often had before that there was nothing fair in nature. It wasn't enough that he was wealthy and a good-looking devil, but his genetic heritage had also bestowed upon him an athletic physique he maintained with almost no effort at all. It was a good word to describe him, she thought. *Effortless*. Everything he was, everything he did, was effortless.

Almost everything, at any rate.

"Mind if I take a shower?"

He always asked. And, as always, she replied, "Of course not. I put out fresh towels for you."

He looked back over his shoulder at her, wearing a small half-smile. "I'm getting predictable."

It wasn't the first time Lyssa had wondered if he could read her mind. He hadn't even been looking at her, for Christ's sake! She worked herself into a sitting position, banking pillows behind her. The sheet was pulled to her waist, so that only her very long, very pale hair veiled her naked breasts.

"Everybody has habits," she said lightly.

His eyes narrowed, though the faint smile remained. "I suppose." He paused, then added, "You're very beautiful."

The remote consideration in his voice was hardly designed to flatter or even please her, so Lyssa merely shrugged and said, "Thanks. Maybe it's just the male sex that's predictable. You all seem to like leggy blondes."

"In your experience?" he asked politely.

She wondered if he was making one of his sardonic references, this time to her somewhat checkered past, but chose not to question. With this man, she had learned not to look too deeply. "Sure," she said. "In the last ten years, not one of the men I've met was even remotely interested in the fact that I got straight A's at Harvard. So I drew the natural conclusion."

He shrugged very slightly. "No one can be expected to assume that a boutique buyer would have a degree in economics."

"Which ought to teach people not to assume."

"Umm. In a perfect world, perhaps." He leaned over and kissed her shoulder lightly, then got to his feet and went into the bathroom, as unself-conscious naked as he was fully clothed.

Lyssa lay there listening as he turned on the shower. He took very hot showers, so within minutes she would see steam come into the bedroom, crawling along the ceiling like some ghostly creature seeking an escape from the room. And only when the mirror above her dresser was fogged halfway down its length would he turn off the shower and get out.

One discovered such things about a lover. Just as she'd discovered that he was an astonishingly sexual creature for so seemingly remote a man, passionate and uninhibited in bed. And not a selfish lover, which had rather surprised her. Also that he never lingered in bed unless he anticipated more sex, and that he never slept here. Never.

She invariably invited him, and he always refused, both of them polite and casual, both pretending it wasn't a conversation scripted in stone.

For more than six months now, the script had remained virtually the same. Two or three nights a week, he either came here or else met her at a hotel somewhere outside town, where they would not be seen by anyone who mattered. At a hotel, they would often have dinner, then go to bed for a few hours, rarely spending the night there; here at her place, there was usually no food in the routine. If she was recently back from one of her buying trips, they usually met every night for several days straight; she was neither young enough nor naive enough to assume he missed her rather than the sexual release while she was gone, and never asked.

Since their affair had begun, there had been only one interval during which the routine had changed: the month following Caroline's death. He had been distant then, even for him. So remote that Lyssa wasn't sure the affair would have resumed at all had she not made the first move and taken advantage of the tension she'd felt building inside him.

As if there had been no interruption in the affair, they went on as before. So businesslike during the day that Lyssa was almost certain no one else had guessed they were lovers—and in Cliffside, that was saying something.

She watched the first wispy tendrils of steam grope their way from the bathroom, and thought of his body, wet and glistening, under the shower's hot spray. There was nothing wrong with his body, absolutely nothing. He was flawless, or so close to it the difference hardly mattered. And there was magic in his fingers. . . .

"Damn. I'm pathetic," she muttered aloud, then sighed and scrambled off the bed. She went into the steamy bathroom, pausing a moment to eye the ambiguous shape of movement behind the shower's frosted glass door. Then, sighing again, she opened the door and slipped inside the hot, steamy cubicle, where his large body took up most of the available space. It was like entering a different world, and for an instant she couldn't breathe.

"What took you so long?" he asked, reaching out to draw her body against his.

Lyssa started to remind him that this was not part of the

routine, but decided not to. Even as long as she'd known him, there was quite a lot of him still marked off as private, and she was certain trespassers into those places would be kicked out of his life with no mercy. What she had with him was little enough, and precarious, but she didn't want to lose it.

"I was gathering my strength," she said instead.

He chuckled, his lips trailing over her cheek and down her throat. "I wonder if you'll ever tell me the truth instead of just what you think I want to hear," he murmured.

Damn him, he is reading my mind!

"Only in business, sweetie," she said, her tone flippant. Deliberately bringing the conversation to an end, she slid her hand down his side, over the smooth, hard flesh of his hip and thigh, then up the front until her fingers found and grasped even harder flesh. It didn't surprise her that he was already aroused, and it didn't particularly flatter her; in public and when they were businesslike, he might have been made of stone for all the reaction she earned from him, but when they were like this, it was almost unconditional how instantly and lustfully he responded to her.

She had more than once wondered if that seemingly primal drive to mate was the price he paid for being so controlled so much of the time.

"This is not smart," he said. "Acrobatics in the shower like a couple of kids." But even as he said it, he was pressing her back against the chilly fiberglass of the stall. The hot water streamed down over her breasts, and he stared down at her, his hands shaping and lifting, thumbs rubbing over her nipples rhythmically.

Those magic hands . . . Her mouth opened under the hungry pressure of his, and she caressed him, stroking him with the quickening rhythm he initiated in her body with his skilled fingers and oddly possessive mouth. It was as if he had been granted absolute knowledge of what would please and arouse and compel, as if nature had given him that as well. Her heart thudded and tension coiled tighter and tighter inside her, and the need to have him became a blind necessity.

She barely felt the wet slide of the wall at her back as he lifted her, or the shower spray beating against her arm and shoulder like tiny fingers. Her legs opened and cradled him, and she whimpered in relief when he came into her. It was an aching completion so consummate it was terrifying, as though this act with this man was the only moment of wholeness she had ever known.

It made panic wash over her even as pleasure did, and she pressed her closed mouth against his shoulder in the effort not to cry out, because she was afraid he'd understand and despise her for it. Almost silent, she took him and the pleasure he gave her, despising herself for the gratitude she felt.

Lyssa was almost limp when he finally eased her back onto her feet, and he had to steady her even though her back was still against the cool fiberglass wall of the stall.

"Whose idea was this, anyway?" she managed, still breathless but trying very hard to stick to her expected flippant role.

"Yours." He kissed her, taking his time about it. Then he gave her one of his small smiles as he reached up and adjusted the spray nozzle.

She sputtered and turned her face away from the spray. "Bastard!"

He chuckled. "Turn around and I'll wash your back for you."

She obeyed, and by the time he was finished with her back and her front and had washed her hair for her as well, Lyssa was feeling limp again and more than a little bit resentful. *Damn him, anyway. Him and his damned magic fingers!*

She returned the favor, hoping he couldn't feel how shaky her hands were as she washed his back. He didn't comment if he did notice, and by the time he turned off the shower and opened the stall door, Lyssa was feeling calmer.

She wrapped a large towel around her body and a smaller one around her hair and went to sit on the edge of the bed as she towel-dried her hair and then combed through it absently with her fingers. He was dressing, and she couldn't help but watch him.

God, I'm really pathetic.

"I heard you had a little confrontation with Griff in town today," she said, trying to distract herself.

Scott didn't ask where she'd heard; in Cliffside, the source rarely made much difference. "It wasn't a confrontation," he said, tucking his shirt into his pants. "He was just asking about that tourist who was killed a few months ago."

Lyssa frowned. "Butler? But that was back in May, wasn't it? I thought Griff had his hands full investigating how that girl came to fall last night."

Scott sat down in a chair by the window to put on his socks and shoes, but paused first to look at Lyssa. "I thought so too. He said he may have closed that other investigation too soon."

"Meaning what?"

"I don't know."

"You didn't even know Butler, did you?"

"No." Scott turned his attention to putting his shoes on.

Lyssa waited for a moment, and when he said nothing more, said, "He is investigating that girl's death, though. Does he think there's some connection between the two deaths?"

"Apparently," Scott said calmly, "he thinks the connection might be me."

"What?"

"He asked me where I was last night, and not because he thought I might have seen something helpful. I can't think of another reason why he'd ask that unless he suspected I was somehow involved."

"Did you tell him you were here?" Lyssa asked.

"No." Scott got up and shrugged into his casual jacket.

"You were here until after midnight," she said slowly.

Scott stood looking down at her, that little half-smile playing around his mouth. "As I heard it, that girl died hours later, sometime before dawn. So it should hardly matter to the sheriff where I was before that. When she died, I was at the house. That's all he needs to know."

After a moment, Lyssa said, "It's your business, of course. But if you should need to tell him you were with me part of the night, go ahead."

"Don't you think I'd sacrifice your reputation without a second thought if I needed to save my own skin?" he asked as if honestly curious.

"No," she replied calmly, "I don't."

His smile widened just a bit, but Scott didn't comment on her faith. Instead, he merely said, "I'll tell the sheriff as much as he needs to know, and no more than that."

"Because you have no intention of making his job easier?"

"Something like that."

Lyssa heard herself give a little laugh that didn't sound very amused. "There's no love lost between you two, is there?"

"None at all." Abandoning that subject abruptly, he said, "Don't forget to go by City Hall tomorrow morning before you come to the house and pick up those papers from the mayor."

"I won't forget."

"I'll let myself out," Scott said.

"Okay. Good night."

"Good night, Lyssa."

He didn't kiss her good-bye, or even touch her. But Lyssa hadn't expected him to, because he never did. Just as he never told her all or even much of what he was thinking. And just as he never slept here, but always returned to that beautiful, lonely house on the cliffs he had shared with Caroline, and to the bedroom he had not shared with her.

One discovered such things about a lover.

NINE

❖ ❖ ❖

JOANNA GOT OUT of her car and studied the place. Neat, very neat. And quiet. So quiet, in fact, that the silence seemed a physical thing, scraping over her nerves. It was fairly early Tuesday morning, and as far as she could see, she was the only visitor to the greenhouse. McKenna's Roses it was called, according to the sign. As she had been told, it was the only one of his businesses that Scott McKenna had chosen to put his name on. Or . . . Caroline's name, perhaps?

It was actually a sprawling collection of three large greenhouses and a small building presumably containing the office and sales space for plant supplies and equipment, and was located roughly between downtown Cliffside and The Inn, situated well back off the coast road and surrounded by woods. And judging by the neatly lettered signs above each greenhouse door, the business wasn't limited to roses.

There was no one around that she could see, and when

Joanna found the door of the nearest greenhouse unlocked, she went inside. This one had been marked *Perennials* and was filled with healthy, fragrant plants and flowers. The variety was unusual in Joanna's experience with greenhouses and nurseries, and everything was in excellent repair. As with all his other businesses, it seemed Scott had hired only the best, most responsible and skilled employees to make certain his property was in superior hands.

She left that greenhouse and went into the next, this one marked *Annuals* and filled with bedding plants and flowers in all stages of growth. Joanna looked around only briefly, again seeing no one, then went back outside and to the third greenhouse, this one marked *Roses*.

Joanna had always loved roses, but when she walked through the front door of this greenhouse, her first reaction was that so many roses in an enclosed space—even one as large as this—were a bit too much. The scent of them filled the air with a cloying sweetness, and she found herself breathing through her mouth for several minutes to lessen the impact. But the flowers were stunningly beautiful nevertheless, bred in every color nature allowed and quite a few created by inventive humans.

As in the other two buildings, the place was immaculate and the plants bursting with health, so despite its seemingly being deserted at the moment, someone obviously took excellent care of the business.

She walked slowly toward the opposite end along a comfortably wide aisle, studying shelves that were staggered in height to give the plants maximum room and light, and noting the complex and undoubtedly expensive sprinkler system. Then, realizing that each rose bore a little brass nametag, she began paying attention to those, reading with an intentness she wasn't even aware of.

Some of the names were familiar to Joanna: Scarlet Knight, Queen Elizabeth, Love, French Lace, Cherish, Tiffany, Peace. But most were strange and exotic, making her wonder who had chosen them and why. Complicata, Sparrieshoop, Madame Hardy, Old Blush, Bewitched, Lady X, Mon Cheri.

She was halfway up the second aisle and moving back toward the front door again when she came to an abrupt stop, staring. The plant was set just a bit apart from those around it and was in a decorative blue ceramic pot rather than black or green plastic like all the rest. And though she hadn't seen a single fallen petal anywhere in the greenhouse until now, a few petals lay about this neat rosebush on the shelf, just as petals had lain around the vase of roses in Joanna's dream. And like those roses, these were a deep, vivid pink, beautifully shaped and just slightly different from any other rose she had ever seen.

She reached out slowly to touch a satiny bloom, and that was when she saw the little brass nametag. *For Caroline.*

"Hi, can I help you? Sorry I wasn't around when you got here, but—"

The man broke off abruptly when Joanna turned to face him, his eyes widening and mouth left open in obvious shock. He had come in from the rear door of the greenhouse and stopped now no more than a couple of steps away from her. He was about forty, with a pleasant face and a stocky build, only his pale blue eyes unusual. He wore faded jeans and a denim shirt, both as immaculate as the greenhouses, and though there was no dirt under his fingernails, Joanna knew he was the green-thumbed expert who ran this place.

"Jesus," he said softly. "They said you looked like her, but . . ."

It had been a few days since Joanna had encountered shock at her appearance, so she was taken aback for a moment. But just a moment. "Hi," she said. "I'm Joanna Flynn."

He nodded slowly. "Yeah, I know. Uh—sorry for staring, but—"

It was Joanna's turn to nod. "It's okay, this has been happening to me for a week now."

"You don't sound like her," he murmured, then shook his head and shifted his shoulders as though throwing off something bothersome. "I'm Adam Harrison. I manage the greenhouse."

She shook hands with him, then nodded toward the rosebush. "I was just admiring all of them, but especially this one. And I couldn't help but be curious about the name. If I remember correctly, roses are named by whoever creates them. Do you happen to know who created this one?"

"I did," he said. "When we opened this place a few years ago, I promised Scott that I'd name the first new plant we developed for Caroline." He shrugged slightly. "So that's what I did. She was the inspiration, after all."

"So it's true that he went into the greenhouse business because Caroline loved roses?" Joanna asked.

Adam Harrison smiled as though he found the subject somehow amusing. "Yeah, it's true. When they were first married, he sent all the way to Portland for roses a couple of times a week. But sometimes they were hard to find, or the variety wasn't good. So he decided Cliffside needed a plant nursery, and brought me up from San Francisco to run it. I'd done some work for his family there, so he knew what he'd be getting."

Another one from San Francisco.

"I see." Joanna couldn't be sure how deeply she could or should probe with this man, but she felt an odd sense of urgency to keep going, to keep asking questions. Because she had dreamed of roses and now found one named for Caroline here, she assumed. Because somehow this place—or perhaps this man—was important in her search for information about Caroline and her death. Otherwise, why would the vase of roses have been a part of the dream? "You seem to find that amusing, Mr. Harrison."

"Adam. Miss Flynn, I find it a scream."

She blinked in surprise at his sardonic tone. "Uh—call me Joanna, please. Forgive me, but—you didn't like Caroline?"

He looked at her for a moment as though weighing her curiosity. Not guarded, as so many others had been, just thoughtful. "I heard you were asking questions about her. Mind telling me why?"

Joanna hesitated, but then, as she so often had since arriving in Cliffside, and, really, for most of her life, she followed her instincts. "Because I look like her. Because ever since I got here, people have assumed things about me, things Caroline would have found familiar. I . . . need to know who she was, what she was like. I need to know more than just her favorite color or the perfume she wore."

He nodded, then shrugged as if the subject hardly interested him. "Makes sense. Okay, then—I'm in the minority, I know, but no, I didn't like Caroline. For all her sweet smiles and soft voice, she was a cruel, destructive woman who did whatever was necessary to get what she wanted, and she didn't care who she hurt."

Joanna heard bitterness in his voice, a lot of it, and it didn't take intuition to tell her a likely reason for it. "So what was it she wanted from you?"

He let out a short laugh. "Complicity. She got it too."

"Complicity in what?" Joanna asked, not sure he'd be willing to tell her that much. But whether it was because she looked so much like the woman he had such strong feelings about or because he had held it all inside him for too long, it was obvious he wasn't going to stop talking now.

"Cheating on Scott. She needed a place to meet her lover, you see, a place unlikely to cause her problems. And I have no doubt she enjoyed the irony of doing it here—a place her husband built for love of her."

Joanna hardly knew what to say. The picture he was drawing was not of the woman so many others in this town had seen, and so she had to believe his view was either twisted by his own emotions or else that only he had seen an ugly side of Caroline's personality—which seemed unlikely but not impossible, depending on just how well he had known her. And Joanna had a very good idea how well he had known her.

"The office has a back room," Adam went on flatly, as if he saw or sensed her doubt, "used mostly for storing the supplies we've no space for out front. She kept a blanket there on an old cot of mine and came here to meet her lover a few times a week."

The storage room of the greenhouse—*and* the old barn? It felt wrong to Joanna, and so she asked, "You mean before Caroline was killed she came here several times a week?"

Adam shook his head. "No, not then. It was about a year ago. Only lasted a few weeks, but hell, cheating is cheating, as far as I'm concerned. She wanted to hurt Scott, that was her reason. Wanted to use this place to hurt him."

"And did she? Hurt Scott?"

Adam let out another short laugh. "You see, Joanna, the problem with Caroline was, she was a coward. Couldn't stand confrontations. So even though she wanted to hurt Scott, she wasn't brave enough to tell him about her affairs. I don't know, maybe just having them satisfied a sick need inside her, that secret knowledge that other men were getting what was rightfully his. Maybe that was what she got off on." He shrugged. "Anyway, I doubt she ever told him. Probably expected her lover to after she'd finished with him. Probably figured he'd be mad enough to want to get even with her after she'd dumped him."

Joanna asked the question quietly. "And did you?"

He didn't seem surprised by her perception. "No." His voice was flat, his face wearing a faint smile that held no amusement. "But maybe one of the others did. I was only one of many, I knew that. I asked her once if she always bedded her lovers in dingy back rooms or cheap motels because of the contrast between that and her husband's fine house on the cliffs. She laughed."

Questions swirled around in Joanna's mind, and she chose one at random. "Why did it end?"

"Because she got tired of me. Because it didn't excite her

anymore. Because I couldn't satisfy her. Because she was ready to move on to the next lover. Take your pick."

"And you weren't tempted to tell Scott?"

Adam's sardonic amusement faded, and he looked away from Joanna at the rose named after his onetime lover. He took a step toward it and almost unconsciously reached out a hand to gently groom the plant, removing a dying petal. "I was tempted. If it had only been a matter of getting back at Caroline, I would have. But I like Scott, and I owe him a lot." Those pale blue eyes, miserable now, shifted their attention back to Joanna. "That's why she picked me, you see. It wasn't just this place she wanted to use to hurt him—it was me too. I was his friend, and I betrayed him as surely as she did." His mouth twisted.

After a moment, Joanna couldn't help but say, "You talk as if you were helpless in her toils."

He shook his head immediately. "No, I don't claim the affair was all her fault. Hell, she didn't rape me. Didn't even seduce me. She just saw I wanted her and she offered, the way you'd offer somebody a ride in your car if you saw them with their thumb sticking up."

It was only then that Joanna understood the truth. Adam Harrison didn't hate Caroline, or at least didn't *only* hate her. He loved her. Even now, more than three months after her death and a year after their affair, he loved her. He was bitter because she hadn't felt the same way about him, but the bitterness hadn't destroyed his feelings for her, only twisted them into complex and obviously agonizing knots. He was torn with guilt about having betrayed Scott, but if Caroline hadn't broken it off, Joanna had no doubt they'd still be using that "dingy" back room.

It also made his willingness to talk to Joanna so immediately and frankly more understandable, she thought. Because she so resembled the woman he couldn't forget, the information he offered so voluntarily was almost in the nature of a confession.

Joanna wasn't a priest, able or willing to offer him absolution—and she wasn't Caroline. Her knowledge of his turbulent feelings for Caroline made her uncomfortable, made her look away from him as one would look away from something too naked to be seen by a stranger.

"I'm sorry," she said.

Roughly, he said, "Goddammit, don't you pity me too!"

She braced herself inwardly and looked at him again, relieved to see only his anger rather than his anguish. "I'm not Caroline," she said very deliberately. "I'm just a woman who looks a bit like her, a woman who's curious about her life."

"And her death?"

Joanna's inner debate lasted only a few seconds, and she couldn't have said what it was that made her certain this man had not been involved in Caroline's death. His aching misery, perhaps, or just her own instincts. All she knew was that her dream had brought her here, to him, and she had to get whatever information he had to give her.

"Yes," she said. "And her death."

"It was an accident," Adam said. "Everybody says so."

"You don't sound so sure." Joanna studied him thoughtfully. "Why?"

He shrugged. "Oh, I think it was an accident—in a manner of speaking. It seems clear she was driving that car, and that she was alone. But I think something was bad wrong the last couple weeks of Caroline's life, that she was worried and she was scared."

"Why do you think that?"

"She came by here three or four days before the accident—and she *never* came by here, not since we stopped using that room behind the office. She had something on her mind, that was obvious. She couldn't be still, kept wandering around the greenhouses like she was looking for something, smoking like a chimney. And she'd bitten her nails down to the quick, I saw that."

Almost unconsciously, Joanna slipped her hands into her pockets to hide her own ragged nails. "She didn't tell you why she was upset?"

A bit of his earlier misery crept back into Adam's pale

eyes, and he shook his head. "No. I didn't give her the chance, to be honest. There were customers here when she arrived, and when they left, I . . . hell, I sort of let it rip, if you know what I mean. I said something sarcastic about royalty visiting the peons, and then I really got nasty. She could hardly get a word in, and I was sure as hell in no mood to listen."

"Was that the first time you'd seen her since . . ."

"Since she stopped taking naps on my cot? Yeah, first time since then we'd been alone. Guess I'd bottled up a few things and had to let 'em out."

Joanna nodded. "So she left without telling you what was bothering her."

He nodded. "God knows why she came to me if it was help she needed. You'd think she would have realized I was still raw and pretty much hated her guts. I mean, wouldn't any man after the way she'd treated me? She should have expected that. Why didn't she expect that?"

It was a rhetorical question, and one filled with guilt. Joanna had heard the same emotion in Griffin's voice, and for much the same reason. She had to wonder if all the men in Caroline's life had felt guilty because they hadn't been there for her at the end. And wondered even more if that had been Caroline's fault. Certainly Adam had loved her, and Griffin might well have for all his denials, yet neither of the men had gone out of their way to help her when she might have needed them most. The way Adam talked, there had been other affairs, other men; had there been? And had she gone to other past lovers in the last days of her life, seeking their help for some problem she dared not confide in her husband, only to find that she had used them up so completely that none of them had been able to find for her even enough caring to offer a shoulder or a willing ear?

"You probably couldn't have changed what happened," she told Adam, not certain of that but knowing it was what he needed to hear.

"Maybe." He shrugged. "I keep telling myself it was her

own fault. You can't treat people like dirt and then expect them to treat you better."

"Most of the people around here seemed to have liked Caroline," Joanna noted neutrally. "Or, at least, had nothing bad to say about her."

"Oh, sure, she could be sweet as honey when she wanted to—it was her public face, as a matter of fact. What most people saw. But I'll bet you haven't found any close friends, especially women. Caroline didn't like other women. She was polite enough, of course—raised that way. Very civic-minded, too, always working for the good of the town. And she worshiped that kid of hers, no doubt about that."

After a moment, Joanna said, "So, when you say she treated people like dirt, you mean she treated men that way?"

For the first time, Adam seemed hesitant. "Some men. I know of at least one other man in Cliffside she turned inside out, and I'll bet there are others. She was . . . too sure of herself and her power, too casual when it ended, for a woman who wasn't used to dumping lovers."

Joanna accepted that opinion with a grain of salt; he was nowhere near objective about Caroline, and a discarded lover was probably not the best person to judge whether she made it a habit to cheat on her husband. Still, the opinion and feelings of at least one other discarded lover might either confirm or contradict what Adam believed of Caroline. And that other lover might have been the one Caroline met in the old barn, possibly right up until her death.

"Will you tell me who that other man is?" she asked him slowly. "I'd like to talk to him."

Adam was shaking his head. "I don't think I should, Joanna. His reputation here in town is a lot more important to him than mine is to me."

Joanna felt a twinge of uneasiness, wondering if it was the sheriff's reputation he didn't want to harm. And wondering if she was ready to hear it if that was true. *Oh God, why does it keep coming back to Griffin? Why can't I believe he didn't love her?*

In any case, she didn't know if she could—or should—convince Adam she could be trusted not to talk about what she found out, so instead asked, "How did you find out about them?"

"He told me. When she dumped him, he got a little drunk and needed somebody to talk to. We're friends, so he came looking for me." Adam's mouth twisted bitterly. "It was months before I got involved with her, so I can't say I wasn't warned."

Months before. So this other lover wasn't seeing Caroline when she died—unless it was a repeat performance. "How an affair would end, you mean?"

"Yeah. She dumped him for no reason, or at least no reason she wanted to give him. Just said it was over and strolled away, avoiding a confrontation the way she always did. And he was in love with her, the poor bastard. He's not over her yet."

Neither are you, Joanna thought. So there were at least two men who had been sexually and emotionally involved with Caroline; had there been others? What about Scott? Had he known or suspected that his wife was unfaithful? And if he had, had he cared?

Joanna had no way of knowing. "Adam, do you have any idea if she was involved with anyone just before the accident?"

"No. She may have been—probably was—but I couldn't say for sure. Only her lover would know."

"This is a town full of gossip," Joanna said wonderingly. "How was Caroline able to hide an affair? Especially if she made it a habit."

Adam shrugged. "I don't know. Maybe she never got caught because she wanted to be."

In a way, that made the most sense to Joanna—if it was true. People with nothing to lose often appeared to have unusual luck, as if fate had a fine sense of irony. If Caroline had indeed wanted—consciously or unconsciously—her husband to discover her infidelity, perhaps fate had determined that she would have to tell him herself.

In any case, Joanna was left with a great deal to think about.

"Thanks for talking to me," she told Adam. "And you don't have to worry. I won't tell anyone about you and Caroline."

"Thanks," he murmured, but not as if he really cared.

Joanna hesitated, wanting to say something else but not knowing what. Finally, she turned and made her way down the aisle toward the door.

"It was a closed-casket."

Startled, she stopped and turned back to look at Adam. He was staring at the rosebush, but then raised his haunted gaze to her. "The service. It was a closed-casket service." His voice was matter-of-fact. "The accident was so bad, she looked . . . there was no way to . . . fix her. So they kept the casket closed. I never saw her again."

And never got to say you were sorry. It also helped to explain, Joanna realized, at least some of the reactions to her here in Cliffside. If only a handful of people had actually seen Caroline's body, then the grieving process for many had no doubt been delayed or hindered. They hadn't been able to see her before burial, hadn't been able to say good-bye in the way so many needed to. Encountering a woman who so resembled Caroline relatively soon after her death must have given rise to even more speculation than Joanna was aware of.

"Talk to Doc Becket, Joanna," Adam said abruptly. "He knew her as well as anyone did."

Joanna wasn't sure if Adam was telling her that Becket had been Caroline's lover, but she didn't want to ask; she accepted the advice without comment. "Thank you, I will. Good-bye, Adam," she said, helpless because there was nothing else she could say.

"Good-bye, Joanna." He turned his head back and resumed staring at the rose named For Caroline, his pleasant face desolate.

She left the greenhouse and got in her car, just sitting there for a few moments before starting the engine. She had to force herself to shake off Adam's pain, to push it away from her, and when she had, what she felt most of all was confused uncertainty.

Who *was* Caroline McKenna? A shy woman—a repressed woman. A serene woman—a woman who nervously bit her nails. A devoted mother—a habitually unfaithful wife. A woman who could bequeath millions so that the town clinic could be improved—yet apparently abandoned her lovers without warning or compunction.

A woman whose marriage was made hollow by the indifference of her husband? Or a woman whose own behavior had caused his cold remoteness?

. . . you assume I'm at fault. That I'm the ogre, the villain of the piece.

And are you?

Why, yes, Joanna. I am. Just because everybody says I'm a cold bastard doesn't mean it isn't true.

But was it true? Joanna wondered now. Was Scott McKenna as remote and uncaring as he seemed? Or was he more sinned against than sinning? Was Scott another man Caroline had left in an emotional shambles, a secret he kept well hidden behind an inherently reserved, seemingly uncaring facade?

"Oh, damn, Caroline, who are you?" Joanna murmured, starting her car at last.

◇   ◇   ◇

"Are you sure?" Griffin asked, rubbing the back of his neck with one hand and holding the phone to his ear with the other. "That isn't what you told me yesterday, dammit."

Doctor Becket sighed. "Griff, you know as well as I do that the longer a body is out in the elements—especially during a wet and chilly night—the harder it is to pinpoint the time of death. You say the girl planned to sneak out of the hotel around eleven-thirty, and you ask if she could have been killed closer to midnight than we originally estimated. Yes, she could have. Anytime between ten P.M. and four A.M. would probably be a reasonable guess. I really can't call it closer than that, not for the record."

"Guesses," Griffin muttered. "Isn't science wonderful."

"It has its limitations just like anything else," Becket said. "Hey, call on the Portland M.E. if you want another opinion."

"No, don't be an ass. Thanks, Doc." Griffin cradled the receiver and sat staring down at the elegant, leather-bound diary lying open on his blotter. "Son of a bitch," he said quietly to himself.

"Having a bad day?"

He looked up at the open doorway of his office, then leaned back in his chair and shrugged. "You might say that."

"I can come back later," Joanna offered.

Griffin shook his head. "No, it's all right."

She came in rather cautiously and sat down in his visitor's chair. "Um . . . about what I said yesterday—"

"If you thought I was still pissed about that," he said, "I'm not."

"Oh? Then how come it feels a few degrees cooler in here than it ought to be?"

"Okay, I'm still pissed. I hate being wrong."

Joanna blinked, then smiled slightly. "Tough on the ego, huh?"

Griffin thought about it, then shook his head. "Not so much that as my knowledge of myself. You showed me something I hadn't seen in myself, and I didn't like it much. You were right—it *was* easier for me to believe Caroline's death was no more than a random accident. I didn't feel quite so guilty when I thought my being there wouldn't have made a difference."

"We can't know that it would have," Joanna reminded him quietly.

"No, but once we accept—once I accept—that something might have happened while she was waiting for me in the old barn, then it becomes a lot more likely that if I'd been there, the outcome might have been different."

"Maybe. But you can't go back and relive that day, not now. So what's the use of feeling guilty? It won't change what happened to Caroline, and it sure won't help you. Let it go, Griffin."

He wondered if he could, but smiled at her anyway. "Okay, I'll work on that. But in the meantime, no matter how I feel about what happened that day, it hardly alters the evidence. She was alone, she was driving, and the car wasn't tampered with or forced off the road. No crime was committed."

Joanna nodded. "Not a legal crime, I accept that. But what about a moral one? What if somebody did cause the accident by upsetting Caroline?"

"Then I'd like to beat the hell out of him," Griffin said unemotionally. "But I can't arrest him."

Her unusual golden eyes searched his face intently, and he had the sudden feeling that whatever she found or didn't find there was going to determine not only the rest of this conversation, but possibly something a lot more important. And the hell of it was, he had no idea what it was she was looking for.

She smiled briefly, the searching look vanishing, and linked her fingers together over her flat middle. "Okay. What about Amber? Another accident? Suicide?"

"What just happened?" Griffin asked slowly.

She looked startled, then wary. "I don't know what you mean."

"Yes, you do. You came in here with something very definite on your mind and then decided not to talk to me about it."

"That's my privilege, surely," she murmured.

"Agreed." He heard tension in his voice and knew she heard it as well. "But I'd like to know why you changed your mind." Her face—very much her own now rather than a mere duplicate of Caroline's, as far as he was concerned—was not one suited to bluff across a poker table;

she didn't like it that he was able to read her so accurately. Still, this time that expressive face told him no more than her words did when she answered slowly.

"Look, I found out something today, something that surprised me. I was going to tell you, but decided not to because it really isn't my story to tell. Besides, it has nothing to do with Amber or your investigation, so . . ."

"It's about Caroline, isn't it?"

Even more slowly, Joanna said, "Not about her death. So it hardly matters, does it?"

"Maybe you should let me be the judge of that."

Her mouth curved in a faint, odd smile. "No, not this time. The story was confided to me, and as far as I can see, it wouldn't help you in any way to know it. So it stays with me. Sorry."

Griffin didn't like it, and he knew that was obvious in his voice. "Well, since thumbscrews and the rack have been outlawed, I can't force you to tell me."

There was a moment of silence, and then she murmured, "So, once again I've messed things up and we aren't pals anymore?"

"Is that what we were?" he heard himself ask.

"I thought so." She looked at him, awareness in her eyes. "Was I wrong?"

For one of the few times in his life, Griffin was unsure. His feelings were too complex to easily define, and a part of him wanted to shy away from examining them. She had secrets she wouldn't share, questions she wouldn't answer, and that bothered him. Who was Joanna Flynn really, and why had she come here?

He had known her only a week—but she was due to leave in another week. That didn't leave a man much time. "It's an old argument," he said finally, "but can a man and woman ever be just friends?"

"I guess that depends on whether they want to be," Joanna said. "Is a friend what you want, Griffin?"

"I have friends. What about you, Joanna? Is there a man waiting for you back in Atlanta?"

For the first time, she looked away from him, not quite nervous but definitely guarded. "Flirting in the sheriff's office. There's probably a town ordinance against it."

"Not since 1879. Answer the question."

"All right. No, there isn't a man waiting back in Atlanta." The golden eyes that met his were unreadable. "It's been a couple of years since I was involved with anybody. Satisfied?"

"Almost." He kept his voice dispassionate. "What ended the last relationship?"

She frowned at him. "I murdered him and buried his body in the rose garden."

"I'm serious."

With a sigh, she said, "Call it basic incompatibility. He thought I needed a life. His. Problem was, I sort of like to think for myself—decide what I'm going to wear or do or say. So the second time he suggested that I not wear pants and try not to just blurt out what I was thinking, I told him to take a walk. A long walk. Satisfied now?"

"Satisfied he was an idiot." Griffin didn't give her a chance to respond to that comment, but went on immediately. "Aunt Sarah would have been proud of you, I'd say." He was backing off and he knew it; Joanna was just wary enough to make him cautious.

With a laugh that sounded relieved, Joanna said, "She would have scolded me for getting involved with him in the first place. You, on the other hand, she would have liked."

He smiled. "Because of my charming ways?"

"Those would have been a plus. No, she would have liked you because she favored dark men with dark eyes. The interesting thing was, none of her husbands were dark. She always said the only really interesting men in the South were blond men."

"Sounds like blatant prejudice to me," Griffin decided.

"Maybe so, but she obviously believed it. All four husbands were blonds."

"And she outlasted all of them. That should have told her something."

Joanna chuckled again, but before she could comment on that, one of Griffin's deputies knocked briskly on the open door and came into the office.

"Sorry, boss," she said, "but I thought you'd want to see this."

He felt his good humor seep away as he accepted the piece of paper. He knew what it was, but asked anyway. "Bad news?"

"It could have been better," she returned wryly.

"Okay. Thanks, Megan."

She left after a brief glance at Joanna, and Griffin read the short message called in by one of his other deputies with a sense of fatalism. As Megan had said, the news could have been better. It could have been a lot better.

"Griffin?"

He looked up to meet Joanna's concerned gaze. "Sometimes," he said, "I really hate being a cop."

After a moment, she said, "I know you told me to butt out of your investigation, but if there's been some kind of breakthrough, I'd really like to know what it is."

He realized that he wanted to talk to her about this, and wasn't sure if it was because he valued her insights and judgment or simply because he found himself wanting to talk to her about everything. Either way, it bothered him.

"I promise I won't share anything with the gossips of Cliffside," she said.

Griffin put the message aside and looked down at the diary lying open on his blotter. "Mrs. Wade came into the office this morning," he said. "She'd been packing up her daughter's things and found her diary." He turned the small book around and pushed it across the desk toward Joanna.

She leaned forward and started to reach for it, then hesitated and looked at him with troubled eyes.

"Yeah, I know," he said. "Mrs. Wade hadn't looked inside, and I didn't want to read it either. But Amber's dead. And if anything she confided in the diary can help us find out what happened to her . . . Anyway, I haven't backtracked—yet. Just read the final entry."

Joanna almost wished she hadn't asked to know what Griffin had found out. But she had asked. Telling herself he was right in saying they needed information to find out what had happened to Amber, she took the diary and began reading the final entry. It was dated Sunday, eleven P.M. Her handwriting had been large, round, and somewhat childish, and she had drawn little hearts over her *i*'s and *j*'s.

Mom and Dad have gone to bed already, but to me the night feels so alive. . . . Has Cain read my note? He must have by now. So he must know how much I love him. How much I need him. And now that he knows . . . Oh God, now that he knows . . . He'll meet me tonight, I know he will. We'll make love in his cottage with the storm all around us, and then we'll go away together. . . . It's supposed to storm all night, but there's a lull now. I'll slip out the terrace door now, while it's stopped raining, I'm sure I can make it. . . . I'm sure the storm will wait for me to reach my love. . . .

Joanna placed the diary gently on Griffin's desk and pushed it back toward him. Melodramatic and self-important as the feelings were, she knew they had been very real to Amber, and she felt so sorry for the girl it made her throat hurt. The desperate pangs of a young love were normal and to be expected at eighteen; dying was not.

"So now we know why she went out that night," Joanna murmured. "And when."

"And who she planned to meet."

"Griffin, she wasn't sure herself that Cain had read the note, so—"

Unemotionally, Griffin said, "Funny that he never mentioned a note, don't you think?"

"Maybe he never got it."

"And maybe he just didn't want to tell me about it. The

same way he didn't want to tell me he left his cottage Sunday night."

"He left his cottage? How do you know that?"

"Somebody saw him." With an index finger, Griffin tapped the message brought in earlier. "Cain drives a silver Jaguar. It's very noticeable—and, due to a faulty muffler, very loud. One of his neighbors had gone to a window to see if the storm was really over or just pausing for a minute. His car backfired, catching her attention. He was heading for the coast road."

"What time was it?" Joanna asked slowly.

"Eleven forty-five, give or take ten minutes."

"But wasn't that too early? I mean, I thought Amber was killed hours later, closer to dawn."

Griffin shook his head. "I just talked to Doc Becket, and he says it could have been anytime between ten P.M. and four A.M. The diary entry tells us she was alive at eleven, so she was killed after eleven and before four. That's the official line. Off the record, Doc says it was probably nearer midnight."

Joanna linked her fingers together and looked down at them for a moment, then returned her gaze to Griffin's impassive face. "Okay, having done it, I know you can walk from Cain's cottage to The Inn in about fifteen minutes—and that's just a leisurely stroll. Hurrying, you could do it in less. So, if she left the hotel within minutes of writing that entry—"

"Which she most likely did," Griffin interrupted. "The storm had died down, but she expected it to start up again. She didn't strike me as the sort who would have wanted to get caught in a downpour, especially on the way to meet a man."

Joanna nodded. "Then there would have been enough time for something to happen before Cain drove away. Time even for her to have walked to his cottage and back— either alone or with him. Maybe time for him to have walked her back to the hotel and then make it back to his cottage, if he hurried. But Griffin, that's assuming an awful lot."

"Yeah, I know. But I have a couple of cold, hard facts as well. Amber died that night. And Cain lied to me about where he was when it happened."

"He might have had a perfectly innocent reason for not telling you the truth."

"Reasons for lying are seldom innocent," he said dryly.

"You know what I mean."

"And you know what I mean. Joanna, I don't want to believe Cain killed that girl—deliberately or accidentally. But I've got a gut feeling she was pushed or thrown over the cliff, and Cain wasn't where he claimed to be. So what am I supposed to think?"

"Maybe he left to get away from her, have you thought of that? Maybe she came to his cottage that night, and to get rid of her he told her he had to go somewhere. So he drives off and she has no choice except to go back to the hotel. And . . . maybe she slipped. Or maybe she jumped."

Griffin shrugged. "Maybe. But if he *did* see her, I want to know why Cain lied about it."

"Because he knew you'd suspect him?"

"He was a suspect anyway, as far as I was concerned, and he knew it. Finding out he lied to me hasn't exactly cleared him in my book."

Try as she might, Joanna couldn't discard the conviction that Amber's death was somehow connected to Caroline's, and to Robert Butler's, and if that was the case, what motive could Cain have had to cause the deaths of three people? It just didn't make sense.

"He might have just lost it," Griffin said, seemingly reading her mind. "Amber wouldn't take rejection well, from all I've heard of her. Maybe she got hysterical and wouldn't let go no matter what he said. Hell, maybe he just shoved her—a little too hard."

"If he did, you'd never be able to prove it in court,

would you? I mean, no matter what happened, you have no real evidence. You can't actually place Cain at the scene of Amber's death or even with her anywhere that night; there were no witnesses to what happened; the postmortem findings say death from a fall. A little churned-up ground might mean a lot—or nothing. So unless somebody breaks down and confesses, you haven't got anything you could take to court."

"That's about the size of it." Griffin smiled without amusement. "No matter what Cain tells me, a confession isn't likely, I'd say. And I have, as you say, no hard evidence that she was murdered. So my final report will likely state that Amber Wade's death was most probably the result of an accident or suicide. That she was most probably alone out there when she went over the cliffs. That I don't know, for sure, what happened out there. And the cold comfort of that her parents can take home with them. Along with her body."

Looking at him, Joanna realized for the first time just how deeply Griffin Cavanaugh felt things. Amber had been a stranger to him, and investigating her death was his job, and yet what ate at him about his inability to fix the blame for her death wasn't professional pride but a very real and deep compassion. Her parents would live the rest of their lives wondering if she had fallen or jumped to her death, would no doubt question and blame themselves for what had happened to their daughter, haunted by the possibility that they might have been able to prevent it—and Griffin knew it. He knew it, and he hated it.

The word these days was *closure*. Griffin wanted to give those grieving parents closure. He wanted to be able to offer them a reason, an explanation for the senseless death of their daughter. He wanted to be able to say to them, "This is what happened . . . and this is why it happened . . . and I'm sorry as hell none of us could stop it from happening."

Joanna hadn't looked deep enough, she realized. She

had picked up on his guilt and anger over Caroline's death, but hadn't seen what was really there. Something deeper and more painful than the events of this last summer.

"You lost somebody, didn't you?" she said slowly. "You lost somebody, and nobody could tell you why."

$\mathcal{T}$EN
✧ ✧ ✧

"$\mathcal{D}$OES IT SHOW SO PLAINLY?" Griffin asked finally, his voice a little rough.

Joanna shook her head. "No." She didn't elaborate, didn't explain that it was something she felt in him rather than something she saw.

"I guess we all carry baggage with us," Griffin said. He linked his fingers together on top of his blotter and looked down at them for a moment, then met Joanna's gaze steadily. "It's been more than twenty years. Twenty-two, as a matter of fact, this past August. I was fifteen. My sister was twelve."

Joanna listened to his voice, stony with control now, and felt a chill because she knew what was coming.

"We were close. Army brats tend to stick together, I suppose because we're always being yanked out of one place and dropped into another. Anyway, we were in a new town and about to start at new schools; we'd just been there a few weeks and had barely met some of the other kids on the base." He paused, then went on, his voice still deliberate. "Lindsey had made a friend of another girl her age, and that day she told our mother she was walking over to play with the girl. Their house was on base, like ours, and it was hardly more than a few blocks away."

Griffin paused again, and this time when he continued it was with more difficulty. "We knew something was wrong within an hour, because Lindsey's friend called asking where she was. But it was three days before her body was found about a mile from the base." His face tightened and those dark eyes were bleak. "She'd been . . . hurt for a long time before she finally died, according to the newspapers. That was how I got the few facts I did, from the newspapers and television. The police and military officials investigating her death wouldn't tell me much of anything, and my parents were so shattered they couldn't see beyond the fact of her dying."

"I'm sorry," Joanna said quietly. "You must have gone through hell."

"I think the worst of it was the sheer bewilderment. It happened so suddenly, without warning. She was alive—then she wasn't. And it was so damned senseless."

"Nobody could tell you why." Joanna was aching inside, for the pain of that boy and the pain of this man. No wonder he felt so deeply about Amber's death; he understood loss all too well.

He shook his head. "There were no answers, no reasons. The authorities found no clues and had no suspects. The investigation went on for months before finally just— fading away. We buried Lindsey. And life went on. But none of us ever got over her death. Hell, we couldn't even get past it, because all we had were questions."

"You never found out what happened?"

Griffin shook his head again. "To this day, the file on the death of Lindsey Cavanaugh is still open down in Texas. There's no statute of limitations on murder."

That must have been the worst of it, Joanna thought. Never knowing for sure what had happened. "Is that why you became a cop? Because you wanted to find the answers for other people?"

"Yes." He didn't hesitate, and there was no doubt in his voice. "If I'd been older or younger at the time, maybe it would have had a different effect on me. Maybe. Or maybe not. I just knew that the worst thing in the world was not knowing *why* you had lost someone. There was no way to move on from there, no way to get past it. I knew right then, that summer, that I'd be some kind of cop."

He shrugged suddenly. "Maybe a lot of my choices were made because of what happened to Lindsey. All I know for sure is that those unanswered questions destroyed my family. My parents split about a year later, still shattered, each of them blaming the other for something neither of them could have prevented. I lived with my dad until I was old enough to join the army myself, but since then I've seen him maybe a dozen times. I've seen my mother twice in the last ten years, Christmas visits that were definitely a mistake. Her house is a shrine to Lindsey, and I'm a stranger to her. Dad retired and moved to Alaska; Mom's living in Florida. They couldn't have put much more space between them if they had measured it out. They're both very, very alone."

One child dead and another emotionally abandoned— and two parents driven apart and left alone. Lindsey's murderer had done more than kill her, Joanna thought. He had killed her family as well. And though Griffin had survived emotionally, he was clearly marked by what had happened.

"Do you believe your parents would still be together if they had known who killed Lindsey?" she asked, because she felt herself that not knowing would have been the most unbearable fact of an unbearable tragedy.

"I believe it's more than likely they would," Griffin answered immediately. "As it was, they had no one to blame except each other. If there had been a villain, someone they could have at least looked at and asked why, then maybe their marriage could have survived her death. Maybe they could have survived it."

"Griffin . . . sometimes there just aren't any answers." Joanna wished there was something else she could say, something more, but in the face of such horrible anguish, words were completely inadequate.

He smiled slightly. "I know that, believe me. Even if they'd found my sister's murderer, we could never have understood why she was killed. And even if I could hand the Wades the name of someone who killed their daughter, the reasons for her death would never make any sense to them either."

"But you'd feel better." She couldn't help wondering, then, if this also helped explain why Griffin was so unyielding in insisting that Caroline's death had been an accident. After all, though an accidental death might leave unanswered questions, they were seldom unbearable ones. Murder, on the other hand, left a host of questions scattered about it, and most of them were unbearable.

"I'd feel useful if I could tell them what happened," Griffin said. "I'd feel I was doing my job. And maybe the Wades could get past the loss of their daughter. Maybe they could even get over it one day."

Joanna nodded, understanding. The problem was, as they had agreed only minutes ago, in the case of Amber's death there wasn't a whole lot he could tell her parents. "It hasn't been forty-eight hours yet," she reminded him. "Just because you can't tell them anything definite today doesn't mean you won't be able to tomorrow."

"Yeah, I keep telling myself that." He looked down at the diary and sighed. "In the meantime, I have to read Amber's diary entries at least from the day they arrived here in town. And I have to talk to Cain."

She didn't envy him either task. "I'll get out of your hair, then," she said, getting up. Since she had decided not to talk to him about what she had learned from Adam Harrison about Caroline, and since he was so obviously preoccupied by the investigation into Amber's death, there was little she could do except to keep pursuing her own exploration of Caroline's life and the days before her death. Until she found something concrete she could hand Griffin, or until she discovered some tangible connection between Caroline and the other two people who had died here, there was nothing she could do to help him.

"Joanna?"

Turning toward the door, she paused and looked at him with a lifted brow.

"You're staying another week, right?"

She nodded. "At least."

"Good."

She left the small office, feeling both pleased and unsettled by that last brief syllable. But her pleasure was short-lived. There were just too many things to worry about. The dream and her reaction to it had only intensified, and the more she found out about Caroline, the less she liked her, and now there were three deaths to be explained rather than the one she had come here to find out about. Joanna had been in town barely a week, and she was more concerned than ever.

Tick. Tick. Tick.

She stood out on the sidewalk in front of the Sheriff's Department and bit her lip, trying to make up her mind. But she couldn't stand still long and finally began making her way toward the main section of downtown stores. She wanted very much to talk to Doctor Peter Becket, but so far hadn't been able to think of a good enough—innocent enough—reason. Griffin had introduced them behind The Inn the morning before as they had stood watching Amber's body being put into an ambulance. But so far, Joanna hadn't encountered the good doctor casually—which was how she seemed to acquire most of her information about Caroline.

She wondered if she could develop something, maybe an upset stomach or some other fairly mild and inexplicable ache just worrisome enough to cause her to visit the clinic. . . .

"Hi, Joanna."

"Oh—hi, Mavis." She nodded at the young clerk from

the drugstore as both of them halted near On the Corner. "Off early today?"

"A couple of hours early, yeah. Um . . . been talking to the sheriff?" Mavis tried to ask the question casually, but only succeeded in alerting Joanna.

"For a few minutes," she confirmed. "He's busy, though."

Mavis nodded quickly. "That poor girl falling over the cliffs Sunday night. I . . . uh . . . I heard it's beginning to look like Mr. Barlow had something to do with it. That he lied to the sheriff about where he was that night."

News really does get around fast in this town. "Where did you hear that?"

"Mrs. Norton came into the drugstore a little while ago—she's my neighbor, you know—and said the sheriff had sent one of the deputies out to her house special just to ask if she'd happened to see Mr. Barlow leave on Sunday night. And she *had*. Just before midnight, when that poor girl was killed. And one of our other customers said he was at The Inn when Sheriff Cavanaugh was questioning Mr. Barlow, and he heard Mr. Barlow say he was at his cottage all night, so . . ."

Deciding that Mrs. Norton must have nearly broken her neck getting into town so quickly to share her tidbit of news, Joanna said, "Whatever Mr. Barlow said, it doesn't necessarily mean he had anything to do with Amber's death, Mavis."

"Oh, but everybody knows how she was chasing after him," Mavis said, her eyes glistening. "And he probably didn't like it. I mean, he *is* involved with Holly Drummond, after all, and you can bet *she* didn't like it. So he probably wasn't at all happy with that poor Amber. I'm sure he didn't *mean* to hurt her, but maybe he just pushed her a little, because she was pestering him, and—"

"It was nearly midnight," Joanna said, making her voice as dispassionate as possible, "and stormy. Which is more likely, Mavis? That anybody would have planned a lovers' tryst out behind The Inn? Or that Amber took advantage

of a break in the storm to go outside and get some air after
being cooped up in the hotel all day and just . . .
slipped?"

"Nobody was likely to see them together on a stormy
night, and they would have wanted to keep it secret because of Holly," Mavis said with a decided nod. "I don't
actually *know* that's true, of course, Joanna, but the sheriff
must have had a good reason to suspect Mr. Barlow. Everybody says so."

It wasn't Joanna's first lesson in the tendency of most
people to believe the worst of others, but she found it every
bit as painful and depressing as she had when the lesson
had sunk in years before. She had been seventeen, still living in Charleston with Aunt Sarah, when an irresponsible
young reporter with an interest in mysterious deaths and a
leaning toward conspiracy theories had turned up in the
neighborhood asking questions about Joanna's parents.

It had gradually emerged that he was convinced that
Alan Flynn had worked secretly as an attorney for organized crime figures, and that the boating "accident" had
actually been a mob hit. Flynn, the reporter claimed, had
been about to turn state's evidence, so he and his wife were
killed.

The story was so absurd that Joanna's strongest emotion had been sheer incredulity. That had been followed by
anger that this stranger had dared to attack her father's
sterling reputation. But then, as she spoke to a neighbor
one day about the matter, she suddenly saw the glistening
eagerness in the woman's eyes, and was shocked to realize
that she wanted to believe the story.

And not only that neighbor, but many of them. People
who had known her parents. Even relatives. They wanted
to believe.

Aunt Sarah hadn't said much about it, but within a few
weeks the house was on the market and they had moved to
Atlanta. And anonymity.

Now Joanna drew a breath and said, "Aunt Sarah always taught me to never assume anything, so I think I'll

wait until the sheriff arrests somebody before I waste too much time speculating about it."

"Is he going to arrest Mr. Barlow?" Mavis asked eagerly.

"I doubt it," Joanna replied dryly, wishing this conversation had never gotten started. "But since I hardly work for the Sheriff's Department . . ."

Obviously disappointed, Mavis said, "I thought maybe the sheriff had talked to you about the case."

Without batting an eye, Joanna said, "Sorry, but I don't know anything. It's been nice talking to you, Mavis."

"Oh, you too, Joanna. Drop into the drugstore sometime, why don't you? I'll buy you a cherry Coke."

"I will, thanks." Joanna watched the younger woman hurry away—not toward her home north of town, but only a few yards down the sidewalk and into another of the town's stores. Obviously, Mavis wanted further discussion on the probable guilt of Cain Barlow. "Damn," Joanna murmured.

"She'll have him tarred and feathered by dark," another feminine voice remarked. "Metaphorically speaking, of course."

Joanna looked around quickly and saw, leaning in the open doorway of On the Corner, the exotic blonde who had mistaken her for Caroline back in Atlanta.

"Hello again," the blonde said. "I'm Lyssa Maitland." A beautiful woman somewhere in her mid-thirties, she was dressed with the same casual elegance Joanna remembered, this time in dark slacks, a silk blouse, and a tapestry vest, with her pale hair worn up. And those very green eyes, Joanna realized suddenly, owed nothing to contact lenses.

"I'm Joanna Flynn."

Lyssa smiled. "Yeah, so they tell me. I must say, I'm glad you're real and not a figment of my overwrought imagination."

Joanna took a couple of steps closer. "It shook me up a bit too. Being mistaken, twice, for a woman I'd never heard of, I mean."

"I imagine it must have." Lyssa studied her with unhidden speculation. "Is that why you decided to come to Cliffside? To find out just who you'd been mistaken for?"

Opting for a brief explanation, Joanna replied, "I'm a research librarian. Shortly after you and Dylan mistook me for Caroline, I was researching and saw her picture in a Portland newspaper. Then I found her obituary. I had some vacation time coming, so I decided to spend it here."

A coincidence that she'd "found" Caroline after having been twice mistaken for her—but not one beyond belief, given her job. And it wasn't a lie, after all; it just wasn't all the truth.

Lyssa apparently accepted the coincidence, because she nodded slowly. "I see. So you're taking sort of a busman's holiday. Researching Caroline."

"Informally, I suppose." Joanna shrugged.

"I work for Scott, you know."

There was no use pretending disinterest to this woman, Joanna decided. "So I was told. Did you know Caroline well?"

"I doubt if anyone knew Caroline well. Except for Scott, of course."

"She lived here all her life," Joanna said. "How could the people around her not know her well?"

Lyssa smiled slightly. "If you ask me, I think she didn't want to be known. It appealed to her vanity to believe that she was an enigma to people. Caroline didn't like her life here, in case nobody's told you that."

"She seemed to keep herself busy," Joanna remarked neutrally.

"Oh, sure. She served on committees and worked tirelessly for the good of the town and generally carved out a place for herself as Cliffside's leading lady."

Joanna couldn't help wondering if it was jealousy she heard in the older woman's voice. "Yet she didn't like her life here?"

"Not much. She couldn't wait to get out of here when she finished high school at seventeen. Went to San Francisco to go to college and didn't last six months. Found herself a very small guppy in a real big pond where being Miss Caroline Douglas didn't mean a whole lot. So she came back home. She'd met Scott there at some society do, though, and he followed her back here."

"She was the only reason he moved here?" *So that was how they met. And the first San Francisco connection?*

Lyssa nodded. "All his family's businesses were in San Francisco, and they pitched a fit when he sold his interest and moved up here. But he didn't care. He bought the old lumber mill and had it turning a profit within six months when it had been in the red for years. Remodeled some old stores here in town and brought Dylan and me up from San Francisco; this was Dylan's hometown and he was glad to come home; I was just eager to be put in charge of a promising business." Lyssa shrugged. "In the meantime, Scott was courting Caroline. Offered her everything, just like a prince in some Cinderella story. As soon as she turned eighteen, she accepted him."

Lyssa, Dylan—more people from San Francisco. It's beginning to look like Butler's being from there as well could hardly mean anything important.

Joanna hesitated, then said frankly, "I heard the marriage wasn't all that happy. So what happened to the glass slipper?"

"I guess it broke." Lyssa shrugged again. "Or maybe it never really fit Caroline after all. She wasn't happy. Didn't like living in a small town but didn't want to give up what she had here. She could have made a much bigger splash in San Francisco as Scott's wife, but I think that bigger pond scared her. Scott was willing to stay here, so they did."

"You didn't like her."

Lyssa appeared thoughtful. "Well, most women didn't. She could be very charming, and there was something about her, a kind of vulnerability, that seemed to appeal to most men, but she didn't waste her energy being anything but polite to other women. That's why you've probably found that most of the clerks and other people here in town who knew her just to speak to her thought she was sweet, or shy—or just real nice. But anyone who knew her better than that most likely has mixed feelings about her."

Joanna hesitated, then said, "Do you think she might have been upset about anything in the last week or so before she was killed?"

"Not that I noticed. Why?" Lyssa's green eyes narrowed. "What are you getting at? That the accident was something else?"

Joanna shook her head. "I heard she seemed uneasy or jumpy before she was killed, and I was just wondering if that was why she lost control of her car that day."

"I guess we'll never know that."

"Yeah, I guess." Joanna felt uncomfortable, but summoned a smile. "Well, it was nice meeting you, Lyssa."

"You too, Joanna."

Joanna turned away from the other woman and continued along the sidewalk toward the far end of Main Street where she had parked her car. She paused on the corner and looked back to find Lyssa still in the doorway watching her, and something about her complete lack of expression made Joanna feel a sudden chill. She turned the corner quickly.

Once out of Lyssa's sight, she paused again, trying to think past her churning uneasiness. She felt as if things were speeding up, as if what had been set in motion months before was building toward a climax. *Tick. Tick. Tick.*

But, dammit, she still didn't know *what* had been set in motion, what it was all about. She didn't even have a clue. All she had was her certainty that if she could only figure out why Caroline had died, she'd understand the rest.

With or without a medical excuse, she needed to talk to Doctor Peter Becket.

✧   ✧   ✧

In his rather cluttered office in the clinic, Doctor Becket welcomed Joanna a bit abruptly, his perpetually tired blue eyes frowning a bit. "Marion said you wanted to talk to me," he said, referring to his receptionist. "Is something wrong, Joanna? Medically, I mean."

She shook her head, sitting down where he indicated in a brown leather chair in front of his desk. "No, I'm fine."

He folded his tall length into the chair behind the desk. "I see. My turn to answer questions about Caroline?"

His voice was mild, but Joanna nonetheless felt awkward and uneasy beneath his steady gaze. "Not if you mind," she offered finally. "It's just that somebody told me you had known her as well as anyone had, and I thought you might be able to tell me something helpful."

"Helpful? In what way?"

Joanna had the idea that Becket was being deliberately obtuse, and it put her on guard. With a slight shrug, she said, "I'm trying to understand her. Who she was, what she was like. I can't really explain why, it's just something I feel I have to do."

"I see," he repeated.

"So, if there's anything you can tell me, I'd really appreciate it."

"I don't think there is anything, Joanna," he said, matter-of-fact. "Oh, I can tell you she was allergic to ragweed and pollen. I can tell you she tended to have one bad cold each year and never got the flu. I can tell you she had a difficult pregnancy but an easy delivery. Does any of that help?"

"Every snippet of information helps, if I feel I understand her better because of it," she told him. "Some people have told me she was shy. Was she?"

"Reserved, I suppose."

"Even with you?"

He shrugged. "I was her doctor, but not her confidant."

Joanna was certain now that the doctor intended to keep whatever intimate and nonmedical knowledge he might have of Caroline to himself, and she was reluctant to push him. Instead, she asked, "Did you talk to her during the week or so before she was killed?"

Becket picked up a pen from his desk and turned it between his long fingers, glancing down at it. "No."

He was lying, and he wasn't very good at it. "Then you wouldn't know if she was upset about anything just before she died," Joanna said.

"No, I wouldn't know about that." He smiled pleasantly. "Sorry I can't be more help, Joanna."

"That's all right." She returned the smile. "Snippets. I get them here and there; most everybody has had something to say about Caroline. The pieces are coming together."

"And what's the picture?" he asked.

"If I had to title it," Joanna said, "I'd call it 'A Complicated Woman.' The usual labels don't seem to fit her very well."

"Usual labels?"

"Yeah. Rich man's wife. Small-town matron. Pillar of her community. Devoted mother. They all fit—but not well."

"Do labels fit any of us well?"

"I suppose not." Joanna felt frustrated once again, but she silently conceded defeat, at least for the moment. She got up. "Thanks for taking the time to talk to me, Doctor."

He rose as well, his pleasant smile not quite reaching his eyes. "It's just Doc, Joanna; I haven't answered to anything else in years. And I'm sorry I couldn't be more help to you."

She lifted a hand in acknowledgment, then left the small office and made her way back down the hall to the receptionist's desk. There were no patients waiting, and Marion was taking the opportunity of a slow afternoon to enter data into the clinic's computer system. She stopped her work and looked up, however, when Joanna reached the desk.

"Any luck?" She was a brisk middle-aged woman with dark hair and very sharp eyes, and practically wore a sign that said she didn't suffer fools gladly.

By now, Joanna simply assumed that everyone knew she

was asking about Caroline; it seemed reasonable, given the gossips of Cliffside—and her experience so far. So she merely shrugged. "Not really."

"I suppose he quoted you chapter and verse of a doctor's responsibility to keep his patient's business to himself?"

"I guess I didn't push hard enough to get that," Joanna confessed. "He just basically said he didn't know anything about Caroline that would be helpful to me."

Marion nodded, unsurprised. "To call him discreet is to disparage the word."

Joanna wasn't about to ask this woman to gossip about whether Becket had seen Caroline outside this office, so she merely said, "Caroline came in here because of her allergies, I hear. Did you know her?"

"To see her, to speak politely to her—yes. But Caroline McKenna didn't have much time for other women."

"I've heard that," Joanna murmured. "Didn't she have any female friends?"

"Not that I know of."

"Did you see her during the week or so before she died?" Joanna asked.

"As a matter of fact," Marion said, "she came in here late one afternoon about two days before she was killed. Wanted to see Doc."

Joanna tried not to show a reaction to that information. "And did she see him?"

"Well, I was about to send her in when we got a call about one of the boys on the high school baseball team hurting his leg sliding into second. Doc grabbed his bag and started out, and when Caroline tried to speak to him, he brushed her off." Marion frowned slightly. "Come to think of it, she followed him out to the parking lot, still trying to talk to him."

Joanna thought of Becket lying about having seen Caroline and wondered if it was because he knew something he hadn't told about her death. Maybe; he'd done the postmortem, after all. Then again, maybe he lied simply because he was yet another man haunted by guilt because Caroline had come to him for help in the last days of her life and he had turned away from her.

"Did she seem upset?" Joanna asked the receptionist.

Marion pursed her lips. "A bit agitated, let's say."

"But you have no idea why?"

"None."

Joanna nodded. "Okay, thanks, Marion."

"Helpful?"

"God knows. But more pieces for the puzzle anyway." Joanna glanced back down the hall toward Becket's office and could have sworn she caught a glimpse of movement, as if, standing in the doorway, he had drawn quickly back out of sight when she had turned her head.

How much had he heard?

"Good luck with the puzzle," Marion said, already turning back to her work.

"Thanks. See you." Joanna left the clinic and walked back toward Main Street to get her car. It was beginning to get dark and there was a chill in the air. Bits of information—"snippets"—and speculation were going round and round in her head, making no sense to her at all. What she needed to do was go back to The Inn, have supper and a long, hot bath, and try to think logically about all she had learned today.

When she reached Main Street, Joanna paused, looking around at a town that seemed so peaceful on this late afternoon in October. Griffin's Blazer was parked at the Sheriff's Department, so presumably he was still in his office. Mrs. Chandler was locking up the library. Lyssa and Dylan stood in front of City Hall talking, both carrying briefcases, and as Joanna watched, they went their separate ways to their cars. Most of the stores in town were still open and would remain so until six or seven, according to individual habit. There were a few people on the sidewalks, going in or coming out of stores, no one in a hurry about it.

Just a peaceful little town. Except that three people had

died violently here since spring. Except that too many of the town's citizens had gazed at Joanna through shuttered eyes, because they either disliked strangers, disliked her questions, or had something to hide.

Just a peaceful little town. *Except that something was wrong here.*

With a sigh, she tried to shrug off the uneasiness that wouldn't leave her alone. Nothing was making much sense to her right now; it was time to call a halt for the day.

Joanna needed to pick up a few things before returning to the hotel, so she walked to the drugstore. In the ten or fifteen minutes she was in the store, she spoke casually to several people, and by the time she came out she felt doubtful about Cain Barlow's future standing in this town. Virtually everyone, it seemed, felt sure that he'd had something to do with Amber's death, and Joanna was convinced that unless Griffin was able to prove conclusively that someone else had been responsible, or that her death had been a tragic accident, then suspicion would hang over Cain's head like a black cloud.

Joanna didn't want to believe Cain had killed that girl, even by accident, but she didn't know if there was anything she could do about the question—except to keep on as she had been, asking questions and trying to understand Caroline.

When she left the drugstore, Joanna walked to her car, which she'd left parked at the end of town farthest from The Inn. She fished in the front pocket of her jeans for the keys, then got in and started the car, automatically fastening her seatbelt even though the drive to her hotel would be fairly brief. Since the car was parked on a slight incline, she didn't have to touch the accelerator to back out onto Main Street; she just put the car in reverse and kept her foot on the brake.

Even before her accident, Joanna had been a careful driver; these days, she was even more careful. It wasn't her habit to drive fast under any circumstances, and she never floored the accelerator. But when she put the rental car into drive and pressed lightly on the accelerator, it went all the way to the floor.

And stuck.

In those first seconds, Joanna tried to get the pedal unstuck by punching at it with her foot, at the same time trying to watch for pedestrians and other cars as the rental car picked up speed through downtown Cliffside. Everything was passing in a blur, her ears were filled with the roar of the laboring engine, and all Joanna could think of was what would happen if she made it past The Inn and Scott McKenna's property south of town.

She had seen the maps. Just as it did north of town, the coast highway ran right along the edge of the cliffs farther south, with only a guardrail to stop a car from going over. It hadn't stopped Caroline's car.

It wouldn't stop this one, either.

Joanna didn't dare take her eyes off the road even long enough to check the speedometer, but she knew she had to be going over fifty when she passed the park at the south end of town.

She'd tried the brake, but other than producing a godawful noise it didn't seem to slow the car, and though she tried to shift down into neutral, the gearshift refused to budge. She wasn't sure, but had the vague idea that if she tried to turn off the ignition while the car was in gear and moving at such speed, it would be like hitting a wall. And despite her seatbelt and the car's airbag, that was something she didn't want to chance except as a last resort.

She passed the turnoff to The Inn just as she heard a siren; either Griffin or one of his deputies was behind her and catching up rapidly. Joanna didn't spare a glance into the rearview mirror, because the coast highway was beginning to wind as it continued past the McKenna property, and it required all her attention just to keep the car on the road.

Then, ahead and on the left side of the highway, she saw a pasture dotted with numerous old-fashioned haystacks. Joanna didn't know if the hay would provide enough resistance to even slow the car, but she did know that her chances were better in that pasture than they would be on the coast road.

The barbwire fence provided little resistance, one post sheering off and the strands of wire snapping as her car hurtled off the road and into the pasture. Joanna felt the car begin to slide as it hit ground still saturated from the weekend rains, and she fought the steering wheel in the desperate attempt to guide it toward the first of the haystacks.

The car hit the small mountain of hay, shuddered, and barely slowed as it plowed through. She continued to fight the steering wheel, aiming for the next haystack. But the car fishtailed, hitting the hay broadside and then going into a spin. The rear end of the car grazed another haystack, the spinning slowed, and then the fourth haystack, finally, provided enough resistance.

The car hit it, again broadside, and shuddered violently. The engine screamed, then died abruptly as the car rocked to a stop. Immediately, hay covered the windshield and windows, and Joanna found herself in the dark.

With exquisite precision, she reached for the key and turned off the ignition. Then she folded her hands in her lap and just sat there listening to her heart pound against her ribs and looking down at the steering wheel, where the airbag remained snugly out of sight.

She was dimly aware of sounds, and then light suddenly as the hay was pushed away from the driver's side of the car. Her door was wrenched open.

"Joanna? Are you all right?"

Griffin's voice was harsh, and the face she looked up into as grim as she'd ever seen it. She wanted to reassure him, to say she was fine, shaken but not hurt at all. But what came out of her mouth, calmly, was what was echoing in her mind.

"That's the third time."

❖   ❖   ❖

"I'm all right, I told you that." Joanna managed a smile as Becket frowned at her. "Really."

"So it seems," he said, laying aside the stethoscope but still frowning a little. "But you've just been through a hell of a shock, Joanna. When the adrenaline wears off, you're going to feel it. I'd rather keep you here in the clinic overnight, just for observation."

"No, thanks."

"Look, at the very least, you're going to be sore as hell by morning, after the way that car jerked you around. If you stay here, we'll at least be able to make you more comfortable."

Joanna shook her head. "No offense, Doc, but I hate hospital beds. I'll be fine."

Becket looked toward the door of the examining room. "Griff, will you try to talk some sense into her, please?"

He hadn't said a word during the entire examination—and hardly a word before that—but now Griffin said very quietly, "He's right, Joanna. You should let them keep an eye on you tonight."

Joanna didn't want to appear obstinate, but no way was she going to spend the night in the clinic, not when she felt perfectly all right. It occurred to her that her calm was a touch unreal, and that she would undoubtedly feel shaky once it wore off, but if she was going to fall apart, she preferred to do so alone rather than under observation.

She looked at Becket and said, "Thanks, but I'd rather go back to the hotel. If I have any problems, I'll call you. Good enough?"

"I guess it'll have to be." He smiled wryly. "But take my advice, at least. You're going to be shaky sometime in the next hour or so. If you eat something hot, it'll help. So will soaking in a hot bath for a while. And then take things easy. Okay?"

"That I'll do."

"Good." He touched her shoulder lightly, then turned away from her and headed for the door. "How's her car, Griff?"

"Totaled," Griffin answered. "And Bill Cook's pasture is in pretty bad shape."

Becket shook his head slightly, but left the room without saying anything else.

Joanna slid down off the examining table. "If my insurance doesn't cover it, I'll pay the damages," she said, peculiarly anxious that Griffin know that.

"Don't be an idiot. Nobody gives a damn about the pasture." His voice was a little rough.

"It seemed my only choice," she said, still anxious. "The pasture or the cliffs. I really didn't want to chance the cliffs."

Griffin pushed himself away from the doorjamb and came into the small room. His face was hard, his dark eyes very intent. When he reached Joanna, he took his hands out of the pockets of his jacket and put them on her shoulders. Without a word, he bent his head and kissed her.

It took Joanna so much by surprise that she didn't get the chance to brace herself—not that it would have helped, probably. The warm, hard touch of his mouth felt instantly right to her, necessary in some way she couldn't explain to herself but could only feel. As if she'd been looking for something desperately important for a long, long time, and had found it unexpectedly when she had stopped looking for it.

His hands left her shoulders to cradle her head, his thumbs stroking across her cheekbones, and she felt herself lean into him with a need beyond reason. Her body responded like some delicate musical instrument to the hand it knew best, to the touch that could coax from it only the purest notes. As if she had been designed, made, only for him. And the certainty of that was something she felt as strongly as the compulsion that had brought her here to Cliffside.

Griffin seemed to feel it as well. There was nothing tentative about his kiss, nothing uncertain, nothing preliminary; it was every bit as unequivocal as the sexual act itself. Possession, pure and simple. And Joanna realized that if there had ever been a question about whether this would happen, there wasn't one now.

He finally ended the kiss, a faint, hoarse sound escaping him when his lips reluctantly left hers. Instead of letting her go, he wrapped both arms around her and just held her. She felt his heart thudding hard and fast, wondered if her own had leaped into that same wild rhythm, and slid her arms around his lean waist. It felt good to be held that way, just simply *good*, and she wasn't tempted to protest or pull away.

"Oh—excuse me. I just wanted to give Joanna my beeper number in case she needs me tonight."

"You have rotten timing, Doc," Griffin said calmly. He kept an arm around Joanna's shoulders as he turned toward the door.

Never easily embarrassed herself, Joanna accepted the card Becket held out to her with murmured thanks. She still had an arm around Griffin's waist and was vaguely surprised at herself for not letting go of him.

"I *am* sorry," Becket repeated, looking at Griffin with a slight smile.

"Forget it." Griffin guided Joanna out the door and down the hall, with Becket following behind them as far as the receptionist's desk.

"I'll have that tox screen for you tomorrow," he reminded Griffin. "It'll be negative, I bet, but at least we'll know for sure."

"Okay, thanks, Doc."

They left the clinic and walked to where Griffin had left his Blazer parked near the doors. It had gotten dark, but the lot was well lit and they were able to see their way clearly. Griffin opened the passenger door for Joanna, and she climbed in. He was about to shut the door when they saw a Sheriff's Department car pull into the lot.

"I'll be right back," he told Joanna, before shutting the door and going to talk to his deputy.

In less than five minutes, he was back, getting into the

driver's side and starting the Blazer's engine. "You're staying at my place tonight," he said.

She was a little startled, both by what was clearly a command and by the harsh tone of his voice, but all she said was, "I'll be fine at the hotel."

Griffin put the Blazer in gear, but kept his foot on the brake, half turning in the seat to look at her. "Doc said you needed somebody to keep an eye on you tonight, and that somebody is going to be me."

"Griffin—"

"Joanna, listen to me." His voice was low now, but still rough. "The accelerator on your car didn't *just* stick, and the airbag didn't *just* fail to deploy. The accelerator was jammed and the entire electrical system was screwed up. Do you understand? It was tampered with. Joanna, somebody tried to kill you."

ELEVEN

✧ ✧ ✧

HE OWNED ONE of the cottages that were spaced along the cliffs between The Inn and the northern end of town. Since it was dark when they arrived, Joanna couldn't get a good idea of how the place looked, and had to assume it was like the others she had seen—relatively small but very well built and attractive, and situated very close to the edge of the cliffs.

She listened to the surf pounding the rocks while he unlocked the door, then followed him inside the cottage. He turned on several lights immediately, and she looked around with interest. They had come in through the kitchen, which, along with the dining area and living room, made up one large and airy space. The kitchen was neat and cheery with its bright color scheme; the small glass-topped dining table boasted woven place mats also in vivid colors; and the living room furniture was the big, over-stuffed kind most men would find comfortable, with neutral colors and plenty of pillows scattered around.

Doors led off each side of the dining area, presumably to bedrooms and bathrooms. There was a rock fireplace in one corner of the living room, and the remainder of that wall—the sea wall, so to speak—consisted of big glass windows and an atrium door opening out onto what Joanna assumed was a deck or patio. The windows were veiled at the moment by draperies made up of some lightweight material in a neutral sand color. In the corner opposite the fireplace was a compact entertainment center with TV and stereo.

Joanna thought the place had probably been professionally decorated at some point in its past, but time had worn down the sharp edges of exactitude and had left pleasantness and comfort behind.

"Nice," she said to Griffin.

He sent her a fleeting smile as he hung his jacket on a rack by the door, but the dark eyes were still grim and Joanna knew he was still thinking about the knowledge that someone had tampered with her car. She was a bit numb herself, unwilling to think very much about that, at least for now.

Griffin left the greatroom, and a minute or so later she heard water running in a bathtub. He came back to her, and before she could say anything, he said, "I know you think you're fine, but Doc was right about the shock *and* about how sore you'll probably be in the morning. Even if you don't agree with either of us, humor us, okay?"

She managed a smile. "Okay."

He nodded, matter-of-fact. "I've put a pair of pajamas in the bathroom for you; they'll swallow you whole, but the pants have a drawstring waist, so you should be able to manage. And while you soak the kinks out, I'll see what I can do in the kitchen. How do you feel about omelettes?"

"I love them," she said. "But you don't have to—"

Griffin turned her toward the doorway leading to the bathroom and gave her a little push. "Go. And take your time."

Joanna went. She found herself in a short hallway, with

a bathroom on one side and a bedroom on the other. Griffin's bedroom, she decided after a brief glance into it. Not only because he'd apparently gotten the pajamas there, but also because the lamplit room just looked like him somehow. Neat and uncluttered, with solid dark oak furniture and a quilt on the big bed instead of a bedspread.

She went into the bathroom, which was also neat, and found that the decorator had used a huge, old-fashioned claw-footed tub to make the most of space in the small room. The tub was filling with hot water and it looked wonderful.

Joanna closed the door and began undressing even before she noticed the dark blue flannel pajamas folded on the vanity. They looked warm and comfortable but weren't exactly sexy, and given her druthers, she would certainly have picked something else—especially after that kiss at the clinic. But she hadn't even thought to suggest that they make a brief side trip to The Inn so that she could pick up a few of her things, and she doubted it would do much good to suggest it now.

Shrugging it off, she finished undressing and climbed cautiously into the big tub. The water was perfect, hot without being too hot, and she felt muscles she hadn't even realized were tense relax. She turned off the faucets and leaned back, resting the nape of her neck against the rim of the tub.

She thought she was fine. She thought she'd handled the shocks of the wreck and the knowledge that someone had tried to kill her very well. But as her body relaxed in the hot water, she felt wetness on her face and realized that she was crying. She didn't sob out loud, but she couldn't seem to stem the flow of tears. They streamed down her cheeks as if a dam had burst inside her.

Fine? She wasn't fine at all. She was shaken and frightened and feeling overwhelmed. Someone had tried to kill her? But why? Because she was asking questions about Caroline? Because she had somehow gotten too close to somebody's secret?

She lay there with her eyes closed, not even trying to stop the tears now and seeing face after face in her mind's eye. Who? Who was so intent on hiding their secret that murder was acceptable to them? She had met so many people since coming here, most of whom had known Caroline; how could she even begin to guess which one of those seemingly ordinary people might have a secret worth killing for?

She didn't know how much time had passed when a soft knock at the bathroom door and Griffin's voice roused her.

"Joanna? Coffee's hot, and supper will be ready in about ten minutes."

She cleared her throat. "Okay."

There was a brief silence, and then he said, "Are you all right?"

She looked at the bathroom door, blurred because of the tears still trickling from her eyes, and had to fight an impulse to tell him the truth. "I'm fine," she said, holding her voice steadier this time. "I'll be out in a few minutes."

"Okay." He didn't sound as if he really believed her, but she heard him move back down the hall toward the greatroom.

Joanna wet a washcloth with cold water and held it against her eyes, repeating the action several times until her eyes felt less puffy and the tears had finally stopped. She was very much afraid it was only a lull, because she felt horribly precarious, but there was little she could do about it.

She got out of the tub and let the water drain while she was drying off, then got into the dark blue pajamas. Griffin had been right; they swallowed her whole. But she managed to tighten the drawstring waist of the pants enough to keep them from falling off her, and rolled up the sleeves of the shirt several times so that the cuffs didn't dangle past her fingertips.

He had also provided a thick pair of socks, and Joanna couldn't help but smile as she put them on. Warm, yes, like the pajamas—and just about as sexy.

She borrowed his comb to straighten her hair a bit, then left her clothes folded on the wicker hamper and went out into the greatroom.

He had built a fire in the fireplace, and the big room smelled pleasantly of wood smoke and cooking. The table was already set. He was in the kitchen, efficiently beating eggs in a bowl, and paused to look at her intently as she came in.

"Feeling better?"

Joanna nodded, not quite trusting her voice. He sounded gentle, more so than she'd ever heard him, and for some reason it made her throat hurt.

He looked at her a moment longer, then nodded toward the counter beside the sink, where a coffeemaker sat. "Help yourself."

She nodded again and went to pour herself coffee.

Griffin watched her as the omelette began cooking. It didn't take any special perception to see that her hands were unsteady, or that her big golden eyes were wet, the lids pink and a bit swollen. She'd been unnaturally calm since the wreck and had accepted the news that someone had tried to kill her with no more than a blink and a somewhat dazed nod, so Griffin had fully expected her to feel the shock sooner or later.

What he hadn't expected was that he would feel this way when he looked at her, seemingly so fragile in the too-big pajamas, vulnerable in a way he guessed was completely alien to her. He was in danger of forgetting about everything but the overwhelming need to feel her against him, warm and real and alive. It was the way he had felt in the clinic, when holding her in his arms had been more important, more vital to him, than anything else.

She sipped the coffee, then turned to look at him. With a slight nod toward the stove, she said, "It smells good."

The omelette did smell good, but Griffin was afraid he'd burn it if he kept staring at her. With an effort, he paid attention to his cooking. "It'll be ready in just a minute.

Why don't you sit down at the table?" His voice sounded normal, he thought.

She accepted the suggestion and sat there with both hands wrapped around her coffee cup, staring down at it. She was too silent, he thought, too still. Sometime in the past few minutes, it had hit her that someone had just tried to kill her, and she was struggling to face that knowledge. He wanted to say something—anything—to banish the haunted shadows from her eyes, to make them smile as they often did, but instinct told him to let her get to the subject of the attempt on her life in her own time and her own way.

When he put a plate in front of her, she began to eat automatically. And it must have been the manners drummed into her by the redoubtable Aunt Sarah, he thought with a flicker of amusement, that enabled her to compliment him in a polite voice on his cooking, because it was fairly obvious she was eating because he wanted her to and that she didn't notice or care how it tasted. He thanked her gravely, however, satisfied that she was eating, and then filled the silence with casual talk she didn't have to respond to about unimportant things.

When they were finished, Griffin sent her into the living room with a fresh cup of coffee despite her—again, automatic—protests, and cleared up in the kitchen himself. He wanted to give her a little time, to not crowd her, because he felt it was very important that she not see him as a cop asking questions when they finally did talk about this, but as a man genuinely concerned about her.

Finished in the kitchen, he turned off the light and carried his own coffee into the living room, which was lit only by the fire and a single lamp at Joanna's end of the sofa. She was sort of curled up, her feet tucked under a pillow beside her, and she looked very withdrawn as she gazed into the fire. But when Griffin sat down about a foot away and set his cup on the coffee table beside hers, she spoke in a measured, careful voice.

"When you warned me not to ask questions about Caroline, were you afraid this would happen?"

"No." He kept his voice quiet. "I didn't believe there was anything in her life—or her death—worth a murder attempt."

Joanna turned her head and looked at him, the firelight igniting golden sparks in her darkened eyes. "And now?"

He drew a breath. "And now, I can't think of a single damned reason why anyone would want to kill you—except that you've been asking questions about Caroline and her death. You haven't made enemies here, Joanna, not as far as I can see. The only thing that makes any sense is that there's some information connected to Caroline that somebody doesn't want you to find. And they're willing to do anything to stop you."

"I haven't found out anything," she said. "Not anything anyone would want to keep me from finding out, I mean. Innocuous things, things that wouldn't have mattered to anyone but her. Things that wouldn't have damaged anyone but her, even in a small town. Except . . . I did find out that Caroline . . . had affairs."

"Was that what you weren't willing to tell me earlier today?"

Joanna nodded. "I talked to somebody. He's . . . still haunted by her, even though their affair ended more than a year ago. He had some pretty brutal things to say about her, but I think he's still in love with her. And he said there were others, at least one other he was certain about because the man confided in him. He wouldn't give me a name, but I think I know who the other man was." She shook her head. "But why would either one of them have gone after me? The first man didn't care who knew about the affair, and the second . . . well, he never admitted to knowing Caroline well, but I can't believe he'd try to hurt me, not because I might have suspected he'd had an affair with her."

Griffin didn't interrupt, realizing that all this was pouring out of her because she couldn't hold it in, because it had gone around and around in her mind since the wreck and she needed to put it into words.

"Caroline saw them both the last week of her life, that was the only thing I fixed on, the only thing that seemed odd. She went to each one of them, maybe needing to talk, maybe needing their help. But neither one gave her the chance to tell them anything. One was too mad at her, the other one in too much of a hurry. And you were too busy."

It wasn't an accusation, just a simple statement of fact, but Griffin felt defensive all the same. "If I'd known she was in trouble—"

Joanna nodded gravely. "I know you would have helped her. The other two men would have, too, I think. She seemed to have had a powerful hold over some of the men in her life."

Again, there was no accusation in her quiet voice, but Griffin felt compelled to say, "I was not her lover, Joanna."

Her gaze searched his face for a moment, but he couldn't tell what she was looking for. Or if she found it. "But there was something there, wasn't there? A reason why she turned to you when she needed help?"

"Maybe," he said. "Once, a long time ago, maybe there was something. Or maybe she sent me that note because I'm the sheriff, the logical person to turn to if she needed help."

Joanna nodded. "I've thought of that, of course. As the sheriff, you might have been her last resort, after those other men turned away. If her problem was something dangerous or illegal, she must have been awfully scared to send you that note."

Griffin shook his head. "Her last resort? She had to know I'd have done my best to protect her if she knew something that could have driven someone to murder. That is what we're talking about, isn't it?"

Joanna returned her gaze to the fire. "That's what we're talking about. Caroline was involved in something, or found out something dangerous, that's what I think. She was nervous at least, probably scared, the last week or so of her life. She didn't come to you right away. To me, that means either that she was involved so deeply in whatever it was that she feared arrest or scandal, or feared that the knowledge she had could have hurt someone she cared about, or that she couldn't make up her mind what to do because *she* had been hurt, betrayed by someone she loved. I also think she was having an affair when she died, or shortly before, so it's possible her lover knows something."

"You're supposing a lot," he reminded her. "There's no proof any of that is true."

"I know. But what else can I do? I'm trying to put a puzzle together, piece by piece. And somebody doesn't want me to see the finished picture. Somebody tried to kill me today."

"And tried to kill you Sunday night."

She turned her head again, quickly, her eyes once more reflecting the firelight in bright sparks. Softly, she said, "You mean Amber died because somebody thought she was me?"

"I wish I could say no." Griffin wanted to touch her, but held himself still. "But nothing else makes sense, Joanna. Aside from the fact that I've known Cain a long time and simply can't make myself believe he could do that just because the girl had a crush on him, today someone tampered with your car. And as soon as that happened, I knew all this had to be connected somehow, just the way you said from the beginning. So what could Amber's connection be? Nothing—except that she looked like you from behind."

"But Amber was killed in the middle of a stormy night. Surely nobody would have just waited outside the hotel on the chance I'd come out?"

"No, I doubt it. But somebody could have been watching from inside the hotel and seen Amber leave. A guest or just somebody who happened to be there that night; there had been several poker games going on, I believe, and quite a few people from the town were there. Or . . . it could have been Cain."

"But you just said—"

"I said I couldn't believe he'd kill Amber because she had a crush on him, not that I believed he was incapable of killing. For a good enough reason, he could have done it. And that might explain why he left that night, to give himself an alibi. Whether or not he knew after he'd pushed her that it was Amber, he couldn't have known we'd find a diary that would offer evidence of the time she left the hotel."

"Then why didn't he give you that alibi when you questioned him? Why did he say he was alone at the cottage all night?"

"If I had an alibi for a murder," Griffin said, "I might think it was smart to hold it in reserve, at least unless and until I became a prime suspect. Especially if, say, I'd spent the night with another woman. He could always say he didn't want to admit that because it would have hurt Holly—and she was sitting right there when I talked to him. Hell, it's even believable. Maybe that's his game."

"Amber sent him a note," Joanna objected. "If he expected anyone outside the hotel, it must have been her."

"If he got the note."

"You're saying he didn't get it?"

Griffin nodded. "On a hunch, I sent one of my deputies out to look around his cottage this afternoon just after you left my office. I wanted to check before I asked Cain about the note. My deputy found Amber's note in an envelope underneath a flowerpot out on his deck. From the condition of it, it was pretty obvious it hadn't been moved since it was left there, and it certainly hadn't been opened."

After a moment, Joanna asked, "Was Cain at the hotel Sunday night? I didn't see him."

"He had dinner with Holly, I know that much. He could have hung around the hotel, especially since it was storming off and on. If he caught a glimpse of Amber leaving the hotel, he could have thought she was you. Followed her out to the edge of the cliffs—and pushed her over before he got a good look at her."

"Now you're supposing," Joanna said.

"Yeah, I know." Griffin swore under his breath. "I've got to talk to him. I've got to make him talk to me, make him tell me where he went Sunday night. And I have to know if he was having an affair with Caroline when she was killed. If he was, he has to know *something*, even if only her state of mind in the days before she died."

"Hasn't he been involved with Holly since before then?"

Griffin nodded. "A point in his favor, since I don't know of many men stupid enough to juggle two women in a small town."

"Cain isn't stupid."

"No. But he's my best suspect right now, Joanna. If he can explain where he went Sunday night, and convince me he wasn't having an affair with Caroline and knew nothing about why she was upset, then I'll knock him off my list for the time being."

"Who else is on your list?" Before he could answer, she said, "Scott, I guess."

"If Amber was killed because somebody mistook her for you—and I believe that's true—and we assume it's somehow connected to Caroline and her death, then he has to be a suspect. I have no proof he was at home like he claimed when Caroline was killed, and he says he was home alone Sunday night with, again, no witnesses to verify. He's another one capable of killing with a good enough reason."

"What would be a good enough reason? It couldn't be just that he found out Caroline was having an affair. He might have chased her down the coast highway because of that, but why try to kill me?" She shook her head. "There's a secret here somewhere, one somebody's willing to do anything to protect. I think if we can just find out why Caroline was afraid, all the rest will fall into place."

"That ought to be a snap," he said. "Know any good mediums?"

Joanna turned her head back toward the fire, a brief smile appearing on her lips. "I have some friends into that stuff. Me, the only medium I know is what's in the middle."

Griffin watched her profile as she fell silent. It was better for her when she was talking, he thought. When she could focus her agile mind on the intellectual puzzle of what was going on in Cliffside. It was the best way, the way most cops operated, and it usually succeeded in lending a bit of detachment when it was desperately needed. But they had talked it through now, at least as far as they could for the moment.

Then, remembering, he said, "When I opened your car door today, you said this was the third time. What did you mean?"

"The third time I've cheated death," she said softly. "But if poor Amber died in my place, I guess it was the fourth time." She looked at him, and that little smile wavered on her lips again. "How many more chances do you think I have left?"

This time, Griffin didn't fight the urge to touch her. He slid across the space separating them and surrounded her face with his hands. Her lips were warm and trembled under his, and he felt the pulse in her neck throbbing rapidly. She made a little sound, then leaned into him, fumbling to push the pillow between them out of the way and turning fully toward him, lifting her hands to touch his chest.

He knew she was vulnerable tonight, knew she might willingly accept something else when it was simple comforting she needed, but when her mouth opened beneath his and her tongue glided along the inner surface of his lips with a featherlight and wildly arousing touch, all he could think of was how much he needed her.

"Joanna . . ." He could barely force himself to lift his mouth off hers long enough to whisper her name, but he needed that, too, needed to say her name, and then he was kissing her hungrily again. One of his hands slipped around to tangle in her silky hair, and the other moved to her back, drawing her closer.

She made another of those throaty, sensuous sounds,

and her back arched beneath his touch. Her instant and total response wrenched a groan from him, yet at the same time brought him at least partly to his senses. He managed to draw back far enough to look at her, his hands moving once more to surround her face.

"Doc isn't the only one with rotten timing," he said huskily. "Joanna, you've had a hell of a day. I can't take advantage of that."

Her eyes seemed huge, still gleaming with moisture, still darkened, but the smile that wavered on her lips was oddly amused. "Thank you," she murmured. "But Griffin, I knew days ago this would happen. Didn't you?"

His thumbs rubbed across her cheekbones rhythmically. "Yes," he admitted. "Still—"

She didn't let him finish, but simply leaned into him once more and pressed her lips to his. Against his mouth, her breath warm, she whispered, "I want you. And I know what I'm doing. Don't make me sleep alone tonight, please."

Maybe some other man could have resisted that plea, but Griffin couldn't. His arms surrounded her, drawing her as close as possible, and his mouth slanted over hers, deepening the kiss. She responded instantly, her arms slipping up around his neck and her upper body molding itself to his. And she didn't feel vulnerable to him, not now; she felt like a passionate woman who knew exactly what she wanted.

She was light when he lifted her from the couch, and it was a stark reminder of how physically delicate she was. The recognition sent a jumble of emotions clashing in his mind. Anxiety because someone had tried—twice—to kill her. Fear for her, because she would be helpless in the grip of almost any man. A sense of protectiveness he had never felt before. And an oddly primitive, iron determination to keep her safe. He had never felt anything like that before. And he had never felt anything like the oddly focused quality of his senses; all he could see or hear or smell or feel was her.

He carried her into his bedroom and set her gently on her feet beside the bed, reaching out one hand to blindly fling back the covers. He couldn't stop kissing her, driven to try to satisfy a need he didn't even understand. Her mouth was warm and wild under his, as if she felt the same hunger for the deceptive simplicity of a kiss.

But it wasn't enough, for either of them. He felt her fingers coping with his belt even as his lifted to unfasten the buttons of the pajama top she wore, and both of them were abruptly frantic to do away with the barriers between them. He took his hands off her long enough to peel the T-shirt off over his head, then pushed the open pajama top off her shoulders. Her naked breasts touched him, the hardened tips like points of fire burning his chest, and Griffin felt more than heard a groan rumble up from somewhere deep inside him.

"Christ, Joanna . . . I want you so much." He hardly recognized the hoarse sound of his own voice. Her eyes gleamed up at him and she moved slightly, rubbing her breasts against his chest, and he thought he'd shatter into a million pieces with the pleasure of it.

He wanted to look at her, to strip her naked and stare at her until he'd memorized every inch of her, but as strong as that need was, the urge to bury himself in her was far more overwhelming. He fumbled at the drawstring waist of the pajama bottoms until it was loosened, allowing the material to slide easily over her slender hips and down her legs, and felt her soft hands against his hips as she pushed his pants and shorts down.

That intimate touch made every muscle in his body tighten in exquisite anticipation, and then the soft, silky skin of her belly pressed against his hardness, and the touch sent a jolt of pure raw desire through him. He felt her shift slightly as she worked the socks off and stepped out of the material pooling around her feet. Somehow, he got rid of his own shoes and socks, kicked them and the pants out of his way.

Griffin lifted her onto the bed and followed her down.

Her body in the lamplight was as beautiful as he had known it would be. As slender and delicate as she was, her small breasts were full and firm, and her hips curved gently in a shape that was all woman. Her eyes gleamed up at him, liquid and sleepy with desire, and her lips were full and reddened from his passionate kisses.

He wanted to tell her what he saw and felt. Wanted to tell her she was the most beautiful thing he'd ever seen, and that he couldn't think of anything but how much he needed her. But he couldn't tell her anything at all, because he didn't trust himself to even try to speak.

Instead, he told her with his touch. He kissed her face, her throat. His hands touched her breasts, stroking the warm, silky skin and examining the stiff pink nipples. His mouth followed his fingers, and the tension and heat inside him surged wildly when she moaned and shifted restlessly in response. He could feel her heart thudding as rapidly as his own, hear her soft, quick breathing and tiny gasps. And the taste of her fed his desire until he didn't think he'd be able to hold back another minute.

His hand slid down over her belly, feeling her quiver, and his fingers combed through the silky blond curls until he found the wet heat that told him she was ready for him. He caressed her for a moment, stroking her sensitive flesh gently until her hips lifted and she made a pleading little sound.

The last threads of his restraint snapped. With a groan, Griffin moved over her, spreading her legs and settling between them. He felt her hands on his shoulders, his back, her nails tiny darts of exquisite sensation, and stared down into her darkened eyes as his body penetrated hers.

She was smaller than he'd expected, tighter, her body admitting him with a reluctance that made the slow joining infinitely pleasurable. He wanted to lose himself in her, to meld the two of them together until they were a part of each other.

The winding, maddening tension built as he began to move, at first slowly. But as she responded, her body moving sensuously beneath his, her moans and husky little sounds urgent, a more primitive rhythm took hold of him. Joanna met his quickening thrusts, her body taut and sinuous, her hands gripping his shoulders. Her face was beautiful in passion, riveting his gaze until she was all Griffin saw, all he could hold in his mind.

It was like being swept up into a storm of sensation, carried along helplessly toward a peak of release that had become an overwhelming necessity. Joanna cried out, and the inner spasms of her pleasure caught Griffin in a caress so shattering that he was blind and deaf to everything except the sheer power of his own blissful climax.

✧   ✧   ✧

"You're a silent lover," he said.

Joanna opened her eyes to find him looking down at her, his head raised and propped on one hand. He had pulled the covers up over them at some point during the last few minutes, and she had been drifting peacefully in the warm cocoon of blankets and him, listening to the distant thunder of high tide battering the cliffs.

"A big change from the rest of the time," she murmured. She couldn't read his face and wasn't sure if her silence had disturbed him or if he was merely making a comment. That rugged face was grave, his very dark eyes—black? blue?—fixed on her face intently.

"Is it . . . usual for you?" he asked almost tentatively.

Joanna thought about the question for a moment. What did he really want to know? For some men, a woman's past sexual history was a topic to be avoided; others wanted chapter and verse—and a comparison with those previous lovers to boot. On the other hand, Griffin might simply be wondering if she thought their experience a unique one.

Slowly, she said, "I went steady with my high school sweetheart for three years; two years in high school and then during our first year of college. We waited until that last year to have sex, and it . . . wasn't very satisfying. In fact," she smiled faintly, "I didn't see what all the fuss was about. I don't know why we were incompatible that way, maybe just because we were young and he didn't have much more experience than I did. In any case, it didn't get any better, not for me. And I suppose my lack of enthusiasm showed. Anyway, we broke up six months later. My next relationship that got as far as the bedroom was the one I told you about in your office. It lasted only a few months. So I don't really know if being a silent lover is usual for me."

She drew a breath. "All I do know is that I never understood how anybody could be . . . overwhelmed by desire—until now."

His free hand reached over to brush back a strand of her hair, then lingered to stroke her cheek gently. His expression still grave, he said, "We did click, didn't we?"

Even the mere touch of his hand on her face sent a surge of heat through her, and Joanna could only smile wryly at what was, on her part at least, quite an understatement. "Yeah, we did." And then she added, "You didn't say much, either. Is it usual for you?"

"No," he replied simply.

Joanna waited, watching him.

"I didn't plan on you," he said, his fingers still moving lightly on her skin as if the feel of it enthralled him. "It was almost like lightning out of a clear blue sky, it was so sudden. So unexpected. When I saw you that first day, when you turned your head—"

"And I looked so much like Caroline," she said.

Griffin's hand stopped moving and rested along her jawline and the side of her neck. His brows drew together just a bit, but his voice remained quiet. "That was my first thought, yes. It had to be. But the differences stood out too. Your voice and accent, your hair and eyes. But the resemblance made me cautious. I don't believe in coincidence, and I had to wonder what you were doing here. Then, later, when I realized you were very methodically asking questions about Caroline, I didn't know what to think."

"So you decided to warn me off?"

"It made me uneasy, Joanna. *You* made me uneasy. I didn't know what you might stir up—and God knows I didn't expect a killer—but I knew many of the people in this town hadn't gotten over Caroline's death."

Joanna merely nodded, silent.

"I didn't expect this to happen, not then," he went on. "I'm not even sure when my feelings began to change, but it wasn't long before you no longer reminded me of Caroline."

She wasn't entirely sure she believed that, but Joanna didn't question him about it. She preferred—very much preferred—to believe that it was her he had taken into his bed tonight, not a stand-in for Caroline.

He smiled suddenly, crookedly. "That's when I realized I was in trouble."

"Swept off your feet?" she murmured, smiling.

"Knocked on my ass," he replied dryly.

Joanna couldn't help laughing.

"I'm not kidding," he told her in a pained tone with something serious underneath. "I'm thirty-seven, Joanna. I'm supposed to be beyond this stuff."

"Stuff?" she inquired innocently.

"You know what I'm talking about. Daydreams. Ridiculous impulses."

Joanna wanted very much to ask him to describe those daydreams and impulses, but she was so surprised by what he seemed to be telling her that all she could think to say was, "Lost in lust, huh?"

Griffin leaned over her suddenly, and there was an unexpectedly fierce glitter in his dark eyes. "I've felt lust," he said. "This isn't it."

She didn't know what she would have replied to that if he'd given her the chance. But he didn't give her the chance to say anything. His mouth came down on hers, hard without being rough, moving with the sensual heat that had so quickly and effortlessly ignited unfamiliar fires inside her, and Joanna lost interest in words.

She fumbled her arms from beneath the covers and reached for him, her fingers blindly exploring a body still foreign to her. It felt wonderful to touch him. He was harder than she had expected, the muscles underneath his smooth skin taut. Her fingers probed his shoulders and back, traced the clean line of his spine, then moved around and stroked the smooth mat of black hair covering his chest. Her fingertips almost literally tingled when she touched him, and a hollow aching inside her grew until it seemed to fill her entire being.

She had thought she was completely exhausted, limp and sated after their first joining, but tension flowed into her now as his mouth seduced her and his hands began to move over her body. She almost jerked when he touched her breast, the burning pleasure stealing her breath and making a helpless little sound of delight purr in her throat.

A silent lover? She was hardly that, not when she couldn't stop or control these disconcertingly primitive sounds of pleasure. But wordless, yes. The way he made her feel was so intense, so overwhelming, that words were beyond her.

His mouth was on her breast now, drawing her into a blind storm of sensation, and his hand slipped down over her belly, finding her mound and the most exquisitely sensitive nerves her body possessed. Joanna knew her legs had parted for him, and she felt the most incredibly voluptuous sense of opening herself to him. It was a kind of abandon she had never known before, and it was wildly seductive.

He stroked her until she thought she'd go out of her mind, until another of those pleading sounds escaped from her throat. Then he was moving over her, and Joanna nearly sobbed in relief. Her thighs cradled him, her arms slipped around him, and she stared up at his taut face as he came inside her.

That sensation was still unfamiliar, being opened and filled by him, feeling him with an intimacy that tugged at all her deepest instincts. And then he was moving, slower this time, and the lingering strokes brought her quickly to the very edge of her endurance. It was wonderful and terrible, what he was doing to her. It made her mindless and turned her body into a creature of nerves and need and desperation. Instinctively, her body tried to quicken his rhythm, but Griffin maintained the maddeningly leisurely pace.

He paid a price for that restraint, she realized on some level of herself. The muscles under her fingers quivered with the strain, his breathing was harsh and uneven, and his face was a mask of raw urgency. But his torment did nothing to soothe her own, and Joanna heard herself making sounds that were completely alien to her. She felt her body undulate with astonishing sexuality to meet his, and knew her nails were digging into his back as the tension inside her reached a height far beyond what she thought she could endure.

He groaned suddenly and thrust into her almost wildly, his restraint snapped. Joanna cried out in fierce elation, the ecstasy sweeping over her in waves and waves of throbbing heat. He shuddered when her body clenched rhythmically around him, and buried himself in her with a harsh sound of overwhelming pleasure as her climax triggered his.

✧　　✧　　✧

When Joanna finally came back to herself, she was wrapped once more in a cocoon of warmth and him. Both his arms were wrapped around her, and her head was pillowed comfortably on his shoulder. This time, she was absolutely positive she lacked the strength to move, and though not sleepy, she drifted along the edge of sleep contentedly.

"Joanna?"

"Hmm?"

"Would you consider going back to Atlanta until all this is settled?"

She raised her head, then levered herself up on an elbow so that she could look down at him and see his face clearly. Before she could respond, he spoke again, his voice low.

"I'm worried about you."

It was very difficult for her to refuse him, but Joanna had to shake her head. "I can't leave before it's over. Even if I wanted to. I can't explain it, but I *know* I have to be here."

His dark gaze searched her face for a moment, and then he nodded reluctantly. "I had a feeling you'd say that. Just for God's sake be careful from now on, will you?"

Joanna smiled. "I'll do my best, I promise." She leaned over to kiss him lightly, then settled down once more at his side. It was still fairly early, but the day had been long and the evening definitely active, and this time she drifted off to sleep.

❖   ❖   ❖

The dream began very much as usual. The sounds of ocean waves crashing and a gradually forming image of that beautiful, lonely house on the cliffs. Then the house sort of faded away into a kind of fog, and other images formed. Misty and tilted slightly, the colorful painting on an easel drifted before her mind's eye. Dimly, far away, she could hear a child's miserable, frightened sobs, the sounds tearing at her heart. A clock ticked softly, steadily. A paper airplane soared on coastal winds, lifting and swooping before coming to rest at last on some kind of boards. Still mistily, an image formed of beautiful pink roses in a vase, with petals scattered all around it. Then it vanished, and the brightly colored carousel horse bobbed and whirled briefly before coming to a stop. It remained there, clear and real, its surroundings vague, while the child's sobs grew closer and more distinct, and the clock's ticking became so loud it echoed.

Don't let her be alone.

The clock was booming now, drowning out everything else until it sounded like an amplified heartbeat, then quicker and quicker—

Joanna sat up with a cry, her arms reaching out for . . . something. She couldn't seem to breathe, and her heart was racing so fast she felt dizzy, and the fear she felt, something akin to terror, went as deep as her marrow and clogged her throat. She could feel wetness on her cheeks, tears shed in pain and grief and regret she could still feel. She wanted to sob with it, to release all the pent-up emotions in primitive sounds of loss.

"Joanna? Honey—"

As soon as she heard his low voice, she began to calm down. The desire to sob wildly faded until it was gone. Her breathing slowed, steadied. Her pulse dropped to normal. The terror inspired by the dream lost its grip on her, and her tense muscles relaxed. When Griffin's arms went around her, she slumped against his hard body.

"We don't have much time," she whispered.

The bedroom was filled with the faint light of early morning, and the frown on Griffin's beard-stubbled face looked more dangerous than usual. "The dream again?"

"Every night," she told him, settling back on the pillow as he eased them down again. "That's one reason I can't leave—the dream won't let me." *Caroline won't let me.* "It's . . . it's moving faster somehow. There's a feeling of urgency there getting stronger every time. Something's going to happen. I know it is. Soon."

He touched her cheek gently, his fingers rubbing away the last traces of her tears. He was still frowning, but his voice was quiet. "If you've been waking up like this every morning, no wonder you feel so strongly about the dream. But it's changing now? There's something different about it?"

"No. Yes. Yes, there is."

More than one thing. Had the carousel lingered longer than usual this time? The paper airplane drifted farther and landed in a different place? And what about that desperate cry—a female voice?—pleading with her not to let *her* be alone. Regan? If this connection was with Caroline, then it had to be Regan, didn't it? *Don't let her be alone.* Not let her be alone emotionally? Or was Regan in physical danger?

It didn't make sense, and Joanna was too shaken to be able to think clearly about it.

"It's virtually the same every night," she replied at last. "The same objects forming and drifting around. But this time, there was something else. A . . . plea that I not let someone be alone. That I not let *her* be alone."

"Her?" Griffin's frown deepened. "You think this connection is with Caroline—is the plea for her? Or from her?"

"I don't know. I think—I *feel*—it's Regan she wants me to help. That Regan's in trouble somehow. But I don't know. All I do know is that the clock is ticking louder, faster, and I know we're running out of time."

$\mathcal{T}$ WELVE

✦ ✦ ✦

$\mathcal{T}$ICK. TICK. TICK.

It was almost constant now, in her head, faster than it should have been, and the urgency of it wouldn't leave Joanna alone. It prodded her to refuse to go to the station with Griffin later that morning and remain under his eye even though she wanted to be with him.

There was something she had to do. Worried about Regan despite Griffin's reassurances that the child was certainly safe at home and not given to wandering far from her own yard, Joanna wanted to walk over to the gazebo this morning, around the time when Regan had told her she normally took a break from her studies. There was no guarantee, of course, that Regan would appear at the gazebo, but Joanna's uneasiness demanded that she see for herself that the little girl was all right. Even if she had to knock on the front door and ask.

"I hope you can get along without your car," Griffin

told her as they rode along Main Street. "I had it towed out of town last night instead of to the local garage."

Joanna looked at him with a little frown, trying to think logically and resisting an urge to chew on her thumbnail. "Didn't you tell Doc it was totaled?"

"Yeah, but it wasn't. A big dent in front where you hit the fence post, and a few scrapes and scratches, that's all the damage caused by the wreck. But as soon as some of my people discovered the tampering, I ordered it towed to a garage a few miles out of town to a mechanic I trust completely. He'll keep it safe and out of sight while we go over it for evidence. However, since I don't want it spread around that somebody tampered with the car, the official reason for the accident is that a short in the electrical system caused the throttle pulse sensor to go haywire."

"The throttle pulse sensor," she repeated. "I guess that's self-explanatory?"

He sent her a little grin. "More or less. It regulates the throttle, which regulates the amount of gas fed to the engine. So if you happen to be in gear when the sensor goes haywire, the engine races wildly. Aunt Sarah didn't teach you about cars?"

"Aunt Sarah viewed cars as things that got her from one place to the next. Which is pretty much how I view them. But I have an excellent memory, and I'll be able to solemnly tell anyone who asks that the throttle pulse sensor in my car went haywire."

Griffin nodded. "Good enough. Tell them also that since the car was a rental and was totaled, we had to send it back to the agency in Portland. It's their headache, after all."

Joanna nodded, but asked, "Didn't anybody drive out there to see the wreck yesterday? I thought that kind of curiosity was a universal trait of humans—nosy or otherwise."

"A few citizens were curious," he admitted. "But my people kept everyone back, so all they saw was your car three-quarters buried in hay. Besides, it was getting dark. I very much doubt that anyone realized it wasn't as badly damaged as we're going to claim."

"Mmm. But won't the killer be suspicious if we seemingly don't realize the car was tampered with?"

Griffin sent her another glance, this one wry. "Small-town cops sometimes miss things. We also tend to look for the most obvious and likely cause of an accident, and it's a lot more likely that your car had the fluke of an electrical short than that it was tampered with in a murder attempt."

"He won't buy that if he knows you at all," Joanna said.

Griffin smiled, but said, "Let's hope he buys it. In the meantime, I'd feel much better if you promised to stay away from the edge of the cliffs and stay out of all cars except this one or a town taxi."

"I'm not planning on taking any chances," Joanna said, feeling a bit guilty for not telling him she intended a stroll over to Caroline's gazebo—which was near the edge of the cliffs. But she didn't want him to worry, and she definitely intended to be careful.

"I wish I could believe that," Griffin murmured. "But I know only too well how hell-bent you are to figure all this out."

Joanna didn't deny that, but said, "I'm not stupid, Griffin. And I won't go racing out of the hotel in my nightgown like some gothic heroine who hears something go bump in the night."

"If I have anything to say about it," Griffin responded, "you won't be spending any more nights alone—and I sure as hell wouldn't let you run around outside in your nightgown. Not without me, anyway."

Joanna couldn't help but smile. "We'd shock the natives. You realize, of course, that we will be—probably already are—fodder for the next hot round of gossip in Cliffside?"

"That did occur to me, yes." He turned the Blazer into the driveway of The Inn and sent her another glance. "Will you mind?"

"Why should I? I don't think we have anything to be ashamed of, especially since we're both unattached and over twenty-one."

"But will you mind?" Griffin repeated quietly.

Joanna looked at his serious profile and wondered if he really was falling in love with her. He had hinted as much last night, after all. And when a man started worrying about a woman's reputation, it usually meant he felt considerably more for her than just lust—at least according to Aunt Sarah.

But neither of them had mentioned the subject this morning, and Joanna wondered now if it bothered him that she hadn't said anything about her own feelings. It was something she hadn't been able to think about much and wasn't yet ready to examine too closely. For one thing, Caroline was still very much in her mind, and until that urgent presence was gone, it wouldn't be fair to Griffin to offer him less than her whole self. It wouldn't be fair to herself, either, because so many of her feelings since she'd come to Cliffside were tied up in this place and the people—and the past.

Until her head was cleared of that, she couldn't be sure of what she really felt.

For another thing, every time she *had* tried to examine her feelings for Griffin, the biggest question in her mind had been Caroline. Maybe Griffin and Caroline hadn't been lovers, but he had admitted that there might have been "something" between them at one time, and until Joanna understood that, she couldn't help wrestling with the fear that his feelings for her were influenced by what he had felt for Caroline. Especially since most if not all of the men in Caroline's life had felt very deeply about her.

Why wouldn't Griffin have felt just as deeply?

"Joanna?"

The Blazer stopped in front of the main doors of The Inn, and as the doorman came toward them briskly to open Joanna's door, she met Griffin's intent gaze seriously. "No,

I won't mind. But what about you? Doesn't the sheriff of a small town have to be above reproach?"

His smile was a bit crooked. "Nobody could possibly reproach me for getting involved with you. Even His Honor asked me the other day what I was waiting for. And Cain asked me Monday if he could paint the heart on my sleeve so everybody could see it. I seem to have made my feelings pretty damned obvious."

Joanna smiled at him, only dimly aware of her car door being opened. "We *could* try to be discreet, you know."

"I don't think that'll be possible," Griffin said and leaned across to kiss her leisurely under the professionally detached gaze of the doorman, who stood holding Joanna's door.

She looked at him a bit dazedly when he finally drew back, and murmured, "Obviously not. Um . . . you said something about not spending any more nights alone? My place or yours?"

He touched her cheek in a brief caress and said huskily, "We'll decide later. Why don't you come into town sometime between twelve and one, and we'll have lunch."

Joanna drew a shaky breath. "Okay. Fine. I'll do that."

"And *be careful* today, will you?"

"Absolutely." It required a tremendous effort for Joanna to turn away and swing her legs from the Blazer, and seeing the patiently waiting doorman—who had obviously heard every word and seen everything—hardly helped her to get a grip on herself. Still, she managed to get out and walk up to the main doors of the hotel without looking back at Griffin and without stumbling over her own feet.

Which she considered something of an achievement.

The lobby was virtually deserted, with Holly at the desk alone when Joanna approached, and the brunette immediately asked, "Are you all right?"

Joanna leaned an elbow on the high desk. "Do I look like a house fell in on me?"

"Metaphorically speaking? Yes."

"Griffin," Joanna said.

Holly matched her guest's pose, leaning her elbow on the desk. Her expression was solemn. "I always considered him a cautious man. But he didn't waste much time with you, did he?"

"I guess you know I spent the night at his place?"

"Well, since Griff didn't try to keep it a secret—I believe he told at least one of his deputies where he was taking you—everybody in town knows, by now. The majority opinion, last I heard, was that you two didn't use that second bedroom at his place."

"We didn't," Joanna confessed.

Holly smiled. "Which is why you look a bit—shall we say—stunned this morning?"

"I was all right until he said good-bye outside a minute ago," Joanna replied, sounding faintly aggrieved. "I suggested we might want to be discreet since he's the sheriff, and he said it wouldn't be possible—and your doorman got an eyeful."

"Ah." Holly nodded in understanding. "Well, it probably wouldn't do much good to try discretion anyway, Joanna. The only betting going on now is whether you'll go back to Atlanta at the end of your vacation or stay here with Griff."

More than a little curious, Joanna said, "And the odds favor—?"

"Griff. We know our sheriff rather well, you see. He's nothing if not determined, and tends to get what he wants. Nobody doubts it's you he wants." Curious herself, Holly asked, "Could you live here, do you think? After Atlanta, I mean."

"Yes." Her response emerged before Joanna even thought about it, surprising her. She had known she liked the town and most of the people she'd met—despite her uneasiness and awareness of trouble here—but she hadn't realized how at home she felt. "Yes, I think I could," she added more slowly.

Holly smiled. "I'm glad. From what I hear, the people around here really like you."

At least one of them doesn't. "Maybe I'm just a small-town girl at heart," Joanna said with a shrug. "Anyway, Griffin and I are not talking about the future at the moment, so I'm trying not to think about it." There were certainly other things to think about. Insistent, worrisome things. *Is Regan all right? Is she in trouble? Dammit, Caroline, what do you want from me?*

"I know how that is," Holly murmured. Her mind was very obviously running along a very specific track, because she added, "Joanna, I know it's unfair to ask you, but does Griff really suspect Cain of having killed Amber?"

Joanna had expected that question sooner or later, so she was able to reply honestly without giving away Griffin's thoughts on the subject. "He has a list of suspects, Holly, and it naturally includes Cain. His job is to eliminate those suspects until he finds out what really happened. Don't worry."

"How can I not? It's all over town that he went somewhere Sunday night and then lied to Griff about that, so of course at least half our eager citizens have convicted him."

"Do you know where he went?" Joanna asked.

Holly made a slight grimace. "No. I . . . think he's avoiding me. He called yesterday to say he'd be out painting scenery most days this week."

"Is that usual?"

"For him to go off painting? Oh, sure, for days at a time. But I know him. There was something in his voice I've never heard before, something evasive. I think he was lying about what he'd be doing."

Joanna thought about it, then said, "He goes to Portland sometimes, doesn't he?"

"Yes. Because of the galleries there, of course. And he has an apartment and studio in the city. He used to spend winters up there and just summers here. But I don't know why he'd have driven up to Portland so late on Sunday night just to work in his studio for a few hours—he was back here early, remember—and if he *had*, I don't know why he would have lied about it to Griff."

Joanna couldn't think of a good reason, either. She wasn't about to tell Holly that Griffin intended to question Cain again, this time in his office. And she certainly wasn't going to mention Griffin's theory that Cain might have gone out so late to meet another woman.

"I don't know what to do about it," Holly confided. "I've always been careful never to back him into a corner, and I'm afraid if I start demanding he account for his time away from me . . ."

Joanna nodded. "I know. Look, if you want my advice, I say be patient for a while longer. Griffin's investigation is still in the early stages; within a few days, we'll all probably know a lot more than we do now. I'll bet Cain had a perfectly logical reason for going out Sunday night, and for not telling Griffin about it, and I bet you'll know what that is before long—without having to back him into a corner."

Holly smiled. "You're probably right."

"Sure I am. Let the town gossip all they want; they'll feel rotten when the truth comes out, and you can gloat."

"Thanks, Joanna."

"Don't mention it." Joanna smiled. "In the meantime, I'm going up to my room for a while, and then I think I'll take a walk."

"Sounds like a good idea. Oh—Joanna?"

On the point of turning away from the desk, Joanna paused. "Yeah?"

"The wreck yesterday—what happened?"

"I couldn't stop the damn thing. Griffin said it was the throttle pulse sensor, whatever that is," Joanna parroted faithfully. "A short in the electrical system apparently caused it to go haywire."

"That must have been terrifying," Holly said sympathetically. "It's amazing you came out of it unharmed. I heard the car was totaled."

"Yeah. And no good to me anymore. We sent it back to the rental company in Portland. From now on, I walk, take a taxi, or ride with Griffin." She smiled. "Good thing Cliff-side is so small; I can go most everywhere I need or want to on foot."

"Handy," Holly agreed. "Well, I'm glad it came out all right. See you later, Joanna."

Joanna lifted a hand in farewell and headed for the ele-vator.

❖   ❖   ❖

Griffin settled into his office chair and immediately called Cain's cottage. He let it ring at least ten times. There was no answer, and no machine since Cain despised the things. He also tended to more or less vanish if he'd found a scene or person he wanted to paint, sometimes for days at a time.

"Hell," Griffin muttered as he hung up the phone. He drummed his fingers on the desk for a moment, then called one of his deputies into the office.

Casey answered the summons, his grave Indian-like fea-tures as impassive as usual. "What do you need, boss?"

"Aside from about a pound of aspirin?" Griffin waved away any impulse his deputy might have had to respond, and said, "The Robert Butler investigation—I want some progress made, pronto. I want you and maybe Lee or Shel-ley to really dig into his background. Find out as much as you can about the guy, even if you have to go down to San Francisco. I'm looking for any connection, absolutely *any* connection, however slight or vague, to somebody in this town. And I want the info as you get it."

"So now there *is* a hurry?" Casey asked.

Griffin remembered his own "no hurry" when he'd first directed that the investigation be reopened, and couldn't help wondering if he might have been able to prevent an attempt on Joanna's life if he had not spoken those words. "Yeah," he said now. "Yeah, there's a hurry. Do whatever you have to do, but get me the details of that guy's life."

"Right," Casey said, unquestioning.

"And one more thing." Griffin drummed on the desk again for a moment, then forced himself to stop when

Casey's dispassionate gaze dropped to watch the restless gesture. "Tell Mark I'd like him to take a run out to Cain's place and see if he's anywhere around, maybe painting outside or something. If Mark doesn't find him there, he's to keep on looking."

"You want an APB?" Casey asked.

Griffin shook his head. "No. Just a casual look around —and no questioning people about him; there's no reason to add fuel to the gossip."

"I'll tell him," the deputy responded, and left the office.

After a moment, Griffin watched his fingers begin to drum on the desk again, and this time he didn't try to stop them.

✧   ✧   ✧

Clouds kept hiding the sun as Joanna walked quickly to the gazebo. Maybe that was why she kept feeling chilled, she thought, because each time the sun vanished, so did the warmth of it. Then again, maybe that wasn't the reason. Maybe it was just her nearness to the cliffs. She was wary, her senses alert for any sign that she was being followed or, indeed, that anyone else was around. She kept back from the edge of the cliffs, but the pounding of the surf against the rocks was a continual reminder of just how close she was.

The constant rhythm of it was like a heartbeat. Like a clock ticking. It seemed to thud in her head and beat against her nerves until she longed for silence just so she could *think* without all the bits and pieces of information and speculation in her head chasing themselves in baffling circles.

Who could have tampered with her car? Doc hadn't been happy with her questions and certainly hadn't been forthcoming with information, but would he have tried to kill her? Adam Harrison had shared his information about Caroline without hesitation, so why would he have gone after her? She supposed he could have had second thoughts later, but still, would those second thoughts have driven him to a murder attempt? And even if Lyssa Maitland *had* stared after her with a peculiar expression on her face, did that even mean anything?

In addition, lots of people had been in town during the several hours Joanna's car had been parked there, and she had talked to most of them about Caroline at one time or another. Many had been guarded or evasive; some had talked easily and openly. No one had seemed dangerous or threatening, as far as Joanna was concerned. But fact and fiction were filled with villains who smiled disarmingly, so how could anyone really know what might lie behind a smiling face?

It could have been anyone. Anyone could have tampered with the car—and unseen.

The town of Cliffside—how was that for a list of suspects?

The problem, Joanna decided as she walked along, was that it was all too easy to imagine any number of people as having a motive, simply because the reason of "protecting a secret" was just too damned vague and opened up too many possibilities. Most people had secrets of one kind or another, but which secrets were important enough to kill for? Surely there weren't many of those in this small town. Surely.

But even if there were few, it didn't narrow the field, because Joanna didn't know what she was looking for. Unless and until she discovered why Caroline had been so uneasy and possibly frightened before she was killed, she didn't have a clue as to the one secret that really mattered.

The gazebo came into view as Joanna came to that conclusion, and she stopped there on the edge of the woods. Regan was in the gazebo, sitting on the carousel horse and gazing out to sea, her small face still, as unexpressive as her father's always seemed to be.

You're why I'm here.

It was crystal clear in Joanna's mind, and she was only surprised she hadn't realized it long before she had. She was here because of Regan. That's why the dream had brought her here, because Regan needed her help.

Don't let her be alone.

Was it a plea from Caroline, placed in Joanna's mind somehow during that instant when both had been in a state of virtual death? Had Caroline cried out for help for her daughter across three thousand miles and death's own void, her terror and desperation in that moment so strong that she had somehow been able to connect with Joanna's subconscious and hurl at her a jumble of impressions and fears?

The subconscious, Joanna knew, dealt with problems in its own unique way. It processed information in ways that were frequently abstract, even surreal. Dream images, for instance, might sometimes be meant literally, but more often were symbolic. Yet in Joanna's dream, most of the images at least *existed* literally, which indicated they had some literal meaning.

The ocean crashing, of course, and Caroline's house were certainly real. The painting had been real. The carousel horse. The roses had been real enough, leading Joanna to the greenhouse where Caroline's rose lived and where her former lover could impart his information. The clock ticking felt very much like time passing—or running out.

But a paper airplane? That image remained a puzzle.

The child crying had to be Regan.

The one person in Caroline's life to whom she had been utterly devoted had been Regan, and it made sense that her concern for her child might be the last desperate thoughts in a mother's mind as death struck—especially if that death was violent and the mother knew her child was threatened.

But by what? Why did Regan need Joanna's help? Because she grieved so for her mother? No, surely the dream would not be filled with such terror if that had been Caroline's main concern. Because she was in danger? Because whatever had so frightened Caroline somehow touched or threatened Regan's safety? That made more sense, at least as much as any of this did. It even lent weight to the admittedly far-fetched idea that some part of Caroline had survived the moment of death to reach out to Joanna; few things in existence were as powerful and all-consuming as a mother's love for her child, and danger to that child would enable most mothers to reach far beyond their normal limits if necessary in the driving need to protect.

Don't let her be alone.

But had she meant that literally, that Joanna shouldn't leave Regan physically? Was the little girl in actual physical danger? Or had Caroline meant that her daughter needed an advocate to balance the remoteness of her father?

"Oh, hell, now what do I do?" Joanna muttered to herself, knowing only that she had to do *something*.

She hadn't spoken very loudly, but Regan turned her head just then, and her small face lightened instantly. Her lips curved in a smile of singular charm, and she said, "Joanna," with obvious pleasure.

"Hi, Regan." Joanna crossed the clearing to the gazebo and stepped inside it, leaning against the railing beside the carousel horse. "How have you been?"

Regan hunched her shoulders slightly, a faint smile remaining. "Okay. I—I got into Daddy's car yesterday and sat there for a while."

Quite a step for a child terrified of cars. Joanna smiled at her. "I'm glad. It was a brave thing to do, facing your fear. Your mother would be very proud of you."

"You're the first one I've told," Regan confessed.

"Not your father?"

"No. He wouldn't care."

Joanna hesitated. "Regan, I hardly know your father, but I'm sure he *would* care."

"He doesn't care about anybody. Mama said so."

"Did she—say that to you?"

Regan frowned a little. "No. I heard her say it to Daddy."

Gently, Joanna said, "Regan, I know it's difficult for you to understand, but sometimes grown-ups say things to each other that aren't necessarily true. Especially when they're angry. Maybe your mama and daddy didn't get along very well, but that doesn't mean either one of them didn't care about you."

Regan's frown deepened. "Mama wasn't yelling at Daddy when she said that."

"Did she ever yell when she was mad?"

"No."

"Then she could have been mad at him when she said that, couldn't she? Even though she didn't yell?"

Regan hunched her shoulders. "I guess so."

"Did she ever tell *you* that your daddy didn't care about anyone?"

"No."

Joanna smiled at her. "Look, Regan, all I'm saying is that things you overhear don't always mean what you think they do. Your daddy's probably the kind of man who doesn't show what he's feeling, but that doesn't mean he doesn't feel. And just because your mama might have been mad at him doesn't mean you have to be too."

After a moment, Regan said diffidently, "Is that why I want to yell at him all the time, Joanna? Because I'm mad at him? Because I wish . . . he had died instead of Mama?"

Joanna wasn't shocked by the question, but the pity she felt for Caroline's child tightened her throat and made it difficult for her to speak. "Honey, I think what you really wish is that there hadn't been an accident at all. You don't wish your daddy dead, you just want your mama back. And since you know you can't have her back, you have to get mad at somebody. He's your daddy—he should have protected your mama, that's what you feel, isn't it? He should have kept the accident from happening."

Regan nodded mutely, her dark eyes shimmering with tears.

"I know that. I felt the same way about my daddy when their boat sank. For a long time, I blamed him, because there was no one else to blame. But, Regan, my daddy did the best he could to save my mama. And your daddy would have done his best if he had been there. But he wasn't there. He was miles away at your house, and he didn't know she'd be in trouble. How could he save her? How could he even help her?"

After a long moment, Regan said, "I'm still mad at him, Joanna."

"I know, honey. But try to think about it, to understand that it wasn't his fault she was killed. In time, I think you won't be quite as mad at him. In time, none of it will hurt so much."

"It won't? Really?" There was a world of bewildered pain in that childish voice, and it nearly broke Joanna's heart.

"I promise you. You'll never stop missing your mama, but in time it won't hurt so much to miss her."

"You still miss your mama and daddy?"

Joanna nodded. "Very much. But it doesn't hurt now. I'll always feel sad, and always wish they could be here with me, but I don't cry myself to sleep anymore."

"I do that," Regan murmured. "Every night."

"It's good to cry, honey. It helps take away the pain."

Regan nodded and fell silent again, watching her own hands running up and down the shiny chrome pole in front of the carousel horse's saddle. Then she turned her head suddenly, and her face was very serious. "Your car wrecked yesterday, didn't it?"

Though she was glad of the change of subject, Joanna was a little startled; adult gossip she had come to expect, but with Regan so cut off from town . . . "How on earth did you hear that?"

"I heard Mrs. Porter telling Mrs. Ames about it this morning," Regan replied, listing her teacher and the housekeeper respectively. "You—you didn't get hurt, Joanna?"

"What do you think?" Joanna lifted her hands in a look-at-me gesture, smiling.

Regan's face remained grave for a moment as she studied Joanna carefully, but then she nodded and smiled. "You look okay. I'm glad."

"Me too. It wasn't really so bad, you know. I just had to drive into a pasture and knock over a few haystacks."

"I'm glad Mr. Cook didn't have his horses in there," Regan remarked.

"You and me both," Joanna responded with some feeling. She studied the little girl for a moment, trying to decide how best to proceed. She still felt very reluctant to question Regan about her mother, but she honestly didn't know where else to go for information. Scott, she supposed—but there was certainly no indication that he'd be willing to talk about his wife.

Still, that lonely house was also a part of Joanna's dream, and it could easily mean more than a simple indication of where Caroline had lived and Regan lived now.

"Joanna?"

She blinked, then smiled. "Sorry. My mind wandered."

"Mama said this was a good place to think," Regan said, turning her gaze back out to sea. "She'd come out here when she wanted to be alone. Do you think . . . she's still here, Joanna? That she's watching over me?"

"I don't know if she's here," Joanna replied honestly. "But I'm certain she's watching over you, Regan. She loved you very much."

They both heard the distant sound of a bell ringing just then, and before Regan could speak, Joanna said, "Do you mind if I walk back to the house with you? I'd like to talk to your daddy, if he's home."

"He's home," Regan said.

Griffin wouldn't like this, Joanna was sure. Scott McKenna was a suspect on his list, and he would doubtless raise hell when he found out that Joanna had talked to the man—alone, she hoped. Joanna was a bit uneasy about the situation herself, given the fact that it was at least possible Scott had tried to kill her the day before.

But she was still convinced that she could find out the truth about Caroline, and she had to talk to Scott if she had any hope of doing that. Of them all, he must have known his wife the best, whether or not he had loved her.

He had lived with her for more than ten years, and the habits and routine of daily life had to reveal the true character of any person.

Joanna and Regan walked side by side through the small stand of woods separating Caroline's gazebo from the big house, and as they neared it, Joanna tried to decide what she would say to Scott.

Did you love your wife?

Did you cause your wife's death?

Did you try to kill me?

She was still uncertain when they walked across the immaculately landscaped yard and climbed the steps onto the porch. Regan led the way through the front door and into a lovely but formal foyer, then down a hallway to the left of the stairs.

"His office is this way," she said over her shoulder to Joanna. "Dylan's office is at the end of the hall, but I think he's in town. And Lyssa only comes here sometimes. So Daddy's by himself right now. I'll take you before I go back to Mrs. Porter."

Joanna didn't object. Though she did feel a bit rueful when Regan opened the door of her father's office and announced without preamble, "Joanna's here to see you."

Alone in the room, Scott rose from behind his desk and looked at Joanna with his usual impassivity. "Joanna. Come in."

Said the spider to the fly.

It was the way she should have felt, but for some reason Joanna's concern about being here faded. She couldn't explain it, couldn't even begin to understand it, but she felt absolutely no threat from Scott.

"I'll see you later, Joanna," Regan said, looking up at her.

"You bet." Joanna watched the little girl turn away without another word for her father and disappear down the hall. She closed the office door and walked across to one of the visitor's chairs in front of Scott's big desk. The room didn't surprise her very much. It was neat and organized and very masculine, with expensive leather-bound books lining the shelves and a gleaming wood floor. The desk was uncluttered.

"Do you think it's wise to see so much of Regan?" he asked.

"Do you care?" she shot back.

Scott actually looked taken aback for a brief instant, but then he shrugged and said something Joanna would rather not have heard. "Touché. Sit down, Joanna."

How can he not care about that little girl? Joanna simply couldn't comprehend it. She sat down and watched him do the same, wondering if she had even a hope of understanding this remote man.

"What can I do for you?" he asked politely.

Burning her bridges, Joanna said, "You can talk to me about Caroline."

Scott leaned back in his chair and gazed at her, seemingly as unsurprised by the request as he had been by her sudden appearance in his house. "Would you mind explaining your excessive interest in my wife?"

"I don't think it is excessive," Joanna replied. "I was interested at first because I look so much like her."

"At first. What about now?"

"Now . . ." Joanna shook her head. "I can't explain; I'd probably sound crazy to you if I tried."

"Try anyway," he invited.

Joanna hesitated, trying to weigh the danger of confiding too much to this man against the import of the information he might possibly provide. Beyond the risk she ran of confiding in precisely the wrong person—the murderer, for instance—the problem was that Joanna had no idea if Scott could or would tell her anything of value. At the same time, he had to be a good source of information about Caroline, and it was clear he wasn't about to talk without knowing her reasons.

Griffin was *definitely* not going to like this.

"Were you in town yesterday afternoon?" she asked him.

Scott lifted an eyebrow in surprise. "No. Why?"

"You were here?"

"No, I was in Portland." His tone was one of infinite patience. "A law firm there handles my legal affairs, and there were documents to go over. I didn't get back here until last night around seven. And I repeat, why?"

An alibi Joanna assumed could have been easily disproven if not true. And though he could have hired someone to do his dirty work, Joanna didn't think it likely that he had. "Someone tampered with my car," she said. "The accelerator jammed, and I couldn't stop it. Went right through the middle of town like a bat out of hell. If I hadn't been able to steer the car into a pasture and into a few haystacks, I probably would have been killed."

Both his brows went up this time. "And you suspect me? Joanna, aside from the fact that I can't imagine why I would try to hurt you, I don't know the first thing about cars beyond how to drive them."

"I see."

"It couldn't have been a simple mechanical failure?"

Joanna hesitated again, mentally apologized to Griffin (not that it would do any good), and said, "We're sure it was tampered with. Which means somebody tried to kill me. And because of that, there's a chance that Amber Wade was killed Sunday night because she was mistaken for me. From behind, we looked enough alike to make that a logical possibility, and so far there doesn't seem to be a reason anyone would have wanted to kill her."

He frowned slightly. "Have you been making enemies here?"

"All I've been doing is asking questions about Caroline."

Scott's frown deepened. "What are you saying?"

"I'm saying Caroline's death may not have been the accident it appeared. Something was going on in her life that last week or so, something that made her uneasy, that frightened her."

"How do you know that?"

"I've been piecing it together since I got here. Talking to people. Asking questions. So far, I haven't been able to figure out what was going on, but I know something was." She paused, then asked, "Did her mood seem different to you before she was killed?"

Scott was still frowning, but answered readily enough. "I was very busy that week, and we hardly saw each other. But . . . the day she was killed, I happened to look out the window in here when she left in her car hardly more than an hour before the accident. I thought at the time that she was upset or angry, because she gunned the engine and pulled out much faster than usual."

Joanna thought about that. Caroline had already sent Griffin the note asking him to meet her, indicating that she had been ready to confide her problem to him. She had, in effect, burned her bridges, so it was entirely likely that she'd been nervous, even frightened that day.

It was also possible that something had happened *here* just before Caroline had left to meet Griffin, something that had upset her even more.

She looked at Scott steadily. "You two didn't have an argument or anything?"

"We never argued," Scott said.

"Never? I find that hard to believe."

Scott's smile was thin and without amusement. "Believe it. It takes feeling for two people to argue."

"And there was none between you and Caroline?"

He shrugged. "It happens sometimes."

"Then why did you stay together? Because of Regan?"

"No. Because there was no compelling reason to separate."

To Joanna, that was a lousy reason to remain in a loveless marriage, and one she hardly understood. She wasn't entirely sure she believed Scott, at any rate. He struck her as a proud man, and proud men generally didn't suffer their wives to conduct affairs, however discreetly. Unless, of course, he hadn't known.

"You told me the day we met that you were the villain of the piece," she reminded him. "Were you?"

He shrugged. "To Caroline, certainly. I was incapable of feeling, she said. I didn't care about anyone except myself. I couldn't make her happy."

"You didn't worship at her feet?" Joanna murmured.

His eyes narrowed slightly, as if she had struck a nerve, but he only repeated, "I couldn't make her happy."

Joanna thought about it for a moment, wondering if her guess *had* been on the mark. If Adam Harrison's experience with Caroline was not unique, then it seemed she had enjoyed being the focus of a man's obsessive love and desire, only to grow bored eventually and break off the relationship. Was that it? Had Scott held on to his wife by showing her a remote face and a cool indifference to her affairs? Had he been the only man in her life who had loved her enough to keep that love a secret she had never guessed?

His remoteness had clearly bothered her, judging by the things Regan had overheard, and possibly had frustrated her. With a husband resistant to her charms, she might in fact have found the marriage more of a challenge than it would have been if he had loved her openly with Adam Harrison's devotion.

It was certainly not the kind of marriage Joanna would wish for herself, but she wondered if, for Scott, it might have been enough. Even if he had known about her affairs, perhaps he had found consolation in the knowledge that she was his in a way no other man could claim, because he was the only one she had not been able to emotionally destroy.

Was that the answer?

Joanna braced herself mentally and said in a very neutral tone, "Was it possible she was having an affair?"

"Likely," he replied without hesitation or visible distress. "But I have no idea who he was."

"And that didn't bother you?"

Scott shrugged again. "I accepted Caroline for what she

was, Joanna. It became . . . obvious early in our marriage that one man couldn't satisfy her needs. She made no secret of that, not to me. Her affairs tended to be brief and relatively infrequent. I doubt there were more than half a dozen during our marriage. As long as there was no gossip, I accepted them."

Joanna nodded, still wondering if she was right about their relationship but not ready to ask or comment just yet. "Would she have told you if, say, an affair was going badly? If she was frightened of a lover for some reason?"

He was frowning again. "Frightened? I don't know, but probably not. She didn't talk about them to me. Acceptance is one thing; I didn't want details, and I made that very clear to her. But I certainly never saw a sign of physical abuse."

"And you have no idea what she was upset about the week she died?"

"I don't know that she was upset. But as I said, we barely saw each other." He paused and then said, "You're convinced her death wasn't an accident?"

Steadily, Joanna said, "Yes, and I'm convinced somebody tried to kill me because I'm getting too close to the reason Caroline died. Whether it was caused directly or indirectly, somebody had a hand in her car going over the cliffs. And I have to find out who that was."

Scott's gaze remained on her face for a long moment, then shifted away. "I'm sorry, but I obviously can't help you." He rose to his feet.

It was a dismissal.

Joanna could have protested, but all she said as she rose was, "Did Caroline keep a diary or journal?"

"No," he replied.

"You're sure?"

"Positive."

She nodded, then lifted a hand when he started to come around the desk toward her. "It's all right—I remember the way out."

Accepting that with a nod, Scott turned instead toward the window near his desk and stood gazing out.

At the door, Joanna paused and looked back at him. "You know, it's funny. Of all the people in this town, all the people who knew Caroline, you're the only one who wasn't shocked, or even surprised, when you saw me."

"I was warned," he said indifferently without looking at her. "I expected you."

She shook her head. "Other people were warned, but they were still surprised when they saw me. But you weren't. I think it was because you hardly noticed the resemblance. Because you had known Caroline inside and out, better than anyone else ever could have. You didn't have to wait and get to know me to see the differences in us. I wasn't Caroline; you knew that. You *felt* that. Because you loved her."

Scott didn't turn around or react in any way. He merely said, "Good day, Joanna."

Had she struck a nerve? Joanna didn't know. But when she left the house, without seeing anyone else, she followed an impulse she couldn't explain and went to the corner of the house where she could see the window of Scott's office. And somehow, she wasn't surprised to see that the window where he stood looked out over what would be, in spring and summer, a lovely rose garden.

❖   ❖   ❖

"Your mind isn't on business," Lyssa said, closing the folder containing the store's inventory lists and leaning back in his desk chair. Not only didn't he have his mind on business, but he was visibly restless—*very* unlike him. She watched him wander over to the fireplace for the third time in ten minutes.

"We can go over the inventory later," he said.

Lyssa would have loved to believe that she was responsible for his distraction, but knew better. He had hardly looked at her since she had arrived an hour ago. "We need to go over everything soon so we'll have a good idea of what the accountants will see next month," she reminded him.

He shrugged, frowning as he gazed into the fire.

"Is something wrong?" she asked tentatively, aware that she was straying from their established script.

"No."

She hesitated, then said, "I'll leave if you want me to."

"We were going to have dinner," he said.

It was one of the nights they usually drove up toward Portland to have dinner, leaving Regan in the capable care of Mrs. Ames. "We don't have to," Lyssa told him.

There was a short silence, and then he said, "I'm a little tired."

Hiding her disappointment beneath a casual smile, Lyssa said, "Okay. I should copy a couple of the disks I brought to the mainframe, though. Do you mind if I work here another hour or so?" She had a computer at the store and also a laptop at home, but all Scott's business information was stored here on his computer—especially important now with the audit he commissioned yearly about to be conducted.

"No, go ahead," he replied. Then, with sudden briskness, he turned away from the fire and headed for the door. "I'll leave you with it."

Lyssa didn't get a chance to say good-bye or even "Okay"; abruptly, she was alone in his office. "So long to you too," she muttered.

It required only a few minutes to start the computer downloading the information she had brought, and while the machine hummed it left Lyssa with nothing to do. She brooded for a short time, then swore under her breath and left the desk, and the office.

She was deviating from the accepted script again and knew it, but she didn't care. She'd never seen Scott so unsettled, and she was determined to find out what was going on. She went upstairs, being quiet because the house was quiet and because she was very aware of trespassing in a way he would certainly not appreciate.

She turned down the hallway leading to Scott's bedroom, but halted in surprise when she realized that the door to Caroline's bedroom was ajar. That door had been locked since Caroline's death, the room undisturbed.

Lyssa crept closer until she could peer inside, and what she saw wrenched at her heart. Scott was sitting on the bed in the ultrafeminine room, one of Caroline's filmy nightgowns in his hands. His head was bowed, and as she watched, he lifted the pale green material to his face, obviously breathing in the ghostly scent of his wife. Abruptly, his broad shoulders began to jerk, and a low, harsh sound of pain escaped him.

Lyssa drew back away from the door and went back down the hall almost blindly. She paused at the top of the stairs, staring at nothing through hot eyes, and whispered, "Damn you, Caroline."

THIRTEEN
✧ ✧ ✧

"*W*HAT THE *HELL* were you thinking of?"

Joanna sat in Griffin's visitor's chair, nodding with perfect understanding of and commiseration with his anger. "I know, it was stupid."

"Then why did you do it? Joanna, Scott is still a suspect as far as I'm concerned, and for you to just waltz over there *alone* and talk to him—let alone tell him every damn thing we've considered as possible—"

"I know," she repeated. "I knew at the time you wouldn't like it. But Griffin—"

He held up a hand to cut her off and almost visibly counted silently to ten. Or twenty. Then he settled back in his chair and took a deep breath. "All I can say is that you'd better have a damned good reason. I'm not kidding, Joanna. Because if Scott had anything to do with Amber's death, you could have just wrecked the case against him."

"He didn't."

"Oh? He told you that, I suppose?"

"He didn't have to." Joanna smiled. "Griffin, I know it'll madden you to hear this, but I know Scott didn't have anything to do with Caroline's death, or Amber's. I have no proof to offer you. I just *feel* it."

Griffin closed his eyes for a moment, then opened them. "I'd like to see the judge's face if you offered that as evidence," he said.

Joanna felt a bit cheered, because his voice was definitely milder than it had been these last few minutes. "Look, I have to follow my instincts, and they say he didn't do it. Of course, I wasn't sure of that until I actually sat there in his office and talked to him, but I knew I had to talk to him sooner or later, and I felt sooner was better. I just . . . I had to *do* something, and that seemed at the time to be the best thing."

Griffin sighed. "Did he tell you anything that might help us?"

"Not really." She thought about it for a minute, then shrugged. "I think I understand his relationship with his wife a little better now, but he doesn't know why—or even if—Caroline was upset before she was killed. And I'll swear he was completely surprised by the knowledge that her death might have been something other than an accident."

"He doesn't have a good alibi for either of the deaths," Griffin reminded her.

"Maybe not, but yesterday when my car was tampered with, he was in Portland. All day, on business. With witnesses."

Griffin frowned, but said, "He could have hired someone to do it."

Joanna smiled. "In Atlanta and other big cities, you could practically look up Thugs-R-Us in the Yellow Pages, but here? Who could Scott hire to do that kind of job? Putting aside the fact that it'd have to be somebody he trusted enough, who'd be willing to do it?"

"You have a point," Griffin admitted.

"And that's not all. Why would Scott want me dead?

Because I've been asking questions about Caroline? As far as I could tell, nothing I found out about Caroline would surprise him—or particularly disturb him. He knew her awfully well, Griffin."

"Okay," Griffin said slowly. "I admit, the thought of Scott of all people waiting outside The Inn in the rain for you to come out boggled my mind. And nobody saw him anywhere around the hotel on Sunday. So consider him off my list, at least unless we find some evidence pointing his way."

"Good. Have you talked to Cain yet?"

"No, dammit, he's made himself scarce."

"Holly said he often goes off painting, sometimes for days," Joanna said.

"Yeah, it's a habit of his. But I've had one of my deputies out all morning looking for him, and there hasn't been a sign."

"You realize a number of the people around here are convinced he killed Amber?"

Griffin nodded. "Another hazard of small towns; once gossip spreads, people tend to make up their minds quickly. I'm trying not to make the situation worse; my deputy isn't asking anyone if they've seen Cain, he's just cruising around town keeping his eyes open."

"So you're stuck until he shows up?"

"Or until I get desperate enough to put out an all points bulletin for him."

Joanna eyed him. "You wouldn't do that."

"Oh yes I would. The mechanic's reported in, Joanna—somebody did a fine job sabotaging your car. And Cain could have done it with his eyes closed; he spends as much time working on the engine of that little car of his as he does painting. I want to know where he was yesterday afternoon. I want to know where he was Sunday night when he claimed to be home alone. And I'm not going to wait much longer for those answers. Not with your life at stake."

"Somebody would have to be awfully dumb to try to

kill me again," she said reasonably. "Yesterday, okay; there was a strong possibility nobody suspected Amber was mistaken for me, so an attempt on my life might not have been connected. But yesterday's attempt failed, and he can't be sure you don't suspect sabotage—which might logically make you wonder if somebody had wanted to kill me instead of Amber. Why would he risk another attempt, right away at least?"

"You're the one who said we're running out of time," Griffin reminded her. "Maybe he has some kind of deadline. Or maybe he's just plain scared that you'll discover his secret."

Joanna sighed and glanced down at the ragged fingernails that were clear evidence of nerves rather than effectiveness. "He shouldn't worry. I don't seem to be getting any closer to finding it." She brooded for a moment while he watched her. "Without knowing who she was involved with when she died, I don't even know where to *begin* looking for that secret."

"Well, in the meantime," he said, "I'm following a different track. You said you believed our dead tourist last spring could have been the beginning of all this, so I'm having my people dig into his background. I told them to pay special attention to any connection, however tenuous, between Robert Butler and anyone here in Cliffside."

"That sounds like a good idea. Any luck yet?"

"No. It'll probably take at least a day or two, and I may even have to send someone down to San Francisco. But if there's a connection there, I intend to know about it."

Nodding, Joanna said, "Maybe that'll give us the key."

"Maybe." He smiled at her. "But for now—are you ready for lunch?"

"Definitely. As long as you aren't still mad at me?"

"Of course I'm still mad at you," he said, rising from his chair and coming around the desk to pull her up from hers. "If you don't stop risking your neck the way you did this morning, I'm going to lock you in my jail." He surrounded her face with his hands and kissed her.

When she could breathe again, Joanna murmured, "How're the beds in there?"

"Lousy. And we'd shock my deputies. So don't make me do that, okay?"

She smiled at him. "I'll be careful, I promise."

"Your idea of careful and mine," he said, "appear to be miles and miles apart."

"We'll argue about it over lunch," she suggested.

✦   ✦   ✦

She ended up spending the remainder of the afternoon with Griffin in his office, mostly because she felt contrite about having upset him earlier. There was plenty to do. For the first time, he let her see all the paperwork on the Butler investigation, as well as Caroline's death, and she was surprised at the amount of paper produced by a police investigation.

The papers themselves, unfortunately, produced no surprises, at least not for her. As Griffin had told her, both deaths appeared to have been accidents, with absolutely no evidence pointing any other way.

Information about Robert Butler began to come in toward the end of the day, but this first stuff at least didn't seem to be useful to them. It was culled from public records, detailing where and when he was born, who his parents had been, where he had gone to school. There was nothing odd in the information, and definitely no connection to anyone in Cliffside.

By five o'clock, Griffin called a halt and suggested to Joanna that they go back to his place. But Joanna said that since they weren't being discreet, her hotel had certain amenities they would both appreciate. Like room service. If, that is, he thought he could walk across the lobby with his dignity intact.

"Let's go," Griffin said.

His bravery was wasted, since the lobby was deserted when they arrived, except for a desk clerk who didn't even look up as they passed.

"The room service waiter will spread the news," Joanna told him as they rode up in the elevator.

"I," he said, "don't care. In fact, I think I'll answer the door wearing a towel, and *really* heat up the gossip."

"You wouldn't," she said.

He would. He did. And he made her stay out of sight in the bedroom, presumably not dressed for a hotel waiter's eyes, while he signed for their supper, tipped the waiter outrageously, and then hustled the young man out in a clearly impatient manner.

"I can't believe you did that," she said, laughing as she rejoined him in the living room of her suite.

Smiling, he caught her around the waist and pulled her against him. "I told you I was feeling ridiculous these days."

Joanna put her hands on his chest, enjoying the feeling of hard muscles and unconsciously stroking the pelt of black hair covering them. "Yes, but I had no idea what lengths you'd go to." Still unwilling to think about her own feelings or question his, she said, "I'm just beginning to get to know Griffin as a lover, you know."

"Griffin as *your* lover," he said, bending his head to kiss her.

She thought it was almost a crime how quickly and easily he could reduce her to a creature of tingling nerves and empty want, but she didn't fight to control how he made her feel. Her arms slid up around his neck, and she rose on tiptoe to fit herself more closely to him, her mouth opening eagerly beneath his.

His hands moved down to cup her buttocks and hold her even tighter against his swelling loins. Against her lips, he muttered, "You're still dressed."

"Mmm. Well, do something about it," she invited huskily. Then she tilted her head back and looked at him. "Our supper's going to get cold."

"To hell with it. We'll send it back to the kitchen to be reheated. The waiter expects it anyway."

Joanna laughed, but she didn't protest when he lifted her in his arms and carried her to the bedroom.

✧　　✧　　✧

"For a couple of intelligent people," Griffin said later, "we haven't been very smart. I assume neither one of us has health concerns, but what about birth control? I'm sorry, Joanna, I didn't even think."

They were on the couch in the living room, both wearing hotel robes as they ate their belated supper—which they had not sent back to the kitchen because they were hungry and it tasted just fine as it was—and watched the news on television.

"I didn't either," she said, "but as it happens, I take those shots every three months. The pill didn't agree with me, and the shots have benefits other than just birth control." She shrugged. "As to health, I know you're a responsible man, so I wasn't worried. And I had a complete physical last summer after the accident, including blood tests. So you don't have to be worried either."

"I wasn't worried, I just thought we should talk about it."

"And you were right." She leaned over and kissed him briefly. "This is a dangerous time for sex."

He touched her cheek as he so often did, and said, "For a woman, there's probably never been a safe time. You always seem to bear most of the consequences."

She chuckled as she drew back. "True enough. But what I can't figure out is how things got so skewed. Do you know that some of the latest research claims that our notions of early man are probably totally wrong? Back when our people were hunter-gatherers and lived in small groups and didn't wear clothes, the thinking goes now, the groups were very likely controlled by the women. Because many species—especially primates—are, in effect, matriarchies."

Griffin grinned at her. "Ah. So, of course, the men had to find ways of asserting control."

Joanna nodded, solemn. "I'm not quite sure when or how the change took place, but whenever you guys got the power, you weren't about to let go of it. Next thing *we* knew, we were wearing utterly absurd things like corsets and bustles and high heels, and were practically sold into slavery when we married—and we *had* to marry, because our fathers certainly weren't going to leave us money or property, and we couldn't get jobs. And now that things are finally getting better, what's happening?"

"What?" he asked obediently.

Joanna frowned at him. "We're criticized constantly. If we work or don't work; if we marry or don't marry; if we have kids or don't. A woman in a position of power, people look at her *clothes,* for God's sake; who looks at a man's?"

"We mostly wear dark suits," Griffin protested. "Boring as hell."

"Umm. Maybe that's the problem. If we went back to our hunter-gatherer days and all went naked—"

"With the hole in the ozone? There'd be a hell of a run on sunblock."

She giggled despite herself. "We're not having a serious conversation here, are we?"

"Not anymore." He grinned again. "I'll just offer a blanket apology for my sex going all the way back to whenever it was we began acting like sexist pigs. Good enough?"

"Well, just remember, I'll have my eye on you. So don't even *think* about reverting."

He saluted her with a hand holding a biscuit. "No, ma'am."

Both chuckling, they went back to eating, absently watching one of those news magazine shows on television. And it was several minutes later when Griffin spoke again.

"Joanna . . ."

She was looking at a chicken leg that appeared to have nothing left to offer, and sighed as she leaned forward to drop the bone onto the plate on the coffee table. Then she leaned back and looked at Griffin. "Yes?"

"You told me that when you saw Regan today, you were sure you were here because of her. To help her."

Joanna nodded. "I was positive."

"Help her in what way?"

"That, I don't know. But if Caroline was terrified enough to reach out as far as she did to plead with me to help Regan, then the threat against her has to be pretty strong, at least in Caroline's mind. To be honest, I was reluctant to leave Scott's house this morning, but I kept telling myself that the only way I could help her was to figure out what her mother was afraid of."

Griffin frowned as he gazed at her. "Why do I get the feeling that with Regan's possible safety in the picture, you aren't going to be nearly as cautious as I want you to be?"

Joanna didn't attempt evasion. Instead, steadily, she said, "If something were to happen to Regan, something I might have been able to prevent, I'd never be able to forgive myself. She doesn't have anybody else, Griffin. Scott doesn't seem to feel a thing for her. She's . . . taken to me. Maybe because of my resemblance to Caroline—but I'd prefer to think that just broke the ice."

"Look, I agree she needs a friend. Maybe she even needs a protector. All I'm asking is that you keep something in mind. You can't protect her if something happens to you."

Joanna nodded. "I know. And I *will* be careful."

He must have heard something rueful in her tone, because Griffin smiled and put his arms around her. "Am I being too much a mother hen?"

"Well, warning me once or twice would have been enough," she replied, grave.

"I just don't want to lose you." He kissed her, then drew back and looked at her, his dark eyes very intent. With his index finger, he traced her eyebrows, the shape of her cheekbones, her nose, her lips. Joanna felt almost hypnotized by his very absorption, and she had the vague feeling she wasn't even breathing.

"And what makes it worse is that I don't really have you," he murmured, his finger still tracing her features as though he were memorizing her. "There's a . . . distance between us, something you won't let me cross. What is it, Joanna? Why are you holding back?"

She tried to concentrate on what he was saying rather than the husky sound of it that her body reacted to like a caress. "I've known you barely a week, Griffin, and a lot has happened. I just . . . I need a little time, that's all."

"Is it only that?"

"No," she answered honestly. "It's . . . everything. I can't explain to you how much of my mind is filled with what's happening here, what happened before I came. The dreams, the questions, the possibilities. Sometimes it's overwhelming. I came here for a reason, because I was compelled to come here, and I just don't have the . . . the emotional energy for more right now. It isn't *you*. It's me."

His hand cupped her cheek, his thumb rubbing across her lower lip slowly. "Then I guess I'll have to be patient a while longer."

Joanna probably would have said something, thanked him or agreed that would be best, but he was kissing her again, and this time it wasn't light or brief or anything but raw hunger. It was a hunger her body felt just as strongly, and she responded to him with the natural instincts of a flower opening to the sun.

She didn't think at all then, and not much in the hours that followed. But by the time they lay close together in her bed in the peaceful quiet of the night, she knew that she didn't need any more time to know that she loved him.

She just needed time to understand what Caroline had meant to him, and to get that other woman out of her head.

And maybe . . . out of his?

✧   ✧   ✧

Griffin left first in the morning, since he had to be at the office early. Joanna told him she'd walk into town later on, that she wanted to stop by the library to talk to Mrs. Chandler and run a few errands—and, yes, she would be careful.

When she left the hotel, it was nearly ten, and she was

unwillingly amused to note how many people in the lobby gave her sidelong glances as she passed through; either the room service waiter had been talkative, or else Griffin had not escaped unnoticed on his way out this morning. Then again, perhaps it had just been the presence of his Blazer parked in the hotel lot overnight that had done the trick.

Life in a fishbowl. Still, Joanna rather liked the feeling of almost everybody knowing each other, and if a certain amount of privacy was lost—okay, if *most* privacy was lost—that still seemed to her a small price to pay for the feeling of community.

She stopped at the library for a few minutes to talk to Mrs. Chandler. It was just small talk, but when she impulsively asked the librarian if she had noticed anything odd about Caroline in the week before the accident, she was surprised by the answer she got.

"Well, just one thing. She came in either that week or the week before and asked me an odd question: Wanted to know how she could find out what countries did *not* have an extradition treaty with the United States."

Joanna frowned. "So she wanted to know where U.S. criminals could go without fearing arrest?"

"That was the information she was looking for. I was puzzled at the time, but people do come in here with odd questions, naturally, so I didn't think too much about it."

"You didn't notice anything about her behavior? I mean, did she seem upset or nervous to you?"

Mrs. Chandler's sharp eyes narrowed slightly. "To be honest, I don't remember. Why, Joanna?"

Joanna shrugged. "I'm just trying to find out all I can about her."

"Forgive me if I doubt that's your reason." The librarian smiled. "But don't worry, I won't demand the truth. Sooner or later, I'll know it."

"One of the benefits of a small town?"

"Well, the truth usually comes out, and when it does everyone knows it. That's not to say, of course, that gossip doesn't get completely out of hand at times. Like now. I wouldn't blame Cain Barlow if he moved back to Portland."

"Have you seen him?" Joanna asked.

"Not for a few days. Not that it's unusual for him to go off painting, but he's not exactly a dense man, and if he knows which way the talk is leaning, it wouldn't surprise me to learn he'd left just to get away from it."

Joanna thought about that as she left the library and walked toward the downtown stores. If Cain *had* left to get away from the gossip, he couldn't have picked a worse time. The faster he cleared his name, the sooner the gossip would die down. Joanna knew Griffin well enough to know that, once satisfied as to Cain's innocence, he would personally see to it that the entire town was made aware of that fact.

But until then . . .

And what about Caroline's question to the librarian? It was beginning to look more and more as if she had indeed been involved in something dangerous. Had she herself committed a crime? Or had she discovered that her lover had done so and was preparing to flee the country? Had that been the final straw for Caroline, finding out that the man she was involved with was about to leave and didn't intend to take her with him?

With Scott eliminated in her own mind, and Cain out of reach at the moment, Joanna couldn't help but think of Doc. Had he been her lover? And if it had been him, what could he have been involved in that had so frightened Caroline? A doctor, of course, had the knowledge and means to kill; had he? And had Caroline somehow discovered that? Joanna hadn't checked so-called natural deaths in Cliffside during the last six months or so—perhaps she should?

Or perhaps Doc had been—maybe still was—involved in something else. As the town's main doctor, he was certainly privy to a great deal of information; could he have been blackmailing someone?

Brooding unhappily over that possibility, Joanna looked

up to realize she was nearly at the cafe. Lyssa and Dylan stood near the door talking, and then the exotic blonde headed across the street toward the store she ran, On the Corner. She saw Joanna as she turned, but just lifted a hand in greeting as she went on.

"Hi, Joanna." Dylan smiled at her. "Can I buy you a cup of coffee? I'm just about to go inside and take a break."

"Sure, thanks." As she preceded him inside, Joanna asked, "A break from what?"

"Wrestling with bureaucratic red tape," he responded. "Scott wants to move forward with all speed to build Caroline's addition to the clinic, and you wouldn't believe the paperwork involved. I just spent the last two hours at the courthouse."

Sitting across from him at a booth, Joanna smiled sympathetically. "You'd think things would be different in a small town, but that sounds just like Atlanta." She looked up as Liz came to their table, and ordered coffee from the waitress. Dylan did as well. It was brought to them promptly and with a cheerful smile from Liz, who asked Joanna if she had recovered from the crash.

"Completely, thanks," Joanna told her. "Didn't even get a scratch."

"Glad to hear it," Liz said with a nod. "God, these modern cars are filled with so much wiring it's a wonder we don't all find ourselves hurtling down a highway out of control. My brother's a mechanic, and he says between all the sensors and other gadgets in these little cars, there's hardly room for a decent engine anymore."

"I think I'll get something bigger next time," Joanna mused. "Maybe a Jeep."

"I like Jeeps," Liz volunteered. Then she rolled her eyes as the cook yelled to her that there was an order waiting. "The master's voice," she muttered, and turned away with her coffeepot.

"Scott told me you'd been in a wreck," Dylan said, shaking his head. "Something about the throttle? Jeez, sometimes I think we'd do better to go back to horses and buggies."

Relieved that Scott had apparently not mentioned the tampering, Joanna laughed and said, "Oh, we don't have to be that drastic. It was just a fluky thing, what happened to me. Anyway, the car's the rental company's headache now, and I'm not going to worry about it."

"Probably smart."

She smiled at him and sipped her coffee. "So, what about your headaches at the moment? I saw the bulldozers beside the clinic and assumed the new addition was well under way."

"Well, Scott more or less jumped the gun when he ordered the lots cleared off. The work had to be stopped while all the necessary permits and paperwork were taken care of. And Doc isn't happy, of course, because with winter coming on, the addition probably won't be finished until next summer and will undoubtedly cost more than the estimates."

"Caroline left a finite amount to cover the costs?"

Dylan nodded. "Probably enough—but maybe not. Of course, Scott would make up the difference."

"Would he?"

"Oh, yeah. Caroline wanted it built, and he'll see to it that it's built."

Joanna hesitated as he drank some of his coffee, then said, "I guess you knew her pretty well."

"I was in and out of the house nearly every day," he said musingly. "So, yeah, I guess I did. She didn't much notice the peons, though."

Joanna felt a little chill and really looked at him, focused on him. "Peons? Surely she didn't feel that way about everybody who worked for Scott?" She couldn't help but think of Adam Harrison and his miserable love for Caroline.

Dylan frowned slightly. "It wasn't contempt, just indifference. She'd grown up with servants in the house, and to her they were virtually invisible; since I have an office in the house and work for Scott, I guess that put me in the same class. There was nothing hateful about it." He smiled wryly. "But feeling invisible isn't the most pleasant sensation."

But handsome men weren't invisible to Caroline—no matter who they were. Joanna knew that as surely as she knew her own name.

"I imagine not," she said slowly. *Another lover? God, did she even sleep with a man her husband saw every day, a man with an office in her own house?* It seemed more than likely, but Joanna wasn't quite ready to ask a blunt question. Instead, she said, "Did you notice anything odd about her that last week? I mean, was she upset?"

"Upset? Caroline was never upset, at least not that I saw." He shrugged. "But I was in and out of Portland that week, so I hardly saw her. Why?"

It was Joanna's turn to shrug. "I just thought she must have been upset about something to lose control of her car that way."

"I've always wondered where she was coming back from," Dylan said. "I mean, so far north of town, and heading back this way, according to Griff. She didn't leave town very often—and in the middle of the day?"

"Maybe she went into Portland to shop," Joanna suggested, not about to mention her planned meeting at the old barn. *Would you know about that place, Dylan? Did you meet her there?*

"She wasn't dressed for shopping in Portland, not that morning," Dylan said. "Caroline always dressed to the teeth if she was going into the city, and not in jeans and a sweater. But maybe she changed later."

"Probably," Joanna said. "Anyway, I guess I've just been looking for a reason when it doesn't really matter."

He was looking at her intently, his face grave and his eyes seemingly without shadows. "You feel a kind of connection with her, don't you? Because of the resemblance?"

"Maybe. It's unnerving enough to find out you look so much like someone else; finding out they died suddenly is an even bigger shock. And . . . Regan seems to have taken to me."

"I feel sorry for that kid," Dylan said, sighing. "Barely see her at the house these days; she's almost like a shadow, vanishing around a corner when you get a glimpse of her."

Deciding to ask at least one blunt question, Joanna said, "Has Scott always been so indifferent to her?"

Dylan immediately shook his head. "Not at all. When she was born, he doted on her. I mean, really doted. Nothing was too good for his little girl. And it was obvious she adored him. Then, about—I don't know—three or four years later, everything changed. At first, I just thought he was working harder than before, going up to Portland and down to San Francisco pretty often; he didn't seem to have time for Regan anymore. Caroline was . . . fussing over her, reading to her, taking her to dancing lessons and to parties at friends' houses.

"I thought she was just trying to make up to Regan for Scott always being too busy for her. But gradually, I realized that Scott's attitude had completely changed toward his daughter. There was no feeling on his face when he looked at her. I even saw him physically push her away a couple of times when she was smaller. After that, she stopped trying to get close to him."

"Do you have any idea why he changed so drastically?" Joanna had an idea. A simple, chilling idea.

Dylan's smile was twisted. "What I know, I picked up from observation, nothing more. I doubt Scott confides in anyone—certainly not me. No, Joanna, I don't have a clue."

Joanna sipped her coffee and brooded. Had Dylan been Caroline's lover? Her last lover? She wanted badly to ask, but in this public place dared not bring up the subject. And what about Scott's emotional abandonment of Regan? Joanna's feelings about Scott were still ambivalent and uncertain, but she was convinced he was a long way from being an unfeeling man. Which left, in her mind, only one explanation as to why he had pushed an adored daughter away.

"Oh, damn," Dylan said suddenly, glancing at his watch. "I have to get back to the courthouse. Joanna, stay as long as you want—my treat."

"Thanks, Dylan."

He slid from the booth, smiling. "My pleasure. See you later."

"Sure." Joanna watched him head toward the cashier to pay, then turned her gaze down to her cup briefly before pushing it away. Griffin was probably wondering where she was, she thought. And if she sat here much longer, she'd undoubtedly be drawn into a conversation with Liz or someone else.

She waited until Dylan had left the cafe and crossed the street to get to the courthouse, then left the cafe herself, waving good-bye to Liz without pausing to encourage conversation.

It was her intention to head toward the Sheriff's Department, skipping her planned errands for the time being, but when she saw Doc come out of the drugstore, she immediately turned in that direction and swiftly caught up with him.

"Doc?"

He stopped and turned, looking at her with brows lifted. "Hello, Joanna. What can I do for you?"

There was no one near them, and the door of the nearest store was closed, so Joanna didn't hesitate. Politeness hadn't been effective on Doc before; maybe sheer effrontery would. "You can tell me the truth," she said. *I'm sorry, but I think I'm running out of time. . . .*

"I don't know what you're talking about." His voice was still pleasant, and he wore a small smile, but his eyes were guarded.

"Oh yes you do. You lied to me about having seen Caroline before she was killed."

His mouth tightened. "It slipped my mind, that's all."

"Did it?" Joanna leaned back against the railing and

crossed her arms, managing a smile. "Or was it just a case of one more man feeling guilty because he wasn't there for Caroline when she needed him?"

"What do you mean, one more man?"

She had his full and complete attention now, and Joanna braced herself inwardly. She didn't like what she was about to do, not one bit, but she didn't have a choice. "Oh, she spread the guilt around, Doc—especially among her past lovers. Don't tell me you thought you were the only one? Even Scott says there must have been at least half a dozen during their marriage."

Doc didn't change expression, but his voice was very soft when he said, "Thanks a lot for telling me."

"Maybe you needed to know." Joanna let the mockery seep out of her voice until there was only weariness. "Maybe you all need to know. Because as far as I can see, not one of you has been able to let her go."

"You don't understand."

"No? Then explain it to me, Doc. Explain to me how she managed to emotionally destroy a man without destroying his obsession with her."

He opened his mouth, then shut it and shook his head. "I can't. She was . . . there was just something about her."

"I guess so." Joanna shook her head. "Destructive yet seductive. Some people would call that the definition of evil."

Doc immediately shook his head. "No, not evil. Caroline was . . . always at war with herself, always struggling. She was never satisfied with what she was or what she had, but always needed more of everything. She was never deliberately cruel, you have to understand that. But she had to get what she wanted, no matter what the cost to someone else."

"She sounds like a spoiled child to me," Joanna observed.

His thin face softened in a way that made Joanna feel nothing but pity for him, and he said, "There *was* something childlike about her, something inherently innocent. Yes, she could be spoiled—but she could also be incredibly generous and loving. That's the Caroline I remember."

"You weren't having an affair with her right before she died, were you?"

"No," he answered almost absently. "It was a couple of years ago."

Joanna didn't bother asking him if he knew who *had* been having an affair with Caroline; the news that he wasn't her only discarded lover had shocked him. "Did she tell you why she needed to talk to you the last time you saw her?"

Doc seemed to come back from a great distance, blinking as he looked at Joanna. "No. I had an emergency—I was in a hurry. She said she needed to talk to me . . . and I brushed her aside."

Joanna sighed, unsurprised by the guilt in his voice. "You weren't the only one, Doc," she said. "Try to remember that. And thanks for telling me the truth."

He nodded slightly, then turned away from her without another word and went on his way.

She remained there for a moment, staring after him, then continued on her interrupted walk toward Griffin's office. He probably wouldn't be happy with her that she had backed Doc into a corner and questioned him, but at least she'd done it in the middle of town under myriad eyes.

There was still a chance that it had been some secret of Doc's that had so frightened Caroline, Joanna thought, but the chance felt slim to her. And she still didn't know who had been Caroline's lover when she was killed. *Unless it was Dylan*.

She was feeling upset and discouraged when she went into Griffin's office and sat down in his visitor's chair, and she knew he saw it. "I hope you have some good news," she told him.

Griffin looked up from the papers covering his desk and smiled wryly. "I don't have any kind of news, good or bad.

Except that Cain's still among the missing. How was your morning?"

Joanna sighed. "Mrs. Chandler says Caroline was in shortly before the accident asking about which countries don't have an extradition treaty with the U.S. So it looks more and more like she was involved in something illegal, wouldn't you say?"

"I'd say the possibility looks stronger," he agreed.

"I also talked to Doc," Joanna said. "And he wasn't a lot of help. He wasn't having an affair with Caroline before she died, but he did a couple of years ago. You don't have to put that in a report or anything, do you? I probably shouldn't have told you."

"That kind of information doesn't belong in a report unless it becomes relevant. And I already knew," Griffin said.

She eyed him thoughtfully. "I seem to recall you looking surprised when I first mentioned the possibility that Caroline might have been having an affair."

"I was surprised. As far as I could tell, there was no talk about Doc and Caroline, so I was startled you could have found out so quickly."

Joanna didn't ask him how he had found out, she merely nodded. "Anyway, I suppose he could have a secret to protect, but I can't see him scaring Caroline in any way—or pushing somebody over the cliffs."

"No, me either."

Joanna was about to mention her meeting with Dylan and her suspicions about him, but before she could, there was a sharp rap at the door and Scott McKenna walked in, closing the door behind him with a deliberate gesture.

Joanna was rather glad she sat to one side and out of the direct line of sight between the two men. She could literally feel Griffin tense, and to call Scott's eyes unfriendly was a bit like calling a diamond hard; the word didn't begin to describe the subject. Definitely uneasy herself, she looked between them and waited.

"Scott." Griffin's voice was cordial, but he didn't get to his feet.

The other man merely nodded, and said abruptly, "According to Joanna, there's some question about Caroline's death. True?"

"True enough. Sit down."

Ignoring the invitation, Scott looked at Joanna. "After you left yesterday, I wondered if I might be wrong about Caroline not keeping a diary or journal. So I went through her things."

"Did you find a diary or journal?"

He shook his head, then reached into the inside pocket of his suit jacket and pulled out a small brass key. "But I found this." He dropped the key onto Griffin's desk and looked at the sheriff once again. "It was in her bedroom desk. I've never seen it before. As far as I can determine, that key fits nothing at the house."

Joanna looked at Griffin. "Somebody told me Caroline bought a little antique box shortly before she died."

"There's no sign of one among her things," Scott said.

Griffin reached for his phone. "Did she get it at One More Thing, Joanna?"

"I think so."

Scott didn't move and watched with no expression as Griffin placed the call.

"Bonnie? Griff. Listen, did Mrs. McKenna buy a small antique box from you last summer? When? I see. Did the box have a lock and key?" He held the small brass key in his palm as he said, "Describe the key for me." Then he nodded, said, "Thanks, Bonnie," and cradled the receiver.

"It's the key to the box?" Joanna asked.

"Or an exact duplicate. The question is, where's the box this key fits?"

"And what did she put *in* the box?"

Scott looked between them for a moment, then fixed his gaze on Joanna. "What makes you believe she had anything to hide like that?"

Since Griffin didn't seem disposed to object, Joanna

said, "It's a guess, Scott. We think Caroline knew something that was dangerous to someone. And she was scared. She tried to talk to a few people here in town in the days before the accident, people she thought she could trust, but for one reason or another, she wasn't able to confide in any of them."

"Why didn't she tell me?" he asked flatly.

Joanna shook her head. "I can't answer that. But we're reasonably sure she was ready to confide in Griffin when she was killed."

Scott looked at the other man. "How are you sure?" he asked.

"She sent me a note, asking me to meet her," Griffin answered readily enough. "I got tied up here and didn't make it. That was the day she died."

Scott's face tightened slightly. "So for once, you weren't Johnnie-on-the-spot."

There was a moment of icy silence. Then, with precise emphasis, Griffin demanded, "What the hell is that supposed to mean?"

Scott shrugged, a smile that was ugly curving his lips. "Why, nothing, Sheriff. I just assumed you were always at the ready when my wife needed something."

Joanna winced slightly, wondering silently how long the tension had been building toward this confrontation. It had to happen, of course, sooner or later. She had known that the day these two men had faced each other on the peaceful sidewalk of Cliffside.

"Look, I don't know what your problem is," Griffin snapped, surging to his feet behind the desk, "but I've had about enough of your bullshit. You want to say something to me? Say it straight out. You want to take me on? Name a time and place outside this office and I'll be there. But in the meantime, why don't you go home and spend some time with that sad little kid of yours. She needs a father a lot worse than I need this hassle from you."

"Then maybe *you'd* better go," Scott muttered, turning away from the desk.

"What?"

He had taken no more than a step, when Scott turned back, the pain on his face so raw that Joanna wanted to flinch away from it, and his voice was ragged.

"I said maybe you should go comfort Regan. God*damn* you, she isn't my daughter. *She's yours.*"

$\mathcal{F}$ OURTEEN

✦ ✦ ✦

$\mathcal{O}$N SOME LEVEL of her mind, Joanna had been preparing herself for Scott's stark words ever since she had learned of his sudden change of attitude toward Regan years before. It was the only thing that made sense, the only reason to explain a father's sudden coldness to a small and innocent child. And given Caroline's history, it was certainly possible.

What Joanna hadn't prepared herself for was her own pain when she heard that accusation leveled at Griffin.

"No," Griffin said. He hadn't glanced at Joanna, but kept his gaze fixed on Scott.

"You think I'd make up something like this? Caroline told me. She *told* me, years ago."

Griffin put his hands on his desk and leaned forward, his eyes unwavering on Scott, and his voice was very quiet. "Listen to me. She lied to you. I don't know why, but she did. There was no affair. We never had sex, not once. There is no possibility that Regan could be mine."

Joanna began to breathe again.

"I don't believe you." Scott's voice was still ragged. "She wouldn't have lied to me about that. Not *that*."

"You want me to take a paternity test to prove it? Gladly. But you take one too. She's your daughter, Scott."

Into the thick silence, Joanna said quietly, "I know you think she looks like Caroline, Scott, but look at her more closely. The shape of her eyes is yours, and her ears. Many of her expressions. And her hands, they're a feminine duplicate of yours. The first time I saw you two together, I thought she resembled you more than Caroline."

Scott stepped back toward the desk and reached out to grip the back of the other visitor's chair. He was looking past Griffin, past everything except his own anguish. His face was white, but his voice was steadier when he said, "I can't have been that blind."

"She blinded you," Joanna told him. "After what she told you, you had to look at Regan with doubt. And once you did that, the damage was done. Caroline must have wanted to hurt you very badly."

After a moment, Scott shook his head, still with that blind expression. "No, not hurt me. She wanted Regan all to herself, and I was in her way. So she said what she knew would make me turn away from the child, what she knew I wouldn't be able to bear."

Doc was right—she had to get what she wanted, no matter what. It rang true to Joanna, that Caroline would have taken that drastic, incredibly selfish and cruel action to have her child's entire focus and love. And it had probably never occurred to her that she would be hurting Regan by depriving her of a father's love; in her mind, her love was enough for Regan. And, to be fair, she had been an excellent mother, devoting herself to her child with lavish attention. But at what cost to Regan?

At what cost to Scott?

Neither Joanna nor Griffin said anything else, waiting silently for Scott to return from whatever distant hell he had been thrown into so suddenly. He did come back, slowly, his eyes gradually focusing on the here and now. And it must have been painfully difficult for such a proud and reserved man to realize how much of himself had been stripped bare in this small office.

He looked at them both, then turned and went to the door. He paused after he'd opened it, and looked back at Joanna. "You were right," he said, and then left the office, closing the door very quietly behind him.

"Right about what?" Griffin asked.

Still gazing after Scott, Joanna murmured, "He was in love with Caroline. No matter what she did, all these years he's been in love with her."

"Jesus Christ," Griffin said, sitting down rather heavily in his chair. "No wonder he's hated my guts for years."

Joanna drew a breath and looked at him. "I guess it never crossed your mind that he might think Regan was your child?"

"God, no. If it had, I would have faced him about it long ago." He shook his head. "Since there was no possibility of that, and since, to me, Regan was so obviously Scott's daughter, I just never considered it. He didn't seem close to the child, but, hell, he didn't seem close to anyone."

Joanna didn't wonder that Scott's indifference to Regan had passed virtually unremarked upon by Griffin and others. Only someone who had spent a great deal of time closer to the family—like Dylan, for instance—was likely to have noticed what had been, in effect, a sudden and drastic change, and to wonder at it.

"But you must have wondered why he suddenly began hating you," she said.

"I just thought—"

"Thought what?"

Griffin hesitated, then swore under his breath. "You said once that there had obviously been *something* between Caroline and me at some time in the past. You were right, in a way. There was something between us."

Joanna waited silently, hoping that she would at last be

able to understand what effect that seductive and destructive woman had had on Griffin—and what baggage he carried now as a result of it.

"I hadn't been in Cliffside long," he said slowly. "I had left Chicago because I was on the verge of burnout, sick to death of all the violent crime I saw day after day. The idea of being a small-town sheriff sounded like heaven, so when I heard about the job when I was in Portland, I didn't hesitate to apply. My credentials suited the town council, and within a couple of weeks, I was moving into the cottage here."

He shrugged. "The first few weeks were almost like a vacation, at least after Chicago. Not one crime reported the whole time. It gave me a chance to catch my breath. I was settling in and getting to know the people here. Caroline was one of the town's leading ladies. Oh, she was young, only married a couple of years, but she seemed to be involved in most everything around here. She seemed shy and a bit fragile, at least to me—and I guess I paid more attention to her than I should have."

"She fell in love with you," Joanna murmured.

Griffin nodded. "Took me completely by surprise when she blurted it out one day when we were alone together at my place. She was out walking, she said, and stopped by to ask me about something—I forget what. Anyway, when she said she loved me, I didn't know what to say to her. I didn't feel that way about her, not at all. To me, she was Scott's wife and way out of my league—and she'd always seemed more child than woman to me."

All that sweet innocence cost you one, Caroline, Joanna couldn't help but think.

"I tried to let her down easily," Griffin went on. "Told her I was to blame for her misunderstanding my feelings. Then I added a few asinine clichés, like she'd realize she had been mistaken, and that we could still be friends."

"How did she take it?"

Griffin rubbed the back of his neck and looked rueful.

"She cried buckets, and the next thing I knew, we were on the couch and I was holding her."

Tears. Jeez, Caroline, was there a trick you didn't *pull on him?*

"Nothing happened," Griffin added a bit hastily, perhaps reading something in Joanna's face. "But at some point I realized that she—wasn't crying anymore. She took my hand and put it—never mind."

"Thank you," Joanna said.

He grinned at her. "All right, all right. But you did ask. Anyway, I managed to get her off my couch and out of the house. After that, things were a little strained between us for a while, but she never mentioned the subject again. And neither did I." His amusement faded, and he added, "She always turned to me if she had some problem, though—and I guess Scott noticed."

"His Johnnie-on-the-spot remark?"

"Yeah. In a way, I guess I got into the habit of making things easier for Caroline whenever I could. Little things, mostly, like getting her permits quickly if she wanted the kids at the school to have a parade, or helping convince the town council her ideas for the community theater were workable. That sort of thing."

"So when you realized Scott hated you . . ."

"I just assumed he knew or suspected that Caroline had been in love with me, and that he resented the time we spent together. I knew it was completely innocent, though, and I made damned sure there were no more private meetings between us. And since I hardly saw Scott, how he felt about me wasn't on my mind very often."

Joanna nodded. "I see. So you felt guilty for not meeting Caroline that last day mostly because you'd gotten in the habit of taking care of her."

"Was that bothering you?" Griffin asked her.

"A little. Caroline had such a strong effect on the men in her life, even long after relationships ended, and I couldn't help wondering . . ."

"If I'd been in love with her."

"It crossed my mind," Joanna confessed. "Even though you denied involvement, I couldn't get past the feeling that there had been something between you. It seemed more than possible. And since the other men who'd cared about her couldn't seem to let go . . . Well. A living rival is one thing—it's hard to fight a ghost." *Especially one haunting you as well as the man you love.*

Griffin rose from his chair and came around the desk to pull her up into his arms. "I thought I'd made myself clear," he said dryly, "but obviously not. Sweetheart, I'd never been in love with anyone until I met you. And I sure as hell didn't fall for you because you faintly resemble Caroline—or anyone else. I've never met anyone with big golden eyes like yours, or that sweet, lazy voice, or the knack you have of pushing everything else out of my mind until all I can think of is you."

A bit dazed, Joanna said, "But . . . it's barely been a week since we met."

"Does that matter?" he asked steadily.

After a moment, she shook her head. "No. Griffin—"

She was interrupted rudely by a sharp rap on the door and then the quick entrance into the office of one of the deputies, who was carrying a thick sheaf of papers.

"Uh, sorry," he said stolidly. "But you wanted the info on Butler as soon as it came in, Griff, and we just got a stack of stuff via fax from San Francisco."

"Casey," Griffin said, "I can't begin to tell you how rotten your timing is."

Joanna couldn't help but laugh a little as she eased out of his embrace. "It's all right, we can talk later," she told him. "Listen, I have a few things to do, so why don't I go back to the hotel and leave you with this stuff."

"It's lunchtime," Griffin protested, the look in his eyes indicating a hunger for something other than food.

"Why don't we have a late lunch," she suggested. "You can pick me up at the hotel at two, okay?"

Griffin's gaze cut to Casey, who was still waiting imperturbably. "I guess it'll have to be. But don't forget where we left off."

"Not a chance," she murmured.

✧   ✧   ✧

The familiar tension tightened around Joanna the moment she left Griffin's office, and she had to marvel at his effect on her. It was literally the only thing that could push her ever present sense of urgency aside, and she felt a brief, craven desire to go back and wrap her arms around him because she didn't know how much more of this anxious tension she could take.

As much as I have to. That was part of it, too, this determination she'd felt since before leaving Atlanta, this compulsion to *do* something. It was wearing her down and frustrating her to no end, but it wouldn't leave her alone.

And maybe that was why her voice was a bit sharper than it should have been when she encountered Dylan again, this time on the sidewalk just a block down from the Sheriff's Department.

"Can I talk to you a minute?" she asked as she reached him. There was no one around them, and she didn't want to miss the opportunity to talk to him without the danger of anyone overhearing them.

"Sure, Joanna. What's up?" His pleasant face wore a smile, but . . . were his eyes just a bit guarded?

Joanna didn't feel she had the time to be subtle, and besides, being direct had worked on Doc. So, bluntly, she said, "Did you have an affair with Caroline?"

For an instant, his face went completely expressionless. But then he smiled faintly. "Asking out of idle curiosity, Joanna?"

She shook her head slightly and repeated, "Did you have an affair with Caroline?"

Dylan glanced down at the briefcase he carried as if he needed to avoid her steady gaze. His face had gone expressionless again, and when his eyes met hers again, they were filled with shadows. "The lady of the manor . . . condescended. Is that what you want to hear? All right, it's true.

I fell like a ton of bricks when I came here to work for Scott. She had grown up while I was away at college and working in San Francisco."

"Did she feel the same?"

His mouth twisted bitterly. "Hell, no. She spent the better part of a year taunting me. Smiling and flirting whenever Scott wasn't around—and keeping just out of reach. She nearly drove me crazy, damn her."

"But you did have an affair." He sounded just like the others, Joanna thought, bitter and resentful—and obsessed.

"If you could call it that." He shrugged jerkily. "We met every day for a week and practically tore each other's clothes off. Then—nothing. She told me it was over, and after that acted as if it had never happened."

Joanna wanted to look away from that hard, bright bitterness in his smile, but forced herself to ask quietly, "Where did you meet?"

He laughed shortly. "In the backseat of my car. Can you beat that? I told her I could afford a room, but she insisted. So I'd drive someplace where we could park off the road and out of sight, and we'd climb in the backseat."

Yet another odd, uncomfortable place, Joanna thought, as if Caroline had punished herself even while seeking pleasure. "Was this recently, Dylan?"

"No, it was years ago, just after I came back here. Now, do you mind telling me why in the hell it's any of your business?" Dylan asked flatly.

Joanna shook her head. "I'm just trying to put the pieces together, that's all. I won't tell anyone, Dylan, you can be sure of that. I just had to ask." She hesitated, then said, "Did Caroline try to talk to you about something the week before she was killed? Something that was bothering her, I mean?"

He frowned. "I hardly saw her that week. I must have gone up to Portland three different times and stayed overnight at least twice. Anyway, she'd gotten damn good at ignoring me, so why would she have wanted to talk to me about anything at all?"

Maybe she wouldn't have. Maybe, by then, she'd learned not to seek help from a discarded lover. Maybe that was when she finally went to Griffin. "I was just wondering," Joanna said. "Trying to find out if she was upset about something that last week."

"Caroline was never upset, I told you that. She was the lady of the manor—never lost her cool."

It sounded as if Dylan's anger and bitterness had outlasted his obsession, but Joanna didn't doubt he'd carry Caroline's scars for a long, long time yet. All her men seemed to.

Joanna smiled faintly. "Well, thanks for being so honest with me."

A bit dryly, he said, "Forgive me if I don't say 'You're welcome.'" No happier with her than Doc had been, Dylan turned and walked away.

With a sigh, Joanna also continued on her way, her thoughts very troubled. How many other men had Caroline used and discarded? Was Cain one of them? Had he been her last lover, despite his relationship with Holly?

Dammit, Cain, where are you?

✧   ✧   ✧

All the way to Portland, Holly kept telling herself she was making an awful mistake. She should have taken Joanna's advice and just waited all this out, been patient until Cain reappeared in Cliffside and settled things. But when she'd gone into town this morning, the talk had reached the point where people had openly asked her if Cain was about to be arrested for Amber Wade's murder.

She had talked to Griff when he had left The Inn this morning, and though his deepening relationship with Joanna obviously delighted him, he hadn't been happy about Cain's continued absence and wouldn't be patient much longer even for the sake of friendship.

Which was why, Holly told herself now, she had to go to Portland. If nobody had seen Cain around town, and his car was gone—which it was, she'd checked—then the most logical place for him to be was at his studio in the city.

Nobody in Cliffside knew about the place except Holly, or, at least, knew where it was. Cain had always been a bit secretive about it. And since he had no phone there because he hated interruptions of any kind while he was working, Holly had no choice except to drive up there.

She didn't know what she was going to say to him. Even as she parked her car and went inside the big converted warehouse where Cain's studio apartment occupied the top floor, she had no idea what was going to come out of her mouth if and when he let her in.

In the lobby, she buzzed insistently, but it was several minutes before Cain's irritated voice came through the intercom.

"What?"

"Cain, it's Holly. Can I come up?"

There was a brief silence, and then she heard the big freight elevator begin to lower toward the lobby. When it arrived, she opened the fencelike barriers and got in. The slow, loud journey up four floors felt interminable to her, and she still didn't know what she was going to say to him.

Cain was waiting for her and opened the outer barrier as she opened the inner one. He actually looked pleased to see her. "Hello, babe. What brings you here?"

"Where the hell have you been?" she heard herself snap.

Both Cain's brows went up. "For the past couple of days? Here."

Appalled at herself, Holly heard that fishwife who apparently lived inside her snarl another question as she stalked past him and into the big open room that was filled with several easels, tables holding cans of brushes and tubes of paint and numerous jars and rags, a draped platform where models could pose, and various other trappings of an artist's work. "Just vanishing with hardly a word to let me face the gossips of Cliffside alone?"

"Oh, have I been tried and hanged?" he asked, bored indifference in his voice. "My being there would hardly change that, Holly. And why don't you just ignore them? The talk will die down soon enough—"

"No, it won't," she said, whirling to face him. "Don't you get it, Cain? You lied to the sheriff about where you were Sunday night, and everyone in town knows that."

He frowned. "How did he find out I lied?"

"Somebody saw your car leave around midnight. Where did you go? Did you come here?"

Cain hesitated, then nodded. "Yeah, I came here."

"Why? To work? What could be so damned important that you needed to slip out in the middle of the night to work on it? And why in God's name did you lie to Griff about it?"

"It was none of his business. Look, I didn't kill that girl—"

"Damn you, I *know* that! I just don't understand all this lying, and why you're hiding out up here when everything's going to hell back home, and why you won't *talk* to me—" She broke off abruptly as her gaze fell on one of the easels that was off to one side of Cain's work area.

It was the painting of Caroline, finished now. And beautiful.

"Or maybe I do understand," she murmured. "How amazingly you've captured her. I guess you did know her well, huh? Very well indeed. You were her lover, weren't you?"

"Yes," Cain said.

✧   ✧   ✧

It was getting cloudy as Joanna walked back to the hotel, and the changing weather exactly matched her mood. She felt as uneasy as the dark clouds scudding across the sky, despite thinking that she might already have done something to help Regan.

She still felt anxious about the little girl, very much so. She still had the nagging feeling that danger lurked somewhere about, and that it threatened Regan. But something *had* changed, and she couldn't help but hope that the change would benefit Regan.

Scott had changed. Or, at least, Joanna thought he had. And she had initiated that change, hadn't she? If she

hadn't told Scott what they suspected, it was likely he
would not have looked through Caroline's things or recognized the possible importance of one small brass key. And
if he had not done that, it was unlikely that the confrontation with Griffin would have taken place, not when the two
men had been avoiding each other for so many years.

So, perhaps Joanna had helped. Perhaps she had, indirectly, helped to give back her father to Regan. Perhaps.

She knew it wouldn't be easy for Scott or Regan, this
sudden change in their relationship. Regan still had a lot of
anger toward her father, some of it about her mother's
death and some, no doubt, born in that small girl inexplicably pushed away from him years ago. But Joanna felt
sure Scott would try to rebuild their relationship, because
any man who had so adored his child once would want
that feeling back again.

She went into The Inn and up to her room, her thoughts
turning to Griffin. She wasn't afraid of Caroline's ghost
anymore, but she was still reluctant to put her own feelings
into words, and she'd been a bit relieved that Casey had
interrupted them. She somehow doubted that Griffin
would like hearing "I love you, but Caroline's still in my
head."

Yet, that was what she'd have to tell him, at least until
this was over. And even then, even assuming that the puzzle was completed and three murders were solved and Regan was utterly safe—even then, Joanna wasn't certain that
the urgent presence in her mind would leave her alone.

She hadn't thought about it until now, but the mere
possibility that Caroline would haunt her forever was distinctly unnerving. Bad enough to be haunted by *any* presence, but . . .

"Not you, Caroline," she heard herself mutter a bit
grimly. "Anybody but you."

Joanna sat on her bed and took a deep breath, pushing
the moment of horrified panic out of her mind. That
wouldn't happen. It would *not*. There was going to be a
happy ending to all this, one way or another. And when it

was over, Joanna wouldn't have anybody in her head except Griffin.

Period.

She sat there for a moment, thinking, trying to capture an elusive something in her mind that was nagging at her. Something she had seen? Something someone had told her? *Damn, what is it?* She got up and went to the dresser, picking up a brush to straighten her hair, then frowned as her gaze fell on her small travel jewelry case. Was that what was nagging at her?

Caroline's necklace. Joanna opened up the case to fish it out, then stared at the delicate piece of jewelry dangling from her fingers. "Damn. I forgot to give this to Regan," she muttered.

She wrapped the fragile chain around her fingers, turning the heart this way and that to catch the light. What lover had Caroline met in the old barn the day she had lost this? Had it been Cain? *Had* he managed to juggle two women in a small town without either of them finding out about the other?

And if he had been her last lover, what could he have been involved in that had frightened her? Or was Joanna all wrong, and Caroline's fear had had nothing to do with her lover?

"Dammit."

Still holding the necklace, Joanna went to her balcony and opened the doors, stepping out into the cool, damp air. She looked off toward the south, toward Scott and Caroline's house, wondering. Wondering.

The dream had brought her here. Led her to many of the places and people she had needed to encounter. And virtually everything in the dream existed in reality. Ocean waves crashing and a big house overlooking the sea—literally existing, and the house might have also represented Dylan and the affair Caroline had conducted with a man in her own house. A painting with lots of color on an easel—literal, and it had led her to meet Cain, to talk to him. But

perhaps she hadn't paid enough attention to the fact that
Cain had painted it, or that it was the painting of a little
girl?

Had she missed the importance of the painting?

"Damn," Joanna said again, frowning. And what about
the other things? The roses, definitely real, had led her to
Adam Harrison; surely they had no meaning other than
that? And the carousel horse existed in Caroline's favorite
place. The paper airplane she'd never been able to figure
out; there hadn't been a sign of a paper airplane anywhere
here in Cliffside.

So—symbolic, maybe?

"Paper. Paper flying. Paper moving," she said. "What
the hell does it *mean*?"

Nothing, to her. The clock ticking obviously meant time
passing. The child crying had to be Regan. She was Caroline's daughter, and besides, there wasn't another child involved in all this.

And the emotions Joanna felt? The fear that clawed at
her throat and woke her with her heart pounding and a
sense of overpowering urgency—what about that? A warning from Caroline? A desperate plea that her child be
helped and protected? Or simply the tangled emotions of a
woman in the instant of her violent death?

No. No, it had to be more than that. Joanna was here
for a reason, she was certain of it. Trouble was here. Danger was here. Or else why had someone tried to kill her?

Sighing, she let her gaze idly roam from the big house in
the distance over the woods between here and there that
hid Caroline's gazebo from view. She could take the necklace to the gazebo and leave it for Regan, she supposed. It
was Caroline's favorite place, after all. . . .

Abruptly, in her mind's eye, Joanna saw the paper airplane again, swooping and soaring all about before coming
to rest—in a different place. That was it. That was what
was different about the dream in the last days. Before, the
plane had landed on the grass; she vividly remembered

green. But the last few times, it had landed somewhere else. Somewhere . . . on boards.

Like the flooring of the gazebo.

✧　　✧　　✧

"I suppose you thought that wouldn't matter to me," Holly said tightly.

"I knew it would matter. That's why I didn't tell you."

"Damn you."

"Holly, listen to me." He didn't attempt to touch her or to come closer, and his voice was quiet, steady. "It was before I knew you, years ago. The first summer I came to Cliffside. And it only lasted that summer."

"But you came back the next summer."

"Not because of Caroline. Because I liked the town. Because it was a good place to paint. I didn't come back because of her."

"You expect me to believe that?" Holly heard herself laugh harshly. "You were so upset by her death, you left for a week. And what about that?" She jerked her head toward the portrait. "You were working on that when she was killed, I know because I saw it in your cottage."

"It was a commission, Holly. Caroline asked me to paint her back in the spring. She wanted the painting for Regan, and she sat for all the sketches. Then we both got busy—and it wasn't finished when she died. Since then, I finished it, and I've about decided to give it to Regan on her next birthday. It's what Caroline would have wanted."

"By all means, let's do what Caroline would have wanted."

Cain's mouth tightened, but his voice remained quiet. "I see we have to get past Caroline before we can settle anything else. Yes, I left after she was killed—but I was getting ready for a showing, you know that. I had to concentrate on work, that's why I came up here then. You were busy holding Scott's hand, and the whole town was practically draped in black—and I had to get away. But it was never because of her. Holly, I was never in love with Caroline. Not even during the affair."

"I wish I could believe that," she whispered. "But I saw the way men treated her. All you men. Watching over her. Taking care of her. Looking at her like she was the most amazing thing. That isn't love?"

"No." Cain drew a breath. "Not from me, anyway, and probably not from many of the others. Shocked? Don't be. Oh, yeah, she had a few lovers over the years, Holly—not just Griff, assuming they had an affair. She told me about them, but she never mentioned sex with him, so I don't know for sure."

It took Holly a moment to ask the question. "She *told* you about them? About her other lovers?"

He smiled faintly. "Shocked again? That was Caroline, Holly—and one of the reasons I found her so fascinating. She looked ultrafeminine and usually acted so sweet and uncertain that men found her charming, but she took and discarded lovers with no more feeling than a female cat in heat. I don't believe she ever understood love, at least not any man's love, and I'm not so sure she ever felt it, even for Griff."

Holly didn't know what she was feeling right then, except relief because his voice was utterly detached and his expression thoughtful.

"I don't know if she was born that way," he went on. "Maybe. Or maybe if she'd had a wider range of choices in her life, maybe if she hadn't married practically out of high school, she might have turned out differently. Then again, maybe it was just her nature. She liked sex. But she didn't like emotion. She was devoted to Regan, I believe that— but there's nothing particularly human about a mother cat's devotion to her kittens, is there? Once the kittens are grown, the mother sees them only as other cats, not related to her; I think once Regan had gotten older, Caroline would have seen her as just another woman—and a rival."

Any idea Holly had entertained that Cain had been in love with Caroline had vanished. "Cain, how could you have an affair with a woman if you felt that way about her?"

"I didn't know her when the affair began—though I learned a lot during the course of it." He shook his head. "And I won't deny I was fairly well obsessed with her that summer. But I was never in love with her, Holly, and when I came back the next year all I felt for her was pity."

Holly couldn't imagine anyone pitying Caroline. "Really?"

He nodded, grave. "She was never happy. Briefly satisfied, but never happy. Not even with Regan."

After a moment, Holly nodded as well. "I'm sorry. I guess I sounded . . ."

"Jealous," he supplied. But he was smiling, the green eyes bright. "Which I'm taking as a good sign, by the way."

"A good sign?"

"Umm. Before we talk about that, can we deal with this lie I told Griff?"

"I hope so," she said somewhat meekly.

Cain came to her, finally, and took her hand. "I didn't tell Griff the truth about where I went that night because you were sitting right there, and I didn't want you to know," he said. "I probably should have told Griff later, but to be honest, it never occurred to me that it would matter."

That made sense to Holly. Whenever he was absorbed in his work, Cain was incapable of noticing much of anything else, and he concentrated fully on the project at hand.

He led her to one of the easels, which was draped with a protective cover. "I've been working on this, off and on, for weeks. I didn't want you to know about it until I was sure I could . . . do justice to the subject." He flipped back the cover with his free hand.

Holly found herself staring at her own portrait. Unposed, it showed her looking out to sea, the wind whipping her dark hair back. As in all his work, the colors were vivid and dynamic, and his "subject" was so alive Holly half expected those lips to move and her own voice to come out of that mouth.

"Cain, it's . . . wonderful," she whispered. "But you said you didn't know enough about me."

"That was the glib answer," he said quietly. "The easiest way to answer a question I wasn't ready to explain. The truth is, I couldn't paint you for a long time because I knew too much about you, saw too much of you. I couldn't see you with an artist's necessary perspective. I was too close to you, too filled with all the facets of you. And until I dealt with my own feelings about you, there was no way I could paint you."

She turned away from the portrait at last and looked up at him, her heart beating fast. "So you've . . . dealt with your feelings?"

His mouth twisted slightly, and those vivid green eyes were suddenly naked. "Well, I've faced the fact that my life would be empty as hell without you in it. I love you, Holly."

Holly drew a breath and then threw her arms around his neck. Against his mouth, she murmured, "Thank God. I've been in love with you for months."

They ended up on the draped platform where his models posed, not a very comfortable bed but adequate for the purpose. And Holly didn't notice any discomfort at all until afterward, when she commented mildly that they might have tried to make it to his bed no more than thirty feet or so away.

Cain glanced around and chuckled. "I guess we might have at that. But it's been days, you know, so you'll have to forgive me for being impatient." He kissed her, lightly first and then more deeply. "You are going to stay tonight, aren't you, babe?"

"It's still the middle of the afternoon," she said, then immediately added, "Of course I'm staying. I left Dana in charge at The Inn."

"Ah." He lifted his head and smiled down at her. "A portent of things to come?"

"Well, I did promise to make more time for us. And Dana can run the place perfectly well from time to time."

She traced his bottom lip with an index finger. "But we'd better go back to Cliffside tomorrow, or find a phone and call Griff. He's not happy with you. You really do need to tell him why you lied to him."

"I must still be suspect number one," Cain said, not as if it bothered him greatly. "I wonder who did kill that girl."

"I don't know, but I hope Griff finds out before the town really does hang you for the crime," Holly said ruefully. Then she frowned up at him. "I heard he's looking for a connection between Caroline's death and Amber's. Do you know if Caroline was involved with anybody before she was killed?"

"Unless she ended it after she sat for the painting," Cain said, "she was having an affair with Dylan York."

✧   ✧   ✧

It would take only a few minutes, Joanna decided as she hurried across the lobby toward the veranda. Griffin wasn't quite due yet, and she could get to the gazebo and back fast if she tried. She knew she should wait for Griffin, but she was too anxious to find out if her guess was correct.

"Hey, Joanna, what's the hurry?"

She paused near the veranda doors and looked with surprise at Dylan. "Just something I want to do. What are you doing here, Dylan?"

"I live here, didn't you know?" He shrugged, clearly no longer as upset with her as he had been when they'd parted in town. "Like Holly, I live in the hotel. Actually, I came back here because Scott told me to take the rest of the day off once I finished at the courthouse. Can I buy you a cup of coffee?"

"Thanks, but I have to be going. Rain check?"

"You bet. And, speaking of rain, it's about to start out there, in case you didn't know."

"I won't melt," she told him, then waved and hurried on, across the veranda and out into the darkening afternoon.

✧   ✧   ✧

"You believed what you were told," Lyssa said quietly, watching Scott pace his office.

"I ought to be shot for believing it," he said, his low voice harsh. "I should have demanded a paternity test instead of just accepting what she said, should have made her *prove* Regan wasn't mine. But I listened to her instead. Listened and believed her. God forgive me, I let Caroline's poison destroy my daughter's love for me."

"Scott, you didn't know it was a lie. How could you?" Lyssa went to him when he paused by the fireplace, and put a hand on his arm tentatively. This wasn't part of the script, not any of it; he had called her less than an hour ago, asking her to come out to the house, and when she arrived he had told her what Caroline had done.

Lyssa was still coping with her own shock. She hadn't liked Caroline one bit, but for any woman to have done to her husband what Caroline had done to Scott was so cruel it almost defied belief.

She didn't quite know how to handle this. Handle him. She had never seen him vulnerable this way, hurting this way, and she wasn't sure how much he would be willing to accept from her. She was reacting out of instinct and her feelings for him, letting them guide her and hoping to hell she wasn't making this worse on him.

He didn't respond to her touch, but continued speaking in that low voice she hardly recognized as his, his face very still but not remote as it usually was. "She knew right where to drive the stake. I already hated him, because I knew she had fallen in love with him. It wasn't lust, like the others, it was love—or as close to it as Caroline could ever get. So when she told me it was his child she'd given birth to, that Regan was his and not mine . . . I was ready to believe it."

Lyssa opened her mouth to say something, then turned her head swiftly when she heard a soft sound from the hall outside the office. "Did you hear . . . ?"

Scott was already moving, striding across the room to the door that was not quite closed, wrenching it open.

At first, Lyssa thought there was nothing there. But then Scott bent, and when he straightened, he was holding a Raggedy Ann doll—the only doll Lyssa had ever seen Regan carry around with her.

"No," Lyssa whispered.

Scott turned his head to look at her, his face gray, just as they both heard one of the outer doors slam. "Oh God, she heard," he said hoarsely.

◇   ◇   ◇

The information faxed from San Francisco was a mishmash of subjects, from Robert Butler's college records to the public records of his various companies and some private records as well, and Griffin got a headache as he read through the stack. He couldn't afford to overlook anything, so he had to read every word.

The late Mr. Butler had been very wealthy, a tough businessman by all accounts. And his companies had enjoyed amazing success. Griffin read of the various successes, patiently, looking for any connection, however slight, to Cliffside or any of its citizens.

It wasn't until he'd almost reached the bottom of the stack that a name leaped off the page at him, and Griffin went tense in complete attention. He read slowly, carefully. Then he read it again. The facts, set down in private papers of Butler's coaxed from his sister by one of Griffin's deputies, were quite clear.

A connection.

Dylan York had worked for Butler years before. And he had stolen money from his employer. A lot of money. Dylan had vanished one breath ahead of discovery, and Butler had been left to explain a lot of creative bookkeeping. He hadn't made a formal charge against Dylan, probably because powerful men like him were accustomed to taking care of their own problems.

Staring down at the page, Griffin speculated. Suppose—maybe during that big business deal his sister had mentioned, or maybe just through information brokers he had hired for the purpose—Butler had somehow heard that

Dylan York lived in Cliffside. And suppose that Butler had come up here, intending to confront Dylan, to face the man who had stolen from him. Suppose they had met, by chance or design, behind The Inn, where Dylan lived, and suppose they had fought.

Speculation, Griffin reminded himself. But it wasn't speculation that Robert Butler had ended up dead on the jagged rocks of the cliffs.

The first death? Griffin's mind leaped ahead, tying together bits of information and speculating where he didn't have facts. Dylan had a job with another rich man; he might well have gotten up to his old tricks. A basically greedy nature would have been sorely tempted both by Scott's wealth and by his habit of delegating responsibility to employees. Over the years, Dylan could have stolen *a lot*.

And maybe Caroline had found out about that, or about Butler's death, probably because she'd gotten close to Dylan. Why not tell Scott? It had to be *because* she'd been involved with Dylan, perhaps so deeply that she hadn't been able to believe his treachery at first.

Later . . . Griffin didn't know. Something had frightened Caroline, either Dylan or what he was doing, and she had decided she needed help. Maybe she'd been able to obtain some kind of evidence, hidden now in that little box no one had seen—and maybe Dylan knew or suspected she had evidence that would put him away for a long time.

It wasn't such a big leap to imagine that Dylan might have come back from Portland earlier than expected that day and discovered Caroline's car at the old barn. Not a big leap to imagine him confronting her, angry and suspicious, and her running away from him in a panic. Not a big leap to imagine one car racing after another down a winding highway until she lost control and went over the cliffs.

And from there, hardly any leap at all to imagine that as Joanna began asking questions about Caroline and putting the pieces together, she would become a threat to Dylan as well. A very dangerous threat.

She was right. She had been right about everything.

"Jesus," Griffin muttered. He looked at his watch and suddenly felt cold. Ten minutes after two. He was late.

He reached for the phone with one hand and with the other opened the bottom drawer of his desk and closed his fingers around the gun he hadn't worn since he'd left Chicago.

FIFTEEN

✦ ✦ ✦

THE COOL BREEZE had become gusty, and the dampness had become droplets of rain by the time Joanna was halfway to the gazebo. She hurried on, automatically staying back from the cliffs, and wished the storm clouds clashing overhead hadn't turned the afternoon dark and eerie, because it seemed to have an odd effect on her mind.

Bits and pieces of information and conversation kept flitting through her mind just as the images in her dream had, and she couldn't seem to shut them out. It was as if her subconscious were searching for something, flipping over the pages of memory. Then, when Joanna was nearly at the gazebo, the correct page was found, the relevant memory surfaced, and she came to a dead stop.

How had he known what she was wearing?

Jeans and a sweater, he'd said. She hadn't been dressed for a trip to town *that morning*, because she'd been wearing jeans and a sweater. But he hadn't been there that morning, Joanna remembered that from the statements in

Griffin's files. He had gone to Portland the day before and had stayed there overnight, returning only in the late afternoon after Caroline's accident. And he couldn't have seen her after the accident, because only Griffin, the rescue people, and Cliffside's doctor had seen her. Identification hadn't been in question, so even Scott had not seen his wife's body that day.

And there had been no mention in the newspapers of how Caroline had been dressed the day she had died.

So how could Dylan have known what she was wearing when she was killed—unless he had seen her earlier that day, perhaps at the old barn . . . ?

Joanna had an almost overpowering impulse to look back over her shoulder, but instead hurried on. She had no way of knowing if he even meant to come after her again, far less that he would make an attempt in the middle of the afternoon, she reminded herself. But if he intended that, then he was probably somewhere between her and the hotel, and she had no desire to try to get past him. No, the best thing to do, she thought, was to keep going, to go past the gazebo and head for Scott's house, where there were people, where she would be safe until she could call Griffin.

But when she burst into the clearing, she saw Regan. The little girl was in the gazebo, huddled on the floor beside the carousel horse, and every line of her small body spoke of pain and grief.

Joanna didn't hesitate; the instinct to go to the child was so strong Regan might have been her own flesh and blood. Just as she stepped up into the gazebo, the skies opened up, rain drumming fiercely on the roof and sheeting downward so hard that visibility was limited to only a few feet.

She knelt beside the child, putting a hand out to touch her gently, thinking only that the little girl had at last given in to her sorrow for the loss of her mother. "Regan? Honey—"

Regan looked up, her small, pale face tearstained, and with a sob threw herself into Joanna's arms. "Not mine," she wailed miserably, her voice choked. "He's not *mine*, Joanna!"

"Not yours? Regan—"

Still sobbing, her voice hardly audible above the sounds of the rain and wind, Regan said, "I heard him talking to Lyssa just now, and he *told* her. He said Mama put a stake in him, and that I wasn't his child. He's not my daddy, Joanna. I don't have a daddy!"

Joanna couldn't know for certain what Regan had overheard, but she had to believe that Scott had been explaining the situation to Lyssa for whatever reason, and that Regan had heard only snatches of it. "Listen to me, honey," she said, making the little girl look at her. "You just heard part of something again, that's all. You didn't hear everything, and so you misunderstood. He is your daddy, I promise you—and he knows he is."

"He said—"

"Never mind what he said. Regan, he's your father. And he loves you, I know he does."

Regan shook her head stubbornly. "No, he's not. Not anymore. I was bad, Joanna, and God took them both away from me."

"Honey—"

"You don't *know*! I thought it was a game, another game, like Mama and me played all the time. I thought she hid the box for me to find. So I got it when she left, but it was locked and I didn't know what was inside. I looked for the key, but I couldn't find it. Then I saw Mama come out here, and I knew she was scared when she didn't find the box, I *knew* it, because her face was all white and she looked like she wanted to cry. And when she left in her car, she was driving awful fast—and she never came back, Joanna! She never came back, and it's all my fault! I brought the box back here after, and put it back in the little hidey-hole where I found it, but Mama never came back. . . ."

Joanna held the sobbing child, thinking how damnably easy it was to miss the most vital clue of all. *I was bad,*

Joanna. A child's guilt, and she should have paid far more attention to it.

"Regan, none of it was your fault—" she began, but was cut off by an eerily casual voice so close it made her jump.

"How very touching."

It was Dylan, and he was holding a gun. He was outside the gazebo but still under the shelter of the roof, resting a forearm on the railing with the gun trained precisely on her.

Joanna managed to get to her feet still holding Regan, and instinctively pushed the child around behind her as she backed away from him. He was smiling, and she'd never realized how terrifying a smile could be until that moment. His eyes were—dead. Just dead.

"Dylan, don't be stupid," she said as calmly as she could manage. "It's over. You think another death could be called an accident? You've been lucky so far, but—"

"Lucky? Is that what you call it?" He laughed bitterly, shaking his head. "I've been looking high and low for that disk for months, and all the time the kid had hidden it here? Jesus."

Disk? Joanna wasn't about to ask. "Let Regan go back to the house," she said without much hope.

Dylan smiled again. "No, I don't think so. See, I heard enough to know the kid ran from the house in a panic, so it seems likely to me she'd maybe get too close to the edge, what with the rain and all. And here you are, Joanna, the living image of her mother, already attached to her—isn't it sweet? I think you're going to try to save Regan, Joanna. And neither one of you is going to make it." He shook his head with a concerned little frown. "Dangerous cliffs we have here. Very dangerous. I believe I'll petition the town council to put up permanent barriers after this latest tragedy."

Regan was utterly silent, her arms wrapped around Joanna, but she was shaking and Joanna had no doubt she was in shock. She surreptitiously slid her hand over Regan's ear and held the child's head close to her side, hoping to shut out the things she didn't need to know about her mother and what had happened. The only thing she could think of to do was stall, to get Dylan talking and keep him talking as long as possible.

"You lied to me about the affair, didn't you, Dylan? It didn't happen years ago. It happened months ago. Just before Caroline died."

He inclined his head slightly in an obscene parody of polite acknowledgment. "Well, I had to lie, Joanna. I didn't want to stick out in your mind as the man closest to Caroline when she died. You might have told Griff before I could get you out of the way, and I couldn't have that. And I knew what you wanted to hear, of course. That Caroline had used me for stud service and then walked away, leaving me in pieces. That is what the others told you, right?"

"How did you know?"

"Because I watched her for years. I watched what she did to her previous lovers. I watched what she did to Scott. I thought all my knowledge might come in handy one day—and it did, the day I decided to seduce the lady of the manor." He smiled. "I knew just which buttons to push, believe me. Caroline found herself used for a change."

Something in his voice when he said that, something eager and pleased, sent an icy chill through Joanna. She drew a breath, and heard the fear in her own voice when she said, "Just get the disk and leave us alone. We aren't a threat to you, Dylan."

"Of course you are, Joanna. You've been a threat from the day you got here—think I don't know that? Asking questions, sticking your nose in where it didn't belong, almost as if you knew . . ." He tilted his head to one side suddenly, curious. "Right from the start, you thought Caroline's death wasn't an accident, didn't you? Why did you think that, Joanna?"

"Caroline told me," she replied. *I have to stall him,* she reminded herself desperately, pushing the fear aside. She had to stall him just long enough to give Griffin the time to reach the hotel—surely it was two o'clock? She didn't dare look at her watch.

His eyes narrowed. "Caroline was dead."

Joanna managed to produce a smile. "Yes. She was. But an odd thing happened, Dylan. Last summer, when Caroline was killed, so was I."

"What?"

She nodded. "I was in a car wreck too. Survived it without a scratch, but a power line fell on my car and I was electrocuted. At the exact same moment Caroline died, so did I."

Dylan scowled, clearly bothered by that information as Joanna had hoped he would be. "A coincidence. So?"

"So there's a connection between us, and I know some of what Caroline knew. She told me, Dylan. She wanted me to help Regan, to come here and make sure she was safe. And she wanted the truth to come out. The truth about you."

With a short laugh, Dylan said, "Sorry, but I'm not buying it."

Joanna held on to her smile. "I don't care if you buy it or not. But I know things, Dylan, things I shouldn't know. I know you used to meet Caroline in the old barn. So you were suspicious that day, when you came back early from Portland and saw her car parked there. You suspected she was meeting someone else, so you stopped and confronted her. But Caroline didn't like confrontations, and she wasn't about to tell you anything, was she?"

"She was jumpy," he muttered, "nervous. I knew she was going to meet someone there, but I didn't know who."

"And you weren't completely sure she had the disk, were you? Not then."

"I thought I'd misplaced it," he said, "until I suddenly realized why she was so nervous, why she flinched away from me like that. She had the disk. That little bitch stole the disk from me."

Joanna drew a breath. "She was afraid of you, wasn't

she? You were rough with her, you controlled her—and that had never happened to her before."

Dylan's smile was self-satisfied. "Scott and the others let her get away with too much. But not me. I showed her who was boss."

Oh, Caroline, you really bit off more than you could handle with this one.

"But that day," Joanna said, still stalling, "you realized she had the disk. And before you could get your hands on her, she ran. Got in her car and drove toward town. And you went after her."

"She was spooked and lost control," he said with a shrug. "By the time I got there and looked, I knew she was gone. So it *was* an accident."

"An accident you caused," Joanna said. "And what about Amber? Did she die in my place, Dylan?"

He scowled. "Another nosy little bitch. She came out onto the veranda that night and saw me. I was looking up at your balcony, trying to decide if I could take the chance of getting rid of you. She asked me what I was doing with a gun." He shrugged. "She must have seen it earlier, when she was wandering around near the game room. I'd been keeping an eye on you before that, so I had it stuck in my belt. Wouldn't you know the bitch would have to get a glimpse of it."

"That's why you killed her? Because she knew you had a gun?"

"She would have told somebody, Joanna, surely you see that?" His tone was eerily reasonable. "Cain probably, since she wanted him in her pants. Or Griff. I couldn't take that chance. Nobody'd even looked at me in suspicion, and I wasn't about to let that change. And what was one more? Especially a silly thing like her." He shrugged again. "She didn't matter. I had too much at stake to see it all ruined. And my luck had held so far. Caroline's death had been an accident, Butler's—"

"Robert Butler? You killed him too?"

Dylan frowned. "I just hit him, that's all. And he fell."

"Another accident? I don't think so, Dylan."

"Think anything you like." He smiled again, the expression even more chilling than it had been before, because there was real admiration in it. "You're smart, Joanna, I'll give you that. And you've got the devil's own luck. Ever since I came back here, I've had my eye on you, but I could never get close enough at the right moment."

Watched all the time, and I never knew. The coldness she felt went bone deep. It was difficult to think past her fear, but Joanna tried. She was still puzzled by the connection between Dylan and Robert Butler, but she could feel his impatience growing and didn't know how much longer she could stall him. Hastily, she said, "You got close enough once. What about my car? You did quite a job on it."

"Not good enough, obviously." He laughed with more than a touch of bitterness and irritation. "But this time, this time I'm going to make sure I get you. And the kid. Then I'll get the disk, and no one will be the wiser."

"Dylan, there's no way you'll get away with another 'accident.' Griffin's on his way here now, and he's suspicious of the other accidents. Very suspicious. He's been checking into them. Sooner or later, he'll find the right connections."

"What connections? He doesn't know shit."

"There's a connection between you and Robert Butler," Joanna said, guessing, hoping there was enough truth in it to make him hesitate. "A reason why you killed him. You may think it's hidden, but Griffin will find it. And once that 'accident' starts to look like something else, he won't give up until he knows the rest. Especially now, Dylan. You think he'd take my death lightly? Think again."

He scowled. "I'll take my chances. Move. Out of there, now."

Joanna didn't move, even though she had caught a faint glimpse of movement some distance behind Dylan. "Forget it. You think I'm going to lead Regan tamely over to the edge and let you push us over? You're out of your mind, Dylan."

He cocked the pistol. "I said move."

"Are you going to be able to explain bullet holes in your 'accident' victims? And they have tests, Dylan. Ballistics tests. They'll know the bullets came from your gun."

"It's Scott's gun," he told her impatiently. "And since I'm wearing a pair of rubber gloves borrowed from Doc, it has his fingerprints on it. Grieving widower shoots daughter and wife's look-alike—news at eleven." He smiled. "The tabloids will love it, don't you think?"

"I think you're insane," she said.

He actually laughed. "No, just determined. I'm tired of working for rich men, Joanna. It's time I got my piece of the pie. Out of the gazebo, or I'll shoot. And I'll shoot the kid first."

"Dylan!"

He jerked and looked past Joanna, his face darkening as he saw Scott standing just a few feet away. Then his face cleared of annoyance and assumed that eerily amiable mask, and he said, "Oh, good, you're here. Maybe I'll kill you too."

"Let them go, Dylan," Scott said, quiet now. He stood in the pouring rain, his clothing drenched and dark hair plastered to his head, but he was still an oddly impressive figure. "It's all over."

"No, it isn't. It can still work," Dylan said, arguing reasonably.

"No," said another voice from behind Dylan, implacable. "It can't. Drop the gun, Dylan."

Instead of doing that, Dylan eased away from the railing, turning slightly so that he could see both Scott and Griffin. He was in the rain now, his blond hair dark from the wetness. He held his pistol negligently, no longer pointed at anyone. "Hello, Griff. I didn't even know you had a gun."

The gun was leveled at Dylan, and Griffin's eyes were very cold. "I was a Chicago cop, remember? And I keep in practice. Don't make me prove it, Dylan. Drop the gun. I know what you did to Robert Butler, why he came after you here. And I'm willing to bet you did the same thing to Scott. The disk will prove it, won't it?"

Dylan's smile was a little sick now, and he began backing away slowly. Toward the edge of the cliffs. "I didn't want to have to leave the country," he said. "I thought about it for a while last summer, but I didn't want to. Without the disk—my record of what I'd done—even those auditors of Scott's wouldn't have been able to find anything wrong. I would have been free and clear. And eventually, I would have given notice to Scott and moved away—and I would never have had to work again in my life. I would have had what I deserved. I would have had what *he* had." He jerked his head toward Scott.

"Drop the gun, Dylan," Griffin told him flatly.

"And go to jail? I don't think so." His mouth twisted. "I was so close. But I couldn't resist the chance to screw the lady of the manor, and look where it got me. She ruined it. Goddamn her, she ruined everything!"

"Dylan, *don't*," Griffin ordered as the other man began to raise his gun.

Dylan's smile was still twisted. "Sorry, Griff." He raised the pistol toward Griffin.

Joanna turned instinctively, making sure Regan couldn't see and closing her own eyes the instant after the bullet caught Dylan squarely in the middle of his chest and sent him staggering backward.

He didn't make a sound when he went over the edge.

For a long moment, they stood as if frozen. Then, as if on a signal, the rain slacked off drastically. Griffin slowly returned his gun to the holster under his arm and walked forward to the edge of the cliffs. He looked over, then turned back toward the gazebo, his face grim.

Scott came forward, but stopped with one foot on the step of the gazebo, his gaze fixed on his daughter. "Regan?"

Joanna felt the child shudder against her, felt those thin

arms tighten around her, but she didn't say anything. This
was between Regan and Scott; they had to do this alone.

"Regan, honey . . . please look at Daddy." His voice
was low, more gentle than Joanna had ever heard it.

Regan turned her head a little, looking at him from
teary eyes. "You said you weren't," she murmured.

"No," he said. "I said I thought I wasn't. For a long
time, I thought I wasn't your daddy. But I was wrong,
Regan. I am your daddy. Please let me make it up to you."

She didn't move, though Joanna felt her arms loosen.
She just looked at him, confused, still shocked by what had
happened here. She was just a little girl, and she couldn't
take in everything she had seen and heard. What she
needed was love and comfort, and when her father held out
his arms to her, every instinct in her small body urged her
toward him.

"I love you, Regan," Scott told her huskily.

Regan let go of Joanna and took a jerky step. Then
another. Then, with a broken cry, she threw herself into
her father's arms. He held her tightly, his eyes closing for a
moment. Then, looking past her at Griffin, who had
reached the gazebo, he said, "I'm taking her home."

Griffin nodded, and stood watching until Scott carried
his daughter through the woods toward their house. Then
he came into the gazebo with a deliberate step and with a
jerky movement pulled Joanna into his arms.

"Christ, you scared the hell out of me," he said thickly
into her hair.

Joanna felt the most marvelous and profound sense of
homecoming in his embrace, and she snuggled closer, glo-
rying in the feeling as she murmured, "Scared myself too. I
should have waited for you, I know, so you don't have to
say it. I was an idiot and a four-star fool and possibly a
moron, and I'm *sorry*, but I just didn't think—"

Griffin raised her head from his shoulder and kissed her.
Hard. "Just don't do it again," he said at last, his voice
ragged. "I earned my first gray hairs in the last ten minutes."

She smiled up at him, conscious of faintly unsteady knees and a slight dizziness and not sure if it was him or the shock. "I'm sorry. Really. But at least it's over, isn't it?"

"More or less," he said.

❖   ❖   ❖

They found the little antique box in Regan's "hidey-hole" beneath a loose board in the floor of the gazebo. The brass key Scott had found fit perfectly, and inside was the small computer diskette containing the details of Dylan's greed.

It would require, Griffin guessed, Scott's entire team of accountants as well as a lawyer or two to get everything figured out, but it seemed that Dylan had found a way to "cook" the books so adroitly that he had been able to siphon off almost two million dollars over the years without leaving evidence behind. A price Scott had paid for putting too much authority in the hands of one man.

As for Dylan, because his schemes had been so intricate, he had been forced to keep the details on some kind of personal record, a practice that had cost *him*. From what he had said to Joanna there at the end, they could only assume that Caroline had somehow discovered what he was doing. She had been at his place frequently, since they were lovers, and had one day, perhaps, stumbled over the information.

In any case, she had taken the disk. She may have gone over the information at her leisure at home, slowly realizing the scope of Dylan's embezzlement. Of course, she should have gone to Scott immediately, or to Griffin, and they could only speculate as to the reasons she didn't.

Somehow, without physical abuse—which would surely have been noticed by Scott and others—Dylan had managed to intimidate Caroline, to keep her more than a little bit frightened of him. Whether by threats of some kind or simply the domination of a stronger mind, he had held her in thrall to him. At some point, it must have occurred to Caroline that her lover was capable of violence, and so she had tried to work up the courage to take some action to free herself from him and expose his crimes.

She had gone to past lovers, one at a time, seeking advice or help. But with the kind of bad timing fate seemed to delight in, she always seemed to approach the wrong man at the wrong time. Or maybe it had simply been a case of "what goes around, comes around." Perhaps her heartless treatment of those men came back to haunt her in the end. And it was likely she didn't go to Scott simply because she hadn't wanted to admit to him of all people that she was involved with a man she could not control.

Finally, she had decided to take the disk to Griffin. Perhaps she had believed she could talk him into keeping her out of it, or perhaps she had come up with some innocent reason for her to have gained access to Dylan's personal records. In any case, she had sent the note and had gone to retrieve the disk from its hiding place in the gazebo.

Regan, looking out the window of her bedroom where she'd been recovering from a summer cold, had seen her mother returning from the gazebo and, though not understanding perfectly, had discerned the panic and anguish on Caroline's face. She knew immediately that she had done something wrong in removing the box from its hiding place, and the guilt of that would probably be with her forever. She never saw her mother again.

The rest of it they had been able to put together fairly well, thanks to Dylan's own words there at the end. And they had his confession— heard by Joanna, Griffin, and Scott—that he had killed Robert Butler "by accident" and Amber Wade with cold-blooded intent.

So at last Griffin could offer those grieving parents a reason, no matter how incomprehensible, for their daughter's death.

It took the rescue team nearly two hours to bring Dylan's body up from the jagged rocks where it lay, and by then the news had spread around Cliffside like wildfire. The curious came out to see, even in the misting rain that had continued to fall, and it naturally wasn't long before a number of people swore they'd always thought there was something suspicious about Dylan.

Par for the course.

In the meantime, Griffin had finally gotten word from Cain, explaining his lie and the reasons for it. He was, Griffin told him somewhat bitterly, a bit late with the information.

Joanna stayed close to Griffin for the rest of the afternoon, both because she wanted to and because he had announced his intention of not letting her out of his sight until his pulse and blood pressure returned to normal. Which would be a while. She knew he had been badly frightened by how close she had come to being Dylan's fourth victim, and did what she could to reassure him that she was fine.

Perhaps oddly, she *was* fine. Being held at gunpoint by a madman whom she had later seen killed was not exactly conducive to serenity, but she felt very calm, very much at peace. She had a sense of satisfaction that was not only hers, a sense of completion. It was over. Finally, it was finished.

✧   ✧   ✧

Lyssa stood in the doorway of Regan's bedroom and watched silently as Scott sat with his sleeping daughter. He held one of her small hands in his, his head bent over it, and one of his long fingers slowly traced hers as if to explore the shape and texture of them. Finally, he tucked her little hand beneath the covers and just looked at her.

Lyssa waited.

Outside, darkness fell, and the lamp in Regan's room cast a warm circle of light over her and her father. Scott had been sitting by her bed for nearly two hours when he rose and came to the doorway.

"I don't want to leave her," he said.

Lyssa nodded, but said, "Doc said she'd sleep all night after that shot he gave her. Why don't you come downstairs and have something to eat? I told Mrs. Ames to keep something warm in the oven for you."

He hesitated, glancing back at Regan, then nodded and came out into the hall to join her. As they went toward the stairs, he asked, "Where is Mrs. Ames?"

"In her rooms. I told her we'd call if we needed her. She's pretty upset. She liked Dylan."

Scott looked at her, frowning slightly. "How are you?"

Lyssa managed a smile. "All right. It's a shock, of course. I knew him a long time—or thought I did. Is it true, what's going around? Is he really to blame for all those deaths?"

Scott wasn't surprised she had heard that, even though he had said nothing to her; undoubtedly, at least a few people had called the house to talk to either her or the housekeeper in the past couple of hours.

"He's to blame," he replied. "Caroline lost control of her car because of him. Robert Butler stumbled back over the edge of the cliffs because Dylan hit him. And he deliberately pushed Amber Wade over, because she had seen the gun he carried, and he couldn't risk her telling someone about it."

"My God." Lyssa shook her head. "And he stole from you? Embezzled money?"

Scott shrugged. "To me, that seems the least of his crimes. If he had only stopped with that . . . But murder can't be forgotten. Or forgiven."

Lyssa could only agree with that. She went with him into the kitchen, where there was a small table that was rarely used except by the cook, and began pulling covered dishes out of the oven.

"Mrs. Ames obviously didn't want you to starve," she noted ruefully.

"You haven't eaten either," Scott said, and got two plates from the cabinet.

They sat at the small table, companionable in a way they had never been before, and ate in virtual silence. Lyssa didn't know where they would go from here. Or if they would go anywhere at all. Their written-in-stone script had been abandoned earlier today, and she felt somewhat rudderless without it.

She tried to take comfort in the fact that it was her Scott had called today when he had needed to talk, her advice he had listened to before going out to search for his anguished daughter. *She needs love, Scott, your love. You haven't been able to show her for so long, now you'll have to tell her. Just tell her that you love her.*

Judging by the way Regan had clung to him when he had brought her back to the house, it appeared that the little girl was willing to give him the benefit of the doubt, at least for now. But there would probably be rough times ahead; years of neglect couldn't be atoned for overnight.

But Lyssa felt just as much pity for Scott as for Regan, pity and a fierce rage at Caroline for what she had done to them. She had left scars that might never fade, and all because she had been cruelly selfish.

"I should have left her," Scott said suddenly, staring at the glass of wine he had half finished. "Or kicked her out."

He seemed to be reading her mind again, but this time Lyssa wasn't disturbed by it. "You loved her," she said calmly.

Scott's gaze lifted to her face, and he smiled wryly. "I loved her. And hated her. And was . . . consumed by her. It wasn't a normal relationship. It wasn't a normal marriage."

"Then put it behind you. And go on." Lyssa smiled. "You got something wonderful out of it, don't forget that. You got Regan."

"It'll take a long time to win her back. And—I don't know how much she heard out there at the gazebo. Joanna tried to shelter her as much as possible, but some of it probably got through. Most of it she probably didn't understand even if she heard it, but she'll remember the words. And one day, she'll come to me with questions about her mother."

"Maybe," Lyssa said. "Or maybe, by then, she'll know

that even the people we love aren't perfect. Don't borrow trouble, Scott."

He smiled slightly. "You're probably right."

"Of course I'm right. I'm always right."

He reached across the small table suddenly and covered her hand with his. "You've been very patient with me."

"Well, it's been a rough day," she began.

Scott shook his head. "No," he said. "You've been very patient with me."

For an instant, Lyssa was tempted to retreat, to take refuge in lightness and flippancy. But she had a sense that this was a turning point in their relationship, and that if she retreated, they would return to their scripted responses that were safe and casual and unfeeling. And she would lose him.

She drew a breath and fought to hold her voice steady, to allow just a touch of self-mockery to filter through. "Thirty-five is old for a first love. You don't have the illusions to cling to, the dreams to cushion you if things don't work out. You just have patience."

He didn't seem surprised by her confession, but he smiled at her, and his eyes were gentle, even pleased, she thought. "Things are going to be difficult for a while," he said quietly. "Especially with Regan. She'll need a lot of my time. You understand that?"

"Of course I do."

"Then will you be patient a little longer? Give me some time to sort through things, get to know my daughter again?"

Her hand turned under his and grasped it, and Lyssa smiled. "Take all the time you need. I'm not going anywhere."

Scott pushed his chair back and got up. Still holding her hand, he bent down and kissed her, lightly but with feeling. "Thank you," he said.

Lyssa forced herself to let go of his hand when he straightened. "Don't mention it. Listen, why don't you go back to Regan? I'll clear up in here and then let myself out."

He hesitated, then said, "I'd like you to stay, if you would. I'd . . . feel better if you were near. There might be talk, but—"

"There won't be talk," Lyssa said. "I'll tell Mrs. Ames that you're with Regan and I'm staying just in case I'm needed. I'll even bunk down on one of those very comfortable sofas of yours instead of using one of the guest bedrooms. Don't worry. She'll spread the word tomorrow."

Scott nodded, then touched her cheek lightly and said, "Thank you," again. And went upstairs to sit with his sleeping daughter.

❖   ❖   ❖

"There shouldn't be much of a fuss," Griffin said. "The state police will want to have a look at my files, since I shot the suspect, but since he confessed in the presence of three witnesses and then subsequently aimed a cocked pistol at me, I doubt I'll hear anything except congratulations for getting him."

Joanna, sharing with him a thick quilt and a pile of cushions in front of his fireplace, looked at him gravely. "It doesn't bother you, does it? You know you had no choice, that what you did was right."

He nodded. "I won't shed any tears for him, Joanna. He caused the deaths of three people, and he was fully prepared to kill you and Regan. As for how he ended, he aimed that gun at me and forced me to shoot him because he didn't have the guts to commit suicide and we both knew it."

"That's what I thought." Joanna set her wineglass aside with a sigh. "Will all that stuff about Caroline have to come out? I mean, that she and Dylan were lovers?"

"Not if I have anything to say about it." He brooded a moment. "I can't see that her relationship with him has to come into it. She found the disk—no need to say how, since we don't actually know. Hid it. He found out it was gone and threatened her, frightened her so that she lost control of her car. He had no idea where the disk was. Then you showed up here, and he got nervous because you were asking questions about Caroline and he was afraid you'd somehow stumble across the disk. So he tried to kill you—twice."

Joanna smiled slightly. "Cheated death again. Guess I'd better be careful crossing streets from now on, huh?"

Griffin put his glass aside and leaned over her, his expression very sober. "Don't joke about it. God knows I hope you do have as many lives as a cat, but please be careful with them, will you? I don't want to lose you. I don't ever want to lose you."

She slid her arms up around his neck, her fingers sliding into his dark hair. His eyes, she decided, were blue. A very, very dark blue. Darker than sapphires. "You won't," she murmured, lifting her face in a silent plea.

Her mouth opened under the hungry pressure of his, and Joanna felt her senses heating, her thoughts spinning away because they weren't needed. All she needed to do was feel, not think, and she gave herself up to the glory of that.

❖   ❖   ❖

It was dawn when he woke, and Griffin sat up quickly when he realized she wasn't in the bed beside him. He threw back the covers and got up, pausing only to pull on sweatpants and a sweatshirt. He felt a draft of chilly air when he stepped into the still-dark living room, and relaxed when he saw the atrium door slightly ajar and Joanna outside on the deck.

She had the quilt from their bed by the fire wrapped around her, and he could see the collar of his shirt, which was probably all she was wearing under the quilt.

He went outside and joined her, one hand rubbing up and down her back lightly as he leaned against the railing beside her. "Hey, you'll freeze out here," he told her.

She looked at him, clear-eyed and pink-cheeked in the chill of dawn. "I've been thinking about it all," she murmured. "But especially about Dylan. What makes a man like him, Griffin? When does greed become so absolute that killing is easy?"

"I don't know, sweetheart."

She sighed, her breath misting a bit. "It was such a miserable, unimportant crime to cost three lives. Covering up embezzlement. It was just *money*, Griffin."

He shook his head. "No, not to Dylan. It was power. It was . . . a balancing of the scales, giving him what he thought was his due. Of course he was willing to kill to have what he wanted. It was his own image of himself he was protecting, Joanna. Caught, he would have been just another stupid criminal; success meant he was smarter than everybody else."

Joanna nodded slightly and was silent for a moment. Then she sighed again. "So now it's really over. I didn't dream last night. It's finally gone, Griffin. The fear. The urgency. The feeling of not being entirely alone in my own mind. Caroline is gone. I thought so last night—but now I'm sure of it." She looked at him, her expression grave.

Griffin touched her cheek. "I'm glad, sweetheart."

"I couldn't . . . face anything else until she was gone."

"I know."

Still grave, she asked, "Do you know that I love you?"

He smiled slowly. "I was sort of hoping you did. You made me wait long enough to hear it, though."

"I had to get Caroline out of my head," she explained.

"And make sure she wasn't in mine?"

"Something like that."

He bent his head and kissed her slowly. "She was never in my head," he said huskily against her lips. "But you are. God, you are. In my head and my heart and under my skin . . . inside me so deeply you feel like a part of me. Like you've always belonged there. I love you, Joanna."

She made a little sound of contentment. "I love you too."

He lifted his head so that he could look at her, and

stroked her cheek gently with the tips of his fingers. "We should go in. You're cold."

Her smile was so lovely it nearly stopped his heart. "I wanted to see the dawn. It looks so different when you don't wake up scared to death. Just look at it, Griffin—isn't it beautiful?"

It was difficult for him to look at anything but her, but he turned his gaze obediently to the horizon, where black was shading to deep purple, only to become dark blue overhead and then lighten gradually toward the east behind them where the sun would soon rise. It was high tide, so the ocean was roaring and booming as it battered against the cliffs, the morning air laden with salty dampness.

He drew a deep breath. "I fell in love with this place the first time I saw it," he said.

"So did I." She smiled at him again. "I didn't realize it because I seemed to see shadows and tension everywhere I looked, but despite all that, I felt deep inside that this was a beautiful place."

"Then stay here—with me. Marry me." He hadn't intended to ask her, not so soon, but it felt right to him to say it now. "I know you'd be giving up a lot, Joanna, but—"

Her fingers touched his lips lightly to stop him. "What would I be giving up? The city? I don't need it. Family? Aunt Sarah was the last. Friends? I'll make new ones."

"Sweetheart . . ."

"I love you, Griffin," she said softly. "There's nothing in the world I want more than to stay here with you."

He drew a deep breath that did nothing to ease the sweet ache in his chest, and pulled her into his arms. "You won't regret it, Joanna, I promise."

"I know that." Her fingers threaded into his hair, and her smile glowed with more promise than the morning. "I knew that the first time I saw you, even if I couldn't admit it to myself. I looked at you, at the suspicion on your face, and I knew I wouldn't be going back to Atlanta—except to pack."

"I think you're three parts witch," he said huskily.

"And I think I'm just very, very lucky."

Griffin thought he'd been the lucky one, but he didn't argue with her as he lifted her and carried her back to their warm bed.

EPILOGUE

✦ ✦ ✦

IT WAS EXACTLY TWO WEEKS to the day after Joanna had arrived in Cliffside, and a sunny Tuesday in mid-October, when Griffin walked beside Joanna to the peaceful old church at the northern end of town. He walked with her as far as the lovely wrought-iron gate at the side of the church and opened it for her. "You're sure you don't want me to go along?"

Joanna smiled up at him. "I'm sure. This is something I need to do alone."

"Okay." He bent his head and kissed her lightly, understanding without the need for explanations. "I'll wait here for you. Just remember our appointment. Fifteen minutes."

"It shouldn't take me that long."

She walked into the town's oldest cemetery, following one of the neat graveled paths toward a spot she needed no directions to find. Like most everything in Cliffside, the grounds here were well kept, mostly sunny but shaded in several places by huge old oak trees. The ocean could barely be heard from here, yet it could be felt, almost like a pulse in the ground. It was an oddly alive place where the dead had been laid to rest.

It was a place Joanna had avoided until now. She had avoided even thinking about it, because she'd been afraid that the fragile tie between her and Caroline would be severed by the stark reality of a grave and a headstone.

But the connection Joanna had known for so long was gone now, the feeling of it no more than a wisp of memory, and it was time for her to say good-bye to Caroline.

Her grave was as meticulously neat as all the others here, the grass clipped short and still green in October, the marble headstone gleaming. Her name was carved deeply into the stone. *Caroline Douglas McKenna.* The dates of her birth and her death were carved deeply as well. She had not lived thirty years, and she had made his life hell for more than ten of them, yet Scott had had carved *Beloved Wife and Mother* as well—and Joanna doubted he had done it because of convention.

Poor Caroline. She had lived and died with no idea of what she had missed.

On either side of her headstone were affixed permanent flowerpots, and in each one a bunch of her own roses glowed with beautiful color. They wouldn't last long this time of the year, Joanna knew, but there were more grown and tended in the greenhouse to replace these when needed. For Caroline, indeed. Somehow, Joanna didn't doubt that Caroline's roses would bloom at her grave for a long, long time.

"You'll probably hate these," Joanna said conversationally as she bent to lay a bouquet of mixed flowers on the neat grave, speaking aloud because it felt right to. "But I'll let the men in your life bring you roses, Caroline."

She looked at the headstone, her gaze tracing the letters spelling out the name of a complex woman who had, Joanna believed, reached out from death to save her daughter. "You knew Regan was in danger, didn't you? Maybe it was just something you realized in that final moment, that she must have found the box with the disk in it. Or maybe . . . maybe there's a time beyond death when we know what happens to those we left behind.

"Either way, I believe you knew. You knew she'd need help, knew she'd be in danger if Dylan discovered she'd found the disk. And maybe you wanted something else fixed as well. Did you, Caroline? Did you, finally, regret what you'd done to Scott? Did you realize that Regan needed her father back?"

There was no answer, of course, but it didn't stop Joanna from musing aloud, from trying to find a kind of closure in this, the most elusive and intangible part of the whole thing.

"I'd like to think you did regret a few things, Caroline. That you sent me here not only to protect Regan but to at least attempt to heal a few of the wounds you caused. Scott knows the truth about Regan now. Adam had a chance to . . . oh, confess, I guess. And even Griffin doesn't feel so guilty about your death now.

"Even the town is sort of healed, with the truth known. I think your death and Butler's shook up everybody more than they wanted to admit, and then when I came along, looking so much like you and asking questions, it just added tension. Griffin felt it, too, the uneasiness of the town. Maybe a lot of people sensed there was something wrong, I don't know. In any case, things are much better now. Why I came here will probably always be a mystery to some people, but even the ones who seemed so wary of me are smiling and friendly now. This is a nice little town, Caroline. I think I'm going to love it here."

She stood with her hands folded, and smiled somewhat ruefully as she looked at the headstone. "I don't think we would have liked each other much, you and I. I can't say that I liked many of the things I found out about you since I got here. But I don't hate you. You probably couldn't help being the way you were, so what's the use of hating you for it? But I do think your life gave you no pleasure, and that's a real shame. You'd hate pity, so I won't offer you that, but I wish . . . "

What did she wish? Joanna sighed. "I'm glad you asked me to come, Caroline. I'm glad I was able to help—even if the whole thing drove me crazy and scared me more than once. The only thing I regret is Amber. Griffin says it isn't my fault, that Dylan is wholly to blame, but I can't help feeling responsible for what happened to her. I'll have to learn to live with that; the price I paid for coming here, I suppose.

"Regan is fine. She and Scott have a long way to go yet, but the beginning has been promising. She even rode into town yesterday in his car, the first time she's been able to do that. Everybody was glad to see her. And though you probably won't like hearing it, I think Scott will probably end up with Lyssa. She seems to be helping him through all this. You ought to be glad for him, Caroline. He loved you, you know. No matter what you did, he loved you."

Joanna frowned slightly. "I guess that's what I wish, that you hadn't missed out on what he could have given you. I don't know what went wrong first, whether your nature made him go cold, or you got restless because it wasn't easy for him to show his feelings and you . . . needed devotion.

"All I do know is that you missed the most wonderful feeling life has to offer, Caroline. And I do feel sorry for you for that."

She fell silent for a few moments, than smiled wryly. "I know, you don't want my pity. I just hope you're at peace now. I'll keep an eye on Regan, I promise. Good-bye, Caroline."

Joanna turned away and walked back down the path to the church. She felt satisfied, felt a sense of closure. And when she saw the man she loved waiting for her at the curch gate, his eyes lighting at the sight of her, her step quickened eagerly and she thought she would burst with happiness. She didn't look back, not once, because the past was finished.

Only the present mattered. And the future.

ABOUT THE AUTHOR

◇   ◇   ◇

KAY HOOPER, who has more than six million copies of her books in print worldwide, has won numerous awards and high praise for her novels. Kay lives in North Carolina, where she is currently working on her next novel.

FBI Agent Noah Bishop has a rare gift for seeing what others do not, a gift that helps solve the most puzzling cases.

Read his electrifying adventures in three stand-alone novels of psychic suspense from *New York Times* bestseller Kay Hooper, all available now.

STEALING SHADOWS

HIDING IN THE SHADOWS

OUT OF THE SHADOWS

Turn the page for a sneak preview of
STEALING SHADOWS,

the chilling story of a woman who steals inside the shadows of a killer's mind—at the risk of losing her own life.

"Talk to me, Cassie."

She was all but motionless in the straight-backed chair, head bowed so that her hair hid her face. Only her hands stirred, thin fingers lightly tracing and shaping the red tissue petals of the exquisitely handmade paper rose in her lap.

"I think . . . he's moving," she whispered.

"Where is he moving? What can you see, Cassie?" Detective Logan's voice was even and infinitely patient, betraying none of the anxiety and urgency that beaded his face with sweat and haunted his eyes.

"I . . . I'm not sure."

From his position a few feet away, Logan's partner spoke in a low voice. "Why's she so tentative with this one?"

"Because he scares the shit out of her," Logan responded, equally quietly. "Hell, he scares the shit out of me." He raised his voice. "Cassie? Concentrate, honey. What does he see?"

"Dark. It's just . . . it's dark."

"All right. What is he thinking?"

She drew a shaky little breath, and those thin fingers trembled as they held and traced the paper rose. "I—I don't want to . . . It's so cold in his mind. And there are so many . . . shadows. So many twisted shadows. Please don't make me go any deeper. Don't make me touch them."

Logan's already grim face grew bleaker at the fear and revulsion in her voice, and it was his turn to draw a steadying breath. When he spoke, his voice was cool and certain. "Cassie, listen to me. You have to go deeper. For the sake of that little girl, you have to. Do you understand?"

"Yes," she replied forlornly, "I understand." There was a moment of silence so absolute, they could hear the soft crackle of the tissue paper she touched.

"Where is he, Cassie? What is he thinking?"

"He's safe. He knows he's safe." Her head tilted to one side, as though she were listening to a distant voice. "The cops will never find him now. Bastards. Stupid bastards. He left them all those clues and they never saw them."

Logan didn't allow himself to be distracted by the disturbing information. "Stop listening to him, Cassie. Look at what he's doing, where he's going."

"He's going . . . to get the girl. To take her to his secret place. He's ready for her now. He's ready to—"

"Where is it? What's around him, Cassie?"

"It's . . . dark. She's . . . he's got her tied up. He's got her tied up . . . in the backseat of a car. It's in a garage. He's getting into the car, starting the engine. Backing out of the garage. Oh! I can hear her crying . . ."

"Don't listen," Logan insisted. "Stay with him, Cassie. Tell me where he's going."

"I don't know." Her voice was desolate. "It's so dark. I can't see beyond the headlights."

"Watch, Cassie. Look for landmarks. What kind of road is he on?"

"It's . . . a blacktop. Two lanes. There are mailboxes, we're driving past mailboxes."

"Good, Cassie, that's good." He glanced aside at his partner, who grimaced helplessly, then returned his attention to that dark, bent head. "Keep looking. Keep watching. You have to tell us where he's going."

For a few moments there was nothing but the sound of her breathing, quick and shallow. And then, abruptly she said, "He's turning. The street sign says . . . Andover."

Logan's partner moved a few steps away and began talking softly into a cell phone.

"Keep watching, Cassie. What do you see? Talk to me."

"It's so dark."

"I know. But keep watching."

"He's thinking . . . horrible things."

"Don't listen. Don't go too deep, Cassie."

She lifted her head for the first time since they had begun, and Logan flinched. Her eyes were closed. He'd never seen such pallor in a human face before. Not a living face. And that pale, pale skin was stretched tautly over her bones.

"Cassie? Cassie, where are you?"

"Deep." Her voice sounded different, distant and almost hollow, as though it came from a bottomless well.

"Cassie, listen to me. You have to back off. Just see what he sees."

"It's like worms," she whispered, "feeding on rotting flesh. On a rotting soul . . ."

"Cassie, back off. Back off *now*. Do you hear me?"

After several moments she said, "Yes. All right." She

was trembling visibly now, and he knew if he touched her, he would find her skin cold.

"What do you see? What does he see?"

"The road. No mailboxes now. Just winding road. He's getting tense. He's almost at his secret place."

"Watch, Cassie. Keep watching."

Several minutes passed, and then a frown tugged at her brows.

"Cassie?"

She shook her head.

Logan stepped aside quickly and spoke in a low voice to his partner. "Any luck with Andover, Paul?"

"There are five variations on the street name Andover within two hundred miles. Bob, we can't even get to them all, much less cover them effectively. She has to give us something else."

"I don't know if she can."

"She has to try."

Logan returned to Cassie. "What do you see, Cassie? Talk to me."

In a tone that was almost dreamy now, she said, "There's a lake. I've seen the lights shining on the water. He's . . . his secret place is near the lake. He thinks he'll dump her body there when he's done. Maybe."

Logan looked swiftly at this partner, but Paul was already on the cell phone.

"What else, Cassie? What else can you tell me?"

"It's getting harder." Her voice became uncertain, shaky once more. "Harder to stay inside him. I'm so tired."

"I know, Cassie. But you have to keep trying. You have to keep us with him."

As always, she responded to his voice and his insistence, drawing on her pitifully meager reserves of strength to maintain a contact that revolted and terrified her. "I hear her. The little girl. She's crying. She's so afraid."

"Don't listen to her, Cassie. Just him."

"All right." She paused. "He's turning. It's a winding road now. A dirt road. I can see the lake sometimes through the trees."

"Do you see a house?"

"We're passing . . . driveways, I think. There are houses all around. Houses on the lake."

Logan stepped aside as Paul gestured. "What?"

"There's only one Andover Street close to a lake. It's Lake Temple. Bob, it's only fifteen miles away."

"No wonder she's picking him up so well," Logan muttered. "She's never been this deep before, not inside this bastard. The teams moving?"

"I've got everybody en route. And we're chasing down a list of all the property owners on the lake. I'm told this is one of those places where the people name their houses, give them signs and everything. If we get really lucky . . ."

"Keep me advised," Logan said, and returned to Cassie.

"Lake Temple," she said, dreamy again. "He likes that name. He thinks it's appropriate."

"Don't listen to what he thinks, Cassie. Just watch. Tell me what he's doing, where he's going."

Five minutes of silence lasted seemingly forever, and then she spoke suddenly.

"We're turning. Into a driveway, I think."

"Do you see any mailboxes?"

"No. No. I'm sorry."

"Keep watching."

"It's a steep driveway. Long. Winding down toward the lake. I see . . . I think there's a house ahead. Sometimes the headlights touch it. . . ."

"Keep watching, Cassie. When you see the house, look for a sign. The house has a name."

"There—there's the house." Her voice quickened. "It has a sign near the door. The sign says . . . 'retirement fund.' "

Logan blinked, then glanced at Paul, who mouthed, "Typical."

Logan turned back to Cassie. "Talk to me, Cassie. Is he stopping the car? Is this house where he's going?"

Cassie said, "Wait . . . we're going past it. Oh. Oh, I see. There's . . . a boathouse. I think it's a boathouse. I see . . ."

"What, Cassie? What do you see?"

"It's . . . a weathervane on top. On the roof. I can see it moving in the breeze. I can . . . hear it creaking."

"Hear it? Cassie, has he stopped the car?"

She seemed startled. "Oh. Oh, yes, he has. The lights are out. I can see the shape of the boathouse, the darkness of it. But . . . he knows his way. He's . . . he's getting her out of the back. Carrying her into the boathouse. She's so little. She hardly weighs anything at all. Ohhhh . . . ."

"Cassie—"

"She's so afraid. . . ."

"Cassie, listen to me. You can only help her by paying attention to what he's doing. Where he's going." He looked at his partner. "Where the hell are they?"

"Almost there. Five minutes."

"Goddammit, she doesn't have five minutes!"

"They're moving as fast as they can, Bob."

Cassie was breathing quickly. "Something's wrong."

Logan stared at her. "What?"

"I don't know. He feels . . . different about this one. Sly, somehow, and almost . . . amused. He means to give the cops something new. He—oh. Oh, God. He has a knife. He wants to just cut her open—" Her voice was thready with grief and horror. "He wants to . . . he wants to . . . taste . . ."

"Cassie, listen to me. Get out. Get out, *now.*"

Logan's partner stared forward. "Bob, if she stays with him, she might be able to help us."

Logan shook his head, never taking his eyes off Cassie. "If she stays with him, and he kills the girl, it could pull her in too deep, into his frenzy. We'd lose them both. Cassie? Cassie, get out. *Now.* Do it." He reached over and plucked the tissue-paper rose from her fingers.

Cassie drew a shuddering breath, then slowly opened her eyes. They were so pale a gray, they were like faint shadows on ice, strikingly surrounded by inky black lashes. Dark smudges of exhaustion lay under those eyes, and her voice shook with strain when she said "Bob? Why did you—"

Logan poured hot coffee from a thermos and handed her the cup. "Drink this."

"But—"

"You helped us all you could, Cassie. The rest is up to my people."

She sipped the hot coffee, her eyes on the rose he still held. "Tell them to hurry," she whispered.

But it was nearly ten long, long minutes later before the report came in, and Paul scowled at Cassie.

"The boathouse was empty. You missed the fork in the driveway. One branch led to the boathouse, and the other led to a cove less than fifty yards away, where a cabin cruiser was tied up. He was gone by the time we found it. The little girl was still warm."

Logan quickly caught the cup that fell from Cassie's fingers and said, "Paul, shut up. She did her best—"

"Her best? She fucking missed it, Bob! There was no weathervane on top of the boathouse—there was a flag flying above the boat. That's what she saw moving in the wind. And the creaking she heard was the boat in the water. She couldn't tell the difference?"

"It was dark," Cassie whispered. Tears filled her eyes but didn't fall. Her shaking hands twisted together in her lap, and she breathed as though struggling against an oppressive weight crushing her lungs.

Paul said, "Five minutes. We wasted five minutes going the wrong way, and that little girl's dead because of it. What am I supposed to tell her parents? That our famous psychic blew it?"

"Paul, shut your goddamned mouth!" Logan looked back at Cassie. "It wasn't your fault, Cassie." His voice was certain.

But his eyes told her something else.

Her own gaze fell, and she started at the tissue rose he held, its delicate perfection emphasized by the blunt strength of his cop's hand.

Such beauty to have been created by a monster.

Sick fear coiled in the pit of her stomach and crawled on its belly through her mind, and she was barely aware of speaking aloud when she said huskily, "I can't do it. I can't do this anymore. I can't."

"Cassie—"

"I can't. I can't. I can't." It was like a mantra to ward off the unbearable, and she whispered it over and over as she closed her eyes and shut out the mocking sight of the paper flower that now lived in her nightmares.

Ryan's Bluff, North Carolina
February 16, 1999

As towns went, it didn't have much to boast of. It was about as broad as it was long, with more acreage than buildings. There was a scattering of churches and car lots and small stores that didn't call themselves boutiques but charged enough for their plain little dresses to be considered just that. There was a Main Street with a grassy town square, enough banks to make a body wonder where all the riches were, and a drugstore so old, it still had a soda fountain.

Of course, there was also a computer store on Main Street, as well as two video stores and a satellite dish dealership, and just two miles away from the center of town was the very latest thing in movie multiplexes.

So Ryan's Bluff was staring the coming millennium right in the eye.

It was also, on most levels, a small Southern town, so the politics were largely conservative, church on Sunday was the norm, you couldn't buy liquor by the drink, and until the previous year the same sheriff had been voted in at every election since 1970.

In 1998 his son got the job.

It was, therefore, a predictable town by and large. Change came as reluctantly as heaven admitted sinners.

There were few surprises, and even fewer shocks.

That's what Ben Ryan would have said. What he believed, after a lifetime of knowing this place and with generations of family history at his back. This town and its inhabitants could never surprise him.

That's what he believed.

"Judge? Someone to see you."

Ben frowned at the intercom. "Who is it, Janice?"

"Says her name is Cassie Neill. She doesn't have an appointment, but asks if you can spare a few minutes. She says it's important."

Ben's very efficient secretary was not easily persuaded by people without appointments, so he was surprised to hear a note almost of appeal in Janice's voice. Curious, he said, "Send her in."

He was still jotting down notes and didn't look up immediately when the door opened. But even before Janice announced "Miss Neill, Judge," he felt the change in the room. It was as if an electrical current had been set loose, making his skin tingle and the fine hair on his body stir. He looked up and rose to his feet in the same instant, noting Janice's disconcerted expression as she gazed warily at the visitor.

They were all three disconcerted.

The visitor was functioning under an enormous level of stress. That was his first realization. He was accustomed to weighing people, and this young woman weighed in as someone carrying a burden too heavy for her.

She was of average height but too thin by a good twenty pounds, a fact obvious even under the bulky sweater she wore. She might have been pretty if her face hadn't been so thin. Her head was bowed a bit, as if her attention were focused entirely on the floor, and her shoulder-length, straight black hair swept forward as if to shelter her face, the long bangs all but hiding her eyes.

Then she looked at him through those bangs, a quick, surprised glance darting warily upward, and he caught his breath. Her eyes were amazing—large, dark-lashed, and a shade of gray so pale and clear, they were hypnotic. And haunted.

Ben had seen suffering before, but what he saw in this woman's eyes was something new in his experience.

He found himself coming around his desk toward her. "Miss Neill. I'm Ben Ryan." His normal speaking voice had softened, so much so that the uncharacteristic gentleness startled him.

Something else startled him. Ben was a Southern lawyer, a one-time judge, and had been for years involved in politics at the local and state levels; shaking hands with strangers was as natural to him as breathing, and sticking out his hand during an introduction was automatic. Yet somehow this woman not only managed to elude shaking hands with him, she did it so smoothly and with such perfect, practiced timing that there was nothing obvious in the avoidance of physical contact, and nothing at all awkward. He was not left with his hand hanging in the air, and was conscious of no slight.

She simply circumvented the gesture by moving promptly toward his visitor's chair and glancing casually around at his office. "Judge Ryan." Her voice was low and beautifully modulated, the accent not Carolina. "Thank you for seeing me."

When she looked at him doubtfully with another of those guarded, darting glances, he realized that she had probably expected him to be older. More . . . judgelike.

"My pleasure." He gestured to the chair, inviting her to sit, then looked toward the doorway with a lifted brow. "Thank you, Janice."

Janice took her gaze off the visitor finally and, still frowning slightly, backed out of the office and closed the door.

Ben returned to his chair and sat down. "We're pretty informal around here," he told her. "I'm Ben." His voice, he noted in some surprise, was still gentle.

A faint smile touched her lips. "I'm Cassie." Another quick glance at his face, and then she stared down at the hands clasped in her lap. Whatever she had come there to say, it was obviously not easy for her.

"What can I do for you, Cassie?"

She drew a breath and kept her gaze fixed on her hands. "As I told your secretary, I'm new in Ryan's Bluff. I've lived here a little less than six months. Even so, that's long enough to get a sense of who's respected in this town.

Who is apt to be . . . listened to, even if what he says is unbelievable."

"I'm flattered," he said, very curious but willing to let her get to it in her own time.

She shook her head. "I've done my homework. You're descended from the Ryans who founded this town. You left only to go to college and law school, returning here to practice. You became a much admired and highly respected district court judge—obviously at a young age—but chose to retire after only a few years because you felt your true vocation was as a prosecutor. You were elected district attorney for Salem County, and you are very involved in community affairs as well as local and state politics. Your . . . support would count for a lot."

"My support in what?"

She answered his question with a matter-of-fact one of her own. "Do you believe in the paranormal?"

That was unexpected, and threw him for a moment. "The paranormal? You mean ghosts? UFOs? ESP?"

"Specifically extrasensory perception. Telepathy. Precognition." Her voice remained calm, but she was sitting just a bit too stiffly and her clasped fingers moved nervously. She darted another glance at him, so fleeting that all he caught was a flash of those pale eyes.

Ben shrugged. "In theory I always thought it was garbage. In fact, I've never encountered anything to make me change my mind." It was the fairly cynical mind common to many law enforcement officials, but he didn't add that.

She didn't look discouraged. "Are you willing to admit the possibility? To keep your mind open?"

"I hope I'm always willing to do that." Ben could have told her that he himself was given to hunches, to intuitions he found difficult to explain rationally, but he said nothing since it was a characteristic he hardly trusted. By training and inclination he was a man of reason.

Still utterly matter-of-fact, Cassie said, "There's going to be a murder."

She had surprised him again, unpleasantly this time. "I see. And you know that because you're psychic?"

She grimaced, registering the disbelief—and the suspicion of a prosecutor—in his voice. "Yes."

"You can see the future?"

"No. But I . . . tapped into the mind of the man who intends to commit a murder."

"Even assuming I believe that, intentions don't always translate into actions."

"This time they will. He will kill."

Ben rubbed the back of his neck as he stared at her. Maybe she was a kook. Or maybe not. "Okay. Who's going to be murdered?"

"I don't know. I saw her face when he watched her, but I don't know who she is."